Praise for the works

Queerleaders

As Mack interacts with a variety of people, the reader does as well, and Queerleaders challenges us to rethink our own assumptions about cheerleaders and queer people and parents and football players, and to pay attention to their feelings and admit that everybody's feelings are complex and important. The writing is also very clever and I found myself highlighting passages as often as I was smiling or laughing. I can't think of a book I've had more fun reading in a while...

-Smart Bitches Trashy Books

This is a fun, easy, and entirely charming read. Guel manages to create a story that is captivating, relatable, and reminiscent of the movies in which the underdog wins. I cannot believe that this is a debut novel, it's just so good. I cannot recommend this one enough.

-The Lesbian Review

This story dealt with a variety of topics. It was about having that fearful conversation with parents about being gay...not knowing if they will face acceptance or rejection. But it also was about strong supportive friendships and experiencing that first special kiss and first girlfriend. The author actually took the reader through a gamut of emotions from start to finish. There were some laugh out loud scenes as well as heartwarming ones. It was an extremely well written, engaging, and entertaining read.

-R. Swier, NetGalley

This is absolutely, one-hundred percent the queer teen book I wish I had when I was a teen. Mack and Lila are so fun and hilarious and you can feel how great their friendship is from the first page. When Mack attempts to woo all the girls on the cheerleading team, the book breaks into hilarious teen antics and I loved every second of it. I highly recommend this sweet, funny book.

Kate C., *NetGalley*

M.B. GUEL

Other Bella Books by M.B. Guel

Queerleaders
Internet Famous

About the Author

M.B. (they/them) is an author of a couple of novels and several mediocre jokes. Their debut novel, *Queerleaders* (2021 ALA Rainbow List; GCLS 2021 Goldie Award finalist), was published with Bella Books in 2020. Ninety-nine percent of readers said it wasn't the worst thing to happen in 2020.

They grew up between South Central LA and the high desert, and spent the long car rides back and forth writing stories about their dogs, and queer fan fiction. They still live in Los Angeles with their partner, writing queer fiction and making bad crafts.

They also will tell you too much about how to embalm a body, dog breeds, Lizzie Borden and how Jennifer's Body deserved better, if you ask.

M.B. GUEL

BELLA
BOOKS
2023

Bella Books, Inc.
P.O. Box 10543
Tallahassee, FL 32302

Printed in the United States of America on acid-free paper.

First Edition - 2023

Editor: Ann Roberts
Cover Designer: Ally Baldwin

ISBN: 978-1-64247-482-4

PUBLISHER'S NOTE

Acknowledgments

Thank you to every single person who supported me while I was writing this. I couldn't have done this without the immense support I have behind me. Though the ones I have to name by name are the animals who did everything they could to make my life hard while writing this. Sitting on my laptop? Done. Ripping out my power cord? Just another Tuesday. Super special thank you to Taffita Sprinks, Minner Winner Chicken Dinner, Deadly Nedley, Boots-idasical and Corn Chowder.

Dedication

For the trans people that history has tried to erase. You deserve to have silly love stories too.

Somewhere out in the Old West, around 1887

CHAPTER ONE

The sun was at its highest in the sky when there came the distant sound of a wagon rolling down the road. Lou looked up from the fence they were building, leaning against the newly sunken post, with the mallet hanging at their side. Their muscles burned and they could feel the sweat dripping down their face and threatening their eyes. They quickly wiped their face with the back of their sleeve, their hat pushed askew as they squinted into the distance.

No one came down this road unless it was on purpose; it was the reason Lou had chosen this piece of land. Far enough away from the main road and Ghosthallow that they felt safe from any people that might come after them.

Ghosthallow was a small, quiet town, but one that harbored its fair share of secrets. Everyone had something they were hiding. The town was just far enough away from the gold rush to keep the miners away—unless they were the ones running away. Even still, people would usually give up before they reached Ghosthallow unless they were desperately determined.

It became a safe haven for all sorts of criminals and various riffraff. Everyone knew and no one really cared. While they would gossip amongst themselves about this dirty secret or that, they'd never tell an outsider. Never snitch.

That's why when Lou saw the mail wagon slowly rolling toward their ranch, they figured after a few long weeks it finally might be the house plans and supplies they had ordered from Old Man Franklin at the general store. They let their mallet fall to the ground and walked toward the road. Taking their hat off, they ran a hand through their wavy black hair to push it back from their face before adjusting their hat back on their head.

Their property was offset just enough that they didn't have to worry about people riding past it all the time, but they could still monitor it from anywhere. The house itself wasn't much, just a small one-room shack with a bed, fireplace and stove. They had a barn and a wide amount of acreage, much more space than they needed for the few cows and chickens they kept, but they were ready to expand, and a nicer, more spacious house was the beginning.

The wagon stopped just as Lou made it to the edge of the road. They stared at the top of the enclosed wagon, suspiciously free of house supplies. The driver looked down at his ledger, his young face scrunching up as he ran his finger down the list. He scratched at the patchy stubble on his chin and looked back up at Lou.

"Ramirez?"

"'At's me," Lou confirmed, making sure to deepen their voice as they spoke. The driver thrust the ledger at them and jumped off the wagon.

"Sign 'ere. I 'ave to say, I'm glad'a be rid o' this one. Wouldn't stop complainin'."

Lou signed next to their name and handed him the ledger with a frown. "Complainin'?"

"Yeah. Yer in for a handful," he said before banging on the carriage door. "Come on 'en."

Lou could do nothing but stare, confused as to how their house plans could be a handful in any way. Maybe he'd just been in the heat too long and was acting looney. Their confusion only deepened when the carriage door swung open and a girl stepped out.

A pretty girl.

A *beautiful woman*.

Dressed in a simple blue calico dress with dark-brown hair done up in a braid only to be twisted and pinned to the back of her head, Lou couldn't help but stare. She was petite with light-brown skin, and nervous hazel eyes looked up at them as she stood in front of the carriage—nervous eyes that betrayed the purposeful hard look she was trying to give off. Lou noticed her jaw was tight, lips pressed into a hard line as she looked Lou over.

They managed to pull their attention away from her and look back at the driver. "What's this?"

"Well that ain't no way to talk 'bout a lady. I mean, she's a bit on the skinny side but I'm sure you can fatten' 'er up a little."

The woman scoffed and Lou blushed. "No, I mean, I didn't have...Why is she 'ere?"

The driver sucked on his teeth and shrugged. "Yer the one that ordered her."

Lou's first reaction was a guffaw of a laugh. Loud and grating and harsh in a way that made the driver cringe, but the woman's face softened just the slightest. Lou wasn't sure why the smallest twitch of this girl's face was wholly distracting, but they found themself forgetting what they were saying for a moment until they heard the driver suck his teeth again.

Their gaze flickered back to him and they shook their head. The driver pointed at the description of the order next to Lou's name in the ledger.

"Says right 'ere. Wife."

"I ordered house plans. *Plans*. Not a house*wife*."

CHAPTER TWO

Lou snatched the ledger from him and looked at the flowy writing scratched next to their name. They couldn't read very well, but they could read "wife" plain as day. They cursed and rubbed the back of their neck as the driver snatched his precious ledger back. How did Old Man Franklin manage to mess this up? They took their hat off and looked down at it, as if it would help them get some clarity in the situation.

They had gone into the general store and were selecting their plans at the same time as Harry Cross was ordering something from the mail. Old Man Franklin wasn't good at hearing to begin with, or seeing for that matter, and they were both at the counter. Cross had been filling out an address from a newspaper clipping while Lou ordered their house plans from the catalog. There must have been some kind of mix-up.

"Shit."

"So, I'll just get a'goin'. I'll leave y'all to your newly married bliss."

The driver winked at Lou and their cheeks flushed even deeper.

"N-no! We're not. She's not my w-wife," Lou stuttered. The woman stifled a giggle and Lou didn't think they could blush any more, but they proved themself wrong. They took a deep breath. "I didn't order a wife," they defended weakly.

The driver smiled, clearly amused. "Now, listen, I ain't judgin' you. Jus' get 'er to yer home."

"I don' want 'er. Take 'er back where she came from." The woman let out a high, haughty laugh. "No offense, ma'am."

The driver interrupted, motioning for the woman to go with Lou with big sweeping moves of his arms. "I can't. I'm s'posed to deliver a girl. I deliver a girl. No exceptions."

"What am I suppose' to do with 'er?"

"I don' know. You ordered 'er," the driver said, already moving back to the seat of his carriage.

"I'm standing right here!" the woman said with a small, defiant stamp of her foot, arms folded tightly in front of her. "And no one *ordered* me."

Lou remembered themself and took their hat off, bending a little toward her. "You're right, ma'am, so sorry."

Her gaze softened when it landed on Lou, corners of her lips turning up in the barest hint of a smile. Lou suddenly found the air around them blistering with heat. Their collar felt too tight on their neck despite the fact that it was already unbuttoned at the top two buttons.

"Clementine Castellanos," the woman blurted suddenly. Lou just stared at her for a moment as she waved her hand and started over. "You can call me Clementine."

Clementine.

Such a nice name. It sounded like something they'd heard in one of those poems their madre used to read them every night. "Miss Clementine it is then."

Clementine blushed and the heat felt even more sweltering. They pulled on their open shirt collar and watched as Clementine's gaze followed the movement. For a moment, Lou found themself distracted before the useless delivery boy spoke again.

"It's customary to tip, ya know."

Lou's face hardened as they looked back at him, sitting back in his carriage. They dug into their pocket and pulled out a nickel. They went to hand it to him but pulled it back as he was about to grab it. He cussed under his breath.

"Tell me, didja 'ave any other deliveries? Wood, nails, stuff like 'at?" Lou demanded with a raised eyebrow.

The boy leveled them with an angry look before muttering, "It went to Harry Cross. He weren't there so I jus' dropped it off. I'm tol' to deliver, I deliver."

"Thank you." Just like they thought. Lou slapped the nickel into his dirty hand with a huff. They watched as he snapped the reins of his horses and pulled away. Watching his carriage get smaller and inwardly cursing his name was better than dealing with what was standing behind them—a woman—Clementine, who thought she was their wife. Apparently.

Lou licked their lips and brushed their hat off on their pant leg. Now what?

Clementine cleared her throat and they noticed the carpet bag at her feet, probably where all her possessions had been stored for the ride.

"So, I take it you aren't the one who wrote for me?" she said, with a tip of her head.

"'Fraid not, Miss Castellanos," Lou said, blushing as they saw the amusement in her eyes. "I mean, 'fraid not as in, there was a mistake."

"Unfortunately, it seems that way. You still haven't told me your name."

"Oh, Lou," they said, putting their hat to their chest and holding their hand out to her. They suddenly became aware that their sleeves were rolled up and felt their stomach sink. The usually rolled-down sleeves now exposed their thin wrists and the stark white scars that made up the landscape of the dark tan skin on their arms.

They resisted the urge to pull their arm back and the bright smile that graced Clementine's face blinded Lou as she took their hand. Her hand was so small and soft and Lou was embarrassed by how rough and dirty their hand probably felt to her. They started to pull away when Clementine squeezed their hand, holding on to it for just a second longer.

"Nice to meet you, Lou," she said. She dropped Lou's hand and it fell limply back at their side, the warm impression of her fingers still ghostly in their palm. They rubbed their hands on their pants to rid the feeling.

Lou looked back toward their property and crushed the felt brim under their hands. The day was already half gone and they definitely hadn't made the progress on the fence they'd been hoping for. That plus the unexpected guest was really throwing off their day, though they figured "guest" was a strong word.

"Cross ain't that far away. I'll go get my horse and we'll head over there. Don' wanna keep you from your husband any longer 'an I already 'ave."

"Yes, well, I suppose I have no choice in the matter."

"You do, Miss Castellanos, if you don' wanna go to Cross jus' say the word—"

"No, I must," she said quickly, some of the color leaving her face. "The money is needed. Far worse will happen if I don't go to him."

Lou tipped their hat at Clementine and hummed lightly. "I'll be on my way to get Trigger 'en. Be righ' back."

They jogged toward the barn, not wanting to keep Clementine waiting too long. It seemed like she was in trouble, at least that's what was implied, and something in Lou's chest told them to help. It wasn't a good idea, though. They knew they just had to mind their own business and keep out of trouble, but admittedly, they wouldn't mind spending a little more time with her.

Lou shook their head and cleared their throat. No, that was dumb. They had resigned themself to a life of loneliness long ago. It was better off this way, after all. Fewer people to get hurt. They didn't need to be making eyes at anyone's wife. And certainly not Cross's wife.

Messing with Cross was like poking a snake. A big, angry and dumb snake. Lou had heard about him from the girls at the saloon. He had a permanent scowl on his face and a heavy beard marring his features. His pasty skin had patches of angry-looking red that made Lou grimace. He was always chewing tobacco loudly, some of the juice soaking into his beard and staining his shirt. The girls hated him. They said he was dirty and rough, and they always drew straws as to who had to deal with him. Lou could stand up for themself, but they'd rather not get the negative attention of Cross.

They got Trigger from the barn, saddling the tan horse quickly before riding him back to where Clementine leaned against the fence.

"Sorry fer keepin' ya waitin', Miss Castellanos," Lou said, dismounting. They held out their hand for her and she took it with a smile. Lou couldn't help but smile back, but they chose to ignore the sudden flutter of butterflies in their stomach.

"It didn't feel like long," she said, as she picked up her bag from the dirt at her feet.

Lou easily lifted Clementine and her bag onto Trigger. She sat sidesaddle, her bag in her lap, and Lou silently hated their predicament.

"It ain't quite proper to be sittin' this way with another man's wife," they muttered to themself as they gingerly reached around her and took the reins. She didn't seem bothered, choosing to lean into Lou's front, much to their dismay. They got a whiff of her perfume, something flowery, and felt a little light-headed.

"I don't mind," she said cheerfully. They adjusted themself on the saddle and tried not to think about how her scent made them want to both lean forward and throw themself off their horse at the same time.

"All right, then."

They rode in relative silence for a while. Lou was too focused on staying straight in the saddle and not touching Clementine *too* much. But it was proving an impossible task with her in front of them and their arms bracketing her body to reach the reins. The soft press of her shoulder into their chest was proving to be hard to ignore.

"Thank you for giving me a ride," she said, turning her head to look at them. Their faces were far too close.

"Ain't no problem, Miss Castellanos," Lou said with a polite tip of the head. "It'd be too far fer you to walk."

"Just Clementine. You can just call me Clementine. Or Clem. Clemie if we get *real* familiar."

"Miss Clementine then."

"*Just* Clementine."

"Miss Clementine does just fine." Familiarity can only lead to sticky situations, Lou reminded themself, quickly veering the conversation in a different direction. "I'm sorry for the little detour on yer way to yer husband."

"Well, to be frank, I don't mind the detour. Can't say I'm necessarily excited about the match."

Lou shifted. It was rude not to ask her to continue, but it would also be rude to mingle in the affairs of others. Their curiosity won out instead.

"Why would that be? Didn' you write to 'im?" they asked as they ascended a hill, the Cross ranch just becoming visible on the horizon. Wouldn't be much longer now.

She sighed and played with the worn clasp of her carpet bag. "Not exactly. Dad died and turns out he owed a lot of money to some bad men. It was either work the brothel or be sold off to the highest bidder. And if I'm going to have to deal with men my whole life, I'd rather it just be one."

Lou's hands unconsciously tightened on the reins. It was against their principles to make a woman do something she didn't want to do. Part of the reason they ended up fleeing all the way to this godforsaken town to begin with.

"Miss Clementine, jus' say the word—"

"Oh no," she said, grip visibly tightening on her bag as she shook her head. "I'm going through with it. I have to. I need the money, otherwise who knows what…" She took a deep breath and a shaky smile appeared on her face. "I'm sure it won't be all that bad. He could be a very lovely man, after all. I don't know him and it seems unfair to judge, after all."

As if on cue, Trigger stopped in front of Cross's fence. He had a nice cabin a little further back on the property, pigs and chickens roaming aimlessly around the front. Lou got off their horse and helped Clementine down, one hand on her waist and the other taking her hand in their own. Again, Lou couldn't help but think how soft her hands were. A thought that made them pull away just as her feet hit the ground.

She smiled at them in thanks, smoothing out her skirt as Lou began the walk to Cross's front door. They were about halfway up the walkway, Clementine close behind, when there came a loud crack followed by a metallic ping. An overturned bucket beside the pathway suddenly flipped over. The bullet hole might as well have still been smoking. Lou's hand automatically went to the gun on their hip, other hand reaching behind them, making sure Clementine was covered.

"Who dat on mah land?" a voice yelled from the house. The front door banged open, Cross standing there with his gun pointed at them. The large boulder of a man spit tobacco juice at his feet, some getting on his yellowed stained shirt.

"I'm here with your *wife*, sir," they said, forcing back the bile in their throat at calling him "sir."

Cross spit a wad of another tobacco out of his mouth and it hit the dirt just a few feet away from them, the juice splashing, and a drop landing on Lou's boot. They clenched their fists at the side and forced a small smile.

"My wife? What'r you doin' with my wife?"

"There was a mistake with the deliveries. Can she come up to the porch now or are you gonna try shootin' again?"

Cross just grunted and lowered his shotgun. Lou stepped aside to reveal Clementine standing behind them, jaw set again like it had been when she'd first arrived at Lou's. The urge to reach out and comfort her was almost overwhelming but Lou followed her up to the porch instead. They watched Cross carefully, as his eyes roamed over her body and yellow-stained teeth appeared in what must have passed for his smile. His patchy beard glistened with spit and his flour-colored skin looked more raw than usual.

"Now, did they drop off my house plans 'ere? Materials?" Lou asked, eyes still on Clementine as Cross leered at her.

"They were, I had some boy take 'em back into town," he said, completely uninterested in what Lou had to say.

Their annoyance bristled up their spine when Cross leaned close to Clementine and she instinctively leaned back. His big meaty hand came up and stroked some hair behind her ear, his nails jagged and nearly black with all the dirt caked under them.

Lou knew they should just leave. Nothing good would come from sticking around and none of this was their business in any way—even if Clementine was pretty with soft hands and a kind smile, even if she was throwing herself into a situation she didn't want to be in. Lou picked at the skin on their thumb with their pointer finger as they watched Cross grip the back of Clementine's neck possessively and steered her into the house. Hazel eyes glanced back at them once more, big and scared.

"Stop!" Lou blurted. Cross looked at them, smile turning to a scowl. Lou licked their lips, straightened themself to their full five foot ten or so inches and stepped up to the man. Cross was big, but Lou still had a few inches on him. "That's no way to treat a lady."

"She ain't no lady, she's my wife," he said, more tobacco juice leaking from the corner of his mouth.

Don't get involved. Don't get involved. They repeated the mantra Pa always told them. "Keep your head down. Don't get involved in other folks' business. Work hard and keep to yourself."

Lou had ignored the advice before and it almost got them killed. They willed their legs to walk away, turn around and go back to their own ranch. Their own business.

But scared hazel eyes locked with their own again and they couldn't do it. "Mr. Cross," they started, thumbs hooked into the front of their belt buckle. They jerked their head to the side. "Can I talk with you away from the lady folk for a minute?"

"Ain't you a lady folk?"

Lou felt their heart drop a little and their eyes darted over to Clementine. Her brow crinkled just the slightest in confusion and Lou felt like they lost something. They tightened their jaw and stared Cross down.

"I 'ave my own money, my own land and make my own decisions, that makes me folk you oughta give a listen to," Lou said, as their hand subtly moved back toward their gun. It was a risky move, but they just needed him to know they were serious. Years of being pushed around for their presumed gender had given them various ways to deal with it. Most of the time they were just met with confusion and people were too worried about being improper to ask, but other times it had become dangerous, to say the least. And now they felt like they had more to prove. Over the years they had learned men respected guns above all else. Most of the time it didn't matter what they had between their legs as long as they had a gun at the ready on their hip.

Sure enough, Cross grunted and looked back at Clementine briefly before giving her a patronizing pat on her cheek and walking toward Lou. He spat again, narrowly missing Lou's boot, but they didn't even flinch.

"I 'ave a proposition for you, sir," they started, voice deeper. "I'll take the girl off yer hands. How much you pay for 'er?"

"Wha' makes you think I'd be willin' to sell 'er to ya?"

Lou tightened their jaw, eyes darting over his shoulder to find Clementine looking at the two of them with never-ending questions. "I mean, she's a bit skinny, ain't she? 'M sure you could find yerself a wife more fit to bear children."

He grunted and looked back at Clementine. "I wan' twice what I paid. For the inconvenience," he said with a smug grin.

"How much would that be?"

"Hundred bucks."

Lou tried not to blanch. That was nearly all the money they had saved up since they got to Ghosthallow almost a year ago. At least what was left after buying the house. In one poor decision over a pretty girl, they were going to lose all of it.

"Fine," they said, hesitating for only a moment before they reached into their boot and pulled out the wad of cash they always kept there. Better on their person at all times so at least they knew where it was. They held it up between them, pulling it back just a little when he reached for it. They purposefully put their hand out between them for him to shake. "An' you won't be botherin' me nor her about this after. Clear?"

"Yeah," he said, as he took their hand. They shook, eyes never leaving each other and squeezing the other's hand for all it was worth. Lou was sure they had at least one broken bone in their hand now, but they noticed a small wince in his face as he pulled away so at least they gave what they got. He snatched the money from them, undid the roll and quickly counted the bills.

Lou stepped around him and stood at the bottom of the porch steps, smiling up at Clementine. They tipped their hat and smiled softly as they spoke. "Miss Clementine, if I could accompany you back to the horse."

Clementine frowned in confusion, looking between Lou and Cross, who was too busy counting the bills to even look bothered. "But my debt—"

"Has been paid. In double," Lou added as an afterthought. "Now can we please get outta 'ere so that he don't decide to pick up his shotgun again?"

Clementine licked her lips and looked back at Cross before walking stiffly off the porch. As she passed Lou, she brushed lightly against their front, and their stomach flipped. They swallowed thickly and pushed the brim of their hat up a little as they followed her back to Trigger.

She spun back around with a determined look on her face. "Let me get this straight," she said. Hazel eyes bored intensely into Lou's and they were helpless but to remain standing there. They expected to be questioned on whether they were a man or not, but instead Clementine said, "You paid Mr. Cross twice what he paid for me so that I didn't have to stay with him?"

"Yes, ma'am."

"And you did this without even asking me if it's what I wanted?"

Lou shifted uncomfortably and they rubbed the back of their neck. "I um, well I jus' thought…Yes."

Her look hardened for a moment and Lou's gut twisted. Suddenly they were surprised by a soft pair of lips on the corner of their mouth. There and then gone again in an instant. They blinked and looked down at her; the only hint that the kiss had actually happened was the pink tint across her cheeks. If they had a mirror, they were sure their cheeks would be as red as if they'd been working outside without a hat all day. Lou felt sure they could look at Clementine for hours on end, the way her nose curved and her jaw was sharp and led to the elegant lines of her neck.

They were taken out of their daze when Clementine poked Lou hard in the middle of their chest.

"Next time ask me," she said. Her face softened again and Lou was captivated. "But thank you."

There was another sharp sound of a bullet hitting the fence near them and Lou stepped in front of Clementine, hand on their gun as they looked toward the noise.

"Get off mah property!" Cross yelled from inside the house. "Next time I won't be missin'!"

Lou scoffed and turned around to help Clementine onto the saddle. They watched in awe as she climbed onto Trigger herself, forgoing the sidesaddle this time. She reached out for her carpet bag and Lou hesitated before handing it to her. She adjusted the bag behind her, their hand sweating on the reins as they wondered how long it would take to lead Trigger back into town instead of sharing the saddle.

"What are you waiting for?" she asked, cocking her head to the side.

"Um, I'll jus' walk 'em back," Lou said. She tugged the reins back and turned Trigger so that Lou was at his side again.

"Don't be ridiculous, we've ridden on the same horse before and we can do it again," she said airily, as a cheeky smile crawled onto her face. "You are my husband now, after all."

Lou sputtered, feeling their cheeks heat from embarrassment but their chest puffed a bit in pride at the same time. Something about Clementine not presuming Lou was a woman, even though Cross had said, "ladyfolk." Still, they figured she deserved an explanation.

They shook their head, quickly regaining their senses. "I ain't your husband, ma'am."

"Well you certainly aren't my *wife* so you must be my husband."

"I didn't mean it like *that*," Lou sighed, and just decided to get it over with. "I ain't a man, but I ain't never felt like no woman neither. I've always jus' been…me."

"Then how do they reference you?"

"One time in the paper I saw someone who no one could tell if they were a man or a woman and the paper used 'they.' I always kinda liked that."

"Okay," she said with a nod. They could see the thoughts running through her mind like a herd of horses but was thankful she didn't seem to have any more questions.

"O' course, it was 'bout some girlie boy down south. I always been seen as a boyish girl, but I could be a girlie boy too." Lou smirked and pushed the brim of their hat up.

She smirked at them. "In that case you might be the prettiest boy I've ever met."

Lou once again felt themself swell a little in pride and quickly cleared their throat to extinguish it. Their instinct to flirt with her was strong. After all, she was the most beautiful woman they had seen maybe ever, but there was something about the pull Lou could already feel that told them to stay away. They were okay with casual. Casual didn't mean danger. When you started really caring about people, that's when it got dangerous. Clementine just seemed like the kinda person Lou could truly care about.

They pulled themself onto the horse in front of her, adjusting on the saddle and sitting up straight in hopes their bodies might not touch. But even despite their best efforts, they could feel how Clementine pressed against them from their lower back to between their shoulder blades. The spot on the corner of their mouth where Clementine had kissed them was still tingling.

"You paid for me. I'm yours now. That's how it works," she said, looping her arms casually around their waist just as Trigger trotted down the path.

"Miss Clementine, I'm drivin' you into town and you'll be on yer own from there. Clear?" they said as they turned at the fork in the road that would take them into town.

Her grip tightened on Lou's waist. "Wait—why?"

"I ain't interested in a wife and it seems like you weren't truly int'rested in bein' one if you're just doin' it for the money. I did it so you didn' 'ave to be tied to a dirty pig yer entire life. Now you can go home."

Her hands left their waist to cover Lou's on the reins. She moved their hand to the left so that the reins steered Trigger around on the road.

"I don't *want* to go home. I'll go back with you."

Lou scoffed and turned Trigger. "No, 'm takin' you back."

"Lou, there is no way on god's green earth that I ain't gonna pay back my debt, which is to you now. I'm staying."

She jerked Trigger's reins back the other way and the horse snorted in agitation.

"Consider it a gift. Now you can go home 'n not worry 'bout it—"

"I can't…go home," she admitted softly, her hands still over Lou's. "I don't…there's nothing there."

Lou swallowed thickly, clenching their jaw and trying to think of another possible solution.

Clementine's voice came small and broken. "Please."

Lou would have given her anything in that moment to this tiny, beautiful, and perfectly charming little stranger.

"You have the week to find somewhere to go. After a week, you go."

Her arms were back around their waist but in a hug this time. "Thank you thank you thank you," she said into the back of their shirt. Dainty hands gripped their shoulders as she lifted herself in the saddle just to place a kiss on Lou's cheek. "Thank you," she repeated, her breath blowing sweetly across their cheek.

Their whole body felt like it was on fire. "Yer gonna have to stop doin' that, Miss Clementine," Lou said softly, ducking their head to hopefully hide their blush.

"Thank you for letting me stay with you."

"Jus' fer the week. Until you can fin' somewhere t' go."

"We'll see," she singsonged. "Can't just leave my husband all on their lonesome, can I?"

"No. We know." Lou chuckled and shook their head. "An' I ain't your husband."
　　"We'll see."

CHAPTER THREE

By the time they got back to Lou's property, the sun had started to sink below the horizon. It settled behind Lou's cabin, casting an orange halo around it as they rode Trigger up the main path.

The smile had been permanently plastered on Clementine's face since they had started their ride back from Cross's house. She was nothing but grateful to the odd and quiet person on the saddle in front of them. Admittedly Clementine had been quite pleased when she stepped out of the carriage to see her…him… *them* there.

Tall and strong-jawed, with lean muscle apparent under their clothes, and sinewy, almost pretty forearms. Their tan skin, made deeper brown from the sun, accentuated the flecks of gold in their big brown eyes. She never wanted to look away from those eyes. That surprised her. When she thought this was the man who'd answered the ad in the paper, desiring a young, viable wife for only fifty dollars, she had been thrilled. She had been riddled with nerves during the whole carriage ride from the Lenning Ranch to Ghosthallow, afraid she would end up with a cruel husband. But there was no way this person with kind eyes and gentle hands could be anything but sweet.

She thought they were a man at first, young and baby-faced, but a man. Then after wrapping her arms around them, she could just sense a softness that could never be a man. She had never been against being with a woman; in fact, if she were being honest Clem had often daydreamed about it. Women were beautiful and kind and soft. When she thought Lou was a woman, she was still okay with being their wife. Realizing Lou wasn't a man, wasn't a woman, was just *Lou*, well, something about that made Clem's heart flutter and want to be closer to them. Now with her arms around Lou, she felt their broad, strong shoulders and sweet scent and felt herself understand just a bit more. Lou was Lou.

Lou wasn't like anyone Clementine had ever met in the obvious and less obvious ways. Her sister had never conformed to society's rules about how women should dress, so it was less about Lou's appearance and just their *being*. At first she just assumed they were a young handsome man, but Cross's comment made her reconsider.

Imagine her disappointment when it was a mistake and her husband *was* a cruel-looking man with teeth the shade of dead leaves and heavy unforgiving hands, and not the kind rancher on whose doorstep she landed.

Riding on the back of her gracious protector's horse, she couldn't help but be reminded of the tales her mama used to tell her about the Knights of the Round Table. The valiant knights who protected the weak and bought them from their unfriendly-looking husbands.

Not that Clementine was weak. Not in the slightest, and she would remind anyone that tried to argue.

She sat up a little straighter in the saddle and felt the cold metal of the small pistol she had taken from Lefty pressed against her sternum between her breasts, nestled away in case of an emergency. She had considered her options, and she wasn't in a position to refuse the acts of this kind stranger.

She did wonder what kind of cruel game fate was playing by bringing her back to Ghosthallow, a town she had left so long ago she barely remembered it. It felt more like a dream, one where she was running with her sisters through tall grass with the family homestead looming behind them. She wondered if that was still there.

As they got closer to the barn, Trigger began to trot again, so Clementine held on to Lou even tighter. She pressed her cheek between their shoulder blades, feeling the worn cotton of their shirt against her skin. The sharp musk of sweat was unmistakable but there was something under it that made Clementine sigh. Sweet. Like sugar.

"All right, boy," Lou muttered as they got to the barn. Their voice rumbled through their torso and Clementine sighed. Lou cleared their throat and shifted in the seat. "Um, Miss Clementine, I'ma need you to let go if I'ma get off this horse."

"Oh, right, sorry," she said, regretfully dropping her arms from around their waist.

"No worries, ma'am," Lou said as they got off the horse and held their hand out for Clementine. She slid her hand over Lou's, feeling the calluses rubbing against her palm. She suppressed a shiver and cursed to herself.

Now wasn't the time to let herself get carried away with girlish fantasies, even if she couldn't help it. Lou was so pretty and handsome and she wanted to knock their hat off their head while she ran her hands through those thick dark strands. And despite how Lou was being so standoffish and respectful, she'd seen their face when she'd first stepped off the carriage. She could tell when someone fancied her.

She would indulge herself and Lou by letting them help her down from the horse even though she could dismount perfectly on her own. Lou's hand on her waist and holding her other hand was too tempting to pass up. Years of nothing but unkind, possessive touches on her body made her want to lean into the stranger's touch.

"Clementine, please, Lou," she said as her feet touched the ground. She held Lou's hand, keeping them close as she looked up at them.

"Miss Clementine will do jus' fine," Lou repeated with the small tilt to their lips that Clementine wanted to kiss away.

She huffed and pretended to be put out despite how, when they said *Miss Clementine*, the words tripped down her spine and settled low in her belly.

"I'll meet you back at the house after I get Trigger settled for the night," Lou continued as they took Trigger's reins in their hands.

Lou nodded at Clementine and headed back into the barn, leaving her out with the summer heat still settling heavy on her shoulders. They looked like they couldn't get away from her fast enough and it just made her want to follow them. Instead she turned around and headed toward the modest cabin just a few yards away.

She could smell the freshly overturned dirt and the cows and it squeezed her heart like a familiar feeling she hadn't felt in years, like a hug from a long-forgotten friend. It felt like home. It was a terrifying feeling, really. This wasn't her home; she knew nothing of it. Still it felt familiar in a way she hadn't felt in ages. Certainly not on Lefty's ranch where she'd been holed up for fifteen years now.

When she got to the cabin, she gently pushed open the door and blinked as her eyes adjusted to the dark. It was small and modest, one room with a stove in the middle and a stone fireplace to the side. There was a simple table opposite the fire and in the far end, a small bed, tub, and mirror.

She looked around, noting the trunk at the end of the bed and the few books stacked on top of it. She set her bag beside the trunk and picked up one of the books, opening the first page to see a faded pencil inscription.

"My love for you won't fade until the ink disappears from these pages. Your Love, I.S."

The door to the cabin opened and she blushed, quickly setting the book back down like she had never seen it. Lou wouldn't have seen her looking anyway because they were hiding their face behind their hat.

"Are you decent, Miss Clementine?"

Their voice was masked by the hat and she couldn't help but find even that appealing in some kind of way.

"I am," she said with a smile.

Lou dropped the hat and smiled back. "All right, well I'm jus' gonna grab a blanket and be out in the barn—"

"What? Why?"

Lou looked at her like it was the most obvious thing in the world. "It's one room."

"There's plenty of room in the bed." She blushed. "Or I could take the floor. Or the chair—"

"I'll be sleepin' in the barn."

"Then at least let me sleep in the barn. You take your bed."

Lou chuckled and waved away her idea like it was the silliest thing in the world. "I wake up early to work in the barn. I'll just be wakin' you up earlier than you have to. It makes more sense fer me to sleep in there."

"You can wake me up so I can help. I want to help out while I'm here. Help pay off my debt."

"I work alone, Miss Clementine," Lou said, picking up a spare blanket from the end of the bed.

Clementine felt the nostalgic squeeze at her heart again and she sighed. "That's silly when someone wants to help you, but I can't say I'm not used to it. My sister is the same."

"Yer sister must be a mighty reasonable woman."

Clementine couldn't help but laugh, hand on her stomach as she doubled over. "You would never be saying that if you knew her. Well, let me help anyway. Then you'll get done with the chores sooner and there will be more time for *other* things."

"Other things? Like what?" Lou tilted their head like a confused puppy, eyes grown soft.

"Other things like…" She trailed off in thought for a moment, her gaze drifting to the low ceiling before she continued. She considered how nice it would be to lay in a field with Lou, running her hands through their hair while they relaxed. "Like reading or just talking."

Lou actually laughed an honest-to-goodness laugh at the idea of doing something other than work. "That jus' won't do,

Miss Clementine. 'M afraid it would jus' throw off my whole day an' I wouldn't know what to do."

"Lou, you're being stubborn."

"My pa used to call me a mule," Lou said with a wink. "So 'm well aware. I'll see you tomorrow, Miss Clementine. After chores I'll go into town to get the house plans and supply back, if you wanna go in to catch a train home."

"I'll go along with you for the company," she said with a small frown.

"Night, Miss Clementine."

"Good night, Lou."

Lou looked at her one last time like there was something unsaid on the tip of their tongue. But instead they just tipped their hat and started out the door. "Sweet dreams."

At the cock's crow Lou was up, swinging open the gate and letting the cattle out to graze. They got a decent night's sleep, at least the best they could with the hay poking them and Trigger snoring, but there was no way they were going to share a cabin with Clementine. They weren't about to do that to themself or that poor woman.

Clementine still needed to get herself home to find a real husband, and Lou knew too well that being associated with the likes of them never did anyone favors. Plus, Lou was already too attached to her company. *Reading or talking. Well I never.* No, if'n it wasn't going to last, there was no point in getting used to it. Shaking their head ruefully, Lou continued their chores.

Finishing the new section of the fence they were building would have to wait for tomorrow if they were going to make it into town to get the house plans. After feeding Trigger, they headed back toward the house by way of the chicken coop, peering over the side and frowning in confusion when they saw seed scattered on the ground already.

The chickens were pecking happily away, little clucks and scratching sounds of pleasure as they dug through the dirt for their food. Lou ducked their head to get a look in the coop and saw that the eggs had already been collected.

They pushed themself up, hands on their knees, and rubbed the back of their neck as they walked the few yards to the cabin. They knocked, ear pressed against the wood to hear Clementine.

"I'm decent!" she called. "You don't need to knock, you know, it's your own home."

Lou opened the door with their hat on their chest and was hit in the face with the smell of cooking. Clementine was standing at the stove with an amused smile.

She wore a long blue skirt and a simple cream-colored shirt with the sleeves pushed up past her elbows. Her hair was in a long braid and she looked even more amused as Lou just stood there.

"I jus' don't want to intrude, Miss Clementine," Lou said as they walked closer, leaning back against the rough counter and nodding toward where Clementine was piling eggs onto a plate. "W'as this?"

"Breakfast. Ain't you ever heard of it, cowboy?"

Lou watched as she hesitated after "cowboy." There was something sweet about how she bit her lip and they saw her thinking over her words. "Guess I'm jus' not used to breakfast bein' made for me. Did you feed the chickens?"

She smiled proudly and pulled a seat out at the table for Lou, motioning for them to sit down.

"I did."

"You don't have to—"

"I wanted to—"

"My schedule—"

"Will be perfectly fine with one less chore," she said pointedly. "Now eat so we can go into town."

Lou sputtered. They were not used to having someone telling them what to do, not since they'd moved to Ghosthallow, or even before that. But they didn't argue, not after Clementine looked at them with raised eyebrows. They looked down at their plate: pancakes and eggs. Their stomach growled in anticipation.

"You don't have much in the way of food," Clem said, as she cut into her own pancake. "If you don't mind, I can pick up some more supplies when we go into town."

"This looks amazing. Thank you, Miss Clementine. And I suppose we can get a few more things. I usually just have a biscuit or somethin'. I'm not much of a cook."

"Well luckily for you, I'm competent. Lefty mostly used me for cooking so I managed to get some skills under my belt."

Lou wanted to ask who Lefty was and what else he *used* her for, but the faraway look in Clementine's eye told them not to pry. They dug into their food, using the fork to practically shovel it into their mouth. Their time in the Army had taught them to eat a meal fast when the opportunity presented itself, and they'd lived alone long enough to forget that it wasn't polite. Not until they noticed Clementine staring at them with amusement.

They stopped with the fork halfway to their mouth and blushed. They cleared their throat and sat up straight instead of hunching over their plate. "Sorry, ma'am."

"Lou, if you ever 'ma'am' me again, I'm going to string you up by your thumbs to the nearest tree. And don't apologize. I'm just glad you're enjoying the food."

Her smile almost made Lou choke on a mouthful, so they tried to eat just a little slower. For their own safety.

They couldn't help but watch Clementine as they ate, not used to someone being there and bothering with them, trying to feed them. It was an odd feeling that settled warm and deep in their belly, not in an entirely unpleasant way. Lou just couldn't quite put their finger on how it made them feel.

Clementine's eyes looked up and met their own and they looked away, cheeks hot. They didn't like to dwell on unfamiliar feelings, so they pushed it away.

CHAPTER FOUR

Clementine's stomach turned with nerves as they approached Ghosthallow's main street. It had been an easy sixteen years since she'd been here. Since she was forced away from the town. Her hold on Lou's waist tightened and she felt them shift uncomfortably. They cleared their throat and she pressed her cheek between their shoulder blades.

Lou stopped just on the outskirts of town and jumped off. "I'm jus' gonna lead 'im from here," Lou said, as they pushed their sleeves down their arms. "You can stay on."

Clementine was starting to wonder if Lou even liked her very much. Sure there were the little smiles and blushes that she hadn't been able to get out of her mind the night before, but Lou didn't seem to want to be associated with her in any way. Not to mention how they seemed determined to send her away. As far as Clementine was concerned, Ghosthallow was her home. With or without Lou.

Preferably with.

Lottie, her older sister, would tell her it was dumb to get so in her head about someone she barely knew, but *technically* they were engaged to be married so she would let herself get as dumb as she wanted about Lou.

As they passed the sheriff's office, Clementine looked toward it. She wondered if Randall Butz was still the sheriff. He'd taken over after Daddy died, after all. Her heart tugged as she remembered Gayle, her childhood best friend. She wondered if she was still here.

"Alrigh', I have to borrow a cart," Lou said, as they tied Trigger to the rail outside the general store. They held their hand out to help her down and she took it, holding on just a second more than she needed to. Lou handed her a few dollars. "Get whatever you might be needin' from the store. I'll be back 'round in a few."

Clementine looked down at the bills and tucked them into her bodice. Lou's eyes followed the movement as they disappeared into her shirt but quickly looked back up.

"I'll wait for you."

Lou shook their head. "Jus' get what you want from there. I won't be but a few," Lou said, already walking back toward the saloon. "I won't be long now."

She looked back at the general store with a sigh. She and her sisters would find themselves in the store a lot back in the day, Lottie always finding new ways to steal the penny candies. Back then it was run by an ancient-looking old man named Franklin. She briefly wondered if he would recognize her face, but there was no way he was still alive. And if he had somehow managed to trick time, he certainly was senile.

Deciding it was worth the risk, she headed inside to browse. It was as she remembered. Small and dusty, not long and stuffed to the brim like the one she had visited a few times in the city. This one was about half the size, the counter in the far-left corner along with the post office stuffed behind it. Every wall had shelves, different goods and wares on display. She smiled at the old man behind the counter, who squinted at her from behind thick glasses. Her heart stopped for a moment when she realized Old Man Franklin was still kicking it, but quickly saw that there was no recognition behind his eyes.

"Hello?" he said, voice light. "Who might you be?"

"Clementine," she said, striding up to the counter and offering him her hand like he hadn't chased her from the store before. "Nice to meet you. And you are?"

"Call me Franklin," he said, taking her hand. His skin was thin like paper, veins and bones apparent under it. "You new here, then?"

"Um, sort of." She smiled as she took her hand back.

Two men walked into the store and she returned to scanning the shelves, getting a glimpse of them to see if she recognized them. A quick look was all she needed and she turned back toward the shelf, picking up a can of beans, and ears perking up at the men's conversation.

"Didja see that queer tall lady walkin' into the saloon?" one gruffed under his breath. He was a thickset man in worn jeans, held up by leather suspenders, and a sweat-stained work shirt.

The other one chuckled. "Course I seen her. How could I miss 'er?"

"Someone swore they saw 'em pissing wit' a cock behind the saloon."

"No way."

"Yeah, and I'll put money on it it's true," the other man said as they went to the rack next to Clementine's.

"What kinda freak did god let roam this earth?"

Clementine's cheeks burned, her stomach sick that they would be talking about Lou like that. She didn't know Lou very well, but she certainly knew they deserved better than for some idiots to be spouting off and calling them a freak. She spun around so fast they startled and stumbled back a little. Hazel eyes flashed with fury as she took a step closer to them.

"What business is it of yours what's between someone else's legs?" she hissed. The two men looked embarrassed for a moment but looked back at her anyway.

"Why are you listenin' to our conversation?" One of the men sneered.

She looked back over at the shopkeeper who was sorting mail, his back to the whole situation. If she knew any better, she'd say he was deaf since he didn't seem to even notice anything was happening in his store.

Eyes back on the men, she tilted her chin high. "You were havin' a public conversation. Hard not to hear two donkeys braying at each other," she snarled.

"Why you little—"

"Do we have a problem here, gentlemen?" Lou's voice came from behind them.

They turned as Lou slowly walked in between them and Clementine, fingers hooked into the front of their belt, their previously rolled-down sleeves now rolled up, forearms flexing. For the first time Clementine saw an intricate mapping of scars on Lou's arms that weaved amongst each other and mostly healed into stark white lines. Her mouth went dry and she swallowed thickly. She got the strong whiff of hay and something sweet on their clothes and she forgot their predicament for a moment. The men looked between them, dumbly trying to understand the situation. Leather Suspenders spoke.

"Yeah, yer little whore here—"

"That ain't no way to talk to a lady," Lou interrupted. They put their hands on their hips, drawing attention to the two guns holstered there. The men didn't seem impressed, hands moving much less subtly to their own guns.

A click of metal, quick as a flash, and both men stood frozen, eyes wide. In the time it took Clementine to blink, Lou had one gun out and pressed against one man's crotch while the other was pointed right between the second man's eyes. Lou had the same calm look on their face, the men's hands still hovering uselessly over their guns.

"Now. Apologize."

The men didn't say anything, just stared at Lou in shock. Lou pushed the gun's barrel deeper into the one man's crotch so hard that he lifted up on his tiptoes.

"I said, apologize."

Their voice was low and dripping in danger. Clementine felt heat rush through her and she dropped her hand to the corner of the shelves to keep herself upright.

"We're sorry, ma'am. *Sir*," the man with the gun in his crotch said. His voice trembled, eyes wide and not leaving Lou's face. They stared back at them for a moment, the tension of the room thick. Lou sucked their teeth and licked their lips before shoving the men back with the barrel of their guns.

"Git then."

The men wasted no time, scurrying from the general store and out of sight. Clementine let out a sigh, watching as Lou holstered their guns, took their hat off and raked their fingers through dark locks, jaw tensing as they looked over at Clementine. "I can't leave you anywhere, can I?"

"They were being rude."

"People are rude all the time, Miss Clementine," Lou said, placing their hat back on their head.

"But they were talking about y— They were...They weren't very nice men."

Lou gave her a look she couldn't decipher. "I know they were talkin' 'bout me. Doesn't mean you had to jump in there."

"I couldn't just *let* them say those things."

"Why not? Who woulda died?"

She looked back at the store clerk as if he could defend her, but he stood completely oblivious as he continued sorting. She rolled her eyes. "I'm not going to feel bad for defending you. I refuse."

"I don't need no one defendin' me," Lou scoffed evenly, "especially when it leads to me havin' to draw my guns on two men who could very well come back for revenge. I don't need to be on anyone's shit list. You hear me?"

She blushed, a twinge of anger in her stomach. "I was just trying to help."

"Well, I don' need it. I 'ave the cart. Get what you need while I talk to the old man about my house plans."

Lou turned and walked toward the counter, leaving Clementine with her cheeks burning. How dare Lou be mad

at her for *helping*. She cleared her throat and tried to stand a
little taller and appear unaffected, even as shame and curiosity
lingered in the back of her mind.

Clementine sat on the porch of the saloon, watching as
Lou loaded up the cart with some wood beams and planks, a
few buckets of nails, and some other things Clementine didn't
quite recognize. She had to admit, there was a certain level of
entertainment, watching Lou work like this. She had offered to
help, but Lou looked scandalized so she stopped trying.

Watching them put all the items in the cart certainly helped
calm her anger at them for being so stubborn and being mad at
her after she was just trying to defend them.

Their white button-up shirt rolled up to their elbows with
a dark vest over it fit them in a flattering way, material loose
and free around their torso. Their pants hugged them just
right around the ass, the gun belt hanging low on their hips.
Clementine watched Lou pick up one of the nail buckets with
practiced ease. Sweat gathered at the side of their head and she
watched as it rolled down their neck.

She sighed as Lou took their hat off and wiped their arm
across their forehead. She imagined brushing her fingers along
Lou's temple where some curls had gathered, plastered against
their forehead with sweat, and pushing it from their eyes. How
their sweaty skin might feel against her fingers. Against her own
skin.

She shivered and blinked, cursing as she shook herself from
her daze. Was she really this lonely? Or this *desperate*? She hadn't
thought much of dating during her time at Lefty's ranch, more
worried about surviving and just staying out of the way. When
she was much younger and much more foolish, she had dreamed
of being swept off her feet by someone kind and obsessed with
her, but reality taught her better.

She prided herself on being independent, so she hadn't
expected to be lusting after the first beautiful person who
showed her kindness. There was just something about Lou,
something behind those layers that she wanted to peel back,
metaphorically and literally.

She crossed her legs at the knee as Lou put their hat back on and looked at her. Sitting up a little straighter, she smiled as they wiped their hands on their pants.

"You mind havin' dinner in the saloon tonight? I kinda promised the girls we'd 'ave dinner there to make up for borrowing their cart. Odd exchange but..." Lou looked down before they looked back up at Clementine; as if she could say no to those eyes.

"Of course." She smiled as she stood. Absently, she wondered how familiar with the saloon girls Lou really was, but she decided not to voice it.

"All right then," Lou said, holding open the swinging door of the saloon for Clementine. She eyed the "Holster Your Weapons" sign as she walked in and noted the bullet hole in the middle.

It felt like she was hit with a wall of sound as soon as she stepped inside. She could smell the stale beer, and the air was thick with perfume trying to cover the reek of the dirty bodies of the men piled into the saloon after a day of work. She took a deep breath and looked around at the men at tables, drinking large pints of beer and hanging off each other. In the corner was a poker table with a serious-looking group around it, and there were stairs leading up into a separate area, probably where the rooms were. There were also women, beautiful women, standing around and talking to the men. They all had their breasts pressed up to their necks with corsets, beautiful skirts, and boots. Some had silk-looking wraps and ornate hair decorations.

"This way, Miss Clementine," Lou said from beside her, leaning a little closer so that she could hear them over the noise. She stumbled into them when Lou started toward the bar.

She gathered her skirt and followed closely behind Lou, eyes steady on the back of their head as they started through the rough crowd. A man knocked into her and she squeaked, automatically grabbing for the back of Lou's shirt to steady herself. Lou paused and maneuvered her in front of them protectively. Clementine stood a little taller under the attention, particularly noting how Lou's hand hovered over the small of her back until they reached the bar. She leaned against it, elbows on the worn wood, while Lou pressed themself against it next to her.

A blond woman working the bar immediately found them and she wandered over to them, eyeing Lou the whole time. She leaned forward on her elbows, face close to Lou's. "Hey there, handsome. See you decided to come by after all."

"You didn't give me much choice, didja?"

Clementine looked between the two of them and found herself scooting a little closer to Lou as she folded her hands together. Who was this woman? And how did she get so pretty? Clementine looked down at the way her breasts spilled over the top of her corset and looked back up just to see the woman looking at her with an amused smile and raised eyebrow. "Who is this?" she asked, her smile getting wider as she brushed her fingers over the top of Lou's hand. "You didn't tell me you had a friend."

Lou cleared their throat and stood up, pulling their hand away from the woman's. "Veronica, this is Clementine. Clementine, Veronica."

Clementine held out her hand and forced her own polite smile. "Nice to meet you."

"Nice to meet you," Veronica said, looking her up and down as she did. "I see Lou here has settled down."

Lou coughed, their blush matching Clementine's. "Veronica, she's just a friend—"

"Yeah, you have lots of friends here too." Veronica winked at Lou and Clementine felt an unwanted, and frankly unwarranted, flame of jealousy.

"It ain't like that. She's jus' stayin' with me until she can get back 'ome."

Veronica gave them both a skeptical look but asked, "And where's home?"

"Um, I'm not sure yet," Clementine admitted.

"Where'd you come from?"

"Nowhere I can go back to."

Clementine, oddly enough, had always considered Ghosthallow her home. But now she was finally back after years to see it changed just as drastically as Clementine herself. There was no one here that she remembered, it was almost like she'd never been here.

"Why are you here?"

"Do you always interrogate the customers, Veronica?" Lou interrupted, pulling money out of their pocket and sliding it toward her on the counter. "Two beers please. And whatever's for dinner."

"Can't keep her to yourself forever, Lou," Veronica teased, as she went to the other part of the bar to pour the beer.

Lou let out an audible sigh and Clementine wondered how many questions she could ask before Lou stopped answering them.

"Friends of yours?" she tried innocently. She was still getting used to Lou, slowly understanding them and their ways. When she said she had never met anyone like Lou, she meant it. They seemed to work and be as stubborn-headed as every man she had met, but still had the soft comfort of a woman. Though she figured that was just it though, Lou wasn't a man or a woman. Lou was just…Lou. Her heart felt trapped.

"You could say that."

"Oh, I could say a lot of things," she quipped, just as another girl waved at Lou from the other side of the bar. Lou tipped their hat as another woman came up behind them. She slipped her arm over Lou's shoulders, and Clementine couldn't help but gape.

Soft supple tan skin contrasted against her dark red dress with black lace accents. The woman leaned forward and placed a kiss on Lou, red lipstick marking their cheek, though the lipstick soon became less apparent as Lou's cheeks went red. They smiled wider than she'd seen them smile, two dimples popping that made her feel a little weak in the knees. Clementine felt something else. Jealousy? It was the first time she had seen that smile and now she wanted to know how to make it come back.

"Juanita," Lou mumbled, embarrassed. "This is Miss Clementine. Clementine, Juanita."

Dark piercing eyes drew a gasp from Clementine when they turned on her. "Miss Clementine," Juanita said with a sparkling smile. "Nice to meet you."

"Likewise." Clementine smiled through her own emotions.

"Veronica taking care of you two?"

"Very well, thank you," Veronica said, as she slid two steins in front of them, giving Clementine a little wink as she did. She felt Juanita's eyes still on her and looked straight into her scrutinizing look. She had so many questions, her curiosity seizing her brain completely as she tried to file through them. But before anything could come out, Juanita was untangling herself from Lou.

"Well, you two let me know if you need anything else. All right? Want a room for tonight?"

"Um, no," Lou said quickly. "We'll be goin' back to the farm tonight."

"Let me know if you change your mind," Juanita said, squeezing Lou's shoulder one last time before letting her hand fall back to her side. Both women went back to their jobs and Clementine took a long sip of her beer, eyes on Lou, who wiped the lipstick mark off their cheek with their sleeve.

"So, good friends?" Clementine said.

Lou just smirked. "Friends. Everyone needs friends sometimes."

"Mmm, bet you do," she muttered as Veronica slid plates of fried fish with roasted potatoes in front of them.

"If yer so high and mighty, Miss Clementine, how'd you end up in a newspaper lookin' for a husband?" Lou asked, as they stabbed a potato and popped it into their mouth, smug grin still on their face.

Clementine smiled stiffly and delicately cut into her fish. "That's a long story."

"I got nothin' but time for you righ' now, Miss Clementine."

She looked up at Lou to see them leaning their elbow on the bar, body turned toward her and happily chewing on a potato that was far too big for their mouth. Her heart thudded against her ribs at the sight. She frowned at Lou suspiciously, watching as their grin just got wider. Maybe the beer was loosening them up, she mused. *Or the attention.* They had chugged half the stein before they even got their food. Either way, Clementine was more than okay to see Lou's hard exterior soften a little bit.

"I told you, my family owed Lefty money," she said. "Now they don't."

"Seems like there's more of a story there is all. An' ya still haven't tol' me about this Lefty sit'iation."

"How have you never heard of Lefty?"

"Oh I heard a 'im. Ain't no scoundrel round these parts who hasn't. That's why I wanna know how a lady like you got wrapped up in his business."

Her gut seized and she wanted nothing more than to spill everything to Lou. But she had to be delicate about these matters. She reached for her own pint and tipped the glass back, draining half the ale in one long gulp. She heard Lou whistle lowly as she set the glass back down and looked at them with an arched eyebrow. Lou at least looked impressed, gesturing at her with their own stein before taking another gulp.

"My dad wasn't a good man," she admitted softly, wiping some beer from the corner of her mouth. "He was the sheriff but he got too greedy. He was making all kinds of deals with a local gang and when he didn't deliver on a wagon of cash that was supposed to be coming into town, well, they came for blood instead. I wasn't very old. I barely remember our old homestead."

She trailed off, hot tears threatening to press against the back of her eyes as she thought about that night. The screaming, the sobs, the smell of gunpowder in the air followed by eerie silence.

"Then they took me," she whispered. "They took me. One of my sisters managed to get away. The other..." Bile rose in Clementine's throat as she bitterly spit out her name. "Lefty took her at the same time he took me except he sold her off real soon to some man in the city. She washed up on the river not long after that. Anyways, Lefty just waited until I was old enough to sell off for what he was owed."

The touch of Lou's hand covering her own brought her from her thoughts, and she let out a harsh breath. It was a light touch, but she could almost feel the hard calluses on their palm brushing against her knuckles and she shivered. She looked into kind, albeit slightly glassy brown eyes and felt comfort in Lou's smile.

"Well, yer fine fer now, Miss Clementine. You don' 'ave to worry about them no more. 'Kay?" Lou said. Their voice was soft, soothing as they squeezed her hand.

When they went back to their food, it took everything in Clementine's body not to reach out and take Lou's hand again. The comfort it had given her in those few seconds made her heart squeeze.

"What about you?" she asked to keep Lou talking.

They shrugged and spoke through the potato in their mouth. "I 'ad a hard time back home. Now I'm 'ere."

"Where's home?"

"Farther south. Far from 'ere."

"What made you come here?"

"Friend tol' me about it. I promise, I ain't that interestin'."

"You seem pretty interesting to me," she said. Lou just grunted and she could practically see the mask slide over their face.

"Well, guess yer not always right then, Miss Clementine," Lou said with a wink.

She just blushed and went back to her food. She had seen just a glimpse behind that mask, and she would keep trying until she saw the whole thing.

* * *

Belly full of the eggs and thick-cut bacon Clementine had prepared that morning, Lou was putting together the foundation and frame of the house. The plans were on the ground nearby, a small rock on each corner to keep the papers in place as they hammered. The heat beat down on the back of their neck.

Lou's shirt was soaked through, sticking to their back and making it uncomfortable. They could feel the sweat on the back of their neck and in the ends of their hair, threatening to drip into their eyes.

They could hear the soft crunching of earth as Clementine approached them from behind, but they stayed focused on driving the nail into the wood under the hammer. They rolled a nail between their lips that they were holding there, just as they heard the footsteps stop behind them.

They wiped their brow with the back of their arm, the feeling of Clementine's eyes boring into the back of their head. "Can I 'elp you, Miss Clementine?" they asked, turning around.

They could tell that Clementine was already getting too comfortable, even after just a couple of days. Too comfortable to move on, and Lou was determined to have her move on. And it would be easier for her to do that if they weren't acquainted. In any way.

Didn't mean that Lou didn't notice the line of her neck or her jaw. And yeah, maybe they had a dream where they swept Clementine up in their arms and kissed her senseless, only to wake up with Trigger snorting horse spit into their face.

Just more reason for her to leave.

Lou didn't need the distraction. Already it had taken them two extra days to build the new fence, not to mention the house plan mix-up. The imaginary timeline they had set up for themself was completely off, though it was nice to have breakfast made for them every morning. Not that that was any reason to keep Clementine around, but it *was* nice.

It was also nice how she just seemed to accept them without question. Rather, she accepted Lou while still asking about them in a way that made them feel…seen. There had been plenty of people they talked to about their feelings on how they were and how they dressed, but all the questions felt accusatory, like someone was trying to fix them or trying to catch them in a lie. With Clementine, it was like she wanted to get to know *them*, to see *them*, not try and figure them out. Lou was tired of trying to be figured out.

Clementine had the prettiest blush on her cheeks, a metal cup held between her hands. Her eyes looked focused on the nail between their lips, but hazel eyes flickered up to meet their own again.

"Thought you might want some water," she said with a small smile that made Lou's heart flutter for some unknown reason. They coughed. "Don't choke on your nail."

Lou straightened up from the wood beam, back popping. They smiled gratefully as they took it, fingers brushing ever so slightly. "Thank you."

They spit the nail into their palm and took a long sip, letting the cool water soothe their parched throat. As they lowered the cup, they saw Clementine's eyes on their neck. They watched as her eyes quickly flickered back up to their face with an amused smile. At least they knew they weren't the only one preoccupied by this situation.

"I actually had one favor to ask," she admitted, fingers twisting the fabric of her skirt. "I was wondering if I could borrow Trigger for the rest of the day."

Lou frowned and rubbed the back of their neck. "I s'pose. Where're you takin' him?"

"I got a job."

"A job?"

"At the saloon."

Lou choked on their water. "The saloon?"

"The saloon."

"Workin' there?" Lou asked, imagining Clementine in a corset that pressed her breasts over the top and a skirt hitched up on her leg. "W-why?"

"It's the only place that can hire a woman, isn't it?" she said with a head tilt. "The more money I make faster, the quicker I can pay you back."

"I told you, you didn' need to pay me back."

"I want to."

"Listen, Miss Clementine, I don' care really what you do. But I jus' wanna make sure you ain't doin' nothin' that you don' wanna do. I didn' pay for you to get out of one situation you didn't like into another."

Clementine smiled. "While that's very sweet, I promise you this is fine."

"What kinda *work* you gonna be doin' there?"

"Downstairs work," Clementine said with a sly smile. "I won't be upstairs with cowpokes like you if that's what you're asking."

Lou sputtered and cleared their throat. "Yeah, well, I trust Juanita, and Veronica'll keep a good eye on you like they try on me," Lou sniffed.

"I know exactly the kind of eye they keep on you. Can't say that's something I'm looking for at the moment." Her gaze lingered where Lou's shirt was unbuttoned as she mumbled, "At least, not from them."

Lou coughed, the heat of the day suddenly feeling that much hotter. They waved Clementine off. "Yeah, you can take Trigger. He's a little stubborn but—"

"I've dealt with much more stubborn creatures," she said with a wink, as she headed back to the barn. "I'll be back just after sunset."

Lou mumbled nonsense and looked back at the meager beginnings of the house foundation they had started. They picked up another nail and slid it between their lips as they placed it on the wood. They picked up the hammer and held the nail at the base as they pounded it into the wood.

They could hear Trigger's hooves against the dirt and looked up. Clementine was astride the horse, reins in her hands and a smile on her face.

"Bye, Lou!" Clementine called as she trotted past. Lou waved, fighting past the smile working its way onto their lips, instead looking back down at the wood. They went to hit the nail with the hammer just as their eye caught the tin cup with water in it beside them. An image of Clementine smiling at them flashed into their mind again and the hammer slipped, hitting their thumb instead.

"Ah fuck!" they hissed, dropping the hammer and shaking out their hand. They closed their eyes and tilted their head up at the sun for a moment. Maybe it was a good thing Clementine was working at the saloon. The sooner she would be out of Lou's hair, the fewer distractions they would have.

Lou worked on the frame of the house until the sun started to set and it was harder to see. Their body had started protesting, which is how they knew it was time to pack it in. They went inside and cleaned up, but once they were done, they sat at the kitchen table feeling something they had not been used to. Was it...boredom?

They missed Clem's presence, which felt like a bad road to walk. Still they sat there thinking how they missed Clementine and her prattling on about whatever she prattled on about. Lou just liked the sound of her pretty voice filling the cabin and their thoughts.

It was a dangerous feeling to have.

Desperate to distract themself, they set up a fire outside, grabbed the whiskey bottle and pulled Pa's old, dusty guitar from under the bed. They went out to the fire just as the sun was setting. They were noodling around as they saw a horse coming up the road, making their heart leap. They took another swig of the bottle, making them even more light-headed.

They hoped it was Clementine, desperately missing her and caring less about hiding their feelings the more time passed and the more whiskey they drank.

Strumming the guitar, they started playing a new tune they had heard in the saloon not too long ago just as Clementine made it up the long road to their cabin.

"Oh my darlin', oh my darlin', oh my darlin' Clementine," they sang softly to themself as Trigger and Clem got closer. They tipped their hat at Clem as she dismounted near the cabin, and continued strumming.

"What are you playing?" Clem asked as Trigger trotted on his own to the barn and she wandered closer to the fire.

"Jus'a song I heard. New one," they said.

"Sing it for me?"

"I ain't much of a singer," Lou said as they tilted their head and smiled. They took another swig of whiskey as Clem sat down next to them at the fire. She was sitting close enough that they could smell her perfume and it made them dizzy.

"Don't matter," Clementine said, leaning a little into them. "Sing for me."

Lou hummed and considered teasing Clem for a bit, but the liquor in their veins made them playful.

"Oh my darlin', oh my darlin', oh my darlin' Clementine. You were lost and gone forever. Dreadful sorrow, Clementine."

Clementine frowned at the last line. "Sorrow? I don't like this."

Lou smiled toothily and continued, "In a cavern, in a canyon, excavating for a mine, dwelt a miner forty-niner. And his daughter, Clementine."

"How does this end?"

"Oh, Clementine drowns," Lou said, as they continued to strum.

Clem frowned deeper. "This isn't as romantic as I thought it would be when I rode up," she said, resting her elbow on her knee, hand under her chin.

She was beautiful, frown deepening the color of her eyes and accentuating her features. The light of the fire on her complexion made her glow, highlighting her features in the gold Lou had heard rumors of in the hills. Lou felt their heart thump annoyingly in their chest, throbbing almost painfully with affection.

"Oh my darlin', oh my darlin'. Oh my darlin', Clementine. You are lost and gone forever, dreadful sorrow, Clementine."

Clementine blushed and smiled despite her words. "You have to know something more romantic than that."

"You want me to sing you a love song, Miss Clementine?"

The problem was that Lou knew they would sing her a love song if she asked enough. The way that their heart throbbed in their chest just looking at how the fire reflected in her eyes scared them. They hadn't let themself feel this way about anyone in a long time, and the last time it was almost a disaster.

There were people after them, not good people, that made just the very idea of having someone in their life like that feel impossible. They weren't interested in more heartbreak, and Clem was going to leave after she made the money for her debt. They couldn't let themself be caught up in it.

"Well, I wouldn't be against it," she said as she crossed her legs and smiled with a bat of her eyelashes that made Lou blush even deeper. "A girl doesn't hate having a love song sung to her."

Lou wanted to sing every love song they'd ever heard for her, but instead they took another swig of their whiskey. They passed it to Clem who took her own long drink. Lou found it very attractive.

"Maybe someday," Lou teased as they continued to strum.

Clementine rolled her eyes good-naturedly and winked at Lou. "I'll break you."

"That's a mighty promise, Miss Clementine."

"I'd bet on it if I were a betting woman."

Lou's heart beat stronger than they ever hoped as the fire reflected off Clem's eyes, the brightness of them making them feel a little off balance. Clementine was beautiful, there was no going around that. Lou just wished she wasn't so keen on them, that she would find a husband worth making her life better. And that wasn't Lou, even if Lou was convinced their heart had never felt anything like it felt in Clementine's presence.

Still, Lou tried to push it away as best they could. It would be best for them and best for Clementine.

* * *

"Achoo!"

Clementine's ears perked up when she heard the sound, followed by a small sniffle. She stood up straight from where she'd been making the bed as Lou walked in. Well, dragged in more like.

It looked like their limbs were ten times heavier the way they were carrying them. Their face was a little pale, dark circles under their eyes. Lou slid into a chair with a small cough and she strode over to them.

"You're sick," she stated, automatically placing the back of her hand on Lou's forehead and only feeling briefly before Lou swatted her hand away. "You have a fever."

"I ain't got no fever."

They swiped at her hand again weakly. She just wanted to pinch Lou's cheeks, they looked so pathetic.

"Probably from sleeping out in that barn and the summer rain we've been getting," she said, taking their arm and steering them toward the bed. Lou let her for a moment until she tried to guide them down onto it. They pulled their arm away and shook their head.

"'M fine, Miss Clementine. Too hot to be sick."

"Tell that to your body," she said with a hint of amusement. She reached up to feel Lou's neck with the back of her hand and hissed. "You're burning up, Lou. Come on. Get into bed."

"I will not, there's too much to do."

Lou was stubborn but she was determined, an even match if she had anything to say about it. She was already pulling Lou's shirt from where it was tucked into their pants and Lou's weak push at her hands were doing nothing to dissuade her.

"Come on," she said sweetly, as they made a pathetic attempt at tucking their shirt back in. She covered their hands with her own, forcing Lou to look at her as she made her eyes as big and pleading as possible. "Please?"

She watched as all the resolve in their eyes crumbled and they dropped her hands with a sigh. Without even thinking, she continued to undress them, quickly undoing the buttons on their work shirt. It wasn't until their leather suspenders and tight cotton undershirt came into view, a white bandage wrapped tightly around their chest under it, that Clementine realized she was taking their clothes off. This definitely wasn't the way she had imagined this. Not that she had imagined it…

Maybe once. Or twice.

She blushed, her mind going to impossibly dirty places as she pulled the suspenders down their shoulders. Their voice brought her from a moment in her mind where she was straddling Lou and pulling the front of their shirt open.

"I don' like bein' sick," Lou mumbled, as she cleared her throat and quickly pushed their shirt over their shoulders and onto the floor. She noticed that the edges of the bandages dug into their skin, leaving thin red lines of irritation. She ran her hands along the angry skin briefly before remembering herself.

Her heart pounded as she reached for the edge of the bandage. They started out of their sick daze, hands instantly finding hers and jerking them away as they sat up quickly.

"Stop—"

Her eyes caught Lou's and they stopped, fear flashing briefly behind their eyes. She smiled softly at them, trying to reassure them. She had questions. A lot of questions, actually, but there was no way Lou would open up to her the way she craved. Clem needed Lou to know that she would take their secrets to her grave, particularly this one, whatever it was. She wasn't sure she could even articulate it if she wanted. It wasn't hers to articulate though, she figured.

"It's okay. I won't tell…I want to help you."

"I don' wan' you'a think'a me different," Lou whispered.

She shook her head, unable to keep the frown from her face. She didn't know what Lou meant, not specifically, but she understood. She could say she'd never seen Lou this vulnerable, this small and helpless-looking. It was something she was sure Lou hated, but she felt like it was more than that. Probably the reason Lou never undressed near her or would always stand a little taller when they knew Clem was looking at them. Sickness had rendered Lou vulnerable and Clementine felt her heart surge with affection. She actually felt a little faint from the rush of it all.

"You're just Lou," she said simply. "You'll always just be Lou."

A moment passed between them and Clementine felt a new trust form, one she would never dare break.

"A'ight," Lou said, slowly lowering their hands. They reached for their discarded shirt as Clementine began undoing the bandage. Lou moved themself when Clementine got to the last layer, turning their back to her and cradling the shirt to their chest. Clementine let her fingers brush absently again over the red lines left by the bandage as she pulled the last layer away. The question on the top of her tongue was whether the pain was worth it, but one moment later, Lou pulled their shirt back over their head and the question retreated.

Lou turned to lie back down and Clementine continued to undress them, quickly undoing the button of their pants with an even deeper blush.

"Miss Clementine, this is not proper," Lou weakly protested, as they pushed her hands away and finished with their pants, pushing them down their legs until they were just in their undershirt and long underpants that came down to their knees.

"I'm just trying to help," she said, voice a few octaves higher as she pulled the blanket and sheet back on the bed. She gripped Lou's forearms and gently guided them into the bed.

"Now get some sleep."

"There's too much to do," Lou mumbled, even as their face turned into the pillow and their eyelids drooped with exhaustion.

"You're no use to anyone like this," she said as she pulled the covers up to Lou's chin. They promptly kicked them off and Clementine sighed, placing them just over their feet.

"This pillow smells good," they mumbled as they hugged it to their chest, face so completely buried in it that she wondered if they might smother themself.

"Just sleep. I'll bring you some soup. Okay?"

Lou mumbled something incoherent before they went still, their breathing evening out. She couldn't help but smile at how their mouth hung open. She was sure a fly would walk in if they kept it up. With Lou incapacitated, Clementine took her opportunity to press her hand to their forehead again. Definitely a fever. She could feel how clammy their skin was. Her fingers brushed against a strand of dark hair and she blushed. Their hair looked so soft, so inviting. And she had been thinking of running her fingers through it, particularly when they were sweaty after working on the house, hammering away.

It was like her fingers moved on their own accord. She watched, part horrified and part fascinated, as her fingers raked through dark waves. She tugged the silky strands between her fingers, nails just barely scraping against their scalp. The gentle curls bounced back into place even as she pulled them, and her heart fluttered.

Lou's brow furrowed ever so slightly in their sleep and she quickly retracted her hand, waiting to see if she had woken them up. But their brow relaxed again and she let out a small sigh of relief. Her hand itched to move back through that hair, but instead she took advantage of Lou being asleep and pulled the blanket over them and up to their shoulders.

"Sleep," she whispered, brushing her hand over their shoulder briefly. She smiled as she thought of all the things she'd need to get from town to make soup. Maybe just a couple of vegetables to make a convincing one, as she'd just used the last of the carrots. Lou could survive on their own for a few hours. Plus, the further away she was, the less likely it was that she would do something embarrassing again—something that was getting increasingly harder around Lou, it seemed.

* * *

The second day of Lou being sick in bed was also Clementine's second day of working at the saloon. She was tempted to strap Lou to the bed to make sure they stayed there while she was gone instead of getting up to work, like she knew they would try to do. Then the image of Lou strapped in a bed made her corset tighten and she quickly abandoned the imagery.

She hoped a soothing cup of tea would be enough to keep Lou down while she was gone.

Dressing for her job was a little more difficult than she had imagined. She only had a couple of dresses and skirts, simple cotton and nothing fancy, but all the other girls had brightly colored ensembles made of soft silks and velvet. Every outfit was designed to really get a customer's attention. It was like an unspoken uniform. And sure, maybe it was because most of them also worked upstairs, but Clementine couldn't help but feel a little self-conscious pattering about in her old cotton dresses with her baby face, while surrounded by beautiful, high-class-looking women.

She tightened her corset as much as she could, breasts pushed high, but it still didn't have the same effect.

Clementine had always been self-conscious, particularly about her skin. Her dad would always point out how she was darker than her sisters, like it was something to be ashamed of. Most the girls working in the saloon had the same pale skin that she used to envy, fair and light. But she'd gotten over that, she didn't envy it anymore, she loved her skin and how it protected her from the sun in a way that her sisters didn't have, but she was more than aware that the paler the skin, the more desirable you were to men. She knew it was wrong and gross, but still it made her sick.

When she got to the saloon, she smiled politely at Juanita and Veronica, who were both mingling about with the midday crowd. She pulled the sleeves of her shirt down her arms so that her shoulders were exposed. Better than nothing, she figured.

She went behind the bar and Juanita walked over, hand on her hip as she leaned one elbow on the wood. "I'm going to ask you something, but know I don't mean it to be offensive," she started with a kind smile.

Clementine smiled back nervously. "That's a terrifying way to start a conversation."

"You're right, I shouldn't have started out that way. How about, do you want a dress?"

"What?"

"I'm not saying what you're wearing isn't lovely," Juanita quickly said, straightening up. "You're cute. Clearly. But I have a dress that never quite fit me right, and lookin' at you, I'd say it'd fit you like a glove. More on par with what everyone else wears, lots'a lace, you know. What do you say?"

Clementine smiled and pulled her sleeve back up her shoulder as her ears burned in embarrassment. "I would be eternally grateful."

Juanita winked at her and tilted her head toward the stairs. "Okay, let's go."

The upstairs was basically a railed catwalk with rooms looking down into the main part of the saloon. A rhythmic grunting came from behind a closed door and Clementine blushed, hurrying after Juanita as she led her down a short hallway off the main row to a more private room at the rear of the floor.

Juanita pulled a key on a chain out from around her neck and unlocked the door. Clementine followed her in, trying not to seem too nosy as she looked around the room. It was a modest size, but not too small. A plush-looking bed pressed against the middle of the wall, a vanity opposite it. There was a closet with an ornate changing screen next to it, designs hand-painted on to the material like beautiful white birds and Japanese writing, but Juanita passed it and went to a trunk at the end of her bed.

"Make yourself at home, sweetie," Juanita said, gesturing toward the bed as she opened the trunk. Clementine tentatively sat on the edge as she watched Juanita sift through her trunk.

"Your room is nice."

The silence felt too heavy when she had so many questions, and she couldn't sit in it any longer for fear she'd blurt something stupid out—like whether Juanita might know if Lou had scars over the rest of their body like the ones on their arms. Though Clem remembered the vast expanse of nearly flawless skin on Lou's back that she'd seen while undressing them.

"Not bad if I do say so myself. Aha!"

Juanita pulled out a dress wrapped in tissue paper and closed the trunk, setting the package on top. She unwrapped it, then shook it out. It was an almost steel blue, silky dress with black lace and accents. Instead of sleeves there were thick straps and the neck dipped low in the front. Clementine couldn't help but reach out and run her fingers along the fabric.

"You like?"

She pulled her hand back like she'd been burned. "I could *never*. It's too nice."

Juanita frowned a little and thrust it toward Clementine. "Why not? It doesn't fit me. Some guy that was way too hung up on me but bad with eyeballing sizes bought it for me before he went back to his wife in Louisiana. I'll just be glad it's getting some use."

Clementine tucked some hair behind her ear. "I couldn't."

"Just try it on," Juanita said, dropping the dress in Clementine's lap and gesturing toward the changing screen.

Clementine smiled. "All right, I guess it couldn't hurt to try it on."

"Thank you."

She took the dress behind the screen, and Juanita took her place on the bed. She settled the dress over the back of a nearby chair. The screen was tall enough that Clementine couldn't see Juanita behind it, but she could hear the smile in her voice when she asked, "How's Lou been treating you?"

She was thankful that Juanita couldn't see her blush as she took her dress off. "They're very polite."

"*La Sombra del Diablo* my ass." Clementine heard her mutter with a chuckle. "They're definitely not as dangerous as they want everyone to think."

The name sent a thrill through her body and her stomach felt warm. *The Shadow of the Devil.* She could see how the name would invoke fear, a creeping sense of dread, but knowing Lou, it sounded almost...alluring.

Still her jealousy won out. Curiosity crept up her spine and burrowed into her brain. It tugged at her stomach and was making it impossible not to ask. She licked her lips and a question slipped out. "So Lou is a good *customer* then?" she asked breezily. "Come here often?" she added casually.

She was just making conversation after all. She slipped her arms through the shoulder straps of the dress and tightened the corset as best she could before she stepped out from behind the divider.

Juanita's smug smile and raised eyebrow made Clementine's stomach hurt. "They're a great *customer*. Never causes problems. Always polite." She gestured for Clementine to come closer. "Here let me do up the back for you."

She stood in front of Juanita so she could tighten the strings. Skilled fingers pulled the corset together and Clementine looked down at the dress. Juanita gripped her hips and turned her around.

"Wow."

"Does it look okay?" Clementine asked, smoothing her hand along her stomach.

Juanita beamed. "It looks like it was made for you."

"Thanks," Clementine mumbled modestly, a smile turning up the corners of her lips as she looked at herself.

Juanita stood up from the bed and suddenly she was standing very close. She smelled a little like roses and a spice that Clementine couldn't identify. Juanita's hands were on her shoulders and she squeezed. "You look beautiful. Now," she said, turning her toward the door and tapping her ass, "let's go make some tips."

CHAPTER FIVE

Lou was convinced they were surrounded by wildflowers. They felt like they were lying in a bed of wildflowers, their body relaxed and the sun baking their skin.

No. That was a fever.

They remembered the burning in their head and the aches in their body and groaned, waking up just a little. They were in their bed, not a field like they had thought. But it was soft and still smelled lovelier than they had ever imagined. Turning their face into the pillow, Lou took a deep breath and let their lungs fill with the scent of wildflowers.

Clementine, Lou's fever-addled mind allowed them to think. The pillow smelled so good because Clementine used it. And Clementine was so pretty and smelled so good and *maybe* was their wife, although Lou hadn't signed anything so she probably wasn't.

The corner of their mouth still burned from where Clementine had kissed them.

Why did she have to be so pretty? And kind and considerate and…

Honestly, it wasn't fair. Especially when Clementine looked up at them with those eyes.

Lou groaned and turned their head until their face was completely in the pillow. Maybe if they smothered themself it would be better. Then they wouldn't have to worry about continuously shoving her away. Whatever compulsion she had to help Lou right now would end soon anyway and then they wouldn't have to worry about it. That, and Lou just knew she was going to leave soon, no reason to get attached.

They drifted back to a restless sleep, thinking of all the chores they still had to do. Their barely started new house just lay in the sun, probably warping.

Lou woke up again as Clementine came through the door. Their eyes felt itchy and they could only open them a little bit before they shut them with a groan. "Fuck," they muttered to themself, stretching their limbs a little.

They opened their eyes again and Clementine hovered over them, brown hair falling in waves to one side of her neck as her fingers skillfully undid the braid. and brushed through the strands. Their gaze naturally wandered down Clementine's arm, noticing much more of it was visible than usual. They could even see her collarbone and the tops of her breasts over the dress. A different dress. Lou felt their fever come back.

"You 'ave a new dress," Lou said dumbly.

"I do."

"It's pretty."

"It's time for you to get up and get in the bath," Clementine said softly, thankfully not responding to what they said. She reached down and put her hand on Lou's forehead again. "Your fever has gone down some."

They groaned and just pulled the covers up to their nose. "I don't wanna."

"I'll fill it up and then you just have to get in," Clementine said, amusement in her voice. She tugged on the sheet and it slipped from Lou's fingers, much to their annoyance.

"I can't, yer here," Lou said as they curled onto their side to try and get comfortable again.

"I'm drawing the water to warm up. You have some time to get over the fact that you're taking a bath before I wrestle you into it."

Lou imagined Clementine wrestling them into a bathtub. Luckily she was out the door before they could feel embarrassed. They tried to push themself to sit up, body aching. A bath would feel nice, but they looked over at the tub in the corner, no barrier around it, and groaned. They definitely didn't want to be naked around her.

It was bad enough without the gentle, comforting hug of the bandages that they usually kept wrapped around their chest to disguise their breasts. They'd been doing it since they were a pup. The summer of their thirteenth birthday they went to the swimming hole with Henderson's kids, just like they did every summer, but this time when they stripped off their shirt the boys guffawed and told them to cover up their tits. They spent the rest of the summer resentfully watching the boys strip and be free with their flat chests in the sun, charging into the water without a care.

They dragged themself out of the bed and pulled an extra sheet from the trunk at the end of the bed. Gathering some nails and a hammer, they dragged a chair toward the tub. Their muscles protested as they stood up on the chair and began to hammer the sheet to the ceiling so that it hung in front of the tub.

"What are you doing?" Clementine asked, slightly horrified as she walked back in with a bucket.

Lou sneezed and the chair shifted under their feet. They wobbled precariously for a moment before looking back at Clementine. "You wanted me to take a bath."

"Yeah. What are you doing?"

"Fer privacy," Lou said, as if it were the most obvious thing in the world. They finally put the last nail in and carefully got down off the chair. But the look on Clementine's face made them want to get back on it.

"You could have hurt yourself."

"But I didn't, 'm fine," Lou said as they dragged the chair back into place. They heard her scoff as she poured the water into the tub. Lou reached for the bucket. "Let me get the rest."

Clementine slapped their hand away and Lou pulled it to their chest in shock. "I told you I was drawing you a bath. Don't be stubborn."

"I ain't stubborn."

"As a mule."

Lou sat back down on the bed and sighed, trying to relax, even going as far to lie back in the bed. It was clearly the wrong choice because then they fell back asleep, waking up only when Clementine shook their shoulder.

Even with the curtain up, Lou felt awkward getting undressed with Clementine in the room. They slid into the lukewarm water, knees scrunched up to their chest in the tiny tub as they took the soap and flannel square and washed themself. They took a deep breath and a sharp earthy scent pierced through their clogged nostrils and made it feel like they could breathe again. They could hear Clementine moving around the shack, stripping the sheets and putting new ones on, making something on the stove.

"Didja put somethin' in the water?"

"Something my mama used to always use when we were sick. Eucalyptus."

"It's nice," Lou said, as they took another deep breath.

Lou washed as quickly as they could, scrunching their body up and dunking their head under the water.

Clementine had even set aside a towel and a clean pair of long johns nearby. And as much as they hated the idea of Clementine touching their long johns, they were thankful she did because they definitely didn't remember to get them themself. Feeling a little better after their bath, they dried off and slipped into the underwear. Clementine was already wearing her long-sleeve, white linen nightdress, tied delicately in the front with ribbon.

Lou cleared their throat, the long johns suddenly feeling far too tight and revealing. They grabbed their duster to keep them warm in the barn.

"I'll go to the barn, now."

"You'll do no such thing," Clementine said, clearly offended. "You're sleeping in here."

They glanced at the floor. It sure seemed better than trekking out to the barn and sleeping in the hay. They didn't know if their runny nose could take it.

"Fine. I'll take the floor."

"No, you're sick. You're sleeping in the bed," she said as she set a candle on the nightstand next to the bed. The soft glow of the candle cast an orange glow about the room, Clementine's skin practically shining in it. With a small laugh that turned into a pathetic cough, Lou shook their head.

"Miss Clementine, I will not be sleepin' in the bed when there's a lady that needs it. I'll sleep in the chair."

Clementine folded her arms, the action pushing her breasts up so that Lou could see cleavage at the dip of her nightgown. "Lou. You *will* be sleeping in this bed. It'll be fine. I'll be in it too if you must know."

"That jus' ain't proper."

"I don't give a damn about what's proper," she said sternly. "I can certainly keep my hands to myself. So are you afraid you won't be able to?"

She raised a challenging eyebrow and Lou set their jaw, cheeks growing hot. "I don' know what yer suggestin', but I will have no problem keepin' my hands to myself, thank you very much."

"Great, then I don't see a problem." Clementine smiled. She pulled back the covers of the bed and looked at Lou. "Do you want the wall or the edge?"

Lou stared at Clementine for a moment, their whole body urging them to get in the bed. They were sick and exhausted and damn did they want to lie down again despite the fact that they had been sleeping all day. Their eyes were itchy and throat hurt and... "If I'dda known you were gonna insist on this, I would'a got a bundling board. I'll take the wall," they muttered as they slowly dragged themself toward the bed. They could see that Clementine was holding back a smile.

"A bundling board? The bed is small enough. One of us would have been shoved off the side with that thing between us."

Lou just muttered as they slipped into the bed, pressing face first against the wall as tightly as they could. The wood of the cabin walls was scratchy but it would have to do. They felt the thin mattress dip as Clementine crawled into the bed beside them. She blew out the candle and Lou held their body stiff, unable to relax with her beside them. They knew their skin brushing together would be inevitable, and so would the cascade of goosebumps that followed every time Lou touched her. The closeness certainly wouldn't help the silly fancying in their head that they had for her.

They felt her shift and her body just barely brushed against their own. They held their breath. After a few moments, Lou could tell she'd drifted off to sleep from the way her breathing evened out and her body felt heavier behind Lou.

Willing their body to relax, they tried not to think about how they could smell her perfume, if it was even perfume. The soft scent of wildflowers that they'd had been smelling on the sheets all day was a smell they wanted to bury their face in and breathe deeply. Instead they pressed their face harder to the wall, the sickness in their bones finally sending them off to sleep.

Lou woke up with Clementine clinging to them, limbs completely circled around Lou from behind. They shot out of bed as quickly as their sick body would allow, climbing over her and out of the bed. Clementine awoke with a startle, all sleepy-eyed and adorable.

Lou hated it.

They hated how Clementine's body against their own had made them feel safe. How it felt so *right* and good. They hated how it felt right to be held again and hated it even more that it felt right because it was *Clementine*.

She was special. Lou could tell from the moment they laid eyes on her—tough, smart, not to mention beautiful. If Lou really let themself think beyond fancying her, they might admire her. But the idea of fancying her was enough already.

Three years ago, Lou had ridden away from the woman they thought they would spend the rest of their life with. The life they were living had gotten too dangerous, and they weren't about to drag someone else into that.

There had been a bitter sort of relief Lou felt when they left that letter for Inez and rode Trigger farther away than anyone would dare track them. A relief that let Lou know they weren't as keen on staying with Inez as they had originally thought. They could disguise their leaving as the noble thing to do, and they let themself think that, even though they knew a part of them was being a coward.

Now, with Clementine, the last thing they wanted to do was to put them or anyone else in a dangerous situation. Danger followed Lou like a starving cougar in the desert, and there was no way they would turn it on someone else under any circumstances. They had done this to themselves, after all. If that meant being isolated for the rest of their life, so be it.

The next night they shared the same bed, and Lou woke up with Clementine's head tucked under their chin and her arm over their waist. Her arms were still locked tightly around Lou's torso, their legs tangled together and bodies touching.

Lou stiffened and tried to untangle them, but she just held on tighter. Not wanting to wake her, Lou eventually gave up and tried to relax. The scent of wildflowers was overpowering, almost intoxicating, and they found themself nuzzling the top of her head. Most of their sickness was gone, and their sense of smell was almost completely returned.

Clementine sighed in her sleep and nestled her face even more into Lou's neck. They could feel her nose brushing against their throat and swallowed thickly as a pleasant shiver ran up their spine. Really, they should push Clementine off, but they couldn't bring themself to do it. Instead, Lou cleared their throat and tried to shake her a little. "Miss Clementine," Lou whispered.

She shivered and held them tighter. Lou felt hot, the thinness of their own long johns along with Clementine's nightdress doing nothing to hide the way the curves of their bodies seemed to slot perfectly together.

"Miss Clementine," Lou tried again, hand on her waist as they tried to shake her a little more insistently.

Clementine groaned, body shifting against Lou's. "'M tired," she whispered, her breath tickling the sensitive skin of Lou's neck.

"This ain't proper, Miss Clementine. Please."

Clementine sighed and took her time untangling herself from Lou, who let out a breath of relief when she rolled onto her back. "You're really on this proper thing," she said, voice rough from sleep.

Lou quickly got out of the bed by awkwardly climbing over her and moving to where their clothes for the day were folded on a nearby chair. They reached for the binding bandage first, wrapping it tightly around their chest.

"It ain't proper for two unmarried people to sleep in the same bed to begin with. I ain't gonna' be the one ruinin' yer chances at a husband."

"I have a husband. One that clearly doesn't want me," she said, eyebrow raised as she turned on her side and propped her head up on her elbow.

"We ain't signed nothin'," Lou said, putting their shirt on so that Clementine didn't see how their neck and face flushed completely. They were feeling pretty good, truth be told, the relief from the aches and congestion making them positively frisky. Clementine clearly wasn't backing down, so Lou decided they might as well have some fun with it. "I ain't yer husband. Besides..." They turned and smirked at Clementine, eyes ever so briefly flitting to how her nightdress struggled to hold in her bosom. "...I don' think you can handle me anyways."

Shock passed over her face and then settled on smugness again. "I think you'd be surprised with what I could handle."

Lou chuckled and tucked their shirt into their pants, doing them up before slipping their suspenders over their shoulders. "I think you'd be surprised how much of me there is to handle, Miss Clementine."

"If Juanita can handle it, so can I."

"Now now, Miss Clementine, what is that I hear? Are you jealous? That ain't no way for a lady to act."

They watched in amusement as Clementine huffed, rolling her eyes and sitting up from the bed. "I may be a lot of things, but jealous isn't one of them."

Lou just nodded, eyebrows raised in a way to show Clementine they didn't believe her. "Whatever you say, Miss Clementine," they said with a wink. Clementine's cheeks instantly tinted. "Now'at I'm feelin' better, I'm gonna tend to the chores."

As Lou left the cabin, they heard Clementine let out a strangled groan behind them.

CHAPTER SIX

Clementine woke up the next morning, reaching for the empty spot in the bed next to her. The sheets were still warm when she balled them in her fist, eyes slowly blinking open. Sitting up, she saw Lou's shirt still hanging over the chair, so they hadn't gone far. They were probably in the outhouse.

It was early, not as early as she had planned to get up, but early enough. She had the grand idea of helping them with the house. She'd worked at the saloon the day before, but when she got home, she saw how exhausted Lou looked, the lingering sickness slowing them down and making them clumsy. She knew Lou wasn't as far along on the house as they had hoped to be.

The very simple bare framing of the first two walls stood not far from the original cabin, and Lou hadn't stopped complaining about being sick and not being able to work on it. She wanted to help. Feeding chickens and making meals only went so far. Lou had *paid* for her to get away from that horrible man, and she didn't feel like she was contributing enough.

There was also something in the back of her mind that said if she made herself useful, Lou would be less keen on getting rid of her.

She got up and slipped out of her nightgown, pulling a simple cream-and-rose-colored dress over her head. If she was fast, she could get out there before Lou was back in the cabin, and maybe they wouldn't notice.

After tying up her boots, she headed out the front door, stopping in surprise when she saw Lou sitting on the steps of the porch, gazing out toward the horizon where the sun was rising. They had their pants on but were barefoot, a thick woven blanket around their shoulders.

"Lou?"

Lou didn't even look at her, just said a gentle, "Ssh."

Clementine followed their gaze and saw a herd of wild horses grazing in the distance. "Wow," she breathed, slowly sitting beside Lou.

"I haven't seen 'em this close to town in a long time," Lou whispered.

Their arms bumped together and she shivered, the cool morning air sending a chill through her. Lou noticed and immediately took the blanket off their own shoulders, sliding it over hers.

"Now you'll be cold," she said softly. She unwrapped herself and tucked the blanket around Lou's far shoulder so they were huddled together under it. She could practically see the protest about to spill from Lou's mouth.

"Don't," she warned playfully.

Lou huffed but took the other side of the blanket so that it stayed around them. "Wonder what brought 'em out 'ere?"

Most of the horses were brown with a couple of black ones in the middle of the herd. But there was one that caught Clementine's eye, a white-and-black-spotted horse. Even with the distance, she could see how its coat shone in the sun, a splash of speckles across the hindquarters.

"See that black-and-white one?" Clementine whispered, using it as an excuse to lean closer. Lou hummed in acknowledgment. "Those are my favorite kind of horses. My momma had a horse like that and I always wanted one."

As she stared at the horses, she could feel Lou's gaze drift to her. "Beautiful," Lou breathed. Clementine's entire body warmed and she looked down at her lap, feeling her cheeks warm as she looked shyly back up at Lou.

Kind brown eyes looked back at her, the gentlest smile on their face before quickly looking away. She felt the push and pull coming from them and hated it. It made her want to jump into their lap, just take Lou's face between her hands and kiss some sense into them. But as soon as she did that, Lou would take off running.

"Why're you up so early?"

"No reason."

"No reason?"

"I wanted to help. With the house."

"Why?"

"I want to help you. With our...the house," Clementine quickly corrected her mistake but the silence that followed told her that Lou had heard anyway. "I just want to do more to help."

"You do more'an enough, darlin'. Trust me."

"I can always do more."

"Yer company is jus' fine."

"But—"

"Ssh, jus' enjoy this," Lou said, putting their arm around Clementine's shoulders. A thrill went through her entire body at the gesture, and she stayed silent as they watched the sun rise behind the herd of wild horses.

The afternoon at the saloon had been fairly quiet, in the sense that there were no drunken fights by noon. For a small town, there sure was a lot of turmoil.

Clementine could still see hints of Lefty's gang around. The trademark scars on people's faces, one slash across the eye to show that they had wronged the gang. Lefty and his men had threatened her with it plenty of times, but she always knew he wouldn't harm her in that way. He had an odd attachment to her that she wouldn't question—not if it kept her unharmed.

She was cleaning glasses when an older man walked into the saloon. A chill ran through her just at the sight of him. There was something familiar about him she couldn't place; maybe it was the dangerous way he walked. Sparkling blue eyes peered from beneath the brim of his cowboy hat, most of his expression covered by a thick mustache above his lip. He was dressed in an expensive-looking, well-fitted suit and had two revolvers slung low on his hips. Everyone in the saloon seemed to turn and look at him at the same time as his eyes scanned the establishment. With a small twitch of his mustache and a tip of his hat to Veronica, who was nearest the door, he made his way to the bar. Clementine couldn't stop staring.

He pulled something from the inside pocket of his jacket and she tensed for a moment, waiting to see if he would pull out a weapon. She could feel the small revolver hidden between her breasts, a reminder that she had at least some protection. But instead, he pulled out a piece of paper, and her shoulders relaxed. He showed the paper to Veronica and she shook her head, hand on her hip. Clementine noticed Veronica's fingers nervously tapping on the fabric of her dress as he approached.

Clementine made eye contact with Veronica who shook her head slowly, eyes serious.

The man leaned his elbows on the bar, his presence demanding attention, and Clementine finally gave in and smiled her signature smile at him: the one that always either put customers at ease or distracted them enough to at least get their order in.

"Can I help you?"

Blue eyes narrowed on her, a hint of recognition flitting across his face that made her smile falter and blood chill. Her suspicions were confirmed. She must know him from somewhere.

"Well hello, ma'am. I'll just be taking a whiskey, if ya don't mind," he drawled as he tipped his hat at her. His voice was smooth like honey, so smooth that it sent a shiver of distrust up her spine.

"Of course."

She got a shot glass, set it on the bar and poured him a tall shot. He slid two quarters across the counter as he pulled the glass in front of him. He didn't hide how his eyes scanned Clementine from head to toe.

"What might your name be, ma'am?" he asked, glass halfway to his mouth. "I do believe you look familiar."

She felt the blood drain from her face and she shook her head. "I can't say why I would. I'm new in town. You can call me Clementine."

The man nodded slowly. "Clementine. You got a last name to go with that?"

If she seemed familiar, it wasn't for any good reason. This man was either a friend of her father or Lefty. Either way, she didn't need him knowing her proper name. "Cross," she lied, remembering her almost husband.

He took his shot and slid the glass back across the counter to her, looking her up and down again.

"Well then, Miss *Cross*. Mind if I ask you a question? Girl like you workin' a bar after all might be familiar with some'a the faces around here."

"Might I get your name first? If we're getting acquainted and all," she said with a bat of her eyelashes.

His mustache twitched again. "Bernard Burner, at your service, Miss Cross," he said as he slid another couple of quarters across to her. "But most people call me Bad Butch."

The name sent a shiver down her spine, but she busied herself with pouring him another shot. Butch Burner had always been associated with the Castellanos family. That is, right before they were forbidden to even say his name in the house. She didn't know what had happened between him and her father, but she knew it wasn't good.

He finally slid the paper across the table toward her and her heart stopped when she looked at it.

"Now, Miss Cross, I was wonderin' if you've happened to see this man around town," Butch said, studying her face for a reaction. "He's tall with quite the temper. If he's here, he shouldn't be hard to miss."

She hid her emotion, stomach churning as she looked at the Wanted poster.

Reward $3000
Wanted: Alive
Louis Guadalajara
"La Sombra del Diablo"
Wanted for crimes against the country and against the United States Army. Armed and dangerous. Approach with caution.

In the middle of the poster was a picture that was clearly Lou from the waist up, just with their hair cut short to their head, barely peeking out from under their forage hat. It looked like a military picture, a uniform jacket fitting them perfectly with the high collar around their neck.

"Handsome," Clementine whispered, as she fingered the edge of the worn paper, crusty with dirt and deep folds that stretched across Lou's face. She looked back up at the man calling himself Butch.

"Can I keep this?" she asked a little wistfully before she caught herself. She cast a harder edge to her voice. "In case he comes by, is all. My memory for faces isn't so great." Blue eyes searched her face for a moment, and she felt a sinking desperation. "I certainly won't be forgetting a reward that large!" she said, forcing a giggle and batting her eyelashes at Butch in a way she hoped was convincing. Though her heart did stop a little to see the reward money. She wouldn't be human if the thought didn't cross her mind that that much money could make a huge difference in looking for Lottie...but she would never betray Lou. She wouldn't betray anyone.

He seemed to relax slightly, putting a finger to the edge of his hat and giving her a barely distinguishable nod. "Indeed, miss. I'll be staying at the hotel down the street if you see anything suspicious."

"Of course. Thank you for coming by. I'll let you know if I see anything."

Butch nodded once again as he slowly strolled out of the saloon, looking around carefully at every person in there.

Clementine breathed a sigh of relief when he finally left, the swinging doors still moving in his wake.

She stared at the picture, noting how young Lou seemed, without some of the weariness behind their eyes, even in a drawing. Still untouched by the world. She folded the poster up and slipped it into the bodice of her dress, the paper stiff against her skin.

Veronica came up to the bar, perspiration running down her neck. "Did you tell him anything?"

"No, of course not, I would never," she huffed, voice low as she looked around to make sure no one was listening.

"Good," Veronica said, considering her carefully. "I have to tell Juanita." She flicked her wrist so that her fan unfurled with a snap and she could cool herself down.

Clementine leaned forward on the bar and whispered, "What is this about? What did Lou do?"

"Nosy little thing, ain'tcha. The less you know, the better."

"I'm already living with them, Veronica. I can't imagine how I could be any *more* involved with them when it comes down to it. At least in the eyes of the law."

"If you don't know anything, you can't get hanged for being a liar when you tell them you were clueless about Lou," Veronica said. Her jaw was tight, lips in a straight line. "It ain't my place to tell, anyway."

"Not even a hint?"

Veronica gave her a look, and for a moment Clementine thought she would give her just a little something. Instead she shrugged. "Ain't my place."

She walked back to her usual post at the front of the saloon. Clementine put her hand over the dress where the paper pressed against her skin and sighed. Just another secret. Something else to keep her guessing. She went back to cleaning the glasses with a sour feeling in her stomach.

The whole ride back to the ranch, Clementine just kept thinking about the poster of Lou, chafing against her skin. It said they were a wanted murderer, worth more than their weight in bounty money. It made her sick to think that anyone would think that of Lou. *Her* Lou.

No, not her Lou. Lou didn't want to be hers. Sometimes it felt like Lou was so close to opening up to her, admitting something, but they would always clam up and Clementine was left in the same place as before.

When she got back that night, Trigger acted a little nervous the closer they got to the ranch. He threw his head back and snorted, and Clementine had to pat his neck to make him calm down.

As she got closer, she saw why. In the corral behind the barn was a horse, pacing the edges. It was the same one she'd seen the other day, beautifully speckled with black and white, strong muscles apparent under its coat.

Lou was in the middle of the corral, the setting sun silhouetting them against the sky. As Clementine approached, she got off Trigger who instinctively headed toward the barn, but she kept toward the corral. Lou wore gloves, one end of a rope in their hands with the other loose around the horse's neck.

She leaned against the fence and watched as Lou spoke to the horse in low tones. It snorted in response, still pacing the edge of the fence.

"What are you doing?"

Lou noticed her for the first time and smiled, dimples popping and making her swoon.

"I'm breakin' a horse."

As if it were obvious. They dropped the rope and the horse stopped on the opposite side of the corral.

"But why?" she asked, hope lighting up her chest just in the slightest.

"We need a second horse. Can' 'ave you takin' Trigger all the time. I got places to go too, ya know."

She hummed, smile growing. "You're breaking the black-and-white horse."

"Yes."

She smiled even wider, eyes practically radiating affection and Lou blushed deeper.

"What?"

"Nothing," she said quickly. They leaned against the fence next to Clementine with their shoulder. "Just...you're sweet."

Lou scoffed, tipping their hat back on their head. "I'm jus' practical."

She shook her head, folding her arms over the top of the fence, her chin resting on them.

"You are."

"Whatever. Don' matter," Lou mumbled as they looked back at the horse who was sniffing the ground. They pulled their gloves off and stuffed them in their back pockets. "Guess you better start thinkin' of a name, though."

She just watched them, the Wanted poster in her bodice cutting into her skin. She was struck by how enchanted she was by the quiet rancher with soft brown eyes and rough hands. An enigma with a riddled past that she was afraid to ask about. Afraid of shattering the illusion. But there was no way. Lou, who was breaking a wild horse for her, the kind of horse she had always wanted.

Her chest swelled with emotion and she stepped up on the bottom rail of the fence, leaning over just enough to kiss the corner of Lou's mouth. Before Lou could say anything, she hopped off and headed back to the house.

"I'll make dinner," she called over her shoulder, pleased to see Lou looking flustered and staring after her. "Don't track dirt into the house!"

CHAPTER SEVEN

Lou couldn't say it had gotten any easier for them to wake up with Clementine clinging to their middle, though it had certainly gotten less annoying.

After almost a week of sleeping in the same bed, Lou had finally stopped fighting it. They would start the night pressed up against the wall and Clementine would settle in with her back against Lou's, as if they would stay that way. No matter when Lou woke up, whether it just be naturally or startled upright by a nightmare reminding them of the grisly past they had run from, Clementine had her arms wrapped around them.

Ever since they had enlisted all those years ago, Lou had problems sleeping. But somehow, with Clementine against them, they woke up in the night less often. Probably just still weak from being sick, Lou thought, after yet another uninterrupted night of sleep.

The sun came up on Saturday and Lou felt much better. There was still a small tickle in the back of their throat but it wasn't much. Predictably, Clementine was pressed against their back, arms wrapped up and over their shoulders with her head snuggled into the back of Lou's neck. They could feel her breath tickling their skin, but they kept their eyes closed.

For someone so small, Clementine sure was strong. She held them so tightly they weren't sure if they'd be able to get out of it, even if they wanted to.

Instead they just relaxed and tried to go back to sleep. They felt her moving behind them, foot rubbing against the back of their calf. Her nose brushed against Lou's skin and they felt a stirring deep in their belly.

She sighed, and her grip tightened for a moment before loosening a little.

Lou couldn't help the small cough that tickled the back of their throat, chest hurting a moment from the strain.

She sat up behind them and leaned over to look at Lou. Lou could feel the press of her breasts against their back and their stomach tightened. They shifted a little, hoping she would back away, but instead she just leaned over Lou's shoulder, strands of brown hair falling into and tickling the open part of Lou's long johns.

"'Re you okay?" Clementine asked, voice still thick with sleep.

With a small nod, Lou coughed once more to clear their lungs and replied, "'M fine, thanks."

"You don't sound fine."

They turned their head a little to see Clementine just staring, their faces close.

"'M fine," Lou repeated.

"I'll get you some tea," she said, sitting up. They groaned, not thinking as their hand reached for Clementine as she slipped out of the bed. With her body heat gone, a small chill hit their back and they pulled the sheets up to their shoulders.

"I don' need no tea," Lou said, turning in the bed so they could watch as Clementine warmed some water over the stove. Once the kettle was set, she walked back to the bed and sat on the edge. Lou crinkled their eyebrows as she put her hand on their forehead.

"You don't feel like you have a fever," she mused. Her hand moved from Lou's forehead to cup the side of their neck, and their pulse jumped.

They swallowed thickly and remained frozen under her touch. "I tol' you I'm fine, I promise."

She hummed, unconvinced. "Okay, well just have this tea. Then you'll feel better."

She got up again and Lou was suddenly able to breathe freely, as their eyes tracked her movements around the room. Lou shifted in the bed, enjoying the scent of wildflowers that had been following them around lately.

Clementine came back a moment later with a cup of tea, carefully handing it to Lou as they sat up in the bed.

"Thank ya," they said, holding the cup between their hands. Clementine sat on the bed next to them, still staring even though Lou's gaze was trained on the tea. They could see the remnants of the leaves swirling in the bottom and making nonsensical patterns.

Once, when they were still enlisted, Lou had been sitting along the trail drinking their tea when an old woman came over and offered to read the tea leaves. She wore flowing scarves that made a beautiful contrast against her dark skin. Lou figured they were being hustled for a few coins but let her read them anyway.

The woman had sat there hunched over Lou's teacup, muttering to herself as her shawl fell from bony shoulders. Lou watched as the old woman laughed and set the cup back down with the handle facing Lou. She leaned over it again, pointing at what just looked like clumps of wet tea to Lou.

"A horse. You're going to take a long journey," the grizzled woman said. "There's a ring…seems there's a great romance in your future. But something is holding you back…You're hiding something. And if you keep hiding it, you will not find happiness until you die."

Hogwash. Lou had given her the coins anyway.

"What can I do to get you to stay in bed again today?" Clementine asked, head tilted.

Lou couldn't help the smirk that quirked their lips, eyebrow going into their hairline as they looked up at Clementine from

over their cup. Based on the blush on Clementine's cheeks, Lou
was sure that Clementine caught the innuendo too.

"I'm jus' fine."

They took a sip of the hot tea, swirling it in their mouth
for a moment before letting it soothe their throat. There was
peppermint in it, if the way their lungs opened and mouth
tingled could be any indication.

"It's good. Thank you."

Clementine beamed. "Peppermint. I got it from the general
store last time I was in town. Figured it'd help you breathe a
little. Peppermint candies are one of my favorites."

"I don' believe I've ever had them. I'll 'ave to try 'em."

"You've never had them?"

Lou shook their head and Clementine smiled, soft and so
sweet it made their teeth ache.

"That's funny because you…always smell a bit like candy…
sweet."

Their cheeks felt like they were on fire as they smiled,
dimples on full display. Clementine blushed too. Lou's heart
tugged at the sight, suddenly feeling exposed in just their long
johns. They cleared their throat and took another sip of their
tea.

"I promise not to overwork myself, Miss Clementine," Lou
said, drumming their fingers on the side of the cup. They stared
at each other. Their knees brushed, and for some reason, it felt
far more intimate than when Clementine had been wrapped
around them. Lou's eyes got distracted when Clementine's long
fingers came up to push some hair behind their ear.

"I'm holding you to that," she finally said with a coy wink
that just made them grin wider.

"I know better than to be dissapointin' a lady."

"I have to get going for work. Don't make dinner. I'll bring
home some food from the kitchens."

"Yes, ma'am," Lou said softly, as Clementine slipped
behind the sheet still hanging up in front of the bathtub. All
they could see was Clementine from the calf down, but the sun
shone through a window behind her and cast her silhouette up
on the sheet. Lou didn't think much of it, looking over just as

Clementine's nightgown pooled at her ankles. They gazed up her legs to lean thighs behind the sheet, rounding out to the generous swell of her hips and waist before the outline of her breasts.

Lou blushed deeply, coughing in surprise as they looked away.

"Are you okay?" Clementine peered around the edge of the sheet, bare shoulders apparent. They coughed harder, tears forming in their eyes.

"'M fine," they sputtered, getting their coughing under control long enough to take a sip of tea.

Clementine hummed in disbelief as she ducked back behind the curtain. Lou set their cup on the nightstand and fell face first into the pillow.

Lou decided they wouldn't give in to the sweet torture of listening to Clementine sing as she washed herself in the tub. They quickly got dressed and decided their time would best be spent with the horse. They were feeling a certain kind of way that could only be fixed by intense physical labor or a trip to the saloon's upstairs.

The horse was being stubborn and the sooner they broke it, the better. A horse meant freedom and moving on and Lou wanted to give that to Clementine. The idea of her leaving sent a twinge of sadness to Lou's heart, but they shook it off. It would be for the best.

They took one of the horse blankets and the horse out to the corral and decided today was the day the horse would be desensitized. It paced nervously on the edges of the corral as Lou held the blanket in front of them. The horse huffed, its large body shuddering when it finally slowed to a stop.

Lou furrowed their brow in concentration as they slowly approached the horse, blanket up where the horse could see it. Lou relaxed their shoulders and approached the horse's head carefully. They touched the blanket to the horse's neck and when it didn't react, they started rubbing the blanket along the beast's strong neck. They continued rubbing it down to its flank, talking gently as they did.

The horse's tail flicked, one hoof stomping into the dirt. Lou pressed their hand to its neck carefully, long fingers rubbing a pattern into its coat as they settled the blanket carefully on its back.

Once the blanket was in place, a smile bloomed on their face, their hand stroking the neck more confidently. Suddenly the horse threw its head back and kicked out behind it. Lou stumbled backward, landing on their ass with a hard thud as the horse practically pranced away. Almost gloating.

They coughed when dirt flew in their face, quickly wiping it away as they heard a distinct muffled laugh. Clementine leaned on the corral fence in her nice dress, hair falling in curls around her shoulders. The light caught her hair just right so that it looked like gold and Lou felt their breath catch in their throat. They then remembered their embarrassment and stood up from the ground, wiping off their pants as they smiled at her sheepishly and walked over.

"I swear that horse is jus' tryin'a embarrass me now," Lou mumbled, resting their forearms on the rail of the corral in front of Clementine. "It was goin' good until you came along."

"Oh, so now it's my fault," she said through her giggles.

"Yes, Miss Clementine, I do believe it is," Lou said, as they pushed their hat a little further up their head.

"Well, then I better get out of here so you two can focus."

"Didja come up with a name yet?"

"Not yet," Clementine said, her gaze following the speckled horse as it happily munched on a weed it found in the corral. "Can't rush these things."

Lou hummed. They saw something dark blow behind Clementine's eyes, her smile dropping and a frown forming ever so slightly before she shook her head. When she looked back at Lou, they felt their heart stutter in a way it hadn't in years. And when Clementine reached across the rail to wipe some dirt off their cheek, they couldn't help the way they leaned into her hand.

CHAPTER EIGHT

When Clementine was six years old, before she was taken from Ghosthallow, she had a friend: Gayle Butz.

They were inseparable from the first time they met.

Her dad had taken her, Lottie, and Maria over to the Butz's house when Mrs. Butz died. Clementine hadn't wanted to go. Death terrified her, but her daddy said it was time for her to get over that. The world was a bad place, he told her, and you'd be faced with death more times than life, and the only people who made it were the ones who could laugh in the face of it.

Dressed in black, they all took the wagon over to the Butz's where there was already a line coming out the front door. Everyone in town had come by to pay their respects to the corpse of Sarah Butz, beloved wife and mother.

Clementine fidgeted. When it came down to it, she didn't think she'd be able to laugh in Sarah Butz's face. Maybe laughing in the face of death wasn't the way to go. First off, she was far too short to really get in her face, and second, it seemed rude. Laughing in the face of a corpse? No one else seemed to be doing it. She wondered if this was just another lie Daddy had told her.

She could feel the nerves jumping in her stomach, the smell of funeral flowers thick in the air, the sickly-sweet miasma combined with the starched collar around her neck felt suffocating. She held tightly to Lottie's hand as they stood in the line, nervous moisture gathering between their hands. Lottie put her arm around Clementine's shoulders as they walked into the house. Her gaze couldn't leave the wooden coffin in the middle of the room, flowers surrounding the edge of the coffin and spilling onto the floor.

The soft scent of rot lingered under the cloying odor of the flowers, the heat hanging in the air certainly not making it any better. Clementine felt overwhelmed and dizzy. She tugged fretfully at her collar. "Lottie, I don't feel good," she whispered, fidgeting at her side.

"What is it, Lil' Daisy?" Lottie asked softly, pulling Clementine closer. She was the only one who still used the nickname their mama had given Clementine when she was little. It always made her feel better. It was odd seeing Lottie in a dress. She had been running around in pants since she fell and put holes in all her dresses and Daddy didn't know how to fix them.

"I wanna go home," Clementine whined, turning her face into Lottie's arm. At twelve, Lottie had become the only family Clementine could depend on. She fed her and kept her safe since their mama left right after she was born.

Lottie and Maria looked mostly like their dad. They had fair skin, light eyes and wispy brown hair that looked golden in the right light and looked like a direct contrast to Clementine and her thick locks of rich brown, deep hazel eyes and tan skin that only got darker in the sun. Maria always told her that she looked like their mom, but she said it with a disdain that made Clementine cower and wish she could hide the darkness of her skin that made her stand out from the rest of her family. It was a curse to look like her mama, she had decided.

"Get off her, Clementine," Maria hissed, yanking Clementine away from Lottie. "You're such a baby."

"I'm not a baby, I'm six!"

"Leave'r alone," Lottie hissed, pushing Maria by the shoulder. Maria was two years older than Lottie but they matched each other in height already, which Maria hated.

"Girls, stop!" their dad said, low and dangerous as he pulled a flask from his coat. He took a long sip and the sour smell of the whiskey just made Clementine's stomach churn more. "Show some respect."

"Yessir," Clementine said, taking Lottie's hand again and looking at her feet. Lottie tugged her back, letting Pa and Maria walk ahead of them in the line. Lottie put her hands on Clementine's shoulders, kneeling so she was eye to eye with her sister.

"Clemie, why don't you go wait on the back porch?" Lottie said as she brushed some wispy strands of hair from Clementine's face. Her lips twitched in the rare smile she reserved only for her little sister, and she squeezed her shoulders. "We'll meet you out there. Okay?"

"But Da—"

"Won't even notice," Lottie said.

The truth broke Clementine's heart, but she nodded and twisted the cotton of her skirt in her hand again. "Okay."

"I'll come getcha after we view Mrs. Butz. Okay?" Lottie said. Clementine nodded and Lottie planted a kiss on her forehead before standing up and patting Clementine's ass to get her walking toward the back of the house. "Now hurry up."

Clementine nodded again and scurried around the house before her pa could see. She took a deep breath when she was out of sight, the air a little fresher. Sitting on the back porch was another little girl her age that she hadn't met before, knees curled up to her chest and head burrowed into them. She was dressed in all black, hair in messy light-brown curls around her shoulders.

"Hello. Are you okay?"

The little girl looked up, blue eyes red with tears and nose bright and raw. She shook her head as she sniffled.

"Mind if I sit with you?"

The girl shook her head and Clementine sat on the wood of the porch next to her. She picked shyly at the rough boards.

"My mommy used to sit with me when I cried," the little girl rasped. "Now who's gonna sit with me?"

"I will," Clementine said. She looked at the scuffs on the toes of her shoes as she asked quietly, "Is that your mommy in there?"

The girl nodded, eyes focused in the distance. "Yeah. My daddy don't properly know how to curl my hair."

"It looks beautiful." Clementine offered a crooked smile. "My name's Clementine, by the way. Clementine Castellanos."

"My name's Gayle," the other girl said, facing her. "I think your daddy is my daddy's boss. Is your daddy Sheriff Castellanos?"

Clementine just nodded.

"Daddy says he drinks like the devil's chasin' him."

"Sometimes I think the devil is chasin' him. That's why my mama left. Least that's what Lottie says."

"Who's Lottie?"

"My sister."

"So you don't have a mama no more either?" Gayle asked shyly.

Clementine shook her head and hugged her knees to her chest. "No."

"We can have a club. You an' me. And we can be best friends."

Delighted to be part of something and have a new friend, Clementine pulled Gayle's hand into her lap with a toothy smile. "Okay."

"Good," Gayle said, leaning a little into Clementine. "An' we won't let anyone say anythin' about the other one for not having a mommy. That's what best friends do."

"I never had a best friend, before," Clementine admitted.

"Don't worry, I'll teach you everythin' you need to know." She looped their arms together, and they spent the afternoon talking about all the nothing that children usually talk about.

A couple of years later when Clementine was pulled from her home, she thought she'd never see her best friend again.

The days of them sitting in the middle of whatever field, heads bent together as they giggled and weaved flowers into each other's hair, were gone.

So imagine Clementine's surprise when Gayle Butz walked into the saloon, a fully grown woman. Clementine just stared at her as Gayle looked around the saloon. Even though she had been in town for a while, no one from her past had crossed her path. Until now.

After everything that had happened with her family, she didn't know who in Ghosthallow she could trust. Someone had basically signed her family's death warrant, so in her opinion, anyone could be suspect. The only one she'd been hoping to run into was Gayle. And there she was. Same old Gayle.

Only now her hair was in perfect curls around her face, her look impeccable in a deep-blue dress with lace and a hat that matched, small and tilted in the fashionable style on her head. When her gaze landed on Clementine's, they both froze. Clementine's mouth ran dry as she doubted her trust and tried to come up with a million ways to lie her way out of this one. Should she just pretend that she had no idea who Clementine Castellanos was? There was no way that Gayle would believe her. As soon as she saw the recognition in her eyes, Clementine knew it was over.

Gayle slowly made her way to the bar, still staring at Clementine in disbelief. Clementine moved around the bar to the front just as Gayle stood a foot away and they both froze. "Clementine?" Gayle whispered, smile slowly starting to curve her lips. "Clementine Castellanos?"

Clementine quickly looked around to see if anyone caught her last name but no one seemed to know the difference.

"Gayle," Clementine chuckled, overcome with emotions as they reached for each other. Gayle immediately pulled Clementine into a hug and Clementine squeezed her friend tightly.

"I can't believe it's you," Gayle squeaked in her ear. "How long has it been? *Where* have you been?"

Clementine's eyes darted nervously around the saloon again before she walked back, hands pulling Gayle with her, a little more out of the public eye.

"I just got here. Not long ago. How are you? How've you been?" Clementine said, finally focusing back on her friend.

Gayle gave Clementine a look that quickly dissolved into distress. "We thought you were dead, Clementine. We thought you were all dead after they found your pa and after Lefty's gang split for good."

A lump formed in Clementine's throat at the gory memory of her dad hogtied and hanging from a tree, throat slit open and blood gushing out. As if the gunshot wound to the back wasn't enough. She could still remember how it pooled in the dirt under him, congealed and almost black. It had not been a quick death.

She shook the thought from her mind and gave Gayle a watery smile. "Maria, she's dead. Lottie I...I don't know what happened to her. I think she got away." Clementine kept trying to swallow the lump in her throat. "And here I am."

Gayle had tears in her eyes when she pulled Clementine into another hug. "Oh, Clem, I missed you so much."

"I missed you too, Gayle. What brought you in here?"

"I was just comin' by to see if there was anything happening. This town is so boring." Gayle gasped and suddenly pulled back, holding Clementine at arm's length. "Where are you staying? You're staying with me and Daddy now. He's going to be so happy—"

"Wait, Gayle, you can't tell your dad, please."

"Why not? He'll be so thrilled you're not dead."

"He can't. No one can know who I am. I'm sorry, they just can't. I have people looking for me still. We didn't necessarily leave Ghosthallow on good terms. So no mention of my last name to anyone."

"Then why are you here? Why come back if you can't even say your name? Don't you think someone will recognize you?"

"I was sold. To become a...a wife. It just so happened the fella who bought me was from town. Musta been new because he didn't seem to recognize me. Believe me, when the carriage headed for Ghosthallow…well, I was actually hoping to find out anything about Lottie—"

Gayle gasped, scandalized hand on her chest. "You *sold* yourself."

"Oh hush, it's not that scandalous. You know it happens all the time. Aren't many options for single women without families after all. And I'm not much worried about someone finding me. You're the first person I've recognized since I've been here."

"Forgive me. Ain't much different than a girl marrying a dirty old man she don't like for his money I suppose. And you're right, Ghosthallow ain't really a place folks settle. Wait. Are you married? And I wasn't at the wedding?"

Clementine rolled her eyes as they easily fell into the routine of old friends again. "It's not like I planned this! And I didn't actually end up getting married. It's a long story."

"Then where are you staying?" Gayle's eyes went wide again. "You don't…live upstairs?"

"I um…" Clementine paused. "I'm staying with a…with Lou."

Gayle's eyes got wider. "Quiet fella that lives west of the town?"

"Yes."

"Clementine— Then you *have* to come stay with me."

"Why? They're harmless." She was suddenly aware of the poster against her ribs again.

"I heard they're jus' plain mean. Never met a man they didn't threaten."

"Lou isn't like that. Trust me. Jus' stupid rumors."

"Well, I did hear that they've *killed* men before. I *hear* they're dangerous."

"They are none of those things, Gayle, I promise you," she said, reaching for Gayle's hand and squeezing it. "I trust them."

"Only if you're sure."

"I'm more than sure," Clementine said, as she bit back a stupid lovesick smile.

Gayle noticed and wiggled her eyebrows, sliding onto a barstool. "Then I guess you have to tell me all about them."

When Clementine rode up the dirt path to the ranch on Trigger, Lou was once again working the horse. Their white button-up shirt was abandoned, full of dirt and hanging over the fence, leaving them with their undershirt tucked inside their pants and held up with suspenders.

Clementine adjusted herself on the saddle, heat creeping up her collar.

Lou squared off with the horse like they were trying to reason with it and Clementine slid off Trigger, letting him plod toward the barn on his own. As she got closer, she could hear Lou talking softly to the horse.

"Listen, I jus' gotta let 'er see I'm capable. Yer doin' better anyways. No need to get into dramatics, ya hear?"

The horse snorted and pulled a little on the rope. Lou pushed the sleeves of their undershirt up as high as they'd go before moving the stirrup with the rope, and Clementine was mesmerized by the muscles of their forearms flexing under their tan skin. The horse reared its head back, but trotted along the edge of the corral more calmly than before. Lou smiled, still moving the stirrup against its side.

"Good girl," they cooed as they moved the stirrup. The horse came to a stop just as Clementine approached the fence and Lou beamed at her. "This girl'll be ready to ride in no time."

Clementine's cheeks hurt with how wide she was smiling. "Already?"

Lou nodded and let the rope around the horse's nose drop so that they could tip their hat. "I don' mean to brag but..."

Just then, a brightly colored butterfly fluttered past Lou's face and startled the horse. It bucked violently with a loud whinny, eyes wild. It took off at full speed around the corral and Lou was caught off guard, jerking forward and falling to their knees in the dirt. Their hat flew off their head and revealed their ears, hot red with embarrassment.

Slapping a hand to her mouth, Clementine attempted to keep her laughter in but it was too late.

"I tol' you, no embarrassin' me!" Lou yelled at the horse as they jumped to their feet.

Clementine laughed louder as Lou stood, picking up the fallen hat and dropping the second rope tied to the stirrups as they wiped their knees off.

Looking back at Clementine, they smiled crookedly and shrugged. "I swear it was goin' good until you showed up." They ran a hand through their sweat-soaked locks and replaced the hat on their head.

"Was it? Because it looks like that horse has been getting the better of you all day," Clementine said, head tipped in disbelief as her gaze roamed Lou's muddy clothes.

"Jus' a little dirt's all."

"Looks like more than just a little bit of dirt, cowboy." She held up a cloth bag. "Juanita sent me home with some of the buffet from today. Meats and cheese."

Lou leaned closer to Clementine than they usually did. Clementine could smell the dirt and musk and the ever-present sweetness. Clementine took a deeper whiff, feeling light-headed. "You best not be coming into the house with all that dirt."

"You spen' yer day bein' dragged through the dirt fer a lady, and all she says is not to track it in a'house."

Clementine gave them a wry look under the sternness. "If you want to sleep in dirt, go right ahead. But I won't be."

"Miss Clementine, did you jus' call me dirty?"

"Well, I'm pretty sure you're more dirt than me right now," Clementine said, lightly tapping the end of Lou's nose. Lou blushed and ducked their head bashfully. Her fingers rubbed at a spot of dirt on Lou's cheekbone. Her fingers tingled and her stomach tightened.

It was the smallest moment of weakness.

Lou just looked so charming and handsome with their quiet smile and dirty face. She softly pressed her lips to the corner of their mouth. It felt like embers brushing against her lips. She pulled away and Lou immediately took a step back. Their cheeks had never been more flushed, eyes unable to catch Clementine's for too long.

"You can' keep doin' that, Miss Clementine," Lou mumbled, a smile fighting its way onto their face anyway.

"I think I can," Clementine singsonged as she slowly backed away from the fence.

"You sure can't!"

"We'll see," Clementine said, finally turning around, sighing dreamily and walking into the house.

* * *

"How's your outlaw been?" Gayle asked, leaning against the bar. Clementine blushed and ducked her head to hide it, but Gayle just grinned wider.

"They're breaking me a horse," Clementine said with an unmistakable grin.

Gayle squealed and reached across the bar to hold Clementine's hands. "They fancy ya," she said with a wink.

Gayle had been coming to the saloon for all of Clementine's shifts, happy to have her friend back for gossiping and commiseration. It turned out she'd lost her (much older) husband and newborn in a fire a town over and had come back to live with her dad and be a wet nurse. It left her with a lot of time and a lot of grief to escape from. Luckily, Juanita didn't seem to mind that Clementine was chatting with her between helping the customers.

"Sometimes I think they do and then other times..." She wiped the counter down and thought of the Wanted poster that she looked at every time she got dressed. Lou in an Army uniform, crisp and neat. Supposedly a murderer. She leaned forward on the bar to talk quietly. "What have you heard about them? What rumors?"

Gayle looked delighted by the opportunity to gossip, leaning forward on her elbows. "Well, when they first got into town, they didn't talk to no one. We all thought they might be mute. Until we saw them talking up the saloon girls. Juanita 'specially. Pretty sure Lou was living in that saloon at one point."

Clementine's stomach turned uncomfortably as she looked over to where Juanita was talking closely with a man who was practically drooling on her. "What else?"

"I heard Daddy talking about a bounty hunter looking for a man as tall as a shadow and dangerous as a snake. Of course, as far as he knows, Lou is a woman."

"That's what I don't get. Lou is gentle...they could never."

"When they first got here, they did have a few incidents according to Daddy."

"Impossible."

"Swear on my mom's grave, bless her soul."

Clementine hummed, tilting her head at the old wives' tale that could decide Lou's fate. "What did the bounty hunter think this person had done?"

"Apparently they killed American soldiers while they were in the Army. For sport." Gayle looked scandalized as she shook her head. "Can you 'magine?"

"Well, that's definitely not Lou. No way."

"What is Lou's last name?"

Clementine faltered and she realized she didn't know. Their last name was a mystery. She shook her head and Gayle frowned.

"Well there has to be somethin' in that cabin to tell you who they are. Letters, paperwork, anything?"

Clementine thought about the trunk that sat unopened at the end of the bed. She'd never thought to look in it. It sat more like a piece of furniture with a blanket draped over it and books stacked on top.

"Maybe. There might be something."

"I gotta go. Daddy is expectin' me. But I'll be back tomorrow. And maybe you'll have more information on your cowboy." Gayle winked at Clementine and she rolled her eyes good-naturedly.

"See you tomorrow, Gayle."

Her friend walked out and she looked at the clock above the bar, counting down the minutes until she could get a peek in that trunk.

Clementine planned to go straight to the cabin as soon as she got back from the saloon. More time to sift through Lou's trunk.

If she decided to do it.

But later, as she got closer to home, she saw Lou in the corral sitting astride the speckled horse. After walking Trigger back to his stable, she approached the corral just in time to see the horse buck Lou off, and for them to tumble to the ground.

Her heart stopped and she froze until Lou stood up and dusted themself off. She breathed a sigh of relief and remained silent as Lou strode back to the horse. She noticed it didn't have a saddle on, not even a blanket, just the reins hanging loosely against its bare back.

"All right, horse," she heard Lou say, as they took hold of the reins again. "You don' wanna take the saddle, we gonna do it the hard way first. Ya hear?"

The horse stamped its hoof.

Lou grabbed onto the horse's mane and swung onto its back. At least they'd had the foresight to put on some chaps first, a little more protection between them and the ground. The horse threw her head back in protest and snorted, but didn't buck Lou again. Lou clucked their tongue and nudged its side with their heel. The horse turned in a circle and they muttered muted praise as they stroked its neck. They repeated the movement on the opposite side before they nudged the horse to walk forward. The horse threw its head back and Lou kicked its ribs a little harder. The horse reared up on its hind legs and whinnied like it'd been shot. Lou held on for dear life, the muscles in their forearms flexing and drawing Clementine's attention as they gripped the horse's mane and tried to get it under control. The horse took off like a shot across the corral and Lou flattened themself to its back as best they could. The horse reared again, but Lou managed to keep control.

The horse immediately went back into a donkey kick and Lou's hips rolled forward with the movement, still gripping the mane expertly. Their shirt looked practically soaked through, clinging to their body in a way that left little to the imagination as the horse continued to try and buck them.

Clementine couldn't stop watching Lou's hips roll with every movement, their strong thighs keeping them up on the horse. She just couldn't bring herself to look away. Something about how Lou's shoulders flexed as they flowed with the horse made her stomach throb with need. She licked her lips, amazed by how dry they suddenly were.

Finally, after one particularly vigorous buck, the horse settled, nostrils flaring from exertion. Lou waited for a moment before patting its neck. "Good girl," Lou said.

Her stomach clenched again. Lou turned the horse and noticed Clementine against the fence. Their lips widened into a smile, dimples on full display, and Clementine felt herself swoon even more.

Lou tipped their hat in her direction. "Howdy, Miss Clementine."

"Howdy, cowboy," she managed, as Lou slipped off the horse.

"Yer girl is lookin' pretty damn good. Almos' ready."

"Good. You're not hurt?"

"No, ma'am."

"Okay, I'll get started on dinner then," she said a little breathlessly, feeling like she was overheating. She remembered the trunk and stopped, turning back toward Lou. "I um…I was looking for a place to put some of my old dresses. Do you mind if I put them in that trunk at the end of the bed?"

"No," Lou blurted, eyes wide. "I um…It's full. We'll get you 'nother one, all right? You can put yer stuff anywhere else. Take somma my stuff from the drawers. Jus'…don' bother wit' the trunk."

Clementine nodded slowly, curiosity further piqued. "Okay. Don't be out here too long."

"Whatever you say, Miss Clementine," Lou called as they started back toward the horse. Clementine watched their retreating figure for a moment before scrambling into the cabin. Her eyes immediately went to the trunk at the end of the bed.

She was torn.

She didn't want to go against Lou's trust, but she *had* to know. It was torture not knowing anything about them. Groaning to herself, she went over to the trunk, sat cross-legged in front of it and moved the books off it. She pulled away the blanket and looked at the unlocked latch, just calling her name.

A quick peek wouldn't hurt. Lou would never have to know.

Quickly, she undid the latch, the metallic click sounding loud in the empty room. The lid creaked from disuse as she opened it and peered inside. At first glance, it was fairly ordinary, just the smell of dust wafting up from its undisturbed contents. A few books stacked in one corner, some letters and papers in another, and clothing wrapped in brown paper. She reached for the papers first, what turned out to be a stack of letters all tied together neatly.

The writing was a pretty, loopy lettering that she recognized from the books on top of the trunk. She scanned to the end of one of the letters and read, *All my love, Inez P.*

A picture fell out of the stack and Clementine froze. The edges were worn, Lou's serious face peering back at her. They were in their uniform, hair cut short like the Wanted poster, and on their lap was a beautiful woman also looking stoically at the camera.

She had tight curls contained under a bonnet and dark skin with piercing eyes that shined even through the photograph.

Clementine felt a wave of jealousy and quickly put the picture and letters back in their place.

The paper-wrapped clothes caught her eye and she lifted the bundle into her lap, carefully peeling back an edge until she gasped. Behind the paper was the same type of uniform Lou was wearing in the Wanted poster. There was no denying it was them anymore. But this uniform was singed and worn through in a few places; it had definitely seen hard times.

The barn door closed in the distance and Clementine quickly put everything back in the trunk. She closed it and put the blanket and books on top, hoping it looked inconspicuous as she went into the kitchen just as Lou came into the cabin.

Clementine saw how dirty their clothes really were. "Lou, you cannot come into this house with your clothes like that," she chastised, shooing them away. "Go clean up. I'll have dinner ready by the time you're back."

"I'll be jus' fine like this—"

"No, you won't." She spun them around and pushed them gently toward the door. "Clean up."

"Wha'? You want me walkin' 'round outside naked as a jaybird?" Lou asked with a huff. Clementine couldn't help but smirk. Lou smiled back. "Yeah, you'd like tha' wouldn't you, Miss Clementine?"

Clementine blushed, caught. "Just go clean up!"

"Alrigh' alrigh'."

She closed the door behind them, and sighed, her gaze returning to the trunk and its barely hidden secrets.

Clementine couldn't stop thinking about the uniform in the trunk, but mostly she just thought about Inez. She must be the beautiful woman seated perfectly on Lou's knee in the photograph, just like she belonged there. Maybe she did.

She sat on the bed with her back propped against the headboard, Lou lying beside her. The candle on the bedside table flickered and cast a glow over the page in front of her.

She still refused to believe that Lou had done what they said. That they were a murderer. The Wanted poster that she kept on her person at all times seemed to get heavier with each day. She hadn't seen Butch since he came into the saloon, but she knew she should tell Lou he was after them. Something in the back of her mind told her to keep it close to her chest for now, that Lou would bolt at the first sign of danger. On top of all of that was Inez. So tall and pretty and sophisticated-looking. Lou muttered and turned over to face Clementine, brow furrowed as they blinked up at her.

"Sorry, is the light bothering you?" Clementine asked softly, reaching to put out the candle.

Lou quickly shook their head and covered Clementine's hand with their own to stop her. Chills ran up her spine at the touch.

"No no. I's fine. Jus' can't sleep. Wha're you readin'?"

"*Frankenstein*," Clementine said, trying not to focus on Lou's hand that covered hers. She swallowed thickly. "Want me to read you some? Maybe that'll help you sleep."

"Wha's it 'bout?" Lou said, voice thick with sleep and rough. The sound trickled warm in her ear, and she wanted to curl up into it.

"It's about a man who creates a monster. It sounds scary but it's not. Not really. Want me to start from the beginning?"

"No, jus' start wherever you 're, darlin'," Lou said, squeezing her hand and letting it fall to the bed between them.

Clementine licked her lips and read softly. "'Such a man has a double existence: he may suffer misery, and be overwhelmed by disappointments; yet, when he has retired into himself, he will be like a celestial spirit that has a halo around him, within whose circle no grief or folly ventures.'"

Lou snored and Clementine smiled. For someone who acted so tough, Lou looked so soft in their sleep. Gentle and small. Clementine gently brushed dark locks back from Lou's face and leaned down to kiss their forehead.

Lou mumbled a little but didn't wake up, so she smiled to herself, marveling at how soft Lou's skin was under her lips. She closed the book and blew out the candle before sinking down into the bed, tucking herself under Lou's chin. Lou instantly opened their arms for Clementine to fill and they fell into a gentle sleep.

* * *

Lou knocked on the door of the cabin, then quickly put their hands behind their back. Clementine answered the door, brow furrowed.

"You know you don't need to knock on the door of your own cabin, right?"

"I jus' don' wanna walk in on anything improper, Miss Clementine."

Clementine opened her mouth to say something else, but Lou slid their hat off their head and held it to their chest. "I was jus' comin' to tell ya that you can properly meet yer new horse if ya like."

Clementine beamed, hands clasped in front of her with happiness as she quickly slipped on her boots. In a flash, she was pulling on Lou's hand and tugging them to the corral. Lou let Clementine hold their hand until they made it to the corral, then they pulled their hand away and opened the gate.

The horse stood at the opposite end of the corral and Lou went into their side bag, bringing out a few sugar cubes. They took Clementine's hand and dropped the cubes into it, her fingers brushing over the back of their knuckles.

"'Ere. She likes these."

"What a coincidence, so do I," Clementine said as she popped one into her mouth. Her cheeks hollowed as she sucked on the cube for a moment before turning back to the horse.

Lou approached the horse and took the reins, their other hand stroking her nose. They had brushed her out before calling for Clementine, so her coat was soft.

"Now remember. No embarrassin' me," Lou whispered before they led the horse to Clementine. They smiled at Clementine as they got closer. "'Ave you thought of a name yet?"

"Butter," Clementine said simply as she held her palm out, a sugar cube resting delicately in the middle. The horse dipped its head, lips moving over Clementine's palm for the treat.

"Butter?"

"Uh-huh." She nodded and she reached out and carefully petted the horse's nose.

"*Butter?*"

"Do you have a problem with the name Butter?"

Lou looked at the horse that had been dragging them through the mud for the last few days, giving her more hell than almost any other horse they'd ever dealt with. "Jus' never pegged 'er for a Butter, I 'spose. Maybe more like Hell Raiser."

Clementine laughed and fed Butter another sugar cube. "She wasn't *that* bad."

"Well, she weren't that good neither," Lou said, as they tipped their hat back a little. Clementine stared at them a moment, eyes soft and Lou blushed under the look. "What?"

"You broke me a horse." Clementine smiled.

"Yeah?"

"It's very sweet of you."

"It's practical—"

"You say practical, I say sweet."

"I jus' trained the beast outta'er for ya," Lou said, playfully patting Butter's side.

Butter snorted and moved to the side, bumping into Lou and just pushing them a little more toward Clementine.

Lou cursed to themself as Clementine caught them by the open ends of their vest, eyebrow quirked as she looked up at Lou. Their eyes locked and Lou felt powerless but to just stand there, staring. Their hands hung dumbly at their sides as Clementine's seemed to tighten in their vest. Her smile fell slowly as she looked up at Lou, lips slightly parted and pupils blown. Lou swallowed thickly, the collar of their shirt suddenly tightening as Clementine's tongue peeked out and wet her lips.

There were still tiny granules of sugar on Clementine's lips from the cube, clinging on and tempting Lou to lean down and taste, though they were sure her lips were sweet enough even without them. They meant to reach up and gently pull her hand from their chest, but instead they reached up and cupped her chin. Their thumb brushed away a tiny dusting of sugar below a full lip, feeling Clementine's breath on their hand.

Her grip tightened and pulled them down. Their lips just barely touched, rough sugar brushing against Lou's lips and pulling them back into reality.

They pulled away, hands coming up and covering hers. "Miss Clementine," Lou said a little breathlessly. "We can't. It ain't proper."

Her face lit up in embarrassment before her brows furrowed and she chuckled humorlessly. "You're really on this whole being proper thing, aren't you?" she asked, still tightly gripping Lou's vest. "What about this isn't proper?"

"I ain't yer…We ain't courtin'—"

"But we could be. Why couldn't we be?"

"I can't," Lou said, squeezing her hands and slowly pulling them from their vest. "I jus' can't."

Lou's stomach twisted and their heart fluttered, begging them to lean down and close the gap between them and Clementine—to taste the sugar on her lips and gather her in their arms, kiss her senselessly until they were both gasping for air. But at the front of their mind they could never forget being chased from the border with what felt like the entire American Army on their back. Guns and sabers raised all trying to get their pound of flesh from them. They could practically feel the fire of their torches still singeing their hair, and shook their head. It was too much. Too dangerous. They had chosen this life and it was the life they were stuck with.

Once they hadn't listened to their pa about keeping their head down, working hard and keeping to themself. And now look where they were. On the run for years and now barely safe in Ghosthallow. Their safety was tentative at best and anything could compromise it. Lou could never ignore his advice again.

"We can't," Lou repeated, voice tinged with sadness.

Clementine scoffed and pulled her hands away from Lou's. "Does this have to do with Inez?"

Lou's blood ran cold at the name and they shook their head. All the memories of her came flooding back, the pain, the betrayal, the shame.

"How do you know 'bout Inez? Who's been talkin'?"

Clementine crossed her arms, tongue poking behind her cheek in thought.

"I saw her name in one of your books."

Lou frowned as the realization slowly dawned on them. "Did you go into my trunk?"

"I just peeked—"

"Why?" Lou asked, taking a step back from Clementine. "The one thing I asked."

"Well do you blame me?" Clementine asked as she threw her arms up. "I'm living with you and I know *nothing* about you! You won't tell me anything—"

"I tol' you not to go in that trunk! I tol' you not to, tha' should be enough. I let you stay 'ere, no questions asked. An' you couldn't do the same fer me!"

"I just want to know what's going on in your head, Lou! But I can see now you're just jerking me around, playing me like the girls at the saloon on top of being in danger."

The barb lodged in Lou's chest and they shook their head. "Serious? You thin' I'm what? Some kinda player?"

Clementine tilted her chin up in defiance. "Yes."

Lou laughed sadly and shook their head. "Fine. You wanna think that, go right ahead. I ain't gonna stop you. If ya think that little of me. I'll be off fer the evenin' then, Miss Clementine."

Her arms fell limply at her sides, face falling along with them. "Wait, Lou—"

"I'll be seein' ya later."

"Lou! I saw the Wanted posters all around town! People are after you. There's a reward, Lou!"

Clementine pleaded to their retreating back, but Lou just kept their head high as they went to get Trigger from the barn. The news felt like a needle of fear sinking into their chest, but they kept walking. Their heart felt like it was cracked open and bleeding into their chest. Clementine didn't trust them, which was *just fine*. It would make her leave sooner, anyway. But they didn't want to share a bed with her, not after this. And if they stayed on the property, she would go looking for them. They felt a cold chill as Clem's words really sunk in. The inevitable had happened and Lou's pursuers had found them. The reality of their situation settled into detachment. Despite whatever people might be waiting for them, they got on Trigger and headed into town, tears stinging their eyes.

CHAPTER NINE

Clementine couldn't sleep that night. The guilt and anger stewed together in her stomach and made her nauseous. She should never have opened that trunk and she should never have felt so betrayed when Lou didn't want to kiss her.

No. Lou *wanted* to kiss her. She saw it in their eyes, in the way their head bent to meet her just before they decided against it. But why? Why was Lou holding on so hard to this other woman? Where was she? What was their story?

Every time Clementine closed her eyes, she would either see Lou happily in the arms of Inez, or being marched in front of a firing squad. Neither image lent themselves to sleep at all.

She walked herself all the way to the saloon that morning, the exertion and chill morning air burning off some of her anxiety, then headed straight to the coffee to get a kick in the ass before she had to deal with hungover customers looking for some hair of the dog. She poured herself a lukewarm cup and turned back toward the counter. Just as she was taking a sip, Lou walked down the stairs, casually doing up the belt of their pants with their shirt mostly undone and hat crooked on their head.

The nausea that had been brewing in her stomach all night boiled over. She set her coffee cup down on the counter, sure she would be sick.

But she couldn't tear her eyes away, even when Lou froze, belt half through a loop and eyes wide. Clementine just scoffed and rolled her eyes, taking her coffee cup and yanking it off the counter so violently that some of the liquid spilled on her hand as she stomped into one of the back rooms.

She halted when she realized she didn't have a purpose for entering, except to get away from Lou. She put the cup into the wash barrel and paced the floor, fists clenched at her sides.

"They have some *nerve*," she mumbled to herself.

There was a soft knock on the door and Lou's muffled voice followed. "Miss Clementine? You in there?"

"Don't you dare come through that door, Lou!"

"I jus' wanna explai—"

"Ha! I think you've explained *quite* enough. Your general unmade nature says all it needs to."

"Please? Jus' let me explain."

"No!"

"Yer not the only one mad, ya know! You invaded *my* privacy!"

Clementine scoffed loudly for Lou's benefit, despite the blush on her face. There was some scuffling on the other side of the door and hushed arguing before the door opened and Lou stumbled in. Their shirt was still undone, leather suspenders and undershirt apparent under it.

Juanita walked in after Lou, a stern look on her face and a visible hickey on her neck that made Clem narrow her eyes at Lou.

Juanita sighed. "You two work your shit out. But not in front of my customers."

"Juanita…"

She gave Lou a warning look that made them freeze and she shut the door, calling from the other side, "Work it out!"

Lou turned back to Clementine, who just raised her eyebrows. In their slightly ruffled state Lou was adorable, and she hated it especially when she was mad at them. "If you're trying to prove that you're not a player, you're doing a piss-poor job at it."

"I ain't tryin'a prove nothin' to ya. Specially not when you went through my stuff."

"It was…I just…" She chewed on the inside of her cheeks as they tinted from embarrassment. There really was no way out of that one, she had to admit. "Well, you don't tell me anything!"

"You don' tell me nothin' either!" Lou said, hands thrown up at their sides. "I don' know nothin' about you, Miss Clementine. An' that's just fine by me, if you would afford me the same courtesy."

"But I want…" Clementine faltered. "I want to know more. About you."

"Like what?"

"Like how many of these girls are you…have you…Are you intimate with?"

Lou smirked and Clementine wanted to smack it off.

"Miss Clementine, I do believe that is betwixt me an' whatever other willin' participant I get tangled up in."

"For someone always talking about being proper, you certainly have a funny idea of it."

"Sometimes a person needs some companionship. I came to this town a heartbroken young buck, an' I will not apologize fer how I got through it."

She took a moment to look at Lou, features softening. Lou was looking anywhere but at her, cheeks pink like they had said too much. They probably had.

"What happened to Inez?" she asked softly.

She saw Lou visibly swallow and they shook their head. "We jus' weren't right. I left 'er. Came 'ere instead to get away from the people tryin'a hurt me. An' e'ryone aroun' me."

Clementine could practically see the wall building in front of Lou and she took a step closer, hands yearning to reach out and touch them. She let her fingers fidget with her skirt instead.

"Why is Bad Butch walking around town with Wanted posters of you?"

"I ain't seen no posters."

Clementine bit the inside of her cheek, the poster scratching her skin almost begging to be revealed, but it felt like evidence she didn't want to reveal yet.

"I want to help. I want to know more about you, like I said."

"You know enough."

"I don't even know your last name."

Lou's jaw tightened. "Ramirez."

"Okay then, Lou Ramirez," she stuck out her hand toward Lou and smiled. "I'm Clementine Castellanos."

Lou took her hand. Tingles ran up her arms from the touch and she tightened her grip.

"What?" she said with a stiff smile.

A frown interrupted Lou's features for a moment and they tilted their head. "'Re you related to the old sheriff?"

Her stomach flooded with dread. "What do you know of the old sheriff?"

"Rumor has it he and his family came to a bad end."

The flame of rage that constantly simmered in her heart roared to life. "A bad end," she muttered. "Well, Lefty best hoped he didn't leave anybody to avenge him."

Lou chuckled at her ferocity and let their hands drop. "I can' imagine anyone woul' peg you fer an enemy, Miss Castellanos. Though you do tend to snoop."

"Clementine is fine, please."

"Fine, Miss Clementine, it stays then," Lou said as they stuffed their hands in the pockets of their pants.

The silence settled between them as Clementine's anger waned, but she still had so many questions.

Lou's face softened. "I didn't mean to imply—"

"Who is after you? Does this have to do with the uniform in that trunk?" Clementine asked, changing the subject.

"A lil' maybe."

"A little? Or a lot? I know you're wanted. For murder."

"You don' know nothin'. That's just a load'a bullshit. Ain't no bit of truth to it. No one got what they didn' deserve."

"Like what?"

"The less you know the better," Lou practically growled.

She set her jaw and started to undo the corset of her dress.

Lou's eyes got wide and they reached out to stop her. "Miss Clementine, wha' do you think yer doin'?"

She pulled out the Wanted poster, unfolding it and holding it up so Lou could see. "I know more than you think."

Lou's face seemed to harden. "An' that's all you need to know—"

"I'm also here for revenge," she blurted. "I mean, I didn't choose to come back to Ghosthallow. But fate brought me back here and I'm hoping to find my sister. The one that's still alive. That, and bring down whoever sold out my family the day they chased us out of Ghosthallow and murdered my dad and took me and my late sister."

Lou just blinked again, shock written all over their face. "The old sheriff."

Clementine shrugged, throat tight from tears. "You see, it's a bit complicated for me too."

"Miss Clementine, I am sorry that 'appened to you."

"It's in the past," she said, swallowing thickly. "But I just need you to know I understand. You can trust me, Lou. I really, *really* care about you."

Lou ducked their head, lips in a tight line. "My life is far too complicated fer such affairs."

"I'm not just some affair; it's me. Your wife."

"We ain't married. I didn' sign nothin', it ain't been…it ain't been consummated," Lou muttered softly, like they were embarrassed.

"That's not necessarily for lack of trying." She couldn't help but tease, just to watch them bluster. "I haven't been exactly subtle in my fondness of you. Which is why seeing you with Juanita…" She flushed at her admission, wishing she could push the words back into her mouth. Her jealous streak wasn't something she was proud of. Lou sat on a nearby barrel, setting their hat down next to them. They rubbed the back of their neck and rested their elbows on their knees.

"Miss Clementine, I can assure you that Juanita an' I're jus' friends. Not that it's anyone's business but our own."

Relief flowed through her but she couldn't forget the fresh mark on Juanita's neck, or how Veronica would always touch Lou with a familiarity that could only come from one thing. She sucked on her teeth and looked at the wall. "I guess we have different definitions of friends, then."

"Wha' do you want from me?" Lou asked, exasperated. "Yer the one who went nosin' in my shit. Why am I apologizin' an' explainin' myself fer things that happened before I even knew you?"

"You're right. I'm sorry. I'm sorry I went through your stuff. Can you at least understand that when I'm living with someone who people are calling a murderer, I want to know the truth."

"I tol' you, the less you know, the better," Lou repeated, steadfastly evasive. She wanted to shake some sense into them. Instead she folded up the Wanted poster and replaced it in her corset. Lou's gaze followed the movement but they didn't say anything.

She set her jaw and stared at them until their eyes locked with hers. She stared deep into them and in that moment felt a sort of understanding pass between them. Her heart surged and it felt like it was pulling her toward Lou, the stupidly beautiful stranger she had officially claimed as her own but who wouldn't let her love them.

God she just wanted to love them. She just needed Lou to give her something, *anything* to prove that they were willing to work with her even the littlest bit. "Just *tell* me, did you kill people?"

"Yes."

"Did they deserve it?"

"Does anyone?"

"Were they hurting people?"

"Yes."

They just stared at each other for a moment. Clementine cautiously reached for Lou's hand, surprised when they let her lace their fingers together. Her stomach jolted at the contact and she brushed her fingers along the inside of Lou's wrist. She believed everything they said. She couldn't imagine the person she had gotten to know over the past few weeks to be anything but gentle and just. They *broke* her a *horse* for god's sake. Her fingers brushed a little higher up their arm, pushing their sleeve up, to reveal the wicked-looking scars, slashing across tan skin in raised lighter lines. Lou flinched at the touch but didn't pull away.

"Is that how you got these?" she asked, voice soft.

Lou gently pulled their hand back, pushing their sleeve back down their arm. "I do believe that's enough questions, Miss Clementine."

She wanted to reach out and take their hand again, but she took a step back, attempting to do up her corset instead.

"'Ere. Let me help."

They moved behind her where she could feel the heat of their body on her back and she swallowed thickly. They gently brushed her hair over her shoulder, long fingers just barely caressing the sensitive skin on the back of her neck and shoulder, and she shivered. If Lou noticed, they didn't say anything, fingers moving to the strings on the back of her corset. They pulled them tight, tying a knot at the base of her spine.

"'At all right?" Lou's voice came deep and strained.

"Perfect," she said, turning around. Lou was still close, looking down at her. Brown eyes searched her face and she tentatively balled the open part of Lou's shirt in her fists. Feeling bolder, she shrugged one shoulder and looked up at Lou through her lashes with a small smile. "You never did say why you won't kiss me."

Lou chuckled, shook their head and covered her hands with their own. "We live toge'her, Miss Clementine."

"More reason to at least try it," she observed, stomach tingling in anticipation as she took a step closer to Lou.

Their eyes darted to her lips and she licked them in anticipation, tipping her chin up just the slightest. Lou smirked and Clementine got distracted by their dimples for a moment as Lou bent closer. Clementine could practically taste their lips. Lou leaned down and her eyes fluttered shut, lips puckered and ready when she felt Lou's breath tickling her ear.

"Now 'at wouldn't be proper, would it, Miss Clementine," they whispered.

She could feel their lips just barely brushing the shell of her ear and a whine got stuck in her throat. They pulled her hands from their shirt and dropped them uselessly back at her sides as her eyes opened again. Lou already had their back turned and was setting their hat back on their head as they looked at her over their shoulder with that infuriating and stupidly attractive smirk before they headed to the door.

Clementine just gaped at them. "Lou Ramirez!" she managed, hands closing into fists at her sides. "You can't...do that."

"Oh, I think I jus' did, darlin'," Lou said, pressing against the door so that it opened.

She crossed her arms and suppressed a pout. "Will you at least be home tonight?"

"Yes, ma'am," they said with a sarcastic tip of their hat.

"Do not 'ma'am' me, *Ramirez*," she said, following them out the door.

She did a quick look around the saloon like she usually did, but no one she recognized was there except for Gayle at the end of the bar. She looked up and saw Clementine, eyes darting to Lou as she put everything together. A slow smile spread across Gayle's face and Clementine blushed.

Clementine took Lou's hand and tugged. "Are you going straight home?"

"I don' know. Why?"

"There are people looking for you. Where do you think I got this poster? Please? Go home?"

"Miss Clementine, ain't a soul in Ghosthallow gonna be ratting me out to no one. This town's so full o' liars and thieves they wouldn't dare risk it."

"I would just feel better if you were safe at home."

"Lucky fer you, I'm behin' on the house anyways. I'll get myself home."

"Thank you."

Lou leaned their elbows on the bar and smiled like they knew it would get them anything they wanted. She moved behind the bar with a raised eyebrow.

"Can I at least get some breakfas' first, darlin'?"

She fought back her smile. "You can't call me 'darlin' if you're not going to let me kiss you."

"Fine, *Miss* Clementine."

She rolled her eyes and went into the kitchen to get a plate of food. When she came back, Gayle was sitting next to them, staring at them with a dopey grin. Lou was paying Gayle a bit more attention than Clementine felt strictly necessary. She let the plates fall hard on the table in front of Lou to get their attention.

"There. Now eat and get back home before someone sees you."

"Now, now, no need to be cross. I was jus' talkin' to yer friend here." Lou picked up their fork with a lazy smile. "See, I don' even 'ave to be married to ya to 'ave you boss me around."

Clementine blushed and Gayle giggled. Lou looked too damn pleased with themself.

"Don't encourage them," she said to Gayle, wagging a finger at Lou.

Gayle giggled again when Lou winked at her, so Clementine busied herself with cleaning the tables.

Lou stepped back and looked at the house. Well, the beginnings of it. It was just the frame at the moment but certainly a helluva lot closer to being finished than it had been. Maybe breaking the horse had taken a little longer than they thought it would, and wasn't completely necessary, but the look on Clementine's face had been worth it.

Even if it was followed by the discovery that Clementine had gone through their stuff.

Clearly they both had their secrets.

Still, Lou couldn't forget how it felt to have Clementine's hands grasping at their front, lips close and breath mingling. They were sure she'd taste as sweet as she acted (most of the time) and was almost dying to find out if they were right. But it was impossible. Clementine was already in enough danger with her last name. She definitely didn't need to be tied to the likes of Lou. And Lou had had plenty of time on their long walk back from town to remember just how dangerous it was to make their association.

Someone had already come looking for Lou in the place they'd thought was safe. Someone familiar with the town, comfortable there.

After leaving Trigger at the saloon for Clem, Lou had done a cursory search around town for more of those cursed Wanted posters, but none had seemed to make their way anywhere else. Small favors.

Hoping to smooth over some of the tension between them, Lou had stopped in the general store and picked up some of the peppermint candies Clementine liked. They left them in the bag and set it on her pillow where she would see. Their pa would say they were spoiling her. He had always warned them against spoiling women, and they could only imagine what he would say if he heard that Lou had broken her a horse *and* was bringing her sweets.

He had been right about a lot of things like keeping to themselves and minding their own business. If they had, they wouldn't have had to get as far away from the border as they could get. His other advice was to not bother getting entangled with the likes of women, but here they were anyway.

Lou heard hooves coming down the path toward their ranch and looked up to see Clementine riding Trigger, dust kicking up from under the horse's hooves as it walked. The warm feeling Lou got as Clementine approached couldn't be ignored, but they certainly were going to try.

"Evenin', Miss Clementine," Lou called, as they picked up the hammer and put a couple of final nails in the frame of the house.

"Evening," she said as she slipped off Trigger, who followed dutifully along behind her as she got closer to the structure. Lou took their time hammering the last nail, waiting to see if Clementine would move on to the barn or keep watching them like she was.

"You're making a lot of progress."

There was that tentative awkwardness in her voice that happened when someone didn't know if they should be tense or not. They hadn't necessarily left on the best terms, but Lou was willing to forget about it as long as she stayed safe and stopped nosing around in their business.

They stood up and brushed their hands on their pants. They looked back just as Trigger nudged Clementine's back affectionately. The horse had taken to her quickly, just like everyone seemed to do.

"Would you like a tour?" They took their gloves off and stuffed them into their back pocket.

"I would love it," she said as she bounced excitedly up to them. Lou stood in front of the makeshift stairs that led up to the soon to be porch. It was just the beginnings of stairs at the moment, wood planks sticking up from the dirt.

They held out their hand, palm up, and Clementine put her hand in theirs. It felt so delicate and soft in their large rough one. They held her hand gently, like she might break if Lou held any tighter. And maybe it would. They were sure if they let themself hold her hand the way they really wanted to, *something* would break. And there was certainly no time for that.

"Well, Miss Clementine, righ' now yer walkin' up our front step." They noticed the slip of tongue and blushed but hoped she didn't notice. "'Ere is where the porch'll be."

"*Our* porch." She smiled.

Lou just hummed and moved on as she carefully stepped over the frame. Their hands were still clasped, Lou offering support so she wouldn't fall over any of the wood or dirt clods. They gestured to the empty space that was only marked out by a few pieces of wood in the correct shape.

"This'll be the sittin' room, fireplace in between this room'n the kitchen. Then back here we have the first bedroom."

Her grip tightened in their hand. "How many bedrooms are there?"

"Two." Lou shrugged. So maybe they decided to add an extra bedroom? It was just...practical.

Lou led her out of the framing and dropped her hand, immediately stuffing their own into the pocket of their pants.

"Whadya think?" they asked, as they looked at the structure proudly. Building a house was a far cry from the barn they had built with their pa years back, but the basics were there.

"It's already beautiful."

"You jus' wait until it's done," Lou said before quickly correcting themself. "If yer still 'round then."

"Do you want dinner?" she asked, taking a step closer to Lou.

She looped a finger between Lou's shirt and suspenders, pulling lightly on the leather over their shoulder. The action sent a rush of heat to their belly that only roared louder when she looked up at them through her lashes.

"After all," she continued, voice low, "you've been working really hard. You must be starving."

Lou's mouth was dry, but they managed to just smile cooly. "I see what yer tryin'a do, darlin'," they said lowly, their gaze flickering to her lips and back up to her eyes. "And it ain't gonna work."

Clementine's bottom lip poked out in a pout as they took her hand from her suspenders. "You're a cruel person, Lou Ramirez."

"Well, that's certainly what that paper you keep in yer dress says. I'll be in in jus' a bit."

She ran a hand through her hair and Lou hated how attractive it was. They watched as she took Trigger to the stable before starting to clean up their work site, eyes lingering on how the setting sun made her skin glow.

* * *

"Will you read to me again?"

Clementine was still frustrated with them in multiple ways, but she couldn't deny the sleepily mumbled request. She was glad that Lou had at least relented about sleeping in the same bed together. Sometimes they would even let her curl into them before they fell asleep.

She knew she had been wrong to go through their stuff. It was a new low that she hadn't been proud of. While she couldn't justify it, she could explain it by saying she was so desperate to figure out what Lou was running from that she was driven to desperate measures. That burned Clementine, especially with the smug way Lou had come down from the second floor of the saloon.

"Sure," she said, opening up the book she had been reading to Lou every night now for the past couple of days. They almost always fell asleep while she was still reading, softly snoring.

Lou settled in the bed, facing Clementine, a hand on the mattress between them. She sat against the headboard, book open on her lap as she began to read. After a few minutes, she felt Lou's hand bump up against her thigh. It was a simple and accidental touch, but it made her feel like her skin was on fire. Her reading faltered for a moment but she kept going. No reason to make Lou feel awkward about it, as they were probably half asleep and it wasn't like she didn't enjoy it.

Then she felt their pinky brush purposefully up and down her nightgown-covered thigh. She looked at the hand and up at their face. Eyes dark and dangerous stared back at her, in a way that made her melt.

"Keep reading?" Lou asked sweetly. "I like 'earin' yer voice."

She swallowed thickly and nodded, forcing her gaze back to the book. Her fingers trembled as she turned the page, Lou's hand flattening on her thigh and running over the top of it.

She kept reading, voice a little shaky. "'There is love in me the likes of which you've never seen.'"

Lou's hand completed its journey over Clementine's left thigh and continued to the right, their touch leaving a burning path in its wake. Clementine couldn't help how her knees fell open as Lou's hand caressed her opposite hip and sat up in the bed. She pressed up against Lou's front and she could practically feel Lou's skin burning against her own through the thin material of their sleep clothes. Her eyes tried to focus on the page but they were ready to drop the book and kiss Lou the way their lips were begging to be kissed.

When their eyes met, Lou smiled playfully and shook her head. "Keep readin'."

Clementine let out a rattling sigh and looked back at the book. "'There is rage in me the likes of which should never escape.'"

Lou leaned forward, their head dipping and lips landing on her shoulder. Their touch was like molten fire against her skin. She could almost hear her skin burning and popping as Lou pressed hot, open-mouthed kisses along the top of Clementine's shoulder and up the column of her neck.

Her blood pounded with arousal and she could feel how slick she was between her thighs already. Her hands itched to reach out for Lou but they felt frozen on the book. Lou's lips brushed along the shell of her ear and they whispered hotly into it, "Keep readin', darlin'."

She almost melted at the words, a whine building up in her throat. She swallowed it down and started again. "'If I am not satisfied in the one, I will indulge the...the other.'"

She dropped the book on her lap as Lou's teeth scraped against the sensitive skin behind her ear and she turned, hands grabbing fistfuls of Lou's hair and pulled their mouth to hers...

Clementine jolted awake, sweat prickling along her hairline and chest heaving. She blinked into the darkness for a minute, the gentle flicker of the dying candle on her nightstand just barely illuminating the room. She sat up, looking over at Lou who was sound asleep, curled away from Clementine. Their hair was sticking up in their sleep and there was no hint of them ever trying to kiss Clementine.

It had all been a dream.

"S-shit," Clementine breathed out, running a hand through her locks. She closed her eyes and tried to settle the rapid beating of her heart, arousal pounding between her legs. She shifted in the bed uncomfortably and kicked the covers off her overheated body.

Great.

The last thing she needed was to be having these dreams lying in bed next to the subject of them. She leaned over and blew out the candle, plunging the room into darkness. She turned so that she was facing Lou's back, scooting a little forward so that she could get a lungful of their musky scent before clenching her eyes shut and willing herself to sleep.

Clementine was more than a little distracted the next day at work.

Unsurprisingly, she woke up cuddled into Lou, the persistent throb between her legs still there. Usually Lou was up before her, but she'd beat them this time and got up and dressed, deciding to go to work early instead of looking at the object of her affection, who wouldn't give her the time of day. Or worse—would tease her.

The crisp summer air made her shiver, some of her libido dying down with the morning chill. By the time she got to town, the dream was pushed into the back of her mind. She put Butter in the livery at the end of the street and made her way to the saloon. As she pushed the doors open, a familiar voice called out behind her.

"Miss Cross, do you have a moment?"

It took her a moment to remember the name she was giving strangers and she looked up. She saw old Bad Butch leaning against the rail of the saloon, a cigarette smoking between his lips as hard blue eyes drilled into her. It was the first time she'd seen him since he came asking about Lou with the poster, she had half hoped he skipped town. She swallowed thickly but tried to keep her face neutral.

"Mr. Burner," she said, forcing a polite smile onto her face. "How may I help you?"

"Oh, nothin' much," he said, taking a long luxurious drag of his cigarette. "Jus' wonderin' how a girl that bears such a great resemblance to a Clementine *Castellanos* happened to come to Ghosthallow with such a similar name."

Her stomach churned but she kept her smile on her face. She just had to get into the saloon. "I'm sorry, I can't say I know what you're talking about. Now if you'll excuse me—"

"Now now, Miss *Castellanos*," he said as he stepped in front of her to block her way. "I jus' wanna talk particulars."

"I assure you I don't know who you're talking about," she said, a slight waver in her voice. "Now if you'll *excuse* me." She tried to push past him and go into the saloon when he grabbed her upper arm. "Ow!" she hissed as he pulled her uncomfortably close. She could smell his aftershave and the sour tobacco on his lips; it just turned her stomach more.

"Listen here, little girl. I gave you a chance to tell me the truth, but I do not appreciate bein' lied to. I thought you might have gotten smarter over the years but I see you are just the same bratty little girl you've always been."

Clementine's chest inflated with anger and she tried to yank her arm back, but his grip tightened. There was no way she would make it out without a bruise. "Leave me *alone*. Before I start thinking it was you who betrayed my family."

He chuckled, head tilting in a convincing show of amusement, but something flashed behind his eyes. "Oh, don't try and turn this back on me, Clementine. Not when I am certain that you are aligned with a fugitive of the law."

"I don't know what you're talking about. Now let me go."

His fingers dug into her bicep sharply and her face screwed up in pain. "When you tell me what I wanna know, I'll let go," he said dangerously low.

"I do believe the lady tol' you to let 'er go." Lou's voice came from behind Clementine. She felt her stomach drop. Of course they would walk right up to the man who was looking for them.

Butch's eyes moved to Lou over Clementine's shoulder and she watched as recognition dawned in his eyes.

"Guadalajara," he said, straightening up but not releasing his grip on her arm.

"That ain't me," Lou said, hand hovering over the gun at their side.

Butch's eyes flickered to the movement and he smiled. "Now now, don't do anything you'll regret, Guadalajara."

"I could say the same to you. Now unhand Miss Clementine."

He stared down Lou for a moment before releasing her arm. He took a long drag of his cigarette, flicking the long bit of burned-down ashes to the side. She breathed a sigh of relief, instantly cradling her poor arm. Lou stepped closer, a concerned hand resting on the small of her back.

"Now if you'll excuse us," Lou said, stepping in front of her. "I believe we have other business to attend to."

"Now now, Mr. Guadalajara, I do believe your business is with me," he said, tossing the butt of his cigarette to the side. "There is a price on your head and I intend on gettin' it."

Lou chuckled and sidled up to Butch, boots toe-to-toe. "I don't know who you think you are, but I am not who you think I am. My name is Ramirez. I don' know this Guadalajara you speak of. So, if you please."

Clementine felt Lou gently nudging her into the saloon. She reached back and took Lou's hand, trying to pull them in with her.

"Hey, sir, come back here!"

Lou followed Clementine into the saloon, Juanita looking up at them from the bar. Her eyes darted to their joined hands and then back to the door behind them as it swung open. She immediately ran up the stairs. Butch came charging in, gun drawn and pointed at the back of Lou's head.

"Louis Guadalajara, I demand that you come with me."

Clementine felt the panic flare in her chest and she reached for Lou's gun on their belt, but they grabbed her wrist. Their eyes caught, and just the most subtle shake of Lou's head told Clementine to back off.

As soon as the click of his hammer pulling back echoed through the saloon, Juanita was on the catwalk pointing a shotgun down at him.

"Butch Burner!" she called. "You know damn well there ain't no guns allowed in this establishment."

Butch looked up in shock, eyes wide. "Juanita. I thought—"

"Put the gun down, Bernard."

"I thought you were dead," he said, slowly lowering his weapon just the slightest. "How?"

"Ever thought that maybe I wanted you to think I was dead? Now. Gun. Down."

He reluctantly put his gun back in his holster, eyes darting from Lou to Juanita.

"Thank you," Juanita said, gun still on him. "Now I think we should talk, Bernard."

"I think that would be a marvelous idea." His attention focused back on Lou and he said over their shoulder. "Do not try to be foolish and do somethin' like run. Or else you'll find I have no problem using the ones you love to your disadvantage."

Clementine frowned at him as he walked away, only tearing her gaze away once he was upstairs and out of sight. She breathed a sigh of relief and looked Lou over. "Are you okay?" She ran her hands up their arms, checking for any hidden injuries, and held Lou's face in her hands.

"'M jus' fine, Miss Clementine," Lou assured her softly. They turned their head and surprised her by kissing her palm lightly before taking her hands. She shivered and then remembered she was upset with Lou.

"I told you not to come into town. Why are you even here? You should've left me to deal with him—"

"He was hurtin' you," Lou said, their gaze on the bruise forming on Clementine's arm. "I couldn't let 'im hurt you."

"*Why* are you in town?"

"I got bored."

"Really?"

They looked away as they mumbled, "I was worried somethin' might be wrong."

"Stupid, stupid cowboy," she whispered, melting a little and flattening her hand on Lou's chest, fingers playing with the shirt buttons. "Sweet, stupid cowboy."

"I think you should leave town, Miss Clementine."

"Where are we going to go?"

"Not *we*," Lou said, rubbing the back of their neck. "You."

"I'm not going anywhere without you." She looked back up at the room where Juanita and Butch had disappeared. "How do Butch and Juanita know each other?"

"Old war friends, you could say." Lou adjusted their suspenders and moved on quickly. Another story, it seemed, that Clementine would have to get somewhere else. "An' I need you to go, Miss Clementine. Now'at he knows I'm 'ere, he ain't gonna stop lookin' fer me. And he'll use you to get to me."

"If I leave, where are you going?"

"I stay and face my fate."

Her grip on Lou's suspenders tightened. "No. We're both going home. He won't know where to find us."

"Miss Clementine—"

"No. That's final," she said, voice wavering from fearful tears. "I won't accept anything else."

Lou's eyes searched her face for a moment before they nodded once. "All right, darlin'."

They rode their horses back to the house as quickly as possible, dust flying up behind them. The sound of the cows mooing in the distance was the only thing that broke the silence, as they quickly watered and stabled their mounts.

Clementine hated that Lou had come into town earlier and that they had been caught. She couldn't help but feel responsible, guilt weighing heavy on her shoulders. She also couldn't help but be more convinced that Butch knew something about what happened to her family. When they got back, they both retreated to the cabin. Lou pulled a bottle of whiskey from the shelf and set it on the table, sitting down and pouring themself and Clementine a glass.

They had a far-off look that Clementine didn't want to interrupt. Something told her Lou wouldn't take kindly to it. So she sat across from them and drank with them until they finally spoke up.

"I did a lot'a things in the Army I ain't proud of," Lou said, voice low and smoky from the alcohol. "I joined 'cause I wanted to be more'an a rancher. More'an my pa. He always tol' me to keep to myself, and I couldn't listen. So I joined. It was foolish."

"That's not foolish. I get that, wanting more."

Lou chuckled darkly. "If'at was where the whole trouble stopped, I'd be fine. But I couldn't keep to my own business. I made things my business that weren't my business and that's 'ow I ended up 'ere."

"What did you do?" she asked, putting her hand on top of Lou's. "Why is this happening?"

They looked up at her and she swore she saw some truth ready to spill out onto the table between them, but a nearby gunshot startled them.

"Louis Guadalajara, or whoever you are pretendin' to be, come out right now!" Butch shouted. "Are you gonna come out here and duel me like a man? Or are you gonna hide like a coward and die like a coward?"

Clementine stood up from her chair. "How did he find us?"

Lou finished off their whiskey and walked over to the trunk.

"Lou, what do you think you're doing?" She watched them change out their shirt for a fresh one, buttoning it up only halfway. They looked at her as they tucked in their shirt and pulled their suspenders up over their shoulders.

"Now if this goes south, I don' 'ave any kin to send my body to," they said all too casually.

She gaped as they dipped their hands in a water basin and quickly washed their face, drying it with a nearby cloth.

"Excuse me? If you…What are you *doing*?"

There was another gunshot and Butch called from outside, "Louis Guadalajara, I know you're in there! So come out with yer hands up and no one'll get hurt. 'Cept course maybe you."

"I'm doin' what I 'ave to do," Lou said as they pulled a clean vest from a drawer and shrugged it over their shoulders. "I been runnin' long enough. Now my time' as run out, an' I must face the consequences."

Clementine sputtered, guilt and panic gripping at her chest. She reached for them, grabbing fistfuls of their shirt and pulling them close. "You can't go out there. He'll kill you."

"Yeah. Prob'ly." Lou smiled wryly and Clementine wanted to slap them.

"Don't go out there," she demanded, hot tears rimming her eyes and making it harder to see. "You hear me? Do *not* go out there."

Lou's hands that had remained so respectfully at their side for so long, came up and held her waist. She melted into the simple touch.

"Miss Clementine, I'm sorry, but I do 'ave to go out there. Butch Burner ain't gonna be leaving either of us alone until he 'as his pound'a flesh. An' I'm gonna give it to 'im."

Clementine shook her head, throat tight from emotion.

"No, Lou, please." She couldn't form any other words, her own pain making her stupid. "Stay in here. With me. We'll figure it out."

Lou gently took her face between their hands and her breath caught in her throat. Their faces were close and she looked up into Lou's eyes. Light streamed through the window and highlighted the edges of their hair like obsidian, eyes shining specks of gold back at her. She swore she could see every missed moment between them in those eyes.

Their hands were so gentle, calluses brushing against her cheeks and making her shiver. She pressed their foreheads together. It felt like the whole world dropped out from under them in that moment and they were suspended, just the two of them.

"Don' you worry now, Miss Clementine, e'rething is gonna be just fine. Ya hear?" Lou whispered, thumbs brushing over her cheekbones.

"It'll be fine if you stay in here," she tried again, tears streaming down her cheeks.

"You know I can't do that." Lou smiled, dimples popping. "Listen, it's a fifty-fifty chance I get 'em first. Either way, you'll be safe. Jus' don't let 'em take my body, all right?"

She felt like she was going to be sick. If she was a little taller and a little braver, she might tip her chin up and finally kiss Lou right here.

"You can't," she sniffled lamely.

"It's been a pleasure gettin' to know ya, Miss Clementine. Take the land and animals if I can't. I'll be seein' you around."

Lou kissed the corner of her lips so softly that she barely even noticed. Then they kissed the opposite corner, then the tip of Clementine's nose, and finally, their lips lingered on her forehead. She stood there in shock, every inch of her face still tingling from Lou's touch. Her hands slid from their shirt and she blinked, brain trying to catch up with everything else she was feeling.

She looked over just as the door closed and Lou left the cabin.

"Lou!" Clementine called uselessly after them. She quickly wiped the tears from her eyes and growled in anger. Stomping over to the bed, she pulled the shotgun out from under it and charged outside. Butch was standing out in the field and Lou was standing across from him a few yards away.

Both were staring at each other, hands hovering over their holstered weapons. Lou yelled out at Butch, "You know damn well I ain't goin' with you. I should just shoot you fer trespassin'."

"Then why don't you?"

"I have more honor 'an that, I can at least give ya a chance. What're yer terms?"

"Ten paces then shoot. Deal?"

"Deal!"

"You bunch of ridiculous cowboys," Clementine mumbled to herself and ran until she was standing in front of Lou. She stopped and turned her gun on Butch.

"Miss Clementine, get out."

"What the hell is this, Guadalajara? Move your woman."

"I am no one's woman! You two are acting like idiots! Solve this like adults!"

"Listen, girl, I don't know what yer playin' at, but you better be gettin' outta here if you don't wanna get hurt," Butch said, mustache twitching.

For a moment there was only silence and all Clementine could hear was her heartbeat echoing in her skull.

"Go back to the cabin, darlin'. Don' be stupid," Lou said from behind her. "We're jus' fine without you gettin' in the middle."

"I'm not moving until the two of you call off this ridiculous show. Just stand next to each other and measure your dicks instead."

"All right, I've had quite enough," Butch sighed.

Faster than Clementine could even register, his gun was out and smoke was coming from the barrel. The ringing of the bullet through the air made her hair stand on end, ringing in her ears and making the rest of the world sound like it was underwater. The only sound Clementine heard was Lou's grunt of pain, and the heavy thud as they fell to the ground.

CHAPTER TEN

Clementine couldn't help but focus on the blood pooling below Lou's arm. She kneeled in the dirt next to them, one hand on Lou's cheek as she tried to get them to respond. Their face was pale, blood soaking into the ground beneath them and brown eyes dazed, blinking blankly up at the sky.

"Lou. Lou!"

She could hear the crunching of boots in the dirt behind her but still only looked at Lou.

"Talk to me."

"'M...fine," Lou managed, some life coming back into their eyes for a moment. "'M fine."

"You're not," she said, trying to hold back her own tears. "You need help."

"I can...fix it myself." They tried to sit up but Clementine hushed them gently, pressing on their shoulders to keep them down.

"Stay down, please."

She heard the click of the hammer by her ear and looked up just as Butch stepped over them, his figure blocking the sun and his gun pointed at Lou.

"All right, Guadalajara, you will be comin' with me now."

Clementine stood quickly, anger flooding her veins with fire as she stood in front of Butch, her body knocking his gun away from Lou. She pulled her hand back and slapped him hard across the face. His head jerked to the side with the impact, stubbled cheek already reddening.

"You've done enough," she said, poking him hard in the chest. "You played dirty and shot them before it was time. You should be strung up in the nearest tree—"

"I do believe it will be Guadalajara that finds himself at the business end of a hangman's knot, dear littlest Castellanos. Now if you jus' let me take 'im into town..."

She held up her shotgun, surprising Butch by poking it hard into the middle of his chest. He blinked at her and held up his hands at his sides. "Now now, no reason to make a rash decision—"

"Get off my property. You get the *fuck* off my property before I blow a hole in your chest. You're trespassing, no one will blame me for putting a bullet in you. Do you understand?"

"Don't be stupid," Butch said, even as some fear crept into his eyes.

Clementine managed to grin at him, lips pulling back into a snarl as she cocked her gun. "Get. Out."

He backed up slowly, his gaze darting back to Lou every few seconds. "I will be back, Miss Castellanos."

"And I'll be just as pissed!" she said, shooting the shotgun into the sky.

Butch at least had enough dignity left in him not to startle, instead turning around and heading back to his horse. As soon as he was gone, Clementine dropped the shotgun and turned back to Lou, kneeling on the ground. They looked paler, the blood on their arm thick and dark red.

Lou tried to sit up again and Clementine put her hands on their shoulders again, halting their movement. "I tol' you, 'm fine, darlin',," they said, voice thick and strained with pain. "I'll just change mah shirt."

"You stubborn ass," she said as worried tears gathered in the corners of her eyes. "Come on, let's get you inside then I'll get a doctor."

"I don' need no doctor."

They grimaced as they stood slowly, Clementine hovering near them until they were on their feet. What little color that was left in their face drained and she quickly tucked herself under Lou's good arm, arm around their waist, and helped them into the cabin.

She started toward the bed but Lou shook their head. "No, table. I don' wanna lay down."

"Fine," she said, begrudgingly helping them over to the table.

The bottle of whiskey was still there. Lou picked up the bottle, pulled the cap out with their teeth and spit it to the side before taking a long swig. Clementine pulled another chair over next to their injured arm. Setting the bottle down, they undid the buttons of their shirt, hissing as they pulled the shirt down to expose their injury, revealing their soaked and blood-stained undershirt.

She looked at the wound as closely as she could through the tattered sleeve of the undershirt. The bullet had gone through their arm, not directly in the middle but just off to the side. She tried to pull the sleeve away from Lou's arm as best she could, but the tacky blood adhered the fabric to the skin.

"You're gonna have to take this off, cowboy."

Lou shook their head, grabbing the shirt at their shoulder and ripping, the seams giving way. Clementine blinked and helped Lou pull the sleeve all the way off their arm.

"Or…that."

She got up to get a spare rag. She tore it into a long strip and tied off the wound. Lou grimaced but just took another long swig of the whiskey before setting it back down heavily on the table. The liquid sloshed inside, almost threatening to come out of the top.

"I can probably handle this but I'd rather you let me get a doctor."

"No doctor." Lou visibly suppressed a shudder and she made a note to ask them about it later. "Jus' rub some dirt into it and we'll move on. Or get Juanita."

"Lou Ramirez, please tell me you don't actually think rubbing dirt into it is a viable solution," she mumbled, as she went to heat up some water to clean the wound.

"Jus' 'cause I talk like this don' mean I'm stupid, Miss Clementine," they said as they took another big gulp of whiskey. "I'm dumb. Not stupid."

"You're neither," she corrected as she lit the stove. "And I'm not getting Juanita. She's probably the one who told Butch where we live."

"It weren't Juanita. She wouldn't do tha'. She ain't...well, she *probably* ain't too happy for Butch to be back neither."

Clementine could tell there was more to the story than Lou was telling. When the water was warm, she poured it into a basin, carrying it over to the table with some more clean rags, her kit, and some bandages. She could smell the alcohol coming off Lou, and they had definitely drunk at least a third of the bottle on their own.

"Why wouldn't she be happy? Did you know Butch before?" she asked, as she put a rag to the wound. Lou hissed in pain but didn't move.

"Let's jus' say 'er and Butch don' really 'ave the best history." Lou took another swig. "I didn' know Butch but I knew of 'im. Defamed friend of one Sheriff William Castellanos. Honored deputy who had one too many run-ins with the law 'imself and turned bounty hunter. I know 'im quite well."

Clementine continued to wipe at the wound, brow furrowed in concentration. She was brought back to her time in Ghosthallow. The hushed fights between her dad and Butch that she and Lottie would try and listen to from upstairs. Maria would always grab their ears and rat them out, leaving Lottie to get a lashing or two. She swallowed thickly and shook her head. "Did he hurt Juanita?"

Lou licked their lips, bottle raised as they looked off into the distance. Their eyes were glazed over, probably a mix of the pain and the alcohol. "Depends who you ask. Depends if they consider tyin' someone up an' forcin' 'em to make booze and medicines fer ya and...who knows what else, depends if you consider that indecent."

Clementine's stomach dropped at the confession, hand pausing. She watched Lou look at the now half-empty bottle and take another swig despite the way they were swaying in their seat. She reached out and put her hand over the top of the bottle, Lou's mouth getting the back of her hand instead.

"Maybe you should slow down there, Dad," Clementine muttered, mostly to herself.

They frowned and lowered the bottle. "Wha'?"

She blushed. "My dad used to drink a lot. Caused some problems."

"'M sorry, darlin'," they slurred as they dropped the bottle back on the table.

"Not your thing to apologize for. How did you and Juanita meet?"

"I was sent to collect some medicines from 'em. Our camp needed a lot more medicine 'an we 'ad and o' course he charged us an arm an' a leg. Either way I was sent to get it. An' I met Juanita. I helped 'er find a way outta there."

"Did you two come here together?"

"No. She came 'ere first and tol' me that this was the kinda town tha' people came to when they wanna hide."

Clementine dipped the rag back in the basin, the blood flowing out of it in tendrils and painting the water pink. Her mind was split between dressing Lou's wound and taking in all this new information.

"And that's why they're looking for you?"

"Nah, that was jus' the start'a it, darlin'," Lou said, eyes going glassy again.

She pulled out a strip of willow bark from her kit and placed it over the wound before wrapping a fresh strip of cloth over it.

"Wha's that?"

"To help the healing. Something my ma taught me. Came in handy later."

"When you'ere with Lefty?"

"When I was with Lefty."

There were things she didn't want to remember about her time with him—mostly about the things she saw and the wounds she was told to fix, the ones that he had inflicted on people he considered traitors. She learned from a young age not to get on his bad side. She stood to take the bowl with dirty water outside when she felt their hand clasp warm on her wrist. She took a sharp intake of breath and looked down to see their glassy eyes staring up at her.

"Did'e hurt you?" Lou asked, hand tightening on her hip. "I'll kill 'em if'e—"

"I believe that's what got you in this problem to begin with, cowboy." She cupped Lou's cheek affectionately, skin burning under her touch. She frowned and touched the side of their neck to the same effect. "Do you feel okay? You're hot."

Lou smirked.

Clementine gave Lou a playful frown and resisted the urge to lean down and kiss them. Their eyelids were heavy and they just looked so cute. But Lou was fairly drunk and she wasn't sure if her heart could take being rejected again, not when she just had to go through the scare of Lou getting shot.

"I meant physically." Lou looked smug and Clementine pressed their lips with her finger. Before they could speak, she said, "I mean, your skin feels hot. Like you have a fever."

"Don't sound like somethin' that ain't common after gettin' shot."

Their lips ghosted over her finger and she hummed.

"Let's get you in bed," she said, as she carded her fingers through Lou's hair.

"Can't. Gotta stay up in case Butch comes back."

Lou stood, swaying a little. She slid her arms around their waist and hugged them lightly. The wound wasn't too serious, at least, not as serious as it could have been. They were still at risk of infection but it had been a warning shot. Just a reminder that just as this shot was purposefully a warning shot, the next one could be deadly if Butch wanted to carry out "justice" immediately despite the "Alive" on the poster.

"Miss Clementine," Lou said, head falling so their cheek was nestled against the crown of her head. "This ain't proper."

"Shut up, cowboy, and just let me hold you." Her words were muffled by the cotton of their shirt as she breathed them in. The aroma of sugar and the soap she'd been putting in the laundry filled her nose and mouth as she took a shuddering breath and felt a rush of heat to her eyes.

Lou squeezed her a little tighter and her tears fell. "You okay?" they asked.

"I'm sorry. You're the one who's hurt...I just—"

"I's all right. Why don' you go to bed early while I wait up?"

"We'll both wait up," she said, quickly brushing some stray tears from her cheeks.

"Miss Clementine—"

"Come on. Get yourself comfortable and I'll put my nightgown on."

Lou mumbled and took a step back, smirking as they undid their belt. "Yes, ma'am."

She blushed and hesitated a moment before grabbing her nightgown and ducking behind the bathing curtain. She changed and set her dress over the back of a chair.

Lou had moved a chair near one of the front windows and were reloading their pistols, fingers moving a little less delicately in their inebriated state. Clementine pulled another chair over and picked up her shotgun.

"I tol' you you could go'a bed," they said, closing the chamber of their gun with a snap of the wrist.

"As if I could stay up knowing you were up. You're down one working arm right now anyway. Maybe you could tell me more about yourself. We can start easy."

"What do ya consider easy?"

"Why did you *really* join the Army?"

"I weren't given a real choice. It was join or end up at the hangman's tree."

Her heart clenched at the thought. "But why?"

They sighed and slid down in their chair, knees spread wide as they stared diligently out the window. "'At's what happens when you break the law, even if the law is a bunch of hogwash to begin with."

"Which law did you break this time?"

"My pa wasn' a rich man, but he made business with rich men. One offered me a job where I could transport goods. I jus' weren't allowed'a ask questions. Thought it'd be easy. Then I saw that they were the type'a people that considered other *people* to be goods."

"Slaves?"

They grunted and sucked on their teeth. "Yeah. And I wasn't gonna be part'a that so I...well, I *lost* the cargo somewhere near the border. The rich men weren't too happy 'bout that."

"Then you ran? Pretended to be a man and joined the Army?"

"Not...exacl'y." Lou rubbed the back of their neck. "They jus' assumed I was a man an' I didn' correct 'em when they said either I'd hang or volunteer to join the war down at the border. I wasn't ready to leave this earthly plane, I suppose."

"See? You're not dumb."

"Yeah, well, it got me with Butch Burner on mah ass so, it's lookin' kinda dumb right now."

"And somewhere in there you met Inez?"

They shook their head and looked over at her. "Now now, Miss Clementine, I do believe that's enough questions fer the night. 'M surprised you ain't know e'erythin' you need to know from goin' through that trunk."

"I'm sorry, Lou. I really am. I shouldn't have—"

"I know," they assured her with a small smile. "No need to apologize further."

Fidgeting with her nightgown, she mumbled, "I feel like I should apologize more."

"How 'bout you apologize more by goin' to bed while I stay up?" They glanced at the bandage over their arm where blood was slowly staining the surface. "I'll wake you up if anythin' int'restin' happens."

"Lou…" she started to protest, but Lou gave her a look that made her jaw snap shut. Their brows furrowed, eyes sharp and commanding. Why did it make her stomach burn and mouth dry? "Okay, fine," she said haughtily as she stood and put the safety back on her shotgun. "But don't complain to me when you're lonely."

"I won'," they said with a smile, their eyes softening again.

She shot them another look as she went to the bed and lay between the sheets. Her mind was still running a million miles a minute with not only the events of the day, but the drama of it all. She couldn't let herself think about Lou getting shot because then her throat closed up with panic and the idea of losing someone else she loved—no, cared about—was too much. She buried her face in the pillow and let out a deep sigh, wishing Lou was in bed next to her. After a few minutes of restlessness, she finally managed to drift off to sleep.

The next morning, Clementine woke with a start. She immediately felt the other side of the small bed but it was cold. Sitting up, she rubbed the sleep out of her eyes as she looked around the small cabin.

"Lou?"

Her heart leapt into her throat and no amount of swallowing was making it go away. Their boots were missing by the front door, hat off the hook. Maybe they had just stupidly gone to do some chores with their injured arm.

Not wanting to wonder any longer, she got out of the bed and quickly got dressed for work. The first thing she noticed when she stepped outside was the door of the barn was open a foot or so. Hopefully Lou was still in there. Taking a big bite of the apple she had grabbed from the kitchen, she poked her head into the barn. Empty. Her churning stomach wasn't pleased with the apple, so she gave the rest to Butter and gave a carrot to Trigger.

Or tried to, anyway. She stopped in front of Lou's horse, who was pacing back and forth in his stall, and spoke softly to him.

"What's wrong, boy?" she asked. The horse snorted, barely even sniffing the carrot before nudging her with his big head instead. "Where's Lou?"

There was no sign of them outside of the barn save for the open door. The dread in her chest refused to leave as she looked around the barn. She saw a half-moved pile of hay in the corner, sitting on the ground a few feet from the stack. The dirt in the area looked disturbed like there had been some kind of scuffle. She noticed a trail of fresh hoofprints leading out of the barn and gasped.

Clementine had to get to town as soon as possible.

With anxious hands, she saddled Butter in record time and nudged her in the ribs to get her into a gallop. The relentless morning air rushed past her face, stinging her skin but thankfully keeping the concerned tears from falling down her cheeks. She was going to kill Butch if she got her hands on him. Especially if he had hurt Lou.

She couldn't let herself think those thoughts, not if she didn't want to ride through her tears.

The first thing she noticed when she rode into town was the new and freshly printed Wanted posters on the sides of all the buildings with Lou's face on them. She got off Butter to pull them down.

"That son of a bitch," she muttered as she ripped one off the side of the livery. Butter followed her dutifully as she went to the general store, pulling another two off the building.

"Whatcha doin' girl?"

The familiar and grating voice made her turn, only to see the two men that had been harassing her in the general store when she first came to town. She threw them a sarcastic smile.

"None of your business," she said, stuffing the Wanted posters in her saddle bag. One of the men shoved her out of the way before she could close the bag and pulled out the stack of posters she had already collected.

They both grinned, teeth like old, crooked fences, and Clementine could smell the sweat and tobacco as if they'd bathed in it. She reached for the posters but they pulled them away.

"I asked ya," the shorter one said as he took a dangerous step toward her. "Whatcha doin'? 'Cause it looks like you been collectin' pi'tures of yer freak."

She clenched her fists at her sides. The glint of amusement in their eyes gave the men away almost immediately. "Where are they?"

"Prob'ly dead by now," the taller man said with a wicked grin. "Buzzards probably already 'ad their way wit' 'em."

She grabbed the fliers from the shorter one's hands again and he scowled, bumping his chest into hers threateningly.

"You wanna join 'er, girl?" he said as he sucked on his teeth, eyes roaming her up and down. "I bet I coul' find a good use fer ya before I feed you to the buzzards like yer lover. If that freak ain't tainted yer cunt yet."

Her blood boiled and she opened her mouth to retort when someone cleared their throat. There, right beside them was one of the men she had been trying to avoid. The two men took a step back, meek looks on their faces.

"Sheriff Butz," the tall one said with a tip of his filthy hat. "Mornin', sir."

His hair had turned fully gray since the last time she'd seen him. His handlebar mustache twitched with irritation just like she remembered from when she and Gayle would get on his nerves as kids.

"Boys," the sheriff gruffed. He looked at Clementine. "Problem here?"

The tall one said, "No, sir—"

"I was talkin' to the missus," Butz said, shooting them down with a hard glare before looking back at her. "If I heard correctly. Yer lookin' for Ramirez. Correct?"

"Yessir. Do you know where they are?"

Butz looked her over carefully and she squirmed, feeling caught. "I do. You best come with me." He acknowledged the men again, face hard. "An' you two better find somethin' else to do that don' involve bothering young ladies."

The tall man scoffed and the shorter one hit him with his hat, pushing him down the street and away from the sheriff as they retreated. Clementine watched them go before looking back at

Butz. He was still looking at her warily and she wondered if he remembered her. She wondered if she should bother lying to him at all.

"You said you know where Lou is," she said instead, a small smile on her face as she made her eyes bigger to complete the "innocent look," one she had used often in the face of Lefty's men.

Butz gruffed and adjusted his belt. "I do. Follow me, Miss…" he trailed off, holding out his hand.

Clementine sucked in a nervous breath. "Clementine Castellanos, sir."

"I had a feelin'….yer just missin' the pigtails. Yer the spittin' image of your ma. She was a fine woman. One'a the best people I knew."

She blushed. She was never told much about her mom. Everyone always focused on her father, as he was the far more notorious of the two.

"Really?"

"Yep," Butz said a little sadly before motioning for her to follow him. "Come on, I got yer girl here."

She felt her fingers twitch uncomfortably, hearing "girl," but she breathed a sigh of relief and followed behind him to the next building, the sheriff's office.

"How long have they been here?"

"Not long. 'Bout since this mornin'. Burner brought 'er in an' tol' me to hold 'er fer'um."

They walked into the small office, Butz's desk on one side with a door behind it leading to another room and a gun cabinet on the opposite wall. He took a ring of keys out of his drawer and walked into the smaller room.

It was darker and felt more humid for some reason. There were four small cells, two on each side, and only one small-barred window for each. Her gaze automatically went to the far-left cell where a familiar body was lying on the cot. She rushed over to the bars, hands around them like she could pry them apart and set Lou free.

"Lou."

They turned their head, eyes blinking as they woke. Their hurt arm was still cradled against their front, more blood seeping from the bandage, and they had a still-bloody gash over their right eye. Clementine's heart ached.

"Miss Clementine?"

Clementine and Lou burst into relaxed smiles when their eyes met. Lou stood and rushed to the bars, the rough calluses of their hands brushing over hers, the hands she had imagined touching her so many more places.

"Clementine, I'm gonna need to talk to ya when yer done here. An' no funny business. No passin' nothin'."

"Yessir," Lou croaked.

Butz gave them both a curt nod and went to sit at his desk. She pressed herself as close to the bars as she could, almost as if she were trying to push herself through them. Lou smiled happily. Like they weren't in a cage. And her heart fluttered up to her throat at that dimpled smile.

"Pleasure seein' you here, Miss Clementine."

She choked out a small sob and a smile, a tear falling down her cheek. "Sweet talking even from a jail cell."

"'S only proper when a pretty lady come'a visit. Now now, no cryin'."

They pulled their red bandana from their pocket and gently brushed away her tears. Pressing her forehead against the cold bars, she wished she could reach up and kiss them right on the lips. She swore she had the courage right now, not like the other times when she just kissed their cheek.

"How am I not supposed to cry? You're in jail."

Lou chuckled and gently bopped her nose with the bandana. "Here, take this."

"What happened?" she asked, eyes flickering up to the cut on their forehead as she took the bandana. She balled it in her fist and shook her head.

"Well, funny story. I was goin' to bale the hay fer the horses an' uh…that sonavabitch— Excuse my language, Miss Clementine, but'e was hidin' in the barn. Gave me a good crack on'a head and put me on 'is horse."

"Oh, Lou."

She reached through the bars, fingers lightly brushing over the deep cut above their eye. Lou just barely flinched, still smiling.

"I'm sorry."

"Ain't yer fault."

"When can you leave?" she asked, pushing some dark strands behind their ear. She took in their features like she hadn't seen Lou for years, every line of their face slowly being mapped out in her mind. Lou tilted ever so slightly into her touch.

"I can't, darlin'."

"Why?"

"Butch plans on turnin' me in. He jus' left me in 'ere while he settled up his affairs. Then who knows?"

Clementine felt her smile slowly fall. "Who knows *what*, Lou?"

"He could be takin' me back down to the border or he could...jus' be takin' me to the hanging tree," Lou finished with a whisper.

Clementine felt sick, her hands tightening on the bars of the cell. "That's not happening. I refuse to let that happen. Do you hear me?"

They smiled sadly. "I know, Miss Clementine."

"Clementine," Butz said from the doorway. "Time's up."

Butz had poked his head back in, still looking between them and how close they were before mumbling to himself and settling back in his chair out of sight. She shook her head and looked back at them.

"I don't want to go."

Lou took her hand, pulled it through the bars and raised it to their lips, but didn't kiss it. They smiled, their breath tickling her skin.

"I'm afraid we don' have no choice, Miss Clementine." They kissed the back of her hand softly and she felt herself swoon. "I'll be seein' ya around."

"I'll be back. Soon. I promise. Today. When Sheriff Butz lets me."

Lou just smiled wider and let go of her hand. "You know where to find me."

"How can you be so calm right now? I'm having a conniption."

"Ain't much I can do from in here," Lou said, pressing their face between the bars so that they were even closer. "I knew this would catch up wit' me someday. Just do me one favor."

"Anything."

"Don't go messin' with Butch. Ya hear?"

"But—"

"*Miss Castellanos*," Lou implored, "please."

"Fine."

"All right," Butz said, standing in the doorway, "Let's go."

She quickly kissed the corner of Lou's lips and pulled away, the blush on their cheeks apparent even in the low lighting. With one final squeeze of Lou's hand, she managed to pull herself away from the bars. One last look back was all she afforded herself, and it was more than enough to make the tears lodged in her throat sting and choke her. The image of Lou standing with their injured arm cradled to their chest and their face pressed between the bars was more than enough to break her heart.

Butz directed her into the chair across from his desk and went to hand her a handkerchief, but she waved him off with Lou's bandana. "Thanks anyway," she said, as the door closed to the cell area, blocking Lou from view. She sniffled and used Lou's bandana to dab at the corners of her eyes.

"Clementine," he said, leaning forward on his elbows and folding his hands together on his desk. "You're... We all thought you were dead. After we found your pa—"

"Yeah, it was easier if everyone just thought I was dead," she chuckled darkly. "Sorry, I would have talked to you sooner, but I was settling in."

It wasn't a *complete* lie. Mostly she didn't know who to trust anymore and people from her past were a big red flag no matter what. After all, Butz had a lot to gain from her dad's murder since he became the sheriff.

"I'm assuming Gayle knows you're back? Seems like jus' yesterday that you two were knee high runnin' around town together."

"Yes, it's been nice to see her again."

"Alrigh', then," Butz said, with an awkward nod. "Be careful, Clementine. You've always been a smart kid. I assume nothing has changed, just take care'a yerself."

"I will," she said pointedly. "I haven't gotten myself into anything dangerous, I assure you. Lou didn't do any of the things that Butch says they did. I swear, Sheriff, if you just let them go—"

"Ain't mah business," he said with a huff. "And you jus' bein' back in Ghosthallow is dangerous enough."

"My debts are paid."

"Your pa had a lot of enemies."

She clenched her fists in her lap. "I know. Not like he didn't deserve most of them."

Butz just grunted, mustache twitching before he sent her on her way.

She considered going back to work, but Veronica had kindly told her that her tear-stained cheeks and red eyes wouldn't do much for sales. Instead she found herself wandering over to the hotel where she knew Butch was staying.

Lou had said not to go after Butch, but she hadn't said anything about accidentally running into him. Plus, she was her own woman. As she saw it, there was no reason for her to be taking orders from someone who refused to even kiss her. Lou would give her their bandana and probably the shirt off their back if she asked, but they wouldn't kiss her.

She decided the back of the hotel would be the best point of entry. Fewer eyes on her as she came in.

The hotel was at the end of Ghosthallow's long main street. It was two stories, looming over most of the street with big fancy French doors in the front made with expensive-looking glass. Someone had definitely sunk a lot of money into it.

The back was less fancy-looking, just the typical rough-sawn siding with some overhanging balconies attached to the rooms.

She pushed through the back door and it opened to a dark hallway. She passed the general kitchen noise and stopped in her tracks when she heard a familiar drawl from another room.

"I tol' you I would have the money by the end of the week," he snarled. "I have three more days."

"He wants it now," came another voice she vaguely recognized but couldn't put her finger on.

"Well he's gonna have to wait—"

"No one keeps Lefty waiting. I think you know that, Burner," the other voice said, a hint of amusement in his voice. Suddenly she recognized the voice: Junior. He was one of Lefty's main men he sent to do his dirty work. Lefty rarely left the ranch unless he needed to.

Clementine flattened herself against the wall beside the door. There was some more rumbling she couldn't decipher, so she gently and quietly pushed the door open just the slightest bit.

"I cannot get you the money until I return the charge—"

"He wants it by midnight tonight. So you better make it work."

"I don't even know if he has the information."

"You callin' Lefty a liar?"

"No, what'm sayin' is that he may be preoccupied with more important things than where a woman might'a gone some years ago."

"If he says he knows where your woman went, he knows where your woman went. Lefty remembers everyone that's passed through his camp."

"All of 'em?"

"All of 'em."

"Funny, because I would put money on him not knowing where the littlest Castellanos girl is."

At the mention of her name, Clementine's stomach dropped so quickly she felt sick. Every second of silence that ticked by just made it worse.

"Why wouldn't he?" Junior finally said.

"She ain't where he sent her, is what'm sayin'. She was holed up with Guadalajara before I brought him in."

"That sonuvabitch who stole from Lefty all them years ago?"

"That's the one."

"Well shit."

"I could go through the hassle'a bringing him in for the bounty, or I could jus' give him right to Lefty. Let justice be served there."

"Lefty just wants him dead. Once that's done we can consider the fee paid."

"I was hopin' you'd say that."

Junior chuckled. "You're a real bastard, you know that, Butch? So much for a great bounty hunter, you ain't nothin' but a snitch. You'd rat on your own brother if it served ya."

The pieces began to slide into place for Clementine and she gasped.

"What was that?" Junior said. She heard the scraping of chairs from the room but before she could flee, a bullet pinged off the doorframe right next to her face, and she fell back with a small scream. Leaping to her feet, she ran out the back door again.

She was just about to round the corner when she ran right into Butch, throwing her off balance. Pushing past her surprise, she pulled out the small pistol she always kept in her corset and pointed it at him. It wasn't much in the way of intimidation but it would definitely cause him some discomfort.

"*You*. You sold my dad out to Lefty and now you're doing the same to Lou."

Butch just stared at her with cold eyes, one hand on his pistol. "You listen here, little girl, I am sick and tired of you pointin' guns at me. You got away with it once because I owe your dad for a lot, but now I got no reason for lettin' you live once my debt is more than paid. So keep comin' at me and see what happens."

"I will *not* be intimidated by you. You killed my dad and sister."

"I had *nothin'* do to with their deaths, you hear me?" Butch said with his face in Clementine's, her gun pushing into his chest. "An' you best shut your mouth about affairs in which you have no business."

"Dad would be ashamed if he could see you now," she said, her voice shaking and betraying her as her heart practically vibrated from her chest.

Butch laughed, low and cold. "Are you saying he wouldn't be ashamed of you? A harlot of a woman chasing around another *woman* that doesn't want anything to do with you?" he asked, voice calculating and purposeful in a way that loosened her grip on the gun. "You are pulling your skirt up for that criminal and you don't have any idea of what she's capable of. What she's done."

"You know they ain't any more a woman than you are. You're just trying to make them feel small because you're afraid of them."

"I guess you don't want to know—"

"Fine, then tell me. Tell me what the warrant's for."

Butch smiled, slow and oily like a snake. "I guess you could say, it has to do with a woman."

Clementine didn't even notice her hand with the gun had fallen back at her side, all she felt was the world tilting under her and her heart leaping into her throat.

A woman. Of course it did.

Lou with their cocky smile and overconfident swagger. Lou who made a habit of visiting saloon girls and staying all night but *refused* to kiss her. They would hold her hand and kiss her cheek but that was it. And *god* they really had been stringing her along, hadn't they?

"Well now I see you are preoccupied, considering the implications," Butch said as he lit a cigarette. "I'll just leave you be."

She shoved the gun back into her corset between her breasts and marched down the street back toward the jail. Butch was the furthest thing away from her mind at the moment. All she saw was red hot jealousy.

Why was everyone else better than her? More suited for Lou? Lou would rather *pay* for a warm body in bed, than choose Clementine, who was so willing to be with them?

When she walked into the sheriff's station, Butz startled, his feet propped up on the desk and hat tipped over his eyes. "Wha—?"

"I need to see Lou," she said, hands clenched at her sides. "Please."

Butz sighed and got up, taking the keys out of his drawer and unlocking the door to the cells again. She pushed her way through as soon as the lock clicked, her gaze barely adjusting to the darkness as she stepped in front of Lou's cell.

They looked as startled as Butz, and stopped pacing in the cell. They smiled brightly when they saw Clementine, but Lou's smile made her skin burn and anger flare even higher.

"Miss Clementine—"

"Don't you 'Miss Clementine' me. Your warrant. Does it have to do with a woman?"

Lou took their time wandering up to the bars of the cell, tilting their head to the side as they rubbed the back of their neck nervously. "Well—"

"Well, what?"

"It 'as to do with a few of 'em, actually."

She barked out a sarcastic laugh. "Seriously! I should have fucking known." She threw her hands up in frustration, scoffing as she ran an angry hand through her hair. She was bitter and angry and *god*, she felt betrayed. "You're ridiculous, do you know that?"

"Miss Clementine—"

"You pretend to be *proper* when really you're nothing but. It's just an excuse to stay as far away from me as you can," she said, her voice shaking in her anger.

"Miss Clementine—"

"No, fuck you, Lou," Clementine said, turning on her heels and walking right out of the jail. She was over Lou. Officially.

She let the door close behind her and stomped off to the saloon, going straight for the bar. She reached over the counter and grabbed a bottle and a glass, pouring herself two fingers of whiskey before shooting it back. The amber liquid burned her throat, stomach warming and her anger only getting stronger. She smacked her lips and poured herself another glass.

Juanita wandered over to her from behind the bar, a small frown on her face. "Whoa there," she said as Clementine threw back another shot. "Slow down, cowgirl. What happened?"

"Lou," she coughed out, practically slamming her glass back down on the bar. Juanita poured her another, much more conservative shot. "Goddamn Lou and...It's always about a woman with them. A woman who isn't me and..." She took her other shot. "Fuck." She dropped her forehead down onto the bar, empty glass in her hand as she groaned.

Juanita sighed and poured her another. "What's going on with Ramirez now?"

"They were arrested—"

"*What?*"

"Yes, Butch has them in the jail for their warrant. Which *apparently* has to do with a woman. Surprise surprise," she finished sarcastically, waving her glass in the air so that some of the liquid sloshed onto her hand. "It always has to do with a woman."

Juanita looked at her with a small frown. "A woman?"

"A *woman*. A woman that isn't and will never be me," she finished sadly. "They'll kiss and fuck and who knows what else with any woman that isn't me. Suppose I should just get the hint."

Juanita licked her lips and got a clean glass, pouring some alcohol for herself. "I need to talk to you about that. About Lou."

"I don't wanna hear it," she muttered, chin down on the table as she wallowed in her own self-pity. "I get it. Lou doesn't want me. I've spent weeks *distracted* by a person who doesn't even want me when I should have been focusing on what I need to be focused on."

"And what is that?"

"Revenge," she breathed, lips loose from the alcohol. "I'm going to take down whoever sold my dad out to Lefty all those years ago. I should have been looking for them instead of pining after Lou. I had a one-in-a-million chance of being sold to a man from Ghosthallow, yet here I am." She scoffed and looked sadly down at her drink. "I mean, I can't blame Lou. Why would I think they wanted me anyways?"

"If you really think that they don't want you, you're not looking hard enough," Juanita said, topping up Clementine's glass. "And you need to know something before you spiral off into jealousy hell."

"I'm not jealous."

"Sure." Juanita smiled, but it faded just as quickly as it was there.

"It's true."

"Instead of listening to your lies, I'm going to tell you a story instead, okay?"

"Fine."

"What did Lou tell you? Did they tell you about their time in the Army?"

"They told me they joined the Army to avoid being hung as a thief after letting some people go," Clementine said, imagining Lou in their spiffy uniform. "And they told me how they met you."

Juanita nodded. "Lou is *too* sympathetic. It's their biggest flaw. Instead of just leavin' well enough alone, they get involved in things they shouldn't. When they were in the Army, they saw…" Juanita looked away and finished her shot. "War is a horrible thing. It brings out the best and the worst in people. And these men, this Army was raiding the Mexican towns and the men had their way with the women there."

"That's awful."

"The men had brought some women from the village back to the camp with them and were passing them around like pieces of meat. They had one young girl in a tent. She was probably barely even old enough to bleed. And Lou…they killed all the men. All of them that were hurting her."

Clementine felt the sickness stew in her belly and wished that she hadn't drunk so much alcohol. "They helped them."

Juanita nodded. "They were helping an innocent girl. But that's not what their superiors saw. They saw Lou killing their soldiers over a bunch of *savages* as they called us. A savage killing white men to save their own is all they saw."

"*That's* what the warrant is about?"

"They shouldn't have killed them, but I get why they did," Juanita finished sadly, voice thick with emotion. "So yeah, their warrant has to do with a few women. But not the way you might think. Butch is just jealous that Lou is still invited to my bed when he's not."

Clementine stared down into her glass, the liquid reflecting the light and her reflection barely visible in it. Her face was distorted and rippling with the liquid. "Well, shit."

"Shit indeed," Juanita mumbled.

"I just yelled at Lou in a jail cell because they killed bad men?"

"Yep."

"Are you sure they aren't a huge womanizer or something too?" she added, almost hopefully. It felt like a clock was ticking down in the back of her head as she imagined Lou in the cell, wondering what was next.

"Being good with the ladies and a womanizer are two very different things," Juanita said. "And I bet you can guess which one they are."

She felt relief and guilt all at the same time. Relief that she was wrong about Lou and guilt that she was wrong about Lou. Mostly a little seed of pride had nestled in her breast when she thought about Lou doing what they could just to save others. Then not even wanting to talk about it afterward, not a hint of boastfulness for their heroic actions. With the alcohol clouding her mind, all she could do was moan.

"I really messed up." Her head fell onto the table. "Again. Lou's never gonna want anything to do with me now."

"You did mess up," Juanita said bluntly. "Lou is in jail and you're just worried about who they used to kiss?"

Clementine felt shame flood her chest. "You're right. Lou's never gonna want anything to do with me now."

"Nah, Lou's probably in their cell feeling awful and wishing they could come talk to you. Buy you a drink," Juanita said, tapping the half empty bottle with a smile. Despite the smile,

Clementine noticed that it didn't quite reach her eyes. It made her worry about Lou sitting over in that cell. Juanita tapped the back of her hand to get her attention.

She smiled sheepishly. "Thank you, Juanita. You're too nice to me."

Juanita shrugged and winked. "No such thing."

Veronica came through the saloon doors in a huff and rushed up to the bar. Her breasts were heaving, breath coming fast. She opened her mouth to talk but just coughed, so she took Clementine's drink and downed it before slamming the glass down on the table. "We have a problem," she finally gasped.

Clementine sat up straight. "What's that?"

"Lou. Butch took them just out of town, to..." Her gaze darted to Juanita and back at Clementine. "...to the hanging tree."

Her heart stopped right in her chest and her stomach plummeted. "They're gonna—"

"Yep."

"Shit," she breathed, jumping off the barstool and feeling a little unsteady on her feet.

"Fuck me," Juanita said, heading toward the stairs.

"Where are you going?" Clementine called. "Now is not the time to freshen up!"

"I have to get something! I'll meet you there!" Juanita called, as she ducked into her room.

"Let's go," Veronica said, grabbing Clementine's hand and dragging her out of the saloon. "Get your horse. I'll lead you to the tree. Half the town's already there to watch."

Luckily Butter was hitched only a few doors down. Veronica motioned for Clementine to follow her, and they tore down the street, galloping toward where Lou was about to be nothing more than a collected bounty.

CHAPTER ELEVEN

Lou hadn't had a lot of luck in their life.

They had started out pretty all right. Their pa was okay with them not exactly fitting into the role they were expected to as a "girl." They had a good ranch and a good horse. But somewhere there in the middle, somewhere between joining the Army and being forced to run far away or be hanged for war crimes, their luck had run out.

It was hard but they recovered and they felt okay about their life. At first Clementine showing up on their doorstep had felt like a huge burden, but they realized it had been good fortune to have Clementine Castellanos in their life, even if she was destined to leave in the end.

Lou felt privileged to be the cause of those little smiles or the way her eyes crinkled when she laughed.

Yeah, she might have moved on, but Lou was glad to have had her in their life while they did.

They just never figured their luck would run out with Butch fucking Burner. But here they were, sitting on a horse that wasn't theirs, with a rope around their neck.

The rope was thick, the loose fibers sticking into their skin and feeling itchy. They looked out at the crowd that had formed in front of them, all the townsfolk who had given them sideways glances and made snide remarks. Now they all waited to watch them die.

The sun was setting behind them, a purple glow practically radiating from the mountains and reflecting on the dry earth around them. Dry, save for the large, gnarled tree that held the other end of the rope they were tied to.

Many a time they had seen men hanging from it. Sometimes they'd leave them up for days until the buzzards had picked their bones clean. They hoped they wouldn't leave them up, for Clementine's sake, though she seemed to hate them now, so maybe she'd enjoy that.

Lou's heart ached at the thought of her and the last conversation they had. If they could call it that. She had been so angry, so upset.

When they had first heard the door of the jail open, they'd allowed themself to wish that it might be her. They even sat up on their cot hopefully, only to be disappointed when Butch came through the door instead with a new rage in his eyes. Butz opened the jail cell for him and Lou stared down Butch, raising themself to their full height.

Butch stared back at them, pulling some rope off his belt. "All right now, let's go."

"I ain't goin' nowhere with you," Lou spat.

"You don't have much of a choice," Butch said, reaching for their arm. They batted him away but he punched them in their injured arm and they crumpled to the ground with a scream. He rolled Lou on their belly and hogtied them; their hands and legs tugged with cruel efficiency behind their back.

"Fuck you," they growled, pain shooting through their injured arm as Butch managed to lift them onto his shoulder, his shoulder bone sticking into their stomach.

"Hate to disappoint, but I ain't interested in such things," Butch said as he carried them out of the jail. He dropped them into a cart and they yelled in pain, writhing in their bindings as he pulled himself onto the horse pulling the cart.

Lou caught their breath, still reeling from the pain in their arm. The cart bumped roughly along the road and they yelled up at Butch, "Where're you takin' me?"

"It doesn't matter. You ain't gonna be there for long."

Lou lifted themself up as best they could with their hands and legs tied and saw that they were rolling out of the town. They tried to pull at the bonds holding them but the ropes just dug harder into their skin. For a moment they considered throwing themself out of the wagon, but Butch would undoubtedly see them anyway.

They were trying to figure out how to get their hands out of the ropes when the cart stopped. They looked up and their blood ran cold. Lou would recognize those limbs anywhere. The hanging tree.

There were still leftover pieces of rope tied around the branches from where previous prisoners had their corpses cut down, little reminders of how many people had perished there. But Lou's horrified contemplation was cut short when Butch pulled them roughly from the cart, and they fell into the dirt. They coughed, chest and arm aching as they struggled to a kneeling position with their feet and arms tied together.

"Stop movin'," Butch muttered, as he managed to pull them by their bonds closer to the tree, dragging them writhing through the dirt. A crowd had already started to form, probably following them from town as soon as they saw the wagon going toward the tree. Lou coughed again and spit in Butch's direction. He just scoffed and gave them a swift kick to the ribs, knocking the air from their lungs.

They gasped for air, corners of their eyes burning with tears. Clementine.

They'd never get to tell her they were sorry. That they wished they could have married her and kissed her. By the time their breath recovered, Butch was pulling out a large hunting knife and cutting their binds. They struggled for a moment but he kicked them in the stomach again and they curled into the pain, bile filling their mouth. Butch grabbed their wrists while they gasped for breath and retied them, this time in front, and then they were hoisted by their arms into a sitting position.

"Do not do anything stupid," Butch said, as he pulled them to their feet and shoved them toward a horse. He pulled out a gun and held it to their head. "Get on."

They shot him a look over their shoulder and grabbed the horn of the saddle, pulling themself onto the horse. They thought about taking off on the horse and risking a shot in the back but the horse was hitched to the tree. After untying the horse, he led the horse over to a noose hung in the tree, got up on a chair that was beside the tree for these purposes and looped the noose around their neck.

The crowd grew quiet now that the rope was tight on their neck. They swallowed thickly, feeling their muscles push and contract under the rope. The horse moved under them, its body shuddering with a breath as it stomped its foot.

"Ladies and gentlemen," Butch began addressing the crowd with a flourish. "You have before you, one Lou Ramirez, also known by the previous alias of Louis Guadalajara. She is being tried for treason, murder, and deception. Today, she will be hung by the neck until dead from this here tree and then her body will taken back to Texas and laid to rest."

There was an excited murmur amongst the crowd and Lou searched it desperately for a familiar face. Sheriff Butz stood at the front of the crowd, hands flexing and relaxing on the leather of his belt. In the distance, Lou could see some dirt kicking up in the direction of town, and their heart stuttered hopefully.

"So now, Lou Ramirez," Butch continued, "do you have any final words for the crowd?"

Lou licked their lips, swallowing nervously as they watched the speck in the distance grow bigger, eventually revealing the outline of a familiar black-and-white speckled horse.

"I um..." Lou started, the horse shifting under them. "I wanna say sorry. Fer any pain I have caused."

Clementine was racing up to the crowd on Butter, Veronica close behind her. Even with the rope around their neck and death inevitably upon them, Lou still had to smile. "An' I wanna say sorry to Miss Clementine Castellanos, fer being a stubborn mule."

She rode Butter right up next to Lou's horse, who snorted nervously. Butch had his hand on his gun but didn't move to stop her when she grabbed Lou's pant leg and waist, the only thing she could touch.

"Don't you apologize to me for anything," she said, tears swimming in her eyes. Lou offered her a crooked smile and wished they could hold her and wipe the tears from her cheeks. "Lou, you get off this horse right now. Butch! Let them off right this second! Sheriff! Please!"

"It's alrigh', darlin'," Lou whispered, trying to calm her down. "I'm fine. I'm a little tied up at the moment, ya see, but I'm fine."

Butter snorted, hooves beating into the dirt nervously. The horse that Butch had stuck Lou on threw his head back with a snort, tail twitching. Lou was hyper-aware of every move the horse made, since if it decided to take off, they were as good as dead. They looked between the two horses.

"Um, darlin', the horses," Lou started before Butch chimed in.

"Miss Castellanos, I do believe that's enough," Butch said, voice tired.

"You can give me another second," Clementine snarled at him. "You son of a bitch."

The crowd gasped.

Lou chuckled and shook their head. "That ain't proper, Miss Clementine."

Their horses shifted again.

"I don't give a shit what's proper and what's not," she said, turning back to Lou. She reached for their leg, their stomach, their shirt, any bit of them she could reach like she was looking for something to hold on to so she wouldn't drown. Lou sat powerless with their hands tied tightly in front of them and their body weak. They could only lean into her a little bit.

"Miss Clementine," Lou whispered seriously. "Listen to me, darlin'. I wanna say I'm sorry I...I'm sorry I never made an honest woman outta you. You understand?"

They couldn't bring themself to say it. Not here when they were about to be a corpse at the end of a rope. But Lou wanted—*needed*—Clementine to know what she meant to them.

"Lou," Clementine sobbed. "Don't leave me. There has to be something we can do."

"There ain't nothin' we can do. I need to tell ya somethin' I…I need you to know that in my heart, I only 'ave room fer you. An' it was broken an' a mess an' I'm sorry 'bout that but it all belonged to you, Miss Clementine," Lou said desperately, throat aching with unshed tears. "Do you understand?"

She nodded, hands tightening on their pant leg. "I'm sorry."

"Nothin' to be sorry fer, darlin'." Lou managed a small smile, their vision growing blurry. "I gotta go now."

"No, no!" she shouted desperately, turning and looking at Sheriff Butz, who just looked solemnly at a point in the distance. "Do something!"

"I can't, it's the law," Butz said, with a shake of his head.

"Well *fuck* the law!"

She looked back at Lou, her hands visibly shaking, and something flashed behind her eyes. Lou felt Clementine's hand curl in the collar of their shirt and Clementine slowly moved closer to Lou, eyes darting down to their lips.

"Darlin'," Lou tried, lips dry. The horse under Lou snorted again, beating the ground a little more anxiously and Butter shifted under her weight. Their faces were just a hairsbreadth apart, and suddenly the world went still. Lou could smell Clementine's perfume and the hint of whiskey coming off her, sharp and comforting. They could hear her last small intake of breath as she prepared to kiss them, the rumble of the crowd sounding distant now and not just a few feet away. Lou was going to kiss Clementine Castellanos and if that was how they were going to die, well, then it wasn't all that bad. They would be swinging from that rope with a smile on their face because they got to kiss the most beautiful woman in the world before they went.

Lou could feel their lips brushing when Butter neighed loudly, bringing the world crashing around them, and the horse under Lou reared up on its hind legs.

Her hand slipped from Lou's collar and the horse under them shot off, running through the crowd and nearly trampling at least three people in the meantime.

Lou felt everything in slow motion. The way the horse slipped from under them, how they slowly fell through the air and the noose around their neck tightened. Their body jerked violently when the length of the rope reached its end, and suddenly Lou couldn't breathe. It felt like all the air was sucked from their lungs, noose tight around their neck and feet kicking for purchase on anything as their vision turned red.

"Lou!"

"Wait!"

Lou's wildly rolling eyes locked on Juanita getting off a horse, holding something in her hand.

"I have the bounty!" Juanita rushed up to Butch with a proud smile on her face and shoved the money at him. "All three thousand and then some. You can let them go now."

Butch shook his head. "It's too late."

They let out a gurgled sound in an attempt to argue his point, vision getting spotty as they lost air.

Clementine slipped off Butter faster than lightning and looped her arms around Lou's legs to hold them up as best she could. Lou took a gulping breath, lungs on fire as they strained for air. Butch drew his gun and held it at Clementine.

"Miss Castellanos! You are interferin' with the law. Step away."

"The law don't mean *shit*," Clementine gasped, struggling under Lou's weight.

Sheriff Butz stepped between Butch and Clementine, hands up, trying to placate him.

"Mr. Burner, you have your money. Can't you just let Miss Ramirez go?" Butz tried. He motioned to Juanita, Veronica, and Clementine. "A lotta people are upset—"

"She is supposed to hang for her crimes and goddammit I will make her hang," Butch growled, almost feral with spit flying from his mouth as he spoke. "What do I care about the emotions of women when justice is bein' served."

"You don't give a shit about justice!" Clementine shouted from where she was struggling to hold Lou up so they could breathe. "You only want the money for Lefty anyway."

There was a murmuring amongst the crowd and Butch looked around a little nervously. The sun had nearly set at this point, casting harsh shadows over the ground and Butch's face.

"I am here as an officer of the law."

"You bootlicking sonova—"

"But you aren't," the sheriff interrupted. He gave Jaunita a nod and she shot the rope where it was tied to the branch. It broke free and Lou tumbled to the ground on top of Clementine. Lou gasped for air, hands still tied and their vision getting spotty.

"Not no more."

"Old man—"

Butch looked over the restless crowd, finally stuffing the wad of cash in his pocket and putting the gun back in his holster. With one last poisonous look at Lou and Clementine, he was back on his horse and galloping away from the crowd.

Lou gasped for breath, even as relief coursed through them. Weak fingers pulled uselessly at the rope still around their neck.

"Lou, here," Clementine said as she batted Lou's hands away from the rope and loosened it herself. She quickly untied the knot from their hands and the blood rushed back all at once, warm and tingly in their veins, their temples thumping. She reached into their shirt and loosened the binding bandage around their chest. Usually they would protest, but the tightness made it harder to breathe and they were more focused on staying alive than maintaining their appearance right now. Lou took a deep gasping breath, coughing a little and watching as blood sprayed the dirt as they tried to breathe. She sat on the ground and pulled their head into her lap, peppering their face in small kisses and whispering things they couldn't hear above their own heavy breathing.

They could feel and taste Clementine's salty tears on their cheeks, both of her hands cradling their face and keeping them close. Clementine held the back of their head and kept them close.

Their heart fluttered with relief and a thousand emotions they couldn't process yet.

"Oh, Lou," she whispered, pressing their foreheads together. "I'm so sorry—"

"Sshh," they managed with their raw throat. "Le's jus' go home, darlin'."

CHAPTER TWELVE

When they got on the wagon Butch had left behind, Clementine made sure to tuck herself against Lou's side as tightly as she could. She wanted to be as close to them as possible, like they might get kidnapped again if she wasn't touching them for too long. Lou's protests against the cuddling was weak at best, probably because they had nearly died.

Juanita offered to let them stay in a room at the saloon, but Clementine wanted to get as far from the town as she could. Every time she passed someone, she just saw another face from the crowd, someone who did nothing while an innocent person was about to be hanged. She supposed, though, she couldn't blame them. As far as they knew, Lou had murdered all manner of men. They had always been the odd one out in town anyway, so it must not have been much of a stretch for them to assume that they were a criminal on the lam.

Clementine rested her chin on Lou's shoulder, lips brushing over the dirty cotton of their shirt, arms firmly wrapped around their middle. "Feels weird not holdin' the reins," Lou complained, their voice hoarse and rough.

"Shh," she said, nuzzling the side of their neck where an angry purple bruise had already formed, the edges of it red and irritated from the rope. "No more talking for you. Rest your voice."

Lou mumbled but stayed quiet for the rest of the ride.

Clementine could hardly keep her tears at bay, constantly replaying the events of earlier in her head. The emotional back-and-forth had been taxing at best. Just seeing them up on that horse ready to die...

Butch was still out there, probably somewhere in town. She worried he would be at the ranch, but he seemed like the kind of man that needed at least a day to regain his ego and lick his wounds. She couldn't help but wonder how long it would be until someone else came looking for Lou, if it wasn't Butch. Lefty knew they were in Ghosthallow now and they were still wanted by the law, just because they got Butch off their trail for now didn't mean others wouldn't be out looking for them.

She thought back to what Lou had said in the moments before they thought they were going to die. It wasn't a love confession, but it was close. After all, they told her she *had their heart*. That had to mean something more than just the terrified ramblings of a person about to face their fate. Then, the almost kiss. The kiss that would have been, if she hadn't thoughtlessly put two nervous horses next to each other. Her distress had made her reckless.

Still, she couldn't stop thinking about it. Everything felt different now, like they had finally crossed a line they had been standing on the edge of since she'd shown up at the ranch.

But with Lou slumped in the saddle, beaten and exhausted, now was not the time to discuss such things.

They finally made it back to the ranch and rode the cart straight to the barn. Lou slipped off of it first and she watched in concern as their legs buckled a little before they straightened back up. She got off and Lou tried to undo the horse before Clementine shooed them away.

"I'll do it," she said, as she unbuckled the leather.

Lou grumbled, "I ain't useless."

"You've just been through a lot." She slung the saddle over the side of the stall. The horse snorted and went straight for the hay. Lou went over and patted Trigger's nose, his ears twitching as they murmured something to him. Clementine checked to make sure they had water and looped her arm through Lou's. "Come on, let's get you inside."

They complied, letting her pull them into the house. They worked in silence, Clementine automatically drawing them a bath, and Lou going for the half-empty bottle of whiskey on the table.

Usually she would scold them for drinking on an empty stomach, but instead she grabbed one of the leftover biscuits she had covered up in the kitchen and set it in front of them with butter and some preserves.

They moaned in delight as they took the first bite, not even bothering with the butter as they gobbled it up. They grimaced a little every time they swallowed but obviously felt too hungry to care. Clementine wordlessly grabbed them another one and set it on the plate, kissing the side of their head without a second thought. By the time Lou was half done with the second one, the tub was ready and she had begun undoing the bandages on their arm.

The wound didn't seem infected, just red and angry. She lightly gripped Lou's chin and looked into their deep-set and tired eyes and the cut on their forehead. Lou searched her face and she smiled sweetly as she brushed her fingers along their cut. "Does this hurt?"

"Nah."

She squinted in disbelief as she got a better look at the cut—a little swollen, rimmed with dried blood, and their eyes were frighteningly bloodshot. "I don't believe you."

"I promise, Miss Clementine. Ain't nothin'."

"Well, be careful with your arm in the bath. Don't submerge it and clean your eye, please." She let her fingers curl over the back of Lou's ear, pushing some of their hair behind it.

"Yes, ma'am," they said with a tired smile.

Her fingers continued to the hinge of Lou's jaw and traced the strong line to their chin. She couldn't stop touching them, like if she did they might disappear. Some part of her needed to be assured that Lou was actually in front of her and it wasn't some sort of hopeful fantasy.

"All right," she finally said, letting her hand fall to their lap. "I'll be over here."

She placed a soft kiss on their forehead before they could stop her. Lou got up and disrobed behind the sheet while she hurried to do the same. Presenting her breasts to Lou in this state might not be the best idea, so she got undressed and quickly slipped into the bed, trying to distract herself from thinking about Lou, just a few feet away. She wanted to rush to their side and help them with everything, but they would probably die from the impropriety of it all if she saw them naked in the tub.

It felt like forever, but Lou finally made it out of the tub and into some sleepwear and took another swig from the bottle of whiskey before joining her in the bed. She went to get up but Lou waved her off. She ignored them, moving over on the bed so that they could fall more easily onto the mattress.

It always belonged to you. Lou's dying words echoed in her mind and she inched her hand between them on the bed, lacing their fingers as they looked at each other.

"Hey," she whispered, nerves already crackling through her veins and telling her to just go to sleep. But she wouldn't be able to go to sleep with her mind racing like this. Lou hummed, thumb brushing along the side of her hand. She licked her lips and continued, "What you said earlier when you almost…Did you mean all of that?"

Lou searched her face before kissing her hand. They kissed each knuckle softly, never breaking eye contact, and she felt like embers were dancing across her skin with each touch of their lips. Their mouth settled on the back of her hand, and she pressed against Lou until their entwined hands were basically the only thing between them.

"I meant e'ery word," Lou said, voice hoarse. "E'ery single one."

She nodded and kissed the back of their hand gently. "What does that mean now? For us?"

Lou looked pained. "Miss Clementine, I just...There's a lot you don' know about me."

"I would feel the same even if I did. And you said you meant it."

Lou frowned like they were figuring something out in their head. "I jus'...It was a very dramatic situation. Maybe it's jus'...I thought I was dyin'—"

"Okay," she said, hoping Lou couldn't hear the wavering in her voice or how her heart was breaking in her chest from the sudden pivot.

"Let's sleep, darlin', it's too late for these conversations."

"Can I hold you?"

Lou just nodded and she pulled their hand over her waist and tangled their legs together so that Lou's head nestled under her chin. She pressed a soft kiss to the crown of their hair as they settled their arms around her.

"Night," Lou whispered, already half asleep.

"Good night," she breathed. She swallowed thickly and tried not to overthink the conversation for fear she'd lose her mind. She had thought they were making progress but now she felt more confused than before.

Instead, she leaned over and blew out the candle, plunging them into darkness.

Clementine was surprised when she woke up before Lou. Usually they were up with the sun no matter what, but obviously, nearly dying had taken a lot out of them. Instead, their head was still tucked under her chin, breath steady against her neck. She let herself bask in it for a few moments before carefully untangling herself from Lou and getting dressed. There were things to be done and Lou was best left sleeping for as long as they could.

Clementine did the usual chores; most weren't a problem. She was fine with feeding the pigs and cows and chickens, and milking was something she was used to. Everything except for baling the hay. But she still made it work, getting the horses their hay and even brushing them out a little and picking their hooves.

When she got back inside, Lou was still sleeping. Their neck looked worse than the night before. Their entire throat was deep purple with prickles of blood dotting the skin. It broke her heart just looking at it and she knew that it would be hard for Lou to swallow anything that wasn't liquid for a few days at least so she let them be and started making a broth.

She stirred the broth slowly, bits of vegetables and meat trimmings floating in it. She kept thinking about Lou under that tree and couldn't help but shiver. The hopelessness that had settled in her stomach hadn't completely gone away, that sinking feeling that everything was about to crash down around her.

Lou groaned and she looked over to see them blinking at the ceiling. She put some of the broth in a tin cup and sat on the bed beside them.

"Hey, baby," she said, blushing a little at the slip. "I have some broth for your throat. Thought it might help."

"'Anks," Lou whispered, eyebrows furrowing. "Wha' time is it?"

"Time for you to eat and go back to sleep," she said, taking this moment to look at the wound on Lou's arm. It looked like it was healing all right so she went for her kit to change the dressing. Lou's shirt pooled around their waist as they drank.

She set their hand in her lap so that she could reach the wound better, blushing when their hand landed on her bare ankle. Lou didn't even seem phased, more focused on staring down into the cup of broth instead.

"What's wrong?" she asked, as she started to wrap Lou's arm.

"I need to do chores," Lou said, curling their hand around Clementine's knee as she pressed some more bark over the wound.

"I already did them," she said. She tried to ignore the warmth spreading through her and focused on their arm instead. Lou frowned and Clementine nodded. "All of them."

"'Anks," Lou mumbled as they finished off their broth and licked their lips.

She focused on tying off the new bandage. "It's my pleasure." Lou's eyes drooped again and she carded her fingers through dark locks. "Go back to sleep."

"Too much to do."

"No, there's not." She took the cup and gently pushed back on their uninjured shoulder. Lou resisted and she sat up on her knees to get a better position. They looked at her with a playful pout and she gave them a look and put a little more pressure on their shoulder. "Come on, rest."

They shook their head stubbornly, resisting as she put her weight into her hand, leaning a little more over her as she pushed on their shoulder. They smirked before flopping abruptly back to the bed, Clementine falling on top of them with a surprised squeak. A pained chuckle left Lou's lips and she moved to sit up but their arms around her waist stopped her.

She looked down at them, their faces close with and a pretty blush on their cheeks. Their eyes shone as they searched her face, darting down to her lips as they licked their own.

She adjusted herself on top of Lou. "This can't be comfortable," she whispered. Her heart felt like a wild bird fluttering in her chest and begging to be set free, thumping wildly against her ribs and into her throat.

"'S jus' fine, darlin'," they whispered, smiling so wide their dimples showed. Clementine felt like she might fall in them.

Lou's fingers scraped softly up her spine and she shivered. She tentatively traced the edge of the gash above their eye and over their dark eyebrows. Her eyes moved from the wound back to their eyes. She never wanted to part from them, she wanted to stay here with their bodies pressed together and stoking the fire deep in her belly. It made her want to lean down and kiss Lou but she didn't know where they stood, not when Lou had clearly avoided the conversation the night before.

"Will you stay with me?" Lou asked, voice small. "While I fall asleep again?"

"Of course." She rested her head on their shoulder and got comfortable. She gazed at the bruises around their neck, angry and dark. "Do they hurt?"

"Only when I think 'bout 'em. Or swallow. Or move my throat. Or—"

"Okay, stop talking then," she chuckled, gently nuzzling her nose against the bruised skin. She ached to kiss it but let her eyes close instead. And together they managed to slip back to sleep.

CHAPTER THIRTEEN

Wild horses galloped through the plains. Lou stood in the middle of them as they ran past, the rhythm of their hooves shaking the ground and echoing their heartbeat. They could smell the dust and the sweat of their coats, and it filled their lungs with a much-needed cleansing breath. They rode with them, surrounded on all sides by nothing but open land, the landscape blooming beautifully around them as it rose into mountains and flowed into rivers.

Suddenly, red began to seep across the sky like blood in water.

The horses were falling around them. Gunshots echoed around the plains from unknown sources, taking them down one by one. They tumbled down with them, sticky dirt choking their throat.

They were in front of the hanging tree again, but this time there was a revolver in their hand and it wasn't them in the tree anymore. Inez was standing there with a noose around her neck and beside her, Clementine. Both looking scared, both barely staying astride, with the nervous horses under them the only thing that kept them safe.

Lou looked back down at the revolver in their hand. One bullet was all it had, and the sound of that one bullet would scare the horses.

The two women would hang in front of their eyes. One bullet to cut one rope while the other horse spooked and hung the other one. Their legs felt like lead, keeping them in place as Clementine and Inez looked at them desperately.

"You put us here, now you have to get us out," Inez said.

"Lou, we're here because of you," Clementine pleaded. "Please."

Lou didn't know what to do. They couldn't save both of them but they couldn't bear to only save one. Their palms were sweaty and it was hard to get a grip on the revolver. Who to choose, who to save? It was their fault they were in the tree anyway, their fault that they were about to die.

Instead, Lou put the gun to their temple and screamed.

Lou blinked. They were sitting on the horse again. They could feel the scratch of the rope on their neck and the way it just barely pinched their skin to be uncomfortable, just tight enough to make it hard to swallow. Clementine was standing in front of them with her shotgun. She raised it to the sky and shot. The horse bolted from under Lou, the rope stretched to its full length, and they felt their neck crack.

Lou awoke with a jolt, hand clawing at their neck as they gasped for air that hurt their swollen throat.

They felt Clementine's hand on the small of their back and instinctively leaned against her. She was sitting next to Lou, book in her lap. Lou blinked and lay back down with their head near her hip.

She brushed her fingers through Lou's hair in the same way she had the night before when they awoke from a nightmare. Lou focused on the scratch of blunt nails against their skull and let out a breath. That was at least three times now that Clementine had witnessed them waking up from a nightmare. They had tried to play it off but could see the concern in her eyes every time.

Lou took a deep breath, their hand resting near Clementine's hip, daring not to touch her, even though their muscles itched to put their arm around her waist and bury their face into the cotton of her nightgown and breathe her in.

Their throat was still sore, but it didn't hurt to swallow as much as it had. It was getting easier and easier to breathe and their arm felt well enough to move it more. It had only been a couple of days but Lou was getting antsy not working. Most of the time they spent sleeping it was to avoid Clementine, who was looking at them with those sad eyes and hopeful smiles.

She thought Lou didn't see it, but they saw how she looked at them. They knew she wanted to kiss them. And goddammit they wanted to kiss her too. But not like this. Not when Lou was helpless and having constant nightmares. Not when they couldn't protect her. If they were gonna kiss her, they would do it when it was proper.

Lou slung their arm over her hips and pressed their face into her nightgown. Her fingers tugged through their hair and against their temples. It was comforting and the final dregs of their nightmare seemed to evaporate like smoke, but the dread still settled in their stomach, making them feel sick.

"How long have you had nightmares?" she whispered.

"Long enough," Lou said. Just her closeness made them breathe easier. Their mind couldn't help but imagine curling their hand around her hip, pushing it up her side and tangling in her hair and...Lou groaned.

"Do you want some tea or something?"

"I'm jus' fine like this."

"Okay."

"Can you read to me?"

Clementine reached for the book, but Lou didn't even register the words. Her voice washed over them and chased away the bad dreams as they fell back asleep.

The next day, Clementine reluctantly went back to the saloon. She'd found that she missed being behind the bar and slinging drinks for the patrons, not to mention Juanita and Veronica. But she was convinced that the moment she left, Lou would be kidnapped again. Or worse, they would start working even with their injuries.

Lou was talking a little better now and had convinced Clementine with a well-timed smile and a voice low like honey that they were fine and it was time for her to get out of the cabin.

It was probably for the best anyway, since Clementine felt like a ball of sexual tension. There had been several moments over the past few days where she thought Lou might kiss her. But it never amounted to anything. They would look at her lips or move in close but then retreat at the last second leaving her in a huff. Sleeping next to them certainly didn't help, especially not since they had been cuddlier lately. Lou would reach for her at night and pull her close as they drifted to sleep, and while she basked in the intimacy of it, it was getting harder to wake up with Lou's leg between hers and their breath on her neck, but no relief in sight.

There were times she considered leaning down and kissing Lou, but none of the times seemed right. The last time they had almost kissed, Lou was about to die. The high drama of it all had heightened everything. Every nerve and emotion was so raw and vulnerable and *dramatic*. It felt a little weird just to kiss Lou when nothing special was happening. It didn't feel as magical when there wasn't danger involved.

Vaguely, she wondered if the drama and danger had brought them together and now the reality of mundane living would push them back apart. Besides the cuddling and lingering looks, Lou seemed to be extra polite with her. She was always "Miss" Clementine—no more "darlin'"—and they seemed to only touch her when necessary—if they weren't sleeping. She missed the little touches and the way Lou's eyes would sparkle when they called her "darlin'." She wondered if she should stage her own kidnapping to get them to kiss her.

When she walked into the saloon, Veronica and Juanita instantly pulled her behind the bar and handed her a glass of whiskey.

"How are things with Lou?" Juanita asked, passing a beer to a waiting customer without a thought.

"Physically? They're fine," she said, as the two women sighed in relief. She pushed the whiskey away from her and shook her head. "Emotionally, I don't know."

"What do you mean?" Veronica asked, taking Clementine's whiskey.

"I think they might be over me. And maybe they're upset because they blame me for…you know…almost dying. I suppose it was kinda my fault. Plus I feel like they're pulling away from me."

They hummed, nodding as they passed the glass of whiskey between them. Veronica shrugged a shoulder. "They do that."

"What?"

Juanita waved her hand in the air. "Lou is always trying to sacrifice their own happiness for some unknown reason. It's their biggest flaw."

She wanted to defend Lou but she found herself agreeing. "I just thought we were on the verge of something because of the things they said to me before they were about to hang." Her voice trailed off and she stared into the distance. "I'm just worried they didn't mean any of it. That it was just the heat of the moment."

With a chuckle, Juanita finished off the whiskey. "Lou is not a 'heat of the moment' kinda person. Not anymore anyway." She raised her eyebrow and blinked. "What?"

"Seems like there's a story there," she said, putting a hand on her hip, tapping her fingers on the counter.

Juanita and Veronica looked at each other briefly. Veronica shrugged and snapped open her fan. "Everyone makes some rash decisions when they're young."

"Let me guess. Lou's had to do with a girl?" she asked, shoulders slumping when Veronica and Juanita shared a look that told Clementine she was right. "Can't they make a rash decision with *me* too?"

Veronica pulled Clementine into her arms, face pressed to her ample bosom as she held her close. "I know it's hard, but Lou will come around. And when they do, it'll be worth it."

"Mmm, thanks."

"They're a very generous lover—"

"Oh…kay. We're done," she said, standing back up and away from Veronica's breasts. She sighed and Juanita passed her another drink, which she gladly took this time.

"They'll come around," Juanita assured her. "I've seen how they look at you. You've got nothing to worry about. Unless you don't keep away from Butch, who's still lurking around town."

Clementine practically growled at the name as she downed the drink. "I know. I'm worried he's going to come back for Lou since they still have that bounty on their head. Nothing would stop him from trying to get paid twice for Lou. Or that someone else will."

"Butch is more afraid of me than god. He won't touch Lou again."

"Why?"

"He swore he saw my body floating in the river a few years ago. It was by design, I wanted him to think I was dead. So when that idiot came in I just told him it was a curse from my people. That I am brought back for revenge."

Clementine blinked at her for a moment. "You lied to him?"

Juanita giggled. "All I have to do is speak some Spanish and that gringo is sure I'm speaking in tongues. He's an idiot. Honestly it works on most white people, you should try it."

Clementine surprised herself with her own giggle before sobering. "Speaking of that asshole though, I'm still not any closer to finding out who sold out my family since he says he didn't do it."

"You believe him?"

"If he knew anything, he'd try to use it to his advantage."

"Yeah, you're right." Juanita gave her a hopeful smile and squeezed Clementine's arm. "You've only just started, Clem. I might have an idea on how to get people off of Lou. Just give me a few days. Now sling some drinks and talk to the locals. They always know something, maybe they'll know something about your dad."

CHAPTER FOURTEEN

Lou pulled the wooden stool next to the cow, metal bucket between their feet. They rolled their sleeves up to their elbows and sighed, wincing when their injured arm twinged a little in pain.

"You stop this now," they said to their arm as they tried to stretch it out in front of them. They could only extend it about halfway before they pulled it back to their chest. The cow munched happily on her feed, and Lou reached for one of her teats with their good hand. They pulled it and milk hit the side of the bucket with a "ting." It was much harder with one hand, but it wasn't the worst.

They just had to do something that made them feel useful so they weren't just a waste of space around the house, especially now that Clementine was gone all day. It was getting tiresome to just mope around their property. Plus, there was no way they wanted to burden her with all the farm responsibilities. They had not only almost gotten themself killed, but they were making things harder for her. The bare bones of the new house loomed over their property like a reminder of all the work they weren't doing. Time was passing and it was inching closer to winter and Lou was far behind.

They had been fine on their own before. If they got hurt, they still figured it out and did everything for themself, but now suddenly they were soft. Barely doing their work, only using one hand to milk a cow. Clementine had made them soft, had made them half the worker they used to be.

They felt stressed just thinking about it. Refocusing back on the teat in their hand, Lou continued to milk. A few minutes in and they took a look into the bucket only to see a fraction of the amount of milk that they usually had at this point.

Lou groaned in frustration and threw their injured arm out to grab another teat, only to yell out in pain. They pulled their arm back closer to their chest and curled over their knees in pain.

"Fuck."

"Are you okay?" Clementine's voice sounded grating and patronizing in a way that just made the frustration in Lou's chest mount.

"'M fine," Lou mumbled, not bothering to turn around.

"Here, I can finish—"

"I'm fine! I just…I'm fine," Lou snapped.

"Let me just finish this. You go start dinner," she said as she came up behind them. They felt her fingers running through their hair and they leaned into it. Lou even allowed themself to lean back against her legs and look up at her. She looked back down at them and held Lou's cheeks in her hands.

"I 'ate this," they admitted. "I can' just keep sittin' 'round."

"I know," she said, her fingers running lightly over Lou's lips. "You can help by doing easier things. Like cooking."

Lou looked up and got caught in hazel eyes, rimmed with dark green and staring back at them with so much feeling swimming behind them. Lou wanted to dive in but they knew they'd drown. They were no use to her as they were anyway, not in a romantic sense. They had to stop entertaining the foolish fantasy that they could be anything more. It wasn't fair to her and would only lead to heartbreak on both ends.

Clementine leaned down and pressed her lips softly to Lou's cheek, just on the edge of their lips. Lou froze and blinked when she pulled away. They took Clementine's hand and squeezed it lightly. "You 'ave to stop doin' that, Miss Clementine," Lou mumbled.

Instead of staying to watch her face fall, Lou stood and started back to the cabin to cook dinner.

When they went to bed that night, Clementine faced the room and Lou faced the wall, their backs barely brushing. Lou's body was stiff in a purposeful attempt not to touch Clementine. They felt bad about their conversation earlier, but Lou also felt like they had been caught off guard.

Their heart tugged, telling them to apologize and hold Clementine the way their arms were begging to do. But, too stubborn to give in, they curled into themself instead.

* * *

The day had started off normal enough. Lou was standing in the field with the cows, checking to see if any of them were pregnant in case they'd have to make preparations. They were feeling the side of one when the unexpected sound of hooves approaching distracted them.

Lou squinted against the sun, tipping their hat back on their head like it would give them a better view. The rider was too far away to make out details, but they were alone and riding at an easy gallop with dust kicking up behind them as they rode toward Lou. They didn't feel particularly threatened with the guns at their hips and Clementine in town, so they just waited, wishing people would just stop riding up on their land. Maybe someday they could go back to an existence of people always passing by, minding their own business. But today was not that day.

As they got closer, they noticed that the rider was a woman. She was wearing a dark buckskin jacket with detailed beading of flowers along the arms and front, hat perched on her head and a dark shirt tucked into her matching pants.

She barely slowed her horse before slipping off it, spurs clinking against the ground as she landed just a yard away from Lou. Long auburn hair waved on either side of her face, framing pale freckled skin and bright blue eyes. Something about her felt familiar, but Lou couldn't quite put their finger on it.

The woman squinted at them, doing a double take before striding up to Lou with her hand on the revolver at her side. She looked around and behind Lou, who just blinked at her.

"Are you all right?" the woman asked, pulling her long-barreled revolver from its holster. She gasped and tugged down the collar of Lou's shirt to look at the bruise on their neck. "Holy shit." It was fading, but it was still angry and noticeable. "What the *fuck* did he do to you? I swear, if he's hurt a hair on Clementine's head—"

"Ma'am?"

The woman straightened. "I'm here to help you. Where is he?"

Lou scratched the side of their neck as they observed the woman, trying to figure out if she was a threat. "Help me wit'... what?"

"I'm here to rescue you," she said, chest puffing up a little. "Now where's the pervert who's keeping you and my baby sister here? I knew he bought Clementine but I can't believe he's forcing her into this fucked-up sister-wives situation. Are there more of you? Chained up somewhere?" She looked Lou over again. "Are you the one he pretends is a smooth-faced boy? What a fucking sicko."

Lou looked down at their clothes a little self-consciously before shaking their head. This woman seemed right off her rocker. Maybe she had that yellow fever everyone was talking about. But...she'd mentioned Clementine.

"Um, ma'am—"

"I'm not a 'ma'am.' I'm Lottie. Now where's Clementine? Is she okay or is she beat up like you? No offense," Lottie quickly added. "Come on. Let's get all his valuables and get out of here."

Lottie took off like a shot for the cabin and Lou sighed, quickly chasing after her. "Ma'am. Lottie?"

By the time they got into the cabin, Lottie was already going through all the cabinets, pulling out the cans.

"All right. We can't really use this stuff but we can grab a coupla things. Where's the jewelry? Money?" Lottie peered suspiciously at a can of beans before shaking it next to her ear.

Lou sighed as they followed her around the cabin, trying not to spook her. "Ma'am. I'ma have to ask you to stop."

"Come on, just start piling things on this," Lottie yanked the sheet from the bed and laid it in the middle of the floor, tossing some cans on it and then going for the chimney. She shoved her arm into it and felt blindly around. "Where's Clementine so we can go?"

"Ma'am!"

"Lottie!"

Lou turned and breathed a sigh of relief to see Clementine standing in the doorway looking just as shocked as they felt.

"Oh thank goodness, Miss Clementine—"

"Clem! Lil' Daisy!" Lottie turned after pulling a bundle of cash from the chimney that Lou had been saving there. It wasn't much, just a little bit in case something happened. She stuffed it in her back pocket as she stared awkwardly at Clementine.

"Clem," Lottie continued, mouth slightly agape. "You've grown!"

"It's been—"

"Years," Lottie finished before gathering Clementine in her arms.

The two women hugged and Lou let them have their moment while they started to pick things up from the pile in the middle of the room and put them back. They gathered the cans first, taking them back to the cabinet and went back for some of the silver Lottie had found hidden in the kitchen, something Lou salvaged from an overturned carriage one day and had been keeping around since.

"Hey! Stop that," Lottie said. The sister moment must have been over because Lottie walked over to Lou in the kitchen and took the silver plate from their hands. "We can sell this for some cash."

"Lottie, we're not selling Lou's things."

"You've been brainwashed too. Whoever this Lou is, I can take care of him."

"No, I haven't," Clementine tried. Lou reached for another plate but Clementine pointed at them. "No, Lottie's going to put that back."

"I don' mind—"

"What is wrong with you two?" Lottie said, taking both of their arms and gathering them all together in the middle of the cabin. "Don't you get it? I'm rescuing you. Snap out of it." For whatever reason, Lottie put her hand on one side of Clementine's face and the other side of Lou's and pushed their faces together so they were cheek and cheek. She smiled maniacally. "It's taken me years, but I finally found you, Clem. Now let's get out of this pervert's house."

"'M not a pervert, thank ya kindly," Lou said, as they pushed Lottie's hand away from their face and stood up straight. "Now if you'll excuse me, a crazy person went through my house an' I gotta clean it up."

Lottie frowned. "What?"

"That's what I'm trying to tell you," Clementine said, hands on Lottie's shoulders. "This is Lou's house."

Lottie blinked, eyebrows knit together. "It's her place?" She pointed at Lou as they picked up some doilies they'd had in their trunk, something Inez had made them forever ago and they hadn't had the heart to throw away.

"*Their* place, yes," Clementine said.

"But you were sold off to some dipshit looking for a mail-order bride," Lottie said slowly, eyes narrowing at Lou. "Are *you* the perv who bought my sister?"

"No!" Clementine supplied before blushing and rolling her eyes. "I mean, kind of. But they're not a pervert."

Lottie's hand was back on her gun. "I'll be the judge of that."

"Sister?" Lou said.

Clementine put her hand over Lottie's. "Lottie, please. Come on, I'm safe and you found me. We don't need to cause trouble when there isn't any."

Lottie grunted and let her hand fall from her gun, face softening as she looked at Clementine again. She grinned widely and pulled Clementine into another hug.

"Get the alcohol, I have the feeling we have a lot to talk about."

She made herself comfortable at the table, one dirty boot resting on the edge, and started to eat the last of the biscuits that Clem had covered with a dish towel that morning.

Lou sighed and reached for their canned food. There was a tickling of an idea at the back of Lou's mind that maybe this is when Clementine would leave. Their first emotion was a dread sinking in their stomach, but they ignored it. This could be a good thing, if Clem was gone she'd be safe.

"Stop putting stuff away," Clementine said softly as she took some things from Lou's hands. "I'll do it."

Lottie almost protested but Clementine fixed her with a look. "Fine. I'll go finish what I was doin'. Outside," Lou said. They hesitated a moment before pointing at Clementine's carpet bag under the bed.

"Jus' a remindin', Miss Clementine, yer bag is there."

She frowned at them. "What would I be needing that for?"

Lou felt their cheeks heat and their shoulders lifted a little. "I jus' figured now that yer sister is here."

"I won't be needing it," Clementine said with a raised eyebrow.

"Just as well, Miss Clementine," Lou said softly, trying to fight off their smile. "Now, I'ma leave ya be."

Clementine mouthed a "thank you" and Lou tipped their hat, slipping out the front door to give the sisters some time.

CHAPTER FIFTEEN

When the door to the cabin banged closed behind Lou, Clementine felt her mouth go dry and nerves come to the surface. She hadn't really thought about it while Lottie was tearing apart her home and trying to find some fictional man keeping them captive, but her *sister* was here, her sister, whom she hadn't seen since she was dragged off her own land at six years old.

She stayed staring at the door for the moment, the vague sound of Lottie moving behind her grounding her. Lottie was *here*. In her kitchen.

"So, Clem, you gonna keep ignoring me all night?"

She turned around and Lottie had already poured two glasses of whiskey, her own half gone. Lottie kicked out the second chair across from her as a clear invitation to sit down. Clementine sat at the table and cradled the drink in her hands as she looked at Lottie.

It was like staring at a ghost.

Lottie looked exactly like she had when she was twelve. Long, glossy hair that Clementine had always been jealous of and piercing blue eyes that made her that much more effortlessly beautiful. She always looked more like their dad, a paler complexion Clementine had been jealous of as a child. Her father used to make "jokes" about her looking dirty and rub at her skin like he was trying to get her coloring off. He would never do that with her sisters, just tell them good job for cleaning behind the ears. Lottie had matured and Clementine saw scars that she knew hadn't been there before, but she was the same Lottie.

"Sorry, it's just, this doesn't feel real," Clementine said with a shake of her head. "I've been...I didn't know if you were—"

"Alive? Yeah," Lottie said with a sad smile, looking a little pained. "I hid when they came. I ran."

Flashes of that night flew through Clementine's mind— Lottie pushing her and Maria under the bed when they heard the hooves of horsemen rushing the homestead. It sounded like distant thunder, like a heartbeat rising into your throat. It rose until Clementine swore the whole house was shaking with the force of it.

Lottie had looked at Clementine with wide eyes, Maria just staring at the door with tears steadily streaming down her face. Clementine's bottom lip quivered and heavy sobs left her throat as Lottie put her hands on either side of Clementine's face.

"Clem, stay here, okay? You'll be safe," Lottie whispered. The sound of a shot ringing through the air made them both jump and fat tears rolled down Clementine's face. She just nodded and shoved her thumb into her mouth, a habit that had seemed broken until this moment.

Lottie nodded and kissed her hard on the forehead before pulling herself out from under the bed and running for the door.

And that was the last that she had seen of Lottie. She wasn't there when their dad was dragged out and killed while Clementine and Maria were spared to pay for her father's debt. A few months after they got to Lefty's ranch, he sold Maria to a man in a nearby town and she didn't hear anything of her again.

Not until a few months later when she heard they found her floating in the river.

There had been no sign of Lottie since that night Lefty's men raided their home though, and Clementine had always suspected the worst.

Now she was sitting here in front of her. Over sixteen years later and Clementine could still feel all the fear and confusion like it was just yesterday. The resentment that had settled in her chest over the years started coming to the surface again, and she swallowed it down.

"How did you find me?"

Why didn't you come sooner?

Lottie licked her lips and threw the rest of the whiskey down her throat. "I was going to get help but then I realized that... there wasn't anyone that was gonna help us. So, well, I ran. For the hills. And I did what I had to do to survive. Sometimes those things got me in trouble. I always meant to come back and get you though." She shrugged it off and the grip Clementine had on her cup tightened. Lottie's eyes remained glued to the cup in front of her like it held all the answers. "I actually saw you. Not long ago. At Lefty's camp."

Clementine frowned, deciding that she was going to need more whiskey to get through this conversation. Taking the shot, she poured another as she grimaced through the burn.

"Guess the drinking gene skipped one Castellanos, huh?" Lottie deflected.

"When did you see me?" she said, ignoring her sister's comment. "Why didn't you do anything?"

Lottie's brief smile faded. "It was a handful'a years ago now. I was arrested for something stupid. I don't even remember. Maybe petty theft. Anyways I was in the tumbleweed wagon behind some piss-wad of a sheriff, an' they went through Lefty's camp. You didn't notice me but I saw you from afar. You were getting water from a well. I tried to break out of the wagon, Clem, I *tried*. But before I could pick the lock, we were gone and I vowed to go back and get you as soon as I could."

"But you didn't," Clementine said bitterly. "I was still there."

"By the time I got back there, you were gone. I heard you were sold off to some idiot here, and here I am," Lottie finished sadly. She licked her lips again and leaned closer to Clementine, hands reaching across the table. "I came back to save you."

"I don't need saving. Not anymore. I saved myself. I got out from under Lefty's thumb—"

"By selling yourself to an asshole."

"I had no other choice. It was that and get the money for Lefty or he would…marry me himself. And I couldn't. He killed Dad. He killed Maria. I thought he mighta killed *you*."

"Sorry to disappoint, but I'm still here," Lottie mumbled. "Not dead. But not from lack of trying."

Just like that, Clementine felt the resentment that had been swimming on the surface dissipate and she pulled her chair closer to Lottie's so that she could take her hand.

"I'm glad you're here, Lottie," she said, squeezing her hand. "You have to understand I'm just a little surprised."

"Wanna talk surprised? What about finally finding your baby sister and she's married to some weird lady rancher back in your old hometown?"

"We're not married. And they're not a lady. Or a man. They're just *Lou*. And if you can't respect that…"

Lottie raised an eyebrow. "All that's fine, I don't give an owl's hoot, I've met all kinda people, they ain't the first one I've met like 'em. But they *bought* you?"

"No. Well, yes. Kind of. I was supposed to be married to this awful man and accidently ended up here instead. Lou paid him for me and now I live here," Clementine explained.

"But you're not married?" Clementine shook her head and Lottie's frown got deeper. "But they bought you."

"Only to get me out of a worse situation."

"Why are they all beat up? Did you do that?"

Clementine kicked her lightly under the table. "No! That's a long story."

Lottie smiled and poured them both another shot of whiskey. "Well as I see it, we ain't got nothin' but time."

CHAPTER SIXTEEN

Lou made sure to keep an eye out as they rode Trigger back into town.

The last person they needed to run into was Butch. They weren't sure what kind of awkward stalemate they were at, or what he would do if he saw them. To be honest, they didn't want to find out any time soon.

They adjusted the bandana they'd tied around their neck to hide most of the bruising, which was still painfully visible. Tipping their hat at Veronica, who was lounging in her usual spot outside of the saloon, they slid off Trigger and hitched him to the post.

"Well look what the cat dragged in," Veronica purred as Lou smiled.

"Good evenin'," Lou said, voice still scratchy. "Thought I'd pop by for a spell."

"I'm surprised Clementine doesn't have you on a tight leash after all that," Veronica said, looping her arm through Lou's as they walked up the steps to the saloon door.

"Well, she don' necessarily know 'm off the land," Lou confessed as they walked over to the bar.

Veronica gasped and dropped Lou's arm. "You sneak. Clementine is going to kill you—"

"She's with her sister. I'll be back before she even knows 'm gone."

Juanita scoffed as she came down the stairs. "Ramirez, what are you doing away from your girl? Does she know you're here?"

Lou couldn't help but growl a little as they sat on the stool. "She ain't mah girl," Lou insisted as Veronica slipped behind the bar and got them a drink. Juanita raised an eyebrow at Lou, fingers trailing across the top of the bar as she walked closer to them.

"I think all that talk of her 'havin' your heart' says otherwise," Juanita said.

Lou reached out for Juanita's hand and tugged her roughly toward them, their bodies flush and faces close even with Lou sitting down. A satisfying gasp escaped Juanita as their bodies came together, Juanita's hips nestled between Lou's thighs, lighting the fire in their stomach that was telling them to prove her wrong. Prove everyone wrong. Prove to *themself* that they didn't need Clementine.

Growing up not needing anyone but yourself got a helluva lot harder when you found someone you couldn't live without.

Their hand settled on the small of Juanita's back and they gave her a slow smile, eyes purposefully flickering down to her lips.

Juanita's eyebrows just got higher in her hairline. "What are you doing?"

"Jus' showin' ya that I can do whatever I want still," Lou said lowly. "So why don't I prove to you how ain't nobody my girl?"

Juanita hummed and tapped the edge of Lou's hat. "Yeah, but something's telling me this isn't what you want at all, cowboy."

Lou's bravado faded and their shoulders slumped, hand falling away from Juanita as their guilt seeped in. Juanita pushed the front of their hat down to cover their eyes and Lou just grumbled. Juanita was right. They could have slept with her, or any of the girls really, and probably would have had a great time, but there always would have been some little twinge of sadness and they would have undoubtedly thought of Clem.

"You're a fool for her. Anyone with sight can see that you don't want anyone but Clem."

Juanita pulled away from Lou and went behind the bar. Lou quickly took a long draught of their drink. "I ain't no fool."

"You are."

Lou dropped their hat on the bar and ran a frustrated hand through their hair. "She made me soft."

"You've always been soft," Veronica said, before walking over to help a different customer.

"She's right," Juanita whispered conspiratorially as she filled up Lou's glass again. "I'm just sayin', it's time to get your head out of your ass. You already broke Clementine's heart, now you gotta fix it."

Lou swallowed thickly, feeling sick at the idea of hurting Clementine. They knew they had. They could see it in the looks she gave them after they tried to backtrack on everything they had said the night at the hanging tree.

"It's better this way," they said. "She's better off movin' on and findin' someone else."

"She doesn't want anyone else, idiot, she wants *you*. Despite all your brooding behavior and trying to push her away, she still only wants you. Don't you see that?"

"She can' 'ave a good life wit' me. She's only been 'ere a month'r so and look at e'erythin' that's happened."

"Don't you think she has the right to say what would make her life a good one? Not some self-sacrificing rancher with a death wish? Can't you see that she doesn't care about all this bullshit and just wants you?"

Lou's whole face burned as they looked down at their drink, their reflection staring back up at them in the amber liquid. "I ain't good enough."

Juanita practically guffawed. "You're a goddamn idiot, Lou Ramirez, if you think Clementine cares about whatever false value you've put on yourself. That this idiot town has put on you. Is she or is she not one of the smartest people you've ever met?"

"Yeah," Lou admitted begrudgingly.

"And you think she'd be dumb enough to align herself with someone not worth her time?"

They scratched the back of their neck, forgetting the bruise for a moment and wincing when they irritated it. "I get it."

"Do you?"

"Yes," they said, taking their second shot.

"Then kiss her already."

"I can't jus'up and kiss a girl like her," they countered. "It ain't proper—"

"I will bet your horse that Clementine doesn't care. And I know you'd take that bet too."

Lou sighed and shook their head, running their hand over her face. "Life was a lot less complicated when I was on mah own."

"Yes, but also way less interesting."

"I also meant to say, thank you for helpin' when...That night. I woulda died without'cha," they said. "I'll pay you back as soon as I can."

"Don't bother." Juanita shrugged. "It was emergency cash and that's what I used it for. An emergency. If you really wanna repay me, you'll talk to Clementine."

"Alrigh' alrigh', I get it," Lou sighed. "You wan' me with Clementine."

"Yeah. It would make the two'a you a helluva lot less annoying." Juanita winked before pouring Lou another shot.

When Lou got back to the cabin, a little tipsy and a lot more embarrassed by the whole situation, the gentle glow of candlelight was apparent in the windows. They took Trigger to the barn and lay down one of the clean horse blankets over some hay for themself.

A few hours later, they were awoken by the sound of the barn door opening, and their hand went to the revolver still at their hip. They had the hammer cocked and the gun pointed directly at Lottie when they turned the corner to where Lou was lying in the stall.

They breathed a sigh of relief when they saw the familiar face, their wrist loosened a little bit, though they kept the gun pointed in Lottie's direction.

Lottie just raised an eyebrow and put her hand on her hip, the other holding a lantern. "Really, Ramirez? You bring my sister into your love den and then threaten *me*?"

"It ain't a love den," Lou said. They opened their hand and let the revolver hang on one finger against their palm in a show of putting it away. "Though I ain't entirely sure what that is."

Lou put their gun back in their holster and Lottie hummed as she sat across from Lou in the stall. Blue eyes squinted at them and Lou sat up with their legs crossed in front of them.

"So," Lottie started. "My sister lives with you."

"Yes, ma'am," Lou said, voice scratchy from being woken up.

"Gross. None of this 'ma'am' shit."

"Miss Castellanos, then."

"Lottie."

"Miss Lottie—"

"God, just stick with Miss Castellanos, then. What happened to you? It's like someone stuck an etiquette book up your ass."

"'M jus' tryin' to be proper."

"I heard that's your thing," Lottie said, giving Lou a hard look over. They wouldn't let her see them squirm, instead they just stared right back. She looked dangerous and somehow that made her even more beautiful. Lottie ran her tongue over the front of her teeth. "You're livin' with my baby sister but won't marry her. How do you think that looks for her?"

"I told her many a time that she has no obligation to stay 'ere. She's stayin' 'ere because she refused to leave."

"And you tried to kick her out?"

"No. I jus' tol' her she didn't 'ave to stay," Lou clarified.

"Yet you share a bed with her." Lottie squinted suspiciously. "I'm just saying, you're not looking great in this situation, Ramirez."

Lou shrugged, irritation stiffening their shoulders. "'Ave you talked to Clementine about this? These ain't our matters to be discussin'."

"I did. She seems to think you've hung the moon and stars just for her. Even if painfully clear y'all are stuck in some kinda sexless standoff."

"Ain't proper to be discussin' such things." They bristled.

Lottie just rolled her eyes and kicked her feet out in front of her. "Well, you're currently in my bed, so get out because I'm not one to cuddle."

"What?"

"Clementine told me to send you in to go to bed and kicked me out here. So go. Before she thinks I'm interrogating you."

"Ain't you, though?" Lou asked, with a smile.

Lottie just gave them a look and pointedly blew out the lantern. "Good night, Ramirez."

Lou pushed themself up with their one good arm, hay sticking into their palm until they brushed it on their pants. They stretched and shuffled into the cabin just as Clementine was slipping between the sheets.

She smiled, weary and nervous, lips just barely turning up at the corners as they looked at each other. "Hey," she said, pulling the sheet up to her nose. "Lottie's here."

"She is," Lou said, taking their hat off and hanging it on a hook near the door.

"You smell like booze. Did you go into town?"

"Only fer a lil' bit," they mumbled, before stepping behind the curtain to get into their nightclothes.

"Did you see Juanita?" Clementine asked. Lou knew what she was really asking and felt their chest tighten with irritability.

"Well, she works there, don' she?" Lou said as they pulled their long johns on and exited from behind the curtain. They could see Clementine looking them over nervously, like she was waiting for the other shoe to drop. As much as Lou wanted to leave Clementine hanging to prove a point, to make her realize she was better off without them—they couldn't. Big hazel eyes stared at them as they climbed over her and slid into the bed. "I only 'ad a coupla drinks. Nothin' else."

They could feel Clementine relax as they turned toward the wall as had become their custom the last few days. Clementine shifted behind them and Lou could feel her sidling closer.

"Lou—"

"It's late, Miss Clementine."

"I don't *care*, Lou," Clementine said, fingers twisting into the fabric of their shirt. "I just want to talk."

Lou squeezed their eyes shut, remembering everything Juanita and Veronica had said. They should try. They knew she wanted them, and hell, Lou wanted her too. There was still that nagging voice in the back of their head that told them she was better off without them. That she still had a chance at a good life with a good man and Lou would be taking that away from her. Especially since they still had people after them. The Butch situation had ended lucky, but they didn't know how many more times they'd manage to escape their fate.

Slowly, they turned and took their time adjusting their head on the pillow before finally looking at her.

"Miss Clementine," Lou said, unable to ignore the distance and that Clementine smelled like fresh-cut flowers. "I-it's very late. And I promise to talk about this but my bones are weary."

She pouted. "Because you were drinking."

"Because it is the middle'a the night," Lou clarified with a smile.

She relented with a sigh, eyes flickering down to their lips. "You promise."

"I think yer sister bein' here 'as gotten you in the talkin' mood," Lou teased.

Their hands begged to touch her, just to bring her a little closer and feel the press of her body. After all, how long had it been since they let themself touch her? Even longer than they let themself hold her. And if they were going to *try*.

Lou put their hand on the small of her back and pulled her close, arm slung over her hip as they put their chin on the crown of her head. She sat stiff for a moment before cuddling into Lou, one hand tangled in the front of their shirt while the other rubbed the back of their neck.

She sighed, nose nudging the hollow of their throat as they settled into each other. "Don't think one night of cuddling will make me forget about this, Lou Ramirez," Clementine whispered, her words dancing across Lou's skin and making them shiver.

"I know, darlin'." They had missed the way that felt on their tongue when they were talking to Clementine. The pet name seemed to affect Clementine too as she melded herself to Lou. "Night."

"Night," she said.

Lou was sure they got the best night's sleep they'd had in weeks.

The sound of crashing and hushed cursing startled Clementine awake the next morning. She blinked in the direction of the kitchen where she'd heard it and saw Lottie muttering and picking up cups from the floor.

Clementine sat up, running her hand through her hair to tame some of the tangles. "Lottie, what are you doing?"

Lottie looked up at her like she was caught, a half-eaten biscuit hanging out of her mouth. "I was, um, trying to make coffee."

"Why?" Clementine rubbed the sleep from her eyes. "Why are you up so early?"

"Us gunslingers wake up with the sun, Clemie," Lottie bragged as she put some of the fallen cups back in the cupboard. "Always alert, always graceful."

"Where's Lou?" she interrupted, hand unconsciously smoothing over the cold spot in the bed.

Lottie dropped another cup and she cursed. "Rude. I don't know. I saw them around here somewhere. I ain't their keeper."

Clementine swung her legs out of the bed and gathered her clothing to get changed.

"I hate to tell ya, Clem, but your husband is real weird," Lottie said, slumping into one of the kitchen chairs. She gestured toward a plate in front of her, only the remnants of food smeared over the top. "They only left breakfast for me. Weird. Right?"

Clementine stuck her head out from behind the curtain to look at the plate. There was an empty can of corn sitting in front of the plate, a couple of wildflowers stuck in it like a vase. Her heart melted like butter left in the sun too long.

She breathed, "They made me breakfast?"

Lottie shrugged, looking suddenly shifty. "I mean, I guess it coulda been for you."

Clementine got dressed faster and started for the door.

"Wait, Clem! What about breakfast!" Lottie called, as she walked out of the cabin. "I'm still hungry!"

Clementine looked around the property from the front of the cabin, hand shielding her eyes so she could see. She found Lou at the frame of the new house, placing boards along the sides and nailing them up. She did her best to keep from skipping or looking too giddy.

Lou wore the shirt Clementine had ripped the sleeve off, to tend to their wound. They had torn off the other sleeve and tucked the shirt into their pants, suspenders stark against the light-colored material.

Something about being able to see Lou's shoulders made her walk a little faster, and the closer she got, the more she could see their biceps bulging. Lou's eyes flickered to her briefly before returning to the board they were nailing. She couldn't help the smile that stretched across her face. Lou's brow was furrowed in concentration, a spare nail bobbing between their lips as they worked. She could watch them like this all day.

"Mornin', Miss Clementine," they said, still hammering. Their words were muffled with the nail between their lips, but it still hit her right between the legs.

"You made me breakfast," she stated with a smile.

Lou didn't miss a beat. "I did."

"There were flowers."

"There were," Lou said. They finally finished hammering, straightening up as the hint of a smile curled at their lips. They hooked the edge of their hammer in their pocket and put their hands on her hips. "Didja like 'em?"

"I did." She smiled, arms swinging at her sides. "I didn't get to eat breakfast, though. Lottie got there before me."

"I thought that might 'appen when I saw 'er come outta that barn."

They just stared at each other for a moment, all soft smiles and hopeful eyes. Her heart fluttered uncontrollably as Lou licked their lips and looked down at their boots before looking at Clementine shyly. If Clementine could be any more enamored with the handsome rancher, she would be.

Suddenly she forgot how she wanted to talk to Lou about where they were, if they would ever be more, and finally dive into what they'd been inching toward for months. Lou like this, sweet and shy. She would fall for it every time.

"Well, thank you anyways," she said, remembering her words. "It was really sweet."

"Yeah, well, ya'know," they said, adjusting the hat on their head a little. "I jus' wanted to do somethin' nice fer ya."

They found themselves staring again and Lou cleared their throat, straightening a little and running their hands over the front of their pants.

"Actually, Miss Clementine," Lou began, voice breaking a little. "I was wonderin' if you would accompany me on a ride later. I been wantin'a show you somethin'."

Her heart practically tripped over herself as she nodded. Her hands gestured in front of her as she rambled. "Y-yes, that would be amazing. *Great*, I mean."

Lou blinked in what appeared to be disbelief for a moment before the widest smile took over their face, dimples popping. "Great. I jus' need to finish up some things 'ere an' clean up an'...When you get back from the saloon?"

"Perfect." Doubt flickered in her mind for a moment and she frowned. "This is a...Is this a *courting* situation?"

Lou blushed deeply. "I mean...I was hopin'...if you want anyways—"

"I do!" she said quickly, her blush matching Lou's. "Want, anyways. Yes."

"Great," Lou said again, shoving their hands in the back pockets of their pants.

"Well I better get to work," she said with an awkward wave before she turned on her heels and headed to the barn. She felt a squeal of glee building up in her chest but managed to keep it in check until she got to the barn.

When Clementine told Juanita and Veronica that Lou was courting her, Veronica rolled her eyes and exclaimed, "Fucking finally!"

Juanita looked just as smug and laughed at the look on Clementine's face when she offered to give her some hands-on lessons to what Lou liked. Thankfully Clementine was too excited for the friendly ribbing to bother her. Juanita also let her know that Butch was rumored to be camped outside of town, licking his wounds, which meant he wasn't far away, but far enough away that Clementine felt a little safer.

Later, Juanita pulled her into the back room, looking mighty pleased with herself.

"You might want to hold yourself back, Castellanos, you're gonna want to kiss me after I give you this news."

Juanita picked up a newspaper and pointed at the obituaries with a delighted giggle. Clementine read the name under her finger and gasped.

Louis Guadalajara, wanted criminal, dead by hanging in Ghosthallow.

"What's this?"

"Well, the editor over at the newspaper likes to come visit my girls when his wife is visiting her sister. Needless to say he owed me a favor. I also convinced Butz to write up a death certificate for them. They're as good as dead as far as the law is concerned."

"This is fantastic!" Clementine gripped the newspaper in excitement. "Do you think this'll work?"

"It definitely will." Juanita wiggled her eyebrows. "You two don't have anything to worry about anymore."

She barely finished her sentence before Clementine practically tackled her with a hug. The newspaper crinkled between them and the two women squeezed each other while giggling in joy.

"I can't wait to tell Lou. This is a huge help."

"Go home now and tell them now."

"No no, I'll wait. They want to take me riding later tonight anyways and I don't want to interrupt their day. You know how they get with their routine."

Her shift flew by quickly, every customer getting an even bigger smile than usual. Nothing could bring her down. She even went into the general store to get some sweets for Lou before hopping on Butter and heading back to the ranch.

The house was looking a little more together, half of the siding finally up, and Lou was nowhere to be seen. Clementine set Butter up in the stable and went into the cabin where Lottie was sitting at the kitchen table. Still.

This time she was taking her gun apart and cleaning it.

"Have you even left that chair?" Clementine asked Lottie, before going to get a fresh dress.

"Yes," Lottie said incredulously. "I went to get more booze. Duh. And Ramirez was giving me a hard time about taking care of Killer here, so." She gestured to all the parts on the table. "Now I remembered why I never do this. It's a fucking bitch."

"Where is Lou?" Clementine asked. She started to freshen up, washing her face in the basin.

"They're around here somewhere," Lottie said with a dismissive hand wave. "What're you getting all gussied up for?"

"Lou is taking me out riding," she said a little breathlessly as she went back to change her dress.

"Oo, roman*tic*."

"Shut your mouth, it's sweet," she said as she silently marveled at the fact that she and Lottie had somehow fallen back into their sisterly routine even after all this time.

"Sure sure, I'll just sit here while you get all romantic with a dirty cowboy. Hey, while you're here, can we talk about that bruise around Ramirez's neck?"

Clementine felt sick just remembering that night and she sighed as she pulled up her fresh dress. "Bad Butch happened."

"I'm sorry. Bernard Burner? *That* Bad Butch? Dad's best friend?"

"That's the one," she said with a vengeful squint. "He was trying to collect a bounty on Lou. Had them strung up on the hanging tree."

"He almost succeeded, is what I'm hearing."

"Yes. And he's still lurking around town like a smooth-talking mustached snake. He better hope I don't see him. I don't even know if he's waiting to get Lou again, but Juanita just fixed that for us—"

"Where's he staying?" Lottie sucked on her teeth and leaned farther back in her chair.

She would have been more interested in why Lottie wanted to know all this and didn't want to hear the news about Lou, but she heard the sound of hooves approaching and her heart rate picked up.

"Um, he's camping outside of town I think," she said, distracted as she looked out the window and saw Lou walking Trigger to the cabin. "I'm going out with Lou. Don't be here when we get back."

Lottie's eyes practically bulged. "Wow, Clem, you're really jumping in with two feet here, aren't ya?"

"No, not like *that*. It'll...It might be late. I don't want to drag you out of the bed."

"Sure, Clem," Lottie said, giving her a little salute as she walked out the door.

She stopped on the porch, the door closing behind her, as she looked at Lou walking Trigger up to the cabin. He looked freshly brushed, mane tangle free and silky. Lou looked slightly more put together too. A fresh crisp shirt, buttoned at their wrists, not yet rolled to their elbows like they usually did. It was unbuttoned low on their chest, just the peek of their binding teasing at the top. Their suspenders looked newer, the leather less worn, and even their boots looked clean.

"Hello, Miss Clementine," Lou said, using one finger to tip the front of their hat with a smile. She practically swooned right off the porch. "Yer ride is 'ere."

Her mind immediately went to how she'd rather ride Lou than Trigger in this moment, but she cleared her throat instead. "I can see that."

She walked up to Lou, standing so close she could smell the fresh soap on them and see how some of the hairs at the base of their neck were still damp. The sun had just begun its descent and was reflecting off Lou's eyelashes. Her heart refused to settle down, and she had to clasp her hands in front of her to stop herself from reaching out and touching any part of Lou she could reach.

Lou held out her hand to Clementine. "Can I help you onto Trigger?"

"Please," she said, sliding her palm over Lou's open one and feeling the bumps of their calluses against her skin.

Lou helped her up, their hands briefly touching her waist as she got into the saddle. Lou settled behind her, arms naturally moving around her to take the reins.

"Alrigh', the ride ain't that far," Lou said, their lips close to her ear and breath just barely caressing her skin. Lou clicked, kicking Trigger into a gallop as they rode toward the back of the property, past the new house and the cows in the field. Clementine leaned back into Lou a little and felt their arms tighten around her.

She was wrapped in Lou's warmth and scent, and if this was all the ride ended up being, she wouldn't complain. The fields became more untamed, grass longer and wilder. As they rode further, Lou slowed Trigger to a walk.

"This is nice," she whispered. Her head rested in the crook of their shoulder and she smiled up at them.

"We haven't even gotta where we goin', darlin'," Lou drawled.

She gripped one of Lou's arms tightly to her chest. "Still. This is nice."

"It is. Alrigh', we're 'ere."

Just then, they came over the top of a hill that gave way into a deep valley, tall mountains framing half of it and trees sprouting up intermittently. The sun was setting between two mountains and casting a long ray of light down into the valley. Her breath hitched at the sight.

Lou hooked the reins over the saddle horn and hugged her close as their head bent closer to her ear.

"I chose this land fer this view," Lou said softly. "When I was ridin' and lookin' fer property to start the ranch on, I saw this'n knew I had to live 'ere. I was convinced no one'd ever be willin' to ride with me again, but I knew if they did, I'd wanna show'em this. So, here we are."

Clementine's heart grew in her chest. "You haven't shown this to anyone before?"

"Nope, never known anyone I wanted to yet. Until you, anyway."

Clementine about melted off the saddle, her skin prickling with electricity, and reached her arm up and behind her so that she could cup the back of Lou's neck and thread her fingers through their hair.

The good news was bubbling up inside her and she couldn't hold it back any longer.

"Lou, Juanita managed the impossible. She talked to the sheriff and someone at the newspaper and now Louis Guadalajara is dead. You're free from the law."

Lou pulled away a little bit just to look at her, brows furrowed. "Free?"

"They're not gonna come looking for you anymore if they think you're dead."

As realization seeped into Lou, a smile tilted their lips. "Well goddamn."

"I know. It's finally happened."

They chuckled and squeezed her a little bit, hugging her from behind with a laugh. "Thank you, darlin'."

"I just asked for help, Juanita wanted to do this for you."

"For us," Lou breathed, so quietly it almost got carried away on the breeze. Clementine's heart fluttered and she pulled Lou's arms even tighter around her.

They stayed like that, watching the sun set between the mountains as it painted the sky a deep orange and purple until finally going dark. Even after the sun disappeared, they held each other for a moment until Trigger snorted and broke the silence.

"Should we go back'n sit by the fire fer a spell?" Lou whispered against her cheek.

She was tempted to turn her head and kiss Lou right then and there, but before she could, Lou turned Trigger and started back toward the ranch. She reluctantly dropped her hand from behind Lou's neck and held their arm again.

"Miss Clementine, I know tonight didn' last too long. And I jus' want you to know that it has occurred to me 'at I don' really know much about you. An' 'at's my fault. I'd like to take the time t'get to know you a little better."

"Does that mean I get to ask you questions too?"

"If you must."

She wondered what kind of questions Lou might ask. Maybe they wouldn't like her after they knew her better. Licking her lips, she just focused on their strong body behind hers, and how she wanted to turn in the saddle and kiss them, to straddle their lap and get as close to each other as humanly possible, all curves sliding together as they kissed. Hands roaming and Clementine untucking Lou's shirt from their pants.

"Miss Clementine."

Their voice brought her from her daydream, tips of her ears reddening. "Hmm?"

"We're 'ere."

She suddenly noticed they were back at the barn, and she pulled away from Lou so that she could get off the saddle. Lou's hands rested lightly on her waist as they helped her down.

They cleared their throat awkwardly and offered her their arm. They walked to the cabin, stopping just short of the front door. She frowned and turned around, confused as to why Lou wasn't moving.

"I'ma say good night here," Lou said, taking their hat off and holding it in front of them.

"But you live here. I thought we were going to sit by the fire."

"I know, but it ain't proper fer me to go in wit' you after a courtin'," Lou said very seriously. A smile twitched on their lips. "An' I'm jus' gonna put Trigger away and 'en I'll be back in."

"You're coming back anyway?"

"Yes'm." Lou winked.

Clementine watched as they headed back toward the barn. Her heart felt lighter than it had in weeks as she turned around and went back into the cabin, getting the fire started for Lou's return.

The next day, before Lou attended to their chores, they wrote Clementine a note in thick, labored script that read: *Fire pit tonite.*

They couldn't read all that well so writing was about the same; they couldn't wax on poetic like maybe some others could have. And admittedly like they wanted. But it would have to do.

When they were done with their chores, they set up the fire pit with just enough time to wash up before Clementine got home. Their courting the night before had gone above and beyond their expectations. They had expected just a little bit of resistance from Clementine after they had essentially told her it wasn't going to happen. But they sat by the fire the night before and just talked about everything and nothing. Lou learned that Clementine spoke Spanish, French, Shoshoni, and Navajo which just furthered their belief that they didn't deserve her. They could barely speak English and they were so embarrassed by their Spanish they refused to speak it. Sometimes by themselves they'd repeat phrases they remembered from their mother, sayings and memories whispered in the fields and to the horses.

Despite this, Clementine always looked at them with those big, trusting eyes and Lou just wanted to hold them.

Soft.

They thought to themself as they put on a clean shirt and tucked it into their pants. They used a piece of flannel to get as much water out of their hair as they could, running a quick hand through it to tame it and keep it down. They heard the barn door open and saw Clementine walking Butter in. The sun had just set so it was perfect timing.

Lou took a few blankets outside and placed them on the logs they had set up around the fire, even making some tea for them to sip while they were out there. They started the fire just as Clementine made it to the cabin.

"Hey, cowboy."

Lou couldn't help but stare. The dress she wore for the saloon really did look amazing on her, the way it hugged her curves and how it pressed up her breasts.

Lou cleared their throat. "Hello, Miss Clementine. I um, would you still join me by the fire?"

"I've been looking forward to it all day," she admitted. She bounced up to them and kissed them on the cheek, a warmth spreading through them at the touch. "I'm just gonna go change."

Lou watched, a little mooney-eyed as she went into the cabin. They took the time to spread out the blankets a little more and put another log onto the fire. Lou was poking at the fire to get some of the logs to catch when they felt arms encircle them from behind.

Chuckling, they put their hands over Clementine's that were entwined on their stomach. "Darlin'."

"I like it when you call me that," she said, words muffled by their shirt.

Lou turned and wrapped their arms around her waist as they smiled down at her. "It suits you."

They watched as the light from the fire flickered over her face. It would be so easy to kiss her right now, to finally taste the lips they'd been dreaming about. Clem rose onto her tiptoes and Lou cleared their throat, dropping their arms from around her.

It wasn't time yet. It wouldn't be proper. After all, they'd only been courting for a couple of days. "I um…" Lou cleared their throat again nervously. "Here is the fire. Thought we could sit 'ere fer a spell."

"It's lovely." She weaved her fingers through Lou's. She placed a blanket on the ground and draped another over their shoulders before pulling them down to sit, slotting herself between their legs with a happy sigh. They blushed when

Clementine leaned against them, using the blanket to pull them in close and snuggle together.

"Perfect." She smiled as she handed Lou their cup of tea and took her own between her hands.

"Um." Lou straightened their legs and Clementine casually put her hand on their knee, fingers tracing a pattern over the fabric. Their stomach started to turn, mouth going dry as they tried not to focus on her hand. "H-how was yer day?"

"Good," she sighed tilting her head to look up at Lou, her head resting on their sternum. "Has Lottie bothered you at all today?"

"I 'aven't seen 'er." Lou shrugged. Just then they saw Lottie turn down the path toward the ranch. "Speak'a the devil."

They watched as she jumped off her horse near the cabin and walked inside.

"I'm going to tell her she has to find somewhere else to stay, don't worry," Clementine sighed. "She can't sleep in our barn forever."

Our.

The word both terrified and thrilled Lou. "*Our* barn." They dropped their head into the crook of her neck and breathed her in, smiling when she giggled and pulled their arm across her chest. "Since when is it *our* barn?"

"Well, Lou Ramirez, I expect to be a kept woman."

Lou pulled their face away from Clementine's neck so that their faces were close. Her cheeks were tinted, maybe from the fire but Lou bet it was a blush. Her eyes reflected the sparks coming from the fire, a hint of rouge still on her cheeks, and Lou had half the mind to kiss her senseless.

They could feel an invisible force pulling them together, when Lottie's voice rang out. "Hey, Ramirez, we're going to town," Lottie said as she came up behind Lou and pushed their hat so the brim covered their eyes. Lou grumbled at the interruption, pushing the brim of their hat back up and fixing her with a look.

"Lottie, no," Clementine said, turning in Lou's arms to better face Lottie.

"Clementine, yes." She saw Clementine's cup and reached for it, sniffing it before drinking it down. She finished with a satisfied smack of her lips and let the cup fall to the ground. "Now let's go."

Something about Lottie's tone of voice brokered no argument. Lou moved to get up but Clementine gripped their arm tighter and pulled them back down. They squeezed back lightly. "I gotta go."

"No, you don't," Clementine muttered. Clementine gripped their bicep and pulled their arm tighter around her chest. "I like you better here."

Trying to ignore the feel of Clementine's breast pressed up against their arm, Lou looked back up at Lottie. "What're we goin' to town for?"

"I gotta see a man about a horse," Lottie chuckled. Seeing Lou and Clementine not react, Lottie rolled her eyes as her smile dropped. "I know Butch Burner. I convinced him to sit down and talk, to get this whole bounty thing out of the way."

"It's already out of the way, Juanita convinced Butz to write up a death certificate. They're as good as dead."

"You really think Butch is going to give up that easy? It's best we just take care of him and get it over with."

"She's not wrong, Miss Clementine," Lou said just a little regretfully.

"No way," Clementine said. "We're not just going right to him like that. He'll kill Lou."

"No. He won't. I already communicated with him and we agreed to talking. I had Juan shut down the back room of the saloon for our little chat and he knows better than to pull anything under her roof."

Lou sat up straighter. "Since when is it *Juan*?"

"Jealous, Ramirez?"

"'M jus' sayin', you haven't been in town very long."

"I'm real friendly. What can I say?"

Lou rolled their eyes and turned back to Clementine. "It's worth the peace of mind."

"It is," Lottie said. "I think you might have some information he's looking for, Ramirez."

"'Bout what?"

"About Annie. Annie Valentine," Lottie said.

"I might know somethin'," Lou muttered as they remembered back to a time they'd rather forget. It was a time that seemed to be coming up more and more. Before they were sentenced to a stint in the Army and were just helping people escape hellish circumstances. They didn't like giving out information on the people they'd met and helped, as they were always running away from someone or something. They were free now, most of them, and as far as Lou was concerned, their business was just their own. They had a feeling Butch was looking more on the romantic side of things, though. Lou was sure they'd had that same hound dog expression recently. And if Butch got what he wanted and left them alone, Clementine would be safer.

"How'd you know I'd know 'bout Annie?"

Lottie shrugged, evading Clementine's eyes as she scratched the side of her neck. "I may have done some digging around town about you, Ramirez. I asked around about you. How you ended up here."

"'Bout the smuggling? With who?"

"Doesn't matter. I heard from some people who were with you on a coupla trips. Figured you might know some people."

"I do."

"Well, then let's go," Lottie said as she kicked their boot. "He's waiting."

Clementine looked back at Lou, watching as they took a deep breath and smiled their most charming smile. "Come on, darlin', it'll be fine. Anything to make sure he leaves us alone an' yer safe."

Her face dissolved into a soft smile. "You'd do that for me?"

Lou felt taller somehow with Clementine looking at them like that. Like they could take on the world. "Oh surely, Miss Clementine. All ya 'ave to do is ask. There's a mighty long list'a things I'd do fer ya."

The smile turned to a smirk and Lou saw the mischief behind her eyes. She leaned in close. "Like what?"

"I guess you'll jus' 'ave to find out," they whispered in her ear, squeezing her one last time before standing up. "Let's go."

Clementine was not pleased with how the night was turning out. She was supposed to be having a romantic night by the fire with Lou and instead she was in the saloon with her sister and Butch Burner, hoping that Lou wasn't about to get murdered.

She sat at the poker table, arms folded as she looked between Butch on one side and Lou and Lottie on the other. They had taken everyone's guns at the door, but Clementine was still cautious.

The only thing on the table was a full bottle of whiskey and four glasses.

Butch stared steely-eyed at Lou, and they stared right back, arms folded on the table as they leaned forward. The bruises on their neck were still visible, but mostly hidden by the bandana they had tied around it. Anger burned deep in her belly just from the idea that she was sitting at the table with the very man who did this to Lou.

"All right, listen," Lottie said as she poured whiskey in everyone's glass. "All good negotiations start with a drink. So, let's drink. To polite conversations and not getting murdered."

She held up her glass and looked around the table expectantly. Everyone else begrudgingly clinked their glasses together before taking the shot.

"Good. Now." Lottie gestured at Butch before pouring more drinks. "Butch. Tell Lou why you were hunting them down."

His mustache twitched and he gripped his glass tighter. "I'm lookin' for someone."

"An' that's why you hunted me like a dog?" Lou asked with a raised eyebrow.

"No. I needed the money that came from your bounty to pay to one Lefty Lenning in exchange for information." He looked around, suddenly shifty. "That, and I thought that you had killed Juanita."

"So, revenge," Lou said.

"No, revenge was just the cherry on top of the pie," Butch growled as he took his shot.

"What kinda info was so impor'ant that you were about'a kill me fer it?"

Butch leaned back in his chair, face softening a little. "I was in love with a woman called Annie. We woulda been married if it were not for the fact that her father sent her away when he got wind of our relations. No one could tell me where."

"You jus' wanted to know where Annie was?"

"Lefty had his hand in the kidnapping and smuggling business, I know this as fact," he said. "An' the only information I knew was that she passed through his camp. But he wouldn't tell me nothin' until I paid him the money."

"All of this was worth an innocent life?" Clementine interjected.

Butch's eyes turned on her for the first time. "In my defense, little girl, they *are* guilty. Are they not? It was to my delight when I saw their face on that poster. Two birds with one stone, as they say. Get my revenge and get my money all at once."

She gritted her teeth but felt Lou's hand cover hers. She looked at Lou in shock for a moment, but they were still staring down Butch. The touch comforted her and she relaxed back into her seat. Butch's eyes flickered from their hands back up to Lou.

"Gimme one good reason I shouldn't kill you right here at this table," Lou practically growled, leaning across the table a bit. "You almost killed me—"

"And yet here you sit," Butch sighed like he was bored. "All because you have built yourself a band of loyal criminals that will protect you."

"They're called *friends*. If there weren't ladies present—"

"That ain't ever stopped you before, Guadalajara."

Lou stood up so quickly that their chair scraped the floor with a squeak.

Lottie took Lou's arm and pulled them back down into their chair. "Okay, we get it. You both are very tough. Can we get down to business now?"

Lou and Butch stared at each other for a moment longer, the tension thick in the air and crackling like wildfire.

"What's the deal then?" Lou mumbled. "I tell you what I know about Annie and you leave me alone?"

"Somethin' like that," Butch said. "I'll confirm the story that yer dead and make sure no one comes lookin' as much as I can."

"I need ya to shake on it," Lou said, holding their hand out across the table. Butch looked at it once before taking it. "Deal."

"Deal," Butch repeated, lips twitching again. "What do you know about Annie?"

Lou took their shot, lips curling a little bit at the taste. "Annie was sent to an old man named Humphrey. Down 'round the edge of Louisiana. He was a mean man, but we took care'a that and smuggled 'er out. Gott 'er into Alta, California. When I talked to 'er she said somethin' about family."

"But she was safe?" Butch asked, some vulnerability finally showing.

"She was safe."

He nodded once, swallowing thickly and pushing his glass toward Lottie. "Well. I guess I know where I'm headed next."

"Don't you think she woulda found you by now if she wanted to be found?"

"I told her not to contact me for fear someone might see it. Now if you excuse me—"

"Convenient."

"Wait, wait, we need some information from you too," Clementine said. All eyes turned to her and she tensed for a moment, doubt creeping in. She shifted a little before looking back at Butch. "What happened to my dad?"

"Were you not there?"

"No, I mean, who sold him out. To Lefty." She figured if anyone knew, it would be him.

Butch stared back at Clementine, face blank as he tapped his fingers on the top of the table. "Now I'm afraid that is not my information to tell. I was sworn to secrecy."

"Like promises mean anythin' to you. Yer nothin' but a snake," Lou growled. "Nothin' more'an a dirty—"

This time it was Clementine who put her hand on Lou to calm them. Her hand found their knee and she squeezed, feeling Lou relax a little.

"But you know? You know what happened?"

"Not really, no. I know that what happened to your dad was not supposed to happen. But that's all."

"What does that even mean?" Clementine said, more frustrated than before.

"My time here is up, Clementine. I have no information left for you," Butch said, as he stood. He tipped his hat at Lottie. "Good seein' you again, Lottie." He turned to Clementine and gave a curt nod. "Clementine."

"You can't just leave like that! You can't just tell me that and go!"

"I can," Butch said without looking back. "And I will."

He just gave Lou a look before walking out of the room. Lottie rolled her eyes and set her glass at the edge of the table. "He can be really dramatic."

"How do you know him again?" Clementine asked. "Besides drinking with Dad?"

"I've seen him *around*," Lottie said with a dismissive wave. Her face lit up and she grabbed a pack of cards on the table. She shuffled them and moved across from Lou. "Come on, Ramirez. We're going to play a little game."

"What kinda game?" Lou asked, clearly still wound up from their encounter with Butch.

"Poker." Lottie smiled as she dealt the cards. "Strip poker. It'll help you clear your head."

Lou threw back their shot and Lottie immediately poured them another. "Fine."

"Um, Lou," Clementine said, taking their free hand that wasn't holding the shot glass. "I don't know if that's the best idea."

"Why not?" they asked with a frown, already taking the next shot. The glass was barely empty before more alcohol found its way into it.

"Castellanos folk have always been good at cards, or at least acting like they're good at cards," she said, noticing that Lottie was looking far too innocent for her own good.

"'M good at poker too, darlin'," Lou said, giving her a wink. Their eyes already looked glassy, the alcohol clearly getting to them.

"Yes, but—"

"Come on, Clem, if you're going to be marrying this person, I need to get to know them," Lottie said with a smirk. Clementine blushed.

"I didn' sign nothin'," Lou reminded the room. "Least not yet."

Clementine blushed even deeper.

"See, all fun and games," Lottie reasoned. "We'll just do a coupla rounds. Just enough to get Ramirez here to loosen up a little, wash the dirty taste of Butch Burner out of our mouths."

"Exactly." Lou smiled at Clementine, and she knew she'd let them get away with anything. Clementine sighed and folded her arms across her chest as she leaned back against her chair.

"Don't say I didn't warn you, Lou. I tried to tell you."

"I'll be jus' fine, darlin.'"

"Famous last words," she mumbled as she watched another shot go down their throat.

Lottie dealt the first hand and Clementine leaned over to look at Lou's. She sighed. Lou was already in trouble. When they laid their cards down on the table, Clementine wasn't surprised to see Lou had lost.

"Well, well, well, Ramirez, not as good as you seem to think you are, huh?" Lottie said as she took another shot.

"'At was jus' the warm up," Lou slurred. They reached down to take their boot off, undoing the laces with clumsy fingers.

Lottie frowned. "What are you doing?"

"Takin' my boot off. You said strip poker."

"No no. That's not how Castellanos' play strip poker. We don't do weak things like take a sock off at a time. We go for the throat." Lottie smirked wider. "So take your shirt off."

"Lottie," Clementine warned.

"House rules."

"Fine," Lou said, as they undid the buttons. "I'll take my shirt off."

Clementine had seen Lou in their undershirt plenty of times. This really shouldn't be any different. Still, she blushed when Lou unbuttoned their shirt and shrugged it off to reveal their snug undershirt.

"Next round?"

"Next round, Castellanos."

That was how it went on until Lou was slowly unbuckling their belt, looking at Lottie with determined eyes.

"I told ya, Castellanos, I don' back down," Lou slurred.

Clementine had lost count of how many drinks they'd had, but their boots and socks had long ago been thrown across the room, suspenders discarded on the table from the several games they had lost.

"Lou, you don't have to," she hissed, reaching for their hands. Lou batted them away.

"Nope," they said, taking a step away from Clementine. Lottie looked like the cat that had eaten the canary. "I lost. Now I 'ave to face the consequences."

"Lou—" Clementine squeaked as they opened their pants and pushed them down their legs, struggling a little with their chaps still on.

Lottie cackled, head thrown back as she took another drink. "You're going to marry a wild one," she said, with a wiggle of her eyebrows. "Not a bad body, though."

"You will *not* look at their body," Clementine said as Lou's pants landed on the table. She looked over and saw Lou smiling proudly, hands on their hips as they stood there in just their undershirt, long underpants, and chaps. Their body swayed a little from the alcohol and Clementine felt her body heat up.

"Next game, Castellanos."

"No more games!" Clementine said, handing the pants back to Lou who just let them fall to the ground. "I'm getting you both some water."

Clementine rushed out of the room and grabbed the pitcher of water that they kept in the back room of the saloon. She was only gone a minute, but when she'd come back it was like chaos had broken out.

Lou was passed out on the table, face down and bare-assed—though somehow still in their leather chaps—Clementine's entire body flushed and she forced herself to look at Lottie.

"What the *hell*, Lottie?"

"You're welcome," Lottie slurred, with a drunken smile. "We played another game."

"And they lost *that fast*?"

"They said they were gonna lose anyways." Lottie shrugged. She frowned at Lou, snoring on the table. "God that looks comfortable."

"No. We're getting you both home," Clementine said, setting the pitcher of water down on a nearby table. "You're helping me get them on their horse."

"I don't wanna."

"You did this, you're helping."

Her gaze wandered back to Lou's ass, exposed proudly on the dark wood of the poker table as they snored away. The sisters struggled to drag their soggy form upright, Clementine eventually just shoving a bar towel into the back of the chaps to cover up that admittedly great ass. Lou was mostly awake by the time they were pulling them off the table by the arms.

Lou mumbled, letting her put their arm over her shoulders as they shuffled outside to their horses. They leaned close to her, their forehead pressing against her temple.

"Yer so pretty," Lou said softly. She felt herself blush again and she smiled at them. Lou smiled back and nuzzled her cheek. "I'm real fond'a you, Miss Clementine."

"I'm fond of you too," she whispered as they stood next to Trigger.

"I wish I wasn't drunk," Lou said with a small pout.

"Why's that?"

"So I could kiss you." Lou whispered it like a secret, a smile pulling at the corners of their lips. Clementine felt her entire body flush, lips begging to kiss Lou. But they were drunk and she wanted Lou to remember it when they finally kissed. To cherish it the way Clementine knew she would.

"Will you kiss me when you're not drunk?" Clementine asked hopefully.

"Darlin' I've wanted to kiss you from the first moment I saw you."

"Why haven't you?"

Lou hummed, eyes drooping closed. "I wanted it to be right. To be proper. To be perfect."

She stroked the side of Lou's face, her fingertips tracing the high curve of their cheekbone. She lingered on the scar below their eye before she kissed it gently. "Let's get you home."

Clementine hummed as she worked behind the bar the next morning. She hadn't been able to wipe the smile from her face since the night before. Sure it had ended in Lottie getting Lou drunk beyond belief and pantless on the table, but Lou wanted to *kiss* her. They'd finally admitted they wanted to kiss her. That was worth the whole night, even if Butch's information on her dad only seemed to get them further away from the truth.

"What are you so happy about?" Juanita teased when she came from upstairs. "Good night?"

"The best. I think Lou and I are finally getting somewhere. They're courting me now."

"Oh, wow," Juanita said, eyebrows going up into her hairline. "Well, that's great for you, Clem. I'm glad they're finally doing something smart. You two deserve to be happy."

"Tonight I'm hoping to make them dinner and maybe they'll finally let me kiss them." She felt mooney-eyed at the thought.

Veronica came through the front doors and went straight for the bar, eyes on Juanita. "You should see the carriage that just pulled up outside. It looks like money."

"Who is it?"

Veronica shrugged just as the saloon doors opened again and a tall, darker-skinned woman walked in, wearing a gorgeous light purple dress that looked like silk. She practically dripped money as she looked around, her eyes landing on Juanita. Something about her looked familiar and Clementine squinted in thought.

"Oh," Juanita said, quickly moving from behind the bar. "Clementine, can you take inventory please?"

"Who is that?"

"It's no one," Juanita said with a dismissive wave. The woman smiled, starting over to Juanita. "Clem, just do inventory, please?"

Clementine started into the back, eyes still lingering on the woman as she embraced Juanita.

Suddenly it clicked and she stopped in her tracks. Clementine felt her blood run cold and dread settled deep in her stomach. She knew exactly who the woman was—the image in Lou's trunk, the picture of the woman sitting on their lap. Somehow she was even more beautiful in person than in the photo, sitting proudly on Lou's knee with their hands on her waist. It was Lou's lost lover, Inez.

CHAPTER SEVENTEEN

Clementine stood there in disbelief, legs unwilling to move from the spot as she watched Inez interact with Juanita. Her brain struggled to figure out if this was real or some elaborate nightmare. But she could still smell the stale beer and the reek of unwashed customers who had come straight from the mines and farms, so she knew this was in no way her imagination running wild.

"Close up your mouth before you trap a fly," Veronica said in a hushed tone, tapping Clementine's hip.

She shut her mouth quickly and looked over at Veronica, who raised an eyebrow in question.

"Is that who I think it is?"

Veronica looked over her shoulder to take a good look at Inez. "I…Who do you think that is?"

"Inez. Lou's ex."

"Lou's *ex*?" Veronica looked over at Inez quickly before looking back at Clementine, ears almost visibly perked in interest. "She's pretty."

"Great."

Gripping her stomach and a steadying hand on the table, she reached for the glass of beer that Veronica had just poured and downed half of it.

"Hey, that was for the table over there," Veronica complained.

She reached for another glass and poured a fresh beer. Her gaze never left Inez as she slowly walked closely past the women, toward the table Veronica had indicated.

"Are they alive?" Inez was asking, tentatively.

"Yes," Juanita said in a hushed tone, side-eying Clementine as she took her time delivering the beer. "They're here. In town."

Inez put a hand over her mouth, but not before a strangled sob escaped her. "I thought they were dead. I had heard they ended up here and I came, just hoping to see their grave."

Clementine put the beer on the table before moving to another table that was even closer to Inez and Juanita, pretending to clean it, probably not subtly, considering the way Juanita was eyeing her. Juanita gestured at Clementine to leave and she shook her head with a squint. Inez saw Juanita looking over her shoulder and her gaze followed, locking eyes with Clementine, who felt caught, hand hovering over the table and reaching for nothing. Inez looked her over quickly, using a hanky to dab at the corners of her eyes.

"I'm sorry, we're trying to have a conversation here," Inez said, not unkindly. But it still made Clementine bristle with anger.

"Excuse me?" she said, feeling caught and trying to figure out if she should play dumb or just talk to her.

Inez sniffled and crumpled the hanky in a silk-gloved hand. "Don't you have customers waiting?"

She looked over at the empty bar and then around the room where everyone else was sitting and enjoying their drinks.

"Uh…"

Inez's gaze darted to Clementine's breasts spilling out of the top of her dress (so maybe she had tied her corset a little tighter that morning just to see Lou run into a chair) and she cleared her throat with a small blush.

"I mean like upstairs?" Inez said, gesturing up the staircase where a few men were hanging over the balcony railing, practically drooling like dogs and waiting for one of the girls to be done with her current client.

Clementine scoffed, face turning hard as she looked back at Inez. Juanita stepped in quickly.

"Clementine works here at the bar."

"Oh, sorry—"

"Excuse me, I have to do my job," Clementine said briskly, just wanting to get as far away as possible.

They stared at each other for a moment before Clementine realized she hadn't left. She looked around for something to do, finally just grabbing a mostly finished beer from a man's hand and walking quickly back to the bar. He blinked at his empty hand, clearly drunk already, and just shrugged. She practically threw the glass into the pile of dirty glasses and spun to grip the edge of the bar.

Juanita and Inez went back to talking, and Clementine tried her best not to keep looking over. But it was hard with Inez *right there*, a woman she had never known but certainly envied. And now she was back, right when Lou was talking about kissing Clementine.

"I wouldn't worry about it," Veronica said, bumping her hip with Clementine's as she stood next to her at the bar, wiping down a glass. "I've never seen Lou with anyone the way they are with you."

Clementine frowned. "Wait, who else have they been with since you've known them?"

The jealousy over these faceless girls was already blooming hot in Clementine's chest.

"Um, Juanita, I guess. Me." Veronica squinted, then shrugged. Clementine sighed, not comforted. "Inez must have been years ago, I'm sure they're over her by now."

"What if they're not?" she said, fears swimming to the surface and the sickness in her stomach only getting worse. She could practically feel Lou slipping through her fingers when she was so close to finally having them.

Clementine poked her tongue into her cheek in thought and watched Inez and Juanita in deep conversation again. She fiddled with her skirt and wished she could tell Inez to leave Lou alone. She was Lou's *something* after all. They shared a bed together every night. Clementine had just seen them ass-up on a table for Christ's sake!

"All right." She clapped her hands together, bucking up some courage and walking back around the bar. If she wanted to get anything done, she was just going to have to do it. She would have kissed Lou a long time ago if she had just taken matters into her own hands. She marched right up to Inez, head tipped back an embarrassing amount to look up at her. *Was she taller than Lou?* She tapped her shoulder.

"Hello."

Inez stopped midsentence and looked down at Clementine. "Yes?"

Her mouth went dry and she forgot what she'd meant to say. "I'm Clementine. Clementine Castellanos. Lou's…person… someone."

"You're together?" Inez asked, face unreadable.

"Not exactly. No, it's complicated."

Inez smiled fondly. "That sounds like Lou all right," she said, opening up her small clutch and putting her handkerchief back inside. It snapped shut with a metal clasp that looked like money. "Can you tell them that I'm staying at the hotel? And that I'd really like to see them?"

"S-sure," she said, voice falling a little bit. Inez's smile was just so pretty and perfect, making her even more beautiful, face lighting up as she said a quick goodbye to Juanita and headed back out the door.

Clementine stood in place, almost in shock and looked over at Juanita, who was giving her a sympathetic look. "You look sick."

"I *feel* sick," she said, hand on her stomach. It felt like a rug had been pulled out from under her leaving her light-headed and sweaty. She looked up at Juanita and sighed. "Life has really shit timing, doesn't it?"

"It really does, Clem. But don't be discouraged. Lou hasn't talked about her in ages."

"They still have her picture."

Juanita shrugged. "Those suckers are expensive. Don't read too much into it."

It was too late. Clementine was already imagining every horrible situation in her head.

Clementine's stomach churned for her whole shift. Inez had long gone, taking her fancy carriage to the hotel. Still, her expensive perfume hung in the air and made Clementine just feel sicker.

"It's been three years," Juanita told Clementine as she sadly poured a beer for a customer. She sighed and gave the leering man a half-hearted smile before turning to Juanita.

"Absence makes the heart grow fonder, as they say," was all she could muster before going to help another customer.

She thought about Lou's arms around her and how safe and right it felt. But maybe those arms weren't meant for her, maybe she had just been a placeholder for someone else, someone fancier and more sophisticated.

Lou's whispered words and little touches came to mind, and the way they looked at her. Brown eyes so warm and inviting that Clementine was sure she could drown in them, reflecting so much joy and affection at her. Cautious hands that had cradled her like she was the most precious thing in the world.

The knot in her stomach loosened a little. Lou was hers. She saw it in the way they looked at her and maybe Lou was afraid to say it right now, but they were inching toward *something*. And she knew she wouldn't be forgotten so quickly.

She sat on Butter with a renewed confidence as she rode back to the cabin that evening. She would tell Lou what happened. There was no way Clementine would ever keep something like that from them, but she wasn't worried about the results anymore. Lou was *hers*. Fate hadn't landed her on Lou's doorstep for nothing.

After brushing Butter out and making sure she was fed, she slowly made her way into the house to find Lou putting some flowers in the tin can on the table, dinner laid out on two plates.

They straightened up and smiled brightly, dimples popping as they gestured proudly to the food on the table.

"I made ya supper."

Their pants and shirt were dirty, a little dusty from working outside, and Clementine imagined them rushing in from their chores to make sure the dinner was set up in time. There was even a little smudge of dirt on their nose that made her heart flutter.

"I see that." She smiled, all thoughts of Inez gone from her mind. She slipped her arms around their neck, fingers finding the wispy hairs at the base of their neck and body aching to lean up and close the gap between their lips. But Lou's tentative hands on her hips would have to do for now. "Is this another date?"

"If you don' mind, anyways."

"I definitely don't." She frowned for a moment and brushed some hair from Lou's face. "How's your head after last night? How are you not dying?"

"Well, you jus' weren't lucky 'nough to see the mess my stomach made behind the barn earlier," Lou mumbled, ears tinting even brighter.

"Poor thing," Clementine said with a pout.

"It was mah own fault. An' I'm sorry 'bout the state I was in."

She giggled, her own blush creeping up her neck. Lou ass-up at the table had been a problem at the time, but she wasn't about to forget the view.

"I didn't mind all that much. Even if you did let Lottie trick you."

"Mm, how about we jus' forget about last night and eat some supper, darlin'?" Lou said, untangling themself from Clementine, but the grip around their neck just tightened. They chuckled, head ducking a little closer to her. "Now, Miss Clementine."

"What?" she said innocently, hand cupping the back of their head.

Lou licked their lips, eyes downcast to Clementine's before they whispered, "It would be quite improper to kiss you before dinner."

She smirked. "I've never been much to care about what was proper."

Lou's grip tightened on her hips, face just a hair's breadth closer, and she felt her confidence surge.

"Plus just think of it as a continuation of last night. Then you can kiss me *again* after dinner."

"Miss Clementine, I think we both know that once I start kissin' you I won' be able to stop."

She almost passed out right there, heat surging through her body as she stood on her tiptoes. She felt their faces drifting closer, the hint of Lou's breath on her lips.

Suddenly Inez popped into the forefront of her mind, with the memories of when she snooped through Lou's trunk and broke their trust. She couldn't avoid telling Lou about Inez any longer. She didn't want to spring it on them after they kissed. Something about it felt wrong, like she was withholding information from Lou to get what she wanted. Plus, she just wanted to be completely sure that Lou chose *her*.

"Lou," Clementine whispered, reluctantly breaking the spell. Lou hummed, their gaze still on Clementine's lips before flickering up to her eyes. "I um, saw Inez in town today."

Lou's whole body tensed, eyes widened and confused as they pulled away from Clementine, who felt her heart drop a little.

"You saw...'Re you sure?"

She nodded, fingers playing nervously with the back of their collar. "She was looking for you. She wanted me to tell you that she's staying at the hotel and wants to talk to you."

Lou stood a little taller, Clementine falling back from her tiptoes onto a flat heel once more.

"The hotel in town?"

"Yeah. She thought you were dead."

Lou, still looking confused, dropped their hands from Clementine's hips and just stood there for a moment, staring at nothing across the cabin.

"I guess, I should go," Lou said, moving away from Clementine to their trunk to get some clean clothes.

Clementine stood there for a moment, brow furrowed as she tried to understand what had just happened. Lou unbuttoned their dirty shirt and washed up at the basin, something they usually chose to do when Clementine was paying attention to something else, but they didn't seem to mind at the moment. They had a far-off look in their eyes that Clementine couldn't quite explain.

"I...What about dinner?" Clementine said pathetically, pointing at the table.

Lou blinked out of their daze and took her hands in their own. "'M sorry, darlin', I 'ave to go see what all this is 'bout. But 'm sure Lottie won' mind takin' mah place."

With a brief kiss to the back of her hand, Lou went back to the basin and scrubbed their face. Clementine stared, still completely in shock. Lou was leaving to go see Inez. Right after they almost kissed her. A kiss that she had been hoping for. And now...

She watched as Lou shrugged on a nice blue-striped shirt that she had never seen before. The linen looked new and soft, with clean dark-brown pants that were missing the usual holes and work stains their other pairs had. They even slipped on a vest Clementine hadn't seen before, after putting on their suspenders.

"Um," was all she could say as she watched them dig into their trunk and bring out some kind of cologne or aftershave and pat it onto their neck. Then they went to the door, taking their hat off the hook and brushing some dirt off it.

Clementine sprang into action, going up to them and taking their hand. "Should I wait up?" she tried with a small, forced smile. "You know so you don't have to worry about waking me up or..."

They frowned like it was the most ridiculous question in the world. "No, it's fine, Miss Clementine," they said as they settled their hat on their head. "Don' wait up fer me."

With a tip of their hat, they closed the door with Clementine still staring at it, wondering what kind of luck she had. The same sick feeling from before began to creep into her veins and she managed to make it over to the table, collapsing in a chair. She rested her head in her hands, elbows on the table, feeling the frustrated tears mounting, throat closing off.

This was it. Lou was going to get back together with Inez. She could feel it deep down. That gnawing insecurity that had been present from the moment she realized her dad hated her and truly wouldn't have cared if she disappeared. The insecurity that she wasn't *good* enough. And never would be.

She let out a shuddering breath and felt her eyes welling with tears. She sniffled, quickly wiping them away, even though no one was there to see them. Maybe that made it worse in the long run. She folded her arms and hid her head as she cried.

Lou had never seen a ghost in their life, but they figured those who had would say it felt something like they felt now, standing in front of the woman they'd left behind three years ago with only a letter.

When Inez opened her hotel door, the first thing that struck Lou was how she was more beautiful than they remembered. Suddenly they felt like a fool, standing there in their rancher clothes, holding their hat nervously between their hands, though they had always felt like a bit of a fool with Inez.

She was so smart, so sophisticated, straight from France, just gracing the wild country with her presence. Somehow, Lou had caught her eye and they started their whirlwind affair. They loved each other, that much was true, and if Lou could have, they would have married her right then and there.

But fate had other ideas and Lou left with only a note on Inez's pillow before they ran for Ghosthallow. Ran for safety.

Now with Inez standing in front of them, Lou felt everything flooding back, every touch, every kiss. Every passionate moment they had shared. They swallowed thickly, watching Inez's face bloom into a giant, relieved smile. "Hi, Inez," Lou said softly, their own smile slowly turning up their lips. "It's been a while."

"It has," Inez said, stepping aside and gesturing for Lou to join her in her room. With a polite nod, Lou stepped in and Inez closed the door behind them.

Clementine tried to sleep that night but woke up every few minutes thinking she heard Lou come into the cabin, but every time it was either a ghost or the wind, never Lou. It was just short of a miracle the following morning that she managed to get herself dressed and to work in a presentable way. She'd checked in the barn while she was getting Butter to see if Lou had decided to sleep in there instead, but the only person in there was a snoring Lottie cuddling with a half-empty bottle of whiskey.

Veronica and Juanita eyed Clementine warily as she came in that day, being extra nice, and Veronica even poured her a cup of coffee, handing it to her with a sympathetic smile.

"So," Juanita finally said when there was a lull in customers. "How did Ramirez take it?"

"I'm going to guess extremely well since I haven't seen them since they left last night," Clementine said with a stiff, tight-lipped smile. Veronica and Juanita gave each other a quick glance.

"I wouldn't worry about it," Juanita said with a dismissive wave. "It's been years. They have a lot to talk about."

Veronica nodded in agreement. "I mean, Inez thought Lou was *dead*. That's a lot to come back from."

"How hard can it be? She thought they were dead, and now she knows they're alive. End of discussion!" She threw her hands up in the air. "Five minutes."

Juanita sighed and rubbed Clementine's shoulder. "I wouldn't worry, seriously. The way Lou looks at you is like someone that just found a gold nugget in their pan."

Clementine managed a chuckle and looked back down at her hands wrapped around the coffee cup. She wanted to stay positive about the whole thing, but it was so *hard*. She couldn't help but think about the picture of Inez and Lou in their trunk, the saved letters and books with her inscription inside them.

"Yeah, until a bigger nugget comes along," she sighed with a sad shake of her head. Her heart was slowly breaking but she couldn't focus on that.

"Well speak of the devil," Veronica said a little under her breath as the saloon doors opened and Lou walked in. Clementine's heart ached at the sight of them, clothes a little disheveled and a fatigued drag to their gait. As they approached the bar, they unbuttoned the top couple of buttons of their shirt and slid into a seat. They gave Clementine a tired smile that normally would have made her melt, but instead she bristled.

"Mornin', Miss Clementine," they said as they took their hat off and set it on the chair beside them. "Mind if I get some coffee and breakfast?"

She looked up at their warm eyes, face hard as she pointedly looked behind them. "Just for one?"

"I mean, I usually only eat fer one but I 'spose if you'd like to join me—"

"For one it is," she said, turning on her heel and walking into the kitchen to angrily throw some biscuits and gravy onto a plate. Usually she would take time to fish out a few more chunks of sausage in the gravy for Lou, but not today. Today they would just take what was given to them, if they cared. She was sure Inez could figure out a way to get them more sausage. She practically stomped back into the main part of the saloon and threw Lou's plate in front of them.

Lou blinked in shock for a moment before looking back up at her. "Um, thanks," they said, picking up a fork but still looking at Clementine a little cautiously. "How was yer—"

"Where's *Inez*?" she interrupted, boiling over like a teakettle left on the fire too long. She put her hands on her hips and just watched Lou stare at her.

"Inez? She's back at 'er hotel," they said, like it was the most obvious thing in the world.

"Did you two have a nice night?" she asked, voice breaking a little bit so she looked away to compose herself. She was *not* going to let Lou see her cry. Again.

"Miss Clementine," they said, "if you don' mind, 'm very tired an' my brain ain't quite catchin' on 'ere."

"I *bet* you're tired," she muttered as she angrily poured them a cup of coffee. She leaned across the bar, a sickly-sweet smell reaching her lungs as she inhaled. "And by the way, you still smell like her perfume."

With Lou's even more confused look, she stomped into the back room again. She didn't want to see Lou's dumb cute face, because every time she did, she just thought about Inez— Inez kissing them, hugging them, loving them in a way that Clementine hadn't been allowed.

She could go at least a few more hours without being reminded of that fact. She simply busied herself in the back room until Juanita came and told her that Lou had left.

Despite not sleeping the night before, Lou hit a second wind when they rode back to the cabin from the saloon.

Clementine was continuing to give them the cold shoulder but they were too concerned with other matters to truly think about it, particularly Inez and her presence in the town. Their conversations had taken Lou back to a place they thought they'd left. It had been so easy to forget when they were getting lost in their work, in building up the farm. Then when Clementine came into the picture, well, it was even easier to forget everything from their past that had plagued them.

When they got back to the barn, they took Trigger's saddle off and were brushing him when they heard Lottie.

"Hey, Ramirez," she said.

Lou didn't even bother turning around, continuing to curry Trigger's flank. "Yes, Miss Castellanos?"

Lottie placed one hand on Trigger's back. "Are you gonna keep jerking around my baby sister or what?"

"I don' know what yer talkin'—"

"Like shit you don't. Juanita told me some interesting things last night when I was at the saloon."

Lou straightened. "Oh yeah? Like what?"

"Like how your ex is back in town and you spent all night reacquainting yourself with her while Clementine sat in *your* cabin by herself—"

"*Our* cabin," they corrected without thinking, a blush creeping up their neck. "An' you jus' show up after how many years to deal with yer sister's affairs? Does she know 'at yer 'ere on 'er behalf? 'Cause I don' think she'd 'preciate it much."

She squinted at them, poking a finger hard into their chest. "She's my little *sister*."

"She's a grown woman."

"And you're a lying, cheating sonuvabitch," she hissed out, shoving their shoulder. Their injured arm protested a little, but they didn't let it show, their jaw tight.

"These affairs don't concern you, Lottie," Lou said, letting the brush drop to the ground and squaring themself up to her. They stood to their full height and looked down at the woman. "An' you'd be best to remember that or get off my land. Ya hear?"

Lou stared down into hard blue eyes one last time before stepping past her, making sure their shoulders bumped as they stalked out of the barn.

* * *

Clementine had managed to ignore Lou for a couple of days. She spent more time at work pretending not to notice when Lou would look at her. But she was losing her resolve, that was clear, in the way her heart betrayed her with a flutter when Lou came into the cabin with a shy smile. The way it tripped over itself in her chest and made her want to kiss them. Still. Even after she knew Lou had spent the other night with Inez.

She felt like they were in limbo and didn't know which way they would tip, just on the edge of the cliff. Lou's cheeks were red and they held their hat in their hands. "Miss Clementine, I know yer a bit cross wit' me righ' now, but I wanna show you somethin'."

She couldn't help but catch onto their excitement, smile tugging at the corners of her lips. "Cross isn't the *right* word. But sure. What is it?"

Lou held the door open for her and gestured for her to follow. "Come on, it's jus' over 'ere."

They took her hand and led her out past the still incomplete structure of the house they were building and into the woods that lined the north edge of Lou's property. The woods were thin, easy enough to see through and navigate until they got to a river that ran through the middle of it. The river was wide but calm, shallow enough to wade through, but you'd still get soaked.

As soon as they stood on the edge of the river, Lou dropped her hand, pushed their suspenders down their shoulders and pulled their shirt off. She felt her cheeks heat as they began to undo their belt.

"What are you doing?" she asked, even as her eyes hungrily devoured the sight of Lou in just their underclothes.

"We're goin' in the river," they said matter-of-factly as they set their hat on the pile of their clothes and began to pull off their boots. "You ain't gonna wanna go in there with yer dress on."

She raised a challenging eyebrow at Lou. "Are you just trying to get me to take my clothes off, Lou?"

They blushed and paused halfway through pulling their boot off. They blinked and shook their head. "Uh, no, Miss Clementine, 'm jus' sayin'."

She laughed and leaned over to kiss Lou's cheek without thinking. "You dog."

"I..."

She cut them off by undoing the laces at the back of her dress and letting it fall down her shoulders, leaving her only in her thin cotton camisole and pantaloons. She quickly pulled off her shoes and Lou still stood there, blinking in shock.

"Come on, cowboy, what were you going to show me?" she teased, thoughts of Inez far from her mind for the first time in days.

Lou smiled, dimples on full display as they chucked their boot off to the side and took her hand again.

"Come on."

They led her into the river, the cold water sending a shiver up her spine as it swirled past her, thin underclothes doing nothing to protect her from the cold. As they waded through the deepest part of the river where the water came up to her chest, it only took a few moments for her to acclimate to the cold; her mind was mostly focused on how Lou's clothes had gone basically see-through in the water, clinging to their every curve and leaving nothing to the imagination. It was basically just looking at their bare back and binding bandage.

They made it to the other side of the river where foliage from the trees hung over, creating a sort of hideaway at the edge of the river. They held their finger in front of their lips, signaling for her to be quiet as they slowly waded toward the riverbank. They stopped where a branch hung particularly low, leaves grazing the surface of the water, and Clementine stood next to them.

"What are we—"

"Sshh."

Lou lifted the branch to reveal a dozen brown-and-yellow fluffy ducklings floating in a bundle, heads tucked between their bodies and cuddled up to their mom.

Clementine gasped, hands immediately gripping Lou's arm to keep herself from reaching out and scooping one into her hands.

"They're so cute," she whispered, leaning a little closer.

"I been watchin' the eggs fer a coupla weeks now," they whispered back as the mama duck raised her head. "I been waitin' fer them to hatch."

"Can we take them back to the ranch?"

Lou chuckled. "We can try."

The mama duck quacked and the babies began to lift their fluffy little heads. The mama duck spread her wings, neck elongated, and quacked again.

She frowned. "I think she's mad."

Like a flash, the duck launched itself at Clementine, flapping its wings in her face. She squeaked in surprise, fear spiking in her chest as she reacted on instinct and threw her arms up to cover her face. She went to step back but she caught her foot on a river rock and tumbled backward into the water instead.

The cold enveloped her and she was in shock for a moment before she pushed herself out of the water with a gasp for air. She sputtered, moving the hair from her face, only to see Lou practically doubled over in laughter. The duck glared at her for a moment before swimming back under the branch to her babies.

Her cheeks heated and she frowned at Lou. "It's not funny!" she said with a pout.

Lou wheezed, trying to talk but just doubling over in laughter again. She crossed her arms, jaw tight with her hair plastered to the sides of her face. "Lou!"

They couldn't stop laughing, so she splashed water on them instead. Their laughter turned to a shocked gasp as the water soaked them even more. Dark hair in their eyes, they stood in shock.

"Miss Clementine!" they said as they brushed the hair from their face. "That ain't proper..."

She splashed them again, Lou's hand shielding their face a poor defense against the assault. She looked at Lou standing there, completely soaked to the bone and couldn't help but chuckle.

"Now we match," she said. Lou smiled mischievously, a sparkle in their eyes that warned her. She held up a warning finger. "Lou Ramirez. Don't you..."

Lou skimmed their arm across the surface of the water, sending a big wave to slap her in the face. She could hear Lou cackling over her gasps.

"I can't believe you!" she yelled, despite the smile on her face.

"You started it, darlin'."

She raised her eyebrow at Lou and they looked concerned for the first time.

"Now, Miss Clementine..."

She launched herself at Lou, wrapping her arms around their shoulders and pulling them under the water. The two of them went under and when Lou realized what was happening, they straightened. Clementine clung tightly around Lou's neck. She squealed as Lou dipped her again and she locked her legs around Lou's waist to stay above the water.

They both dissolved into a fit of giggles, Lou still trying to splash her. She returned the favor, scooping water directly into their face. They shook their head to get rid of some of the water but she kept splashing them.

Both still laughing, Lou blindly grabbed for her hands. Finally, the splashing stopped and she realized how close they were. Her legs were still wrapped around their waist, their thin undergarments doing nothing to separate them. Lou's hands gripped Clementine's wrists and their faces sobered at their closeness.

A flush of heat surged through her as Lou's hands dropped her wrists and found her hips instead. As the water settled around them, her eyes darted down to Lou's soaked undershirt, sticking to them like a second skin. All the lines of their muscles—firm ropes—spread from their neck to their strong shoulders. She swallowed thickly, eyes flicking back to Lou's. She watched their tongue dart out and wet their lips unnecessarily, their breathing ragged.

The silence between them was thick with tension, Lou's thumbs rubbing infuriatingly teasing circles on her hips. She tangled her fingers in their scalp and pressed closer, feeling every single inch of her body touching Lou in some way.

Then it snapped.

The tension became too much, crackling around them like the air before a thunderstorm and they surged together. Their lips crashed together with the force of a tornado, all the built-up lightning between them finally meeting.

She sighed against Lou's lips, fingers tightening in their hair to the point it must be painful, but she didn't want to pull away, didn't want to waste any space where they could be touching. Lou's mouth molded instantly to hers, one hand cupped the back of her neck, the other finding purchase on her lower back as their lips clumsily found a rhythm.

It was messy and desperate and sloppy, and exactly what she had craved for *months*. Their teeth clashed and lips were nipped as the months of longing finally got some relief.

From the first touch of their lips Clementine's blood pounded with arousal, and when Lou's tongue slipped between her lips, she groaned. Lou pressed her against a nearby boulder and kissed her jaw. She wanted to protest when Lou's lips left her own but she felt their teeth scrape against her pulse point and her head tipped back to give them more access.

Her fingers raked through wet locks, hips tilting into them as their lips traveled across her collarbone. They bit down on the pronounced bone before soothing their tongue over the bite and sucking. Clementine could barely think with the heat crawling over her skin and between her thighs.

She pulled Lou's face back to her own while Lou's hands gripped her thighs, squeezing the flesh there as they kissed. The cold water from the river did little to cool her overheated body, and she was sure she would combust at any moment, the way Lou kissed her.

She wanted to rip all her clothes off and tell Lou to take her right there, to tell them that she was theirs, and theirs only, and would do anything for them. But back at the forefront of her mind was Inez, probably in her fancy hotel room thinking about Lou.

Clementine slowed their kisses, eyes squeezed shut and not wanting it to end. When she pulled away from Lou, they leaned back in and Clementine had to put a finger over their lips to stop them. Dazed brown eyes blinked open, pupils dilated, and lips swollen. Lou kissed the tip of Clementine's finger, their faces still close.

"Miss Clementine—"

"Inez," she said simply, the name off her lips enough to break her heart. "What about Inez?"

Lou's face fell, brow furrowing in confusion as their hands traveled to safer territory on her hips. "What?" Lou blinked, still dazed with their eyes fluttering down to her lips.

"Inez," she repeated painfully. "What are you and her?"

Realization dawned on Lou's face, as they slumped and their grip loosened. "Oh," they said simply, cheeks reddening.

Her heart broke all over again and she chuckled without humor. "That's what I thought."

She unwrapped her legs, sliding back into the water and heading toward the shore where their clothes were.

"But, Miss Clementine! We haven't...It's not—"

"It's fine, Lou," she said, not bothering to turn back as she quickly slipped her dress back on. Tears pooled behind her eyes, throat strained as she swallowed thickly. "I let it get too far. I... it's fine, Lou."

Without turning around, she walked back to the cabin alone.

Clementine was wringing her hair out with a towel when Lottie stormed into the cabin. She had a bag over her shoulder and a smirk on her face as she looked over Clementine's soaked form.

"Hey, Clem," she said, dropping the bag on the floor with a thud. "We're almost ready. What the fuck did you do?"

"Almost ready for what? Lou and I..." She could still feel Lou's lips pressed against her own, the arousal coursing through her veins. She cleared her throat and forced a smile. "We were looking at baby ducks."

Lottie frowned but waved it off with her hand. "Okay, whatever. Well, we're leaving."

"Hey, you're not going anywhere. And neither am I."

"Why? Isn't Ramirez being a total cow pie to you? I just finished a job and I got the money to get out of Ghosthallow. You and me."

Clementine ran her fingers through her wet hair. Her heart was a jumbled mess of emotions at the bottom of her ribs, but she didn't want to fall apart yet. She wasn't even sure if she should be upset or overjoyed.

Lou had *kissed* her.

Their bodies had been pressed together, nothing between them, and Lou's lips—*god* their lips. The now hidden bruise on her collarbone throbbed with the reminder. But the question of

Inez still hung in the air, and Lou hadn't done anything to ease that worry.

"Where would we even go?" she sighed.

"Wherever we want. The big city! Think of it, Clem," she said, eyes lighting up with excitement. "We could get jobs there, and then we can go wherever we wanted! It doesn't matter."

Clementine ran a hand through her hair. It didn't seem like the worst option at the moment. She didn't want to stay here with a broken heart. Plus if she left first, Lou wouldn't get a chance to leave her. She would beat them to the punch.

"I don't know, Lottie."

"Well, think about it. We can leave after this week. Okay?"

"Yeah."

Lottie kissed the side of her head, and she smiled weakly. Just as Lottie was picking up her bag and leaving the cabin, Lou came in, eyes only for Clementine. Lottie scoffed and pushed past them, muttering as she did.

The door shut behind Lou, and Clementine felt a little sick just looking at them. Their shirt was hanging open, undershirt still soaked, and hair still clinging to the sides of their face.

"Miss Clementine."

She sighed and tried to rub some of the disappointment from her eyes. "Lou."

"Miss Clementine," they repeated, taking a step closer to her. "You 'ave to understand, I—"

"Lottie said we could leave." She didn't want to hear whatever sorry excuse Lou had for her. She didn't want to hear Lou tell her they loved Inez and could never love her. To know it was one thing, but to hear it would destroy her.

"What?"

"Lottie has money and it's enough that we can leave," she said again, voice even. "I'd make sure you get paid what you paid for me and we could call it even. I just..." Clementine put her hands on her hips and she looked up at the ceiling, swallowing thickly before looking back at Lou. "I'm going to go unless there's a reason I should stay."

Her voice had a hopeful lilt to it that she didn't want, the silent plea for Lou to ask her to stay. To tell her she was the one and Inez would be leaving soon.

Lou's eyes searched her face and they shook her head slowly. "Miss Clementine...I don't understand."

"Is there a reason I shouldn't go with Lottie? Is there a reason I should stay?"

Lou's face dropped and they looked down at the hat clutched between their hands by the brim. The silence got heavier with each second, weighing them down and suffocating them.

"I guess there ain't," they finally said, brown eyes looking up at her.

She nodded, ignoring how her heart had turned into a clawed creature, trying to crawl out of her chest. "All right then." She squared her jaw, determined not to cry as she looked back up at Lou. "Now if you'll please excuse me, I want to take a bath."

"I...okay," they whispered, turning around like a kicked puppy and walking out the door.

Clementine sobbed and she waited for a moment before going out to the barn where Lottie was. Lottie looked up from the bag she was packing and Clementine nodded once.

"All right then. Let's go."

* * *

Lou found it easy to step back into their role with Inez. It was easy to offer their arm and walk her about town like they had before everything went to shit. Before Lou left, they thought they were in love. They probably were. Except Inez had asked them to go to France with her, to escape the rough West and live with her as a kept person.

They knew that Inez couldn't wait to dress them in fancy suits and take them to all these uppity parties she talked about. Just the thought made Lou pull the collar of their shirt away from their neck in discomfort.

Inez had never asked them to be anything but themself, but Lou still felt miniscule standing next to her. With the way she dressed them up, it felt like she had an idea of a better version of them, one that Lou wasn't sure existed. They couldn't compete with her silk dresses and lace parasols. It was lucky that they had time to clean their boots before coming to see her. But the fact was, that life wasn't their style.

They liked working on the ranch and the dirt under their nails. They felt accomplished after a day of work that left their shoulders aching but strong. Inez wasn't much made for ranch life and that had been fine. Lou liked being around her.

Clementine was easy to be around too, but in a different way. Loving Clementine had come so naturally that it felt like a mistake, like something would go wrong at any moment.

Their stomach ached at the thought of her leaving. They didn't want her to, but it was best for her. She wouldn't have even asked Lou if she should stay if she hadn't wanted to leave anyway. Lou was doing her a favor.

Inez's grip tightened a little on Lou's arm, and they brought their attention back to her. Lou smiled, hoping they hadn't missed too much of what Inez was saying before their mind wandered. They had finally made it back to the front of Inez's hotel, some people not hiding their stares. Lou didn't blame them. Lou was the town pariah walking around with an obviously rich woman. Neither of them blended in.

"Are you all right?" Inez asked, fingers brushing lightly over the back of Lou's hands.

"'M fine. Jus'…thinkin'."

"About Clementine?"

Lou blushed, doing her best to keep their smile at bay. "Nah."

"You've never been a good liar, Lou Ramirez," Inez said as they took a seat on the bench at the hotel back porch.

Lou wiped their hands on the front of their pants, nervously playing with a loose thread. "Yeah, well, guess I never got much practice in."

"You were always too honest for your own good," she said, voice light like a song. "Except for when you left that letter."

Somehow in the past few days, they still hadn't talked about the letter. Not really. They had danced around it, referencing it only as a hiccup in what was supposed to be their story.

"Why did you come 'ere? Why come all 'is way? Did you want me go back wit' you?"

Inez smiled sadly. "Closure. I thought you were dead. I asked everyone I could think of about you, if they knew where you went. But you're like a ghost. Just disappeared."

"Yeah well, I didn' wan' anyone'a find me."

"Not even me?"

They pulled at the string again, the silence falling heavily over them before they smiled at her. "Well, you know I ain't got no problem with pretty ladies findin' me."

She tilted her head with a small, exasperated smile despite the blush on her cheeks. "I also know you divert to flirting when you don't want to answer a question."

They chuckled and shook their head. "I didn' wan' you to find me. Yer right. But it was because I didn' wan' ya to get hurt. They were after me, an' I knew they'd come for you too."

"I could have gone with you. I could have taken you to France where no one would have found you. You knew that. That's why I figured you didn't want me around anymore."

Lou rubbed the back of their neck. "You know France ain't much for me...An' I'm sorry. I shoulda told ya to your face instead'a disappearin'. I was a coward."

"There are a lot of words I would use to describe you but coward's not one of them," Inez whispered, like it was a secret. She winked and shrugged. "It's fine, really. I wasn't expecting that when I came here. I'm just thrilled that you're even alive."

"Yeah, well, lotta people 'ave tried to remedy that since. Ain't had that much luck, obviously."

"Then maybe you should stop trying to get killed. For Clementine."

"I'm not sure why you'd say that."

"I know you love her."

Lou's face burned even harder, a reply that was only sputtering leaving their lips as they tried to form a response. "I ain't...it ain't...love."

"You don't half-ass anything. Let alone when it comes to women."

"Well, I don' know about that."

"Look at me, please."

Lou forced themself to look up at Inez, a stray piece of hair falling into their line of vision before Inez pushed it away. She cupped Lou's face and smiled. "Tell me what you're thinking."

"I do," they admitted softly. "I do love 'er. I think. But I ain't been proper with 'er. I *bought* 'er for god's sake. She pro'bly jus' feels like she owes me somethin'. Plus, I came to Ghosthallow to be alone. To escape. I knew there were people after me. I couldn' bring anyone else in'o it. I'm meant to be alone forever."

"I promise you, she doesn't care. You didn't buy her on purpose. You helped her out of a situation." Inez chuckled, patting Lou's cheek lovingly.

"I really fucked this one up, Inez. I been so hot 'n cold with 'er that I doubt she even wants anything'a do with me anymore."

"If she feels about you the way I think she does, you don't have anything to worry about."

"What makes ya think that then?"

"I've seen how she talks about you. How she protects you. That's love."

"Well, I guess we'll see."

Inez smiled and put her hand over Lou's. "Now I better go so I can pack and catch my carriage back on the road tomorrow. Will you write this time?"

"I will. I promise."

"Good. I'll hold you to that." Inez leaned forward and kissed Lou softly. They smiled against her lips as she pulled away. "I will always love you, Lou. Just let me know if you ever need anything. Okay?"

"A'right. I'll write."

"Good luck," Inez said with a smirk, and headed into the hotel. Once Inez was gone, Lou mounted Trigger and rode at a full-speed gallop to get back to the ranch. They didn't know when Clementine was leaving, but they wanted to tell her how they felt right away. They wanted to scoop her into their arms and kiss her senseless.

But the closer they got to the barn, the more they knew something was wrong. They could sense it.

Even then, their heart still dropped when they got back to the cabin and all evidence of Clementine was wiped clean. She was gone.

CHAPTER EIGHTEEN

Lou ricocheted aimlessly about the cabin for a few minutes, an unsatisfying activity when you could get from one wall to the other in about five strides. But they paced, heart racing and mind struggling to catch up with the situation.

Clementine…was gone.

The carpet bag she kept under the bed was gone, the stray dress usually left drying over a chair was missing and even the bed was made neatly with one pillow in front of the other instead of two pillows next to each other like they usually did.

It was as if she'd never been there.

Lou felt sick. They didn't want to believe it. They didn't want to admit that she was gone, and they had managed to chase her out.

They went out to the barn, hoping to see Butter standing there with her big head sticking out of the stall in greeting, like she always did. Trigger followed along behind them, and he stuck his head over the door of Butter's empty stall like he was looking for her, snorting in discontent before turning back to Lou.

"I know, boy," they said, patting his neck. He pushed his face into their chest and they set one hand on his long nose, the other under his jaw. "I know."

He whinnied and turned back toward the barn door. Lou's gaze flicked wildly around the barn as if hoping to find a solution within, then they swung themself into Trigger's saddle and headed for the road.

When they got to the saloon, they hitched Trigger up to the post, a little disappointed not to see Butter there. They went inside, automatically searching for Clementine but instead landing on Juanita, who was marching up to them with a determined look on her face.

"Have you seen—"

The slap across the face was sharp and unexpected. Their head whipped to the side, cheek on fire until they slowly turned to face Juanita, who crossed her arms angrily.

"I ain't sayin' I didn' deserve that. But what exactly was 'at for?" Lou said, rubbing their cheek.

"You told Clementine to leave, you dumbass."

"I didn' tell 'er to leave. She asked me if she had anythin' to stay fer and she wouldn'a asked me that if she weren't already itchin' to move on."

"You're a donkey's behind. She wanted you to tell her to stay!"

"Then why didn' she jus' tell me that?"

"You are the single *thickest* person I've ever met. You just went and sabotaged the best thing that ever happened to you. I hope you know that."

Lou's stomach dropped as they watched Juanita go back behind the bar. Clementine was gone and it was their fault. But she should have told them. They should have…

Lou's mouth went dry and they took a beer off a tray Veronica carried and tipped it back. The liquid slopped down the corners of their mouth and onto their shirt, but they couldn't bring themself to care.

* * *

Clementine stared into the measly flames of the fire, watching as the tips flickered lazily up to the sky, and she wished that she had asked Lou how to build a better fire. The thought of Lou simultaneously angered and saddened her. She pulled her blanket tighter around her shoulders and missed them for another moment before letting the anger take over.

They had to camp out for the night before making it to the big city. Butter whinnied from nearby, and she absently wondered if the horse missed Trigger the same way Clem's heart ached for Lou.

She jumped a little when Lottie unceremoniously dropped another pile of sticks onto the fire. She rolled her eyes and reached for another stick as the fire smoked and struggled to stay lit under the barrage of fuel. She poked it to encourage it to grow again.

"I don't know how you've survived this long on your own."

Lottie shrugged and shoved her hands into the pockets of her buckskin jacket. "Me neither, to be honest." She looked at her and lightly kicked the bottom of her shoe. "Hey. What's up? You look like someone shit in your biscuits."

Clementine threw her a look and scooted over a little on the log so Lottie could sit next to her. "Nothing."

Lottie just stared at her for a moment and she sighed. "Just Lou."

"Aw, Clem." Lottie put her arm around Clementine's shoulders and pulled her close. She rested her head on Lottie's shoulder. "Listen, Ramirez don't know what they're missing. Okay? They're just as thick as a mule, and you're better off without them."

"They're not thick," was all she could say, eyes still trained on the glowing fire.

"Anyone would have to be thick to pass on you, Clem."

She looked up at Lottie and her sister was giving her a soft smile. She couldn't help but smile back. She put her cheek on Clementine's head and they both stared into the flames.

The initial feeling of awkwardness from having her big sister back in her life was gone, and they'd managed to shift into the natural pattern of sisterly behavior. If Clementine didn't let herself think about it, it was like they had never been apart.

"It's okay, we'll find you another hot rancher to marry for their money," Lottie said, with another squeeze. "Do you have a preference? Man? Woman? Or…neither?"

Clementine snorted and shook her head. "There's no preference. They have to be…" She scratched the side of her neck. She thought of Lou smiling at her, slow and easy, sun setting behind them and eyes sparkling with the final shreds of daylight, hat slightly crooked on their head after running long fingers through their hair. "…kind, soft, handsome. Sweet…"

Lottie gagged. "I don't need to know *that* much, Clem."

She pulled a bottle of liquor from somewhere and took a long swig before handing it over to Clementine. "Here. Nothing like some questionable liquor to get you over a breakup."

Tipping the bottle against her lips, Clementine took two large gulps, eyes watering as she endured the burning. She coughed and handed it back to Lottie, the warmth of the whiskey already spreading through her veins.

"There we go," Lottie said as she rubbed Clementine's back.

Clementine shook her head. "You know, I should actually be thanking you."

"Well obviously." Lottie smiled. "I mean, for what?"

"For helping me get my head out of my ass. For getting me out of there so I wasn't distracted by Lou anymore. I had always planned on getting away from Lefty and paying off whatever debt I owed to him, and then going back and getting the truth about what happened when Dad died."

Lottie shifted a little, looking down into the flames. "Why do you need to know? He died. We didn't. Now we're here."

"It's more than that. I want revenge," she said seriously. "I sold myself off. I sold off my *body* as a mail-order bride just for the chance to get away from Lefty. That's how bad it was."

"You know, Dad was worse than I think you remember."

"He was a drunk and he was mean but he was still our father. He and Maria were our family."

"You really don't remember?"

"Worse than Dad beating you every night? Being drunk and angry all the time? Just for darin' to even look like mama?" Lottie asked bitterly.

"I still wasn't free, Lottie."

They both looked at the flames before Lottie asked, "What do you remember? Of that night?"

"I remember you putting me under the bed. I remember the screaming and Lefty taking me and Maria out. I remember you were already gone and...Dad trying to run and getting shot in the back."

Recalling the memories felt like pulling at painful barbs deep in her skin. The things that happened that night had haunted her for years. She'd wake up sweating or the sound of a gunshot would set her on edge or into a spell, and gunshots weren't uncommon on Lefty's ranch. She had eventually figured out a way to soothe herself and the nightmares had subsided, even while the gunfire didn't.

"What did Lefty do to you while you were with him?"

She shook her head, not wanting to bring up the memories again. If she went digging, some things about Lou were bound to pop up too.

"It wasn't always too bad. There just came to be a point when I was too disgusted with myself to handle it anymore."

Lottie's face hardened, fist clenching. "I'll kill 'em."

"Lottie—"

"For putting his fucking hands on you—"

"Lottie! It's fine!" She took her sister's hand. "It's okay, I promise. Whatever horrible thing you're thinking it...That wasn't it."

Lottie looked at their joined hands. "You promise?"

"Yes."

Lottie nodded and looked back at the fire, expression unreadable. She stood and stretched. "All right. Imma go set up the tent."

Clementine wasn't sure she trusted Lottie to set it up but she let her do it anyway, allowing herself a few more minutes to wallow in her self-pity.

* * *

Lou had started getting used to how the room spun. They peered at the half-empty liquor bottle in front of them through blurry eyes and groaned. They really thought they had drunk more than that.

Licking their lips, they clumsily reached for the bottle again, but a hand came out of nowhere and swiped it off the table. With a growl, they looked up and saw Juanita staring back at them, unamused.

"It's time for you to sober up," Juanita said, setting a cup of coffee on the table.

Lou scoffed as they sat back in their chair, legs falling open and arm slung along the back of another chair.

"'M jus' fine, darlin'," they said, trying to bring some of their bravado back.

They purposefully looked her up and down before smirking, eyes dropping drunkenly. All Juanita had to do was raise an eyebrow and Lou felt properly chastised.

"You're embarrassing yourself."

Lou flapped a dismissive hand and grunted, looking back at their empty glass, mouth dry as the desert. They gave her big pleading eyes and pushed the glass toward her with the tips of their fingers.

"Jus' one more?"

Juanita gave them a half a shot. "That's all you get for the rest of the night."

"Fine." Lou took the drink and held it closely to their chest like a precious thing—the thing that was supposed to distract them from remembering that Clementine was gone, but so far drinking was just making the pain worse. They were convinced that all they needed was this little bit more to numb the pain.

They stared down into the amber liquid and heard the chair across from them slide out. Juanita sat down, purposefully setting the liquor bottle as far away from Lou as possible. At least she looked sympathetic to Lou's situation. "You have to go after her."

"She don' wan' me no more. Wha's the point?"

"The point is, you have to let her know how you really feel."

The tears pressing behind Lou's eyes burned and they willed them to go away. The saloon was far too crowded for them to break down now. They didn't want to look soft in front of the whole town, especially not over a woman.

They cleared their throat and drank the rest of the liquor instead. "Nah," Lou said, voice thick. "She don' want a dumb rancher like me anyway. She 'an get a man in the city that'll take care'a 'er the way she deserves."

"Lou Ramirez, you're a dumbass, but you're not dumb. We've been through this a thousand times. She doesn't want anyone else; she wants you. And yeah, you fucked up, but that's why you have to fix it instead of sitting here and drowning your sorrows in liquor. She's probably halfway to the city right now, and you have to go talk to her."

Lou was quickly losing the battle to keep the tears at bay, feeling them creeping into the corners of their eyes and rolling down their cheeks. They allowed themself a sniffle and shook their head. "I jus'…" They blinked, vision blurry from unshed tears. Their insides felt like mush, emotion making it hard to form a proper sentence. "She's jus' so beautiful an' I like 'er so much. What if I mess it up?"

Juanita clucked her tongue sympathetically and moved next to Lou, pulling their head against her chest as the tears fell. They sniffled pathetically, their hands balled into fists in an attempt to control what they were thinking. The tears fell hot from their eyes, and they were drunk enough to bury their face into Juanita's dress. She cradled the back of their head as their shoulders shuddered with sobs.

"I know, you stubborn thing. We're going to take you upstairs and let you sleep this off and then tomorrow you're going to go after her. Okay?"

Lou nodded, sniffling again as they slumped in the chair. Juanita patted their back and pulled away, taking their hand so that she could lead them upstairs to her room. They collapsed into the bed with a groan, the room spinning, and they barely registered Juanita putting a bucket on the side of the bed for them to throw up in before drifting off to sleep.

* * *

The city was one of the biggest Clementine had ever seen. A couple of times, Lefty had taken her into a nearby town when he needed her to be a translator between him and the Chumash, but other than that, she had been kept at his camp. When she and Lottie got to the city and a streetcar rolled past them on a track, she was more than a little awestruck. She hadn't seen one in real life before, just the drawing in the paper once.

The sound of Butter's hooves on the pavement startled her for a moment, and she looked over at Lottie, who was staring down every person they passed. There were fancy-looking men and women in fine suits and dresses, strolling along the main street.

Even from the outskirts Clementine could tell the city was sprawling, blocks upon blocks of buildings, storefronts with elaborate displays in the windows, and carts of goods being driven up and down the streets.

"Don't get too enamored, Clem," Lottie muttered, their horses walking side by side. "It's nothing but a bunch of freaks in the city."

Clementine adjusted herself in the saddle. She thought she saw Lou for a moment and her heart jumped, but she did a double take and they were gone. Did she really miss Lou so much that she was hallucinating now? She shook her head, disappointment settling into her stomach as Lottie led them to a saloon. From the outside, it looked twice the size of the one in Ghosthallow. Jaunty piano music and the sound of a bustling crowd poured out the window as they dismounted.

"All right, here." Lottie tossed a leather bag of money to Clementine. "Get us a room and then you can wander around or whatever you want. I have something to do."

She turned away and Clementine scoffed. "Lottie! Where are you going?"

Lottie turned and said, "I told you I have shit to do! I'll be back tonight."

Clementine grumbled, frustrated, but went into the saloon to get a room. She was tired and wanted to get a little cleaned up after the ride.

With her bag tight in her hand, she tried to get a good look at the people around her without being obvious. While she was sure they weren't all freaks like Lottie had said, saloons weren't known to harbor the finest of folks. There was a bald man behind the counter who looked at her through small gold spectacles, and wore a white shirt under a red silk scarf with ornate embroidery.

She smiled her most charming smile at him. "Hello, I'd like to inquire about a room."

"For one?" he asked, voice scratchy.

"Two. I'm with my sis…ter of mercy. We're on our way to a new Spanish mission," she said, unsure of how much information she should actually give away to a stranger.

The man looked at her for a moment before grunting. He reached down and took a key out from under the counter before sliding it to her.

"That's two dollars a day. Don't include breakfast. That's fifty cents a day. Won't be no…business going on upstairs. You understand? That's reserved for the girls that pay rent here."

Clementine gasped, offended, as she reached out and took the key.

"We are servants of the *Lord*, sir," she said as she started up the stairs. She turned to look back at him to see if he was watching her but she breathed a sigh of relief to see he had moved on to someone else.

When she got up to the room, she locked it and took a quick inventory of her surroundings. The space was simple and clean, if a little worn, with a high ceiling and a window that looked down on the plank sidewalk below. Clementine put some of her clothes in the drawers provided and tried to make the time pass faster. She used the porcelain washstand and cleaned up from the road, sighing with relief, and even tried to take a nap. But she had gotten to the point where there was nothing left to do.

She couldn't help but feel useless pacing around, locked up in the room while she should be figuring out more about where Lefty was. Ever since the fire had been reignited under her, she didn't want to just sit around. Plus, the more time she had to think, the more often Lou would sneak into the forefront of her mind—someone she definitely didn't want to think about.

Veronica once told her locals knew all the ins and outs of the town, so Clementine made sure her dress looked nice and headed down into the saloon. She looked around as she descended the stairs, taking in the scene. In every bar, there was a man who knew of Lefty Lenning. It was just a fact.

In one corner sat a group of men playing poker, all with serious faces and darting eyes. The other tables were dotted with men just sitting and drinking or shoveling a meal into themselves, some slumped over and some involved in what looked like intense conversations. Saloon girls wandered around, flirting with men and sitting on their laps.

Clementine spotted a man at the bar who looked worse for the wear, tall and lanky with scars across his face, one a shiny looking slash over his eye. Clementine would bet her horse that it meant he was one of Lefty's men. They all had the same scar. More than once she had watched Lefty's barbaric ritual of taking a hot knife fresh from the fire and pressing it over a new recruit's eyes to brand them. She could smell the sizzling flesh and hear the screams like it was yesterday.

There was a point when she knew all the men that came in and out of Lefty's, but she didn't recognize this one from her time at the ranch, so she figured he wouldn't know her either. She surreptitiously tugged at her corset, pressing up her breasts a little more, and sauntered down to him. A man like that would have her answers.

She added a little sway to her step as she approached. Leaning on the bar with her elbow, she looked him up and down, standing close enough so that he would notice. He looked over at her mid-sip, an oily smirk crawling over his face.

"Well, hello there, little thing," he said as he set his glass down. He smiled and Clementine saw that the remaining teeth he had were cracked and black. She suppressed a shiver and smiled back at him, playing with the ends of her hair. "You lost?"

"No, just thought I'd come by and see what was going on in this saloon," she said, batting her eyelashes up at him. "I'm just so thirsty."

"I can help with that," he said, signaling the bartender for another drink and sliding it in front of her.

"Why, thank you," she simpered. "What's your name, cowboy?"

"Folks call me Bear."

She smiled as she took the small glass of whiskey in her hands, looking at him over the rim as she took a sip. His gaze seemed to have a hard time choosing between her breasts and her eyes, and she wanted to crawl out of her skin.

"Well now, that's my favorite animal. What are you doing in town, Bear?" she asked innocently, voice purposefully higher, drawing out her words. "You look like a big important man."

His chest puffed up and it looked like he was trying to flex. "Well, my work ain't nothin' a woman can understand much of, but let's just say I'm a supplier of sorts."

She bristled inside, but her smile widened and she put her hand on his arm, squeezing his bicep. "A *supplier*? Sounds like hard work."

"Oh, it is. I work fer a very important man. Ever heard of Lefty Lenning?"

He grinned like Clementine was supposed to be impressed so she pretended to swoon, hand on her chest as she gasped. "Not *the* Lefty Lenning."

She marveled at how easy it was to manipulate men when you had breasts, and she tapped the side of her glass with her fingers. He smiled smugly.

"Sure is. I help him get goods in and out of town."

"Do you mean like smuggling? In *this* town? It seems so busy. I can't imagine what it takes to get things out of here. That sounds so naughty."

"That's what most people would think. That's why it's genius. We just load things on and off the train he controls every night. Easy as pie and right under everyone's noses."

"Wow," she said, dropping her hand from his arm and throwing back the rest of her whiskey. She had the information she needed and wanted to get away from him as soon as possible. "Well, I must go now."

He frowned and grabbed her arm. "Wait! We were just startin' to have some fun."

He jerked her forward so she was against him, grin wide and breath reeking of whiskey and something else dark and rank. She tried to pull away but he gripped her tighter. She panicked for a moment before she came up with the perfect solution, schooling her features into a big pout.

"I would love to have some fun tonight, stud, but I'm afraid my curse just came," she said, grimacing and putting her hand on her stomach to emphasize the fact that she was bleeding and in pain. He practically shoved her away with a frown of disgust and she rolled her eyes, turning around and heading toward the door.

She loosened her corset as she walked, adjusting her breasts again and making sure that her gun was securely between them. The train station was across the city and Clementine followed the road with its gaslit street lamps.

Her heels clicked against the hard-packed earth. It was odd not to have dust kicking up under her skirt with each step, tickling her nose. Although the city smelled different, it didn't necessarily smell better. There was still the underlying reek of horse shit and liquor soaking the streets, but above that there was a subtle smell of gas and fumes. Smokestacks rose up not too far from the city, and Clementine wondered if that was where the smell came from. Even in the fading daylight she could see the black smoke rising into the air.

She heard the train before she saw it. The station sat at the edge of town, a good-size wooden building, and through the windows she could see nice couches for waiting passengers.

No one was taking the train this late at night, but still there was a wagon behind the caboose, men who looked like nothing more than shadows in the dim light loading boxes into the back. Clementine quickly ducked into a nearby alley, hiding herself in shadow as she watched. A large hulk of a man with long, greasy-blond hair tied back in a ponytail and an eyepatch over his left eye, walked from the other side of the train, supervising the work.

It was unmistakably Lefty. Her blood ran cold just at the sight of him. She could practically smell the reek of alcohol coming out of his pores and the ever-present smell of grease and filth on his pasty white skin.

Now was her time to move. She reached for the gun in her corset and started toward them. Suddenly there was a hard grip on her arm and she was jerked back. Her hands balled into fists and she swung wildly, ready to fight, when someone grabbed her wrists and slapped a palm over her mouth.

"Clem, it's me," Lottie hissed.

She frowned and blinked, Lottie's face swimming into view in the inky darkness. She pushed away Lottie's hand from her face. "Lottie?"

"Yes! What the hell are you doing here?"

She pulled away from Lottie roughly. "I figured out how to get to Lefty."

"Well, you're done. Go back to the room."

"No. This is just as much my fight as it is yours, you know."

"It's too dangerous," Lottie said, grabbing her arm again and dragging her out of the alley and toward the hotel. "Come on."

"No!" She ripped her arm from Lottie's grip again. "I'm doing this."

"No way."

"You can't just hide me away like this!"

"I can, you're my baby sister—"

"I'm not a *baby* anymore, Lottie, I grew out of that stage when you were off doing god knows what, and I was with Lefty. You can't just shove me under the bed anymore."

Lottie paused, both of them remembering the night their father died, Clementine cowering while Lottie ran. Lottie growled in frustration and stuffed her hands in the pocket of her jacket. "I can't...if anything goes sideways, you get out of there. Do you hear me?"

Clementine put defiant hands on her hips but sighed. "Fine."

"Thank you." Lottie looked back at the men, who were still loading things. She jerked her head to the side for Clementine to follow and went down the street. She caught up with her sister, unable to tamp down her excited smile. "All right, so what are we gonna do?"

Lottie rolled her neck. "I'm going to pretend to be a buyer. Go to the station, ask to see the big man, all that jazz. He'll be alone because his crew will be unloading and he's a dumbass. Once he's by himself..." She made a violent gesture across her throat with her finger. "He's gone."

"We can't kill him. We need to know exactly what happened that night."

"Our family died, that's what happened!" Lottie said, exasperated, throwing her arms in the air. "Can't we just kill the asshole and move on?"

"No, *I* can't. We're getting answers."

"Yeah. We'll see."

* * *

Lou could see the city rising in the distance, still a hard day's ride away, but attainable at least. The buildings rose up toward the sky, some bigger than any buildings they had ever seen. They couldn't quite see it yet, but they saw the black smoke spewing into the air from the three stories of ugly factories looming behind the city, staining the sky. They scoffed and pulled their bandana over their face. Their stomach fluttered with excitement and nerves, and they adjusted themself on the saddle.

They missed Clementine with every bone in their body. They thought they were soft before, but really all they could think about was her and how devastated she looked when they told her she shouldn't stay. They should have gathered her up in their arms and kissed her senseless right there. Instead they just let Clementine leave, and now they had to follow her into the big city—pleading for a second chance.

They had only been through cities a couple of times, mostly with Inez. She'd liked the shopping, the entertainment, and the luxuries a city brought—things Lou wasn't necessarily interested in, but they didn't mind being there with Inez.

Still, their heart belonged in the country, preferably with Clementine if they could fix their fuck-up. And Lou was determined to fix it.

Clementine watched Lottie tuck her hair up under her hat and spread some dirt along her face where a five o'clock shadow would be. She snorted, raising her eyes as she pulled on her boots.

"That looks nothing like whiskers."

"Trust me. From far away and at night, no one will know the difference," she said, popping the collar of her jacket and adjusting her hat. She lowered her voice almost comically. "All right. Let's go."

Clementine picked up the shotgun Lottie had given her from within the voluminous folds of her skirts, keeping it hidden until it was time. They traveled along the darker roads to an alley just a block or so from the supply train, huddling together behind a barber shop.

Lottie turned to her and nodded toward the other side of the street. "Wait over there until I give the signal."

"What's the signal?"

Lottie flicked the back of her ear with her finger and darted off. Clementine rolled her eyes but nodded in agreement.

She'd just tucked herself behind some crates that were stacked in the alley when Bear, the guy from the saloon, approached Lottie. Clementine shivered at the sight of him.

Lottie nodded and he nodded back. Clementine couldn't hear what they were saying, but he looked nervous, looking over her shoulder and keeping his distance, until Lottie showed him some cash. He looked back to where the train was loading and leaned close to her, snatching the cash. He then ambled off toward the train, and she looked back toward where Clementine was hidden, thumb up.

After a few moments, Clementine watched as Lefty Lenning turned the corner, a man behind him with a large shotgun cradled in his arms.

"Shit."

They hadn't planned for two.

Clementine finally revealed the shotgun, pulling it from under her skirt, making sure it was cocked and ready to go. She watched Lottie rest her hand subtly on the butt of her gun, and she waited until she saw Lottie flick the back of her ear. With one deep breath, she walked quickly in the shadows along the edge of the alley, shotgun raised and aimed at Lefty.

When she was about a yard away, the man with Lefty startled and quickly turned, leveling his sights at Clementine. Lottie pulled her gun and shot him in the head. At the same time, Clementine shot Lefty in the kneecap and watched him fall to the ground with a grunt of pain.

Clementine scrambled to pick up the thug's gun while Lottie shoved Lefty onto his back. "Put your hands where I can see them."

Lefty bared his teeth in a growl, hands up near his face as he looked up at Lottie. Clementine stood next to her, and Lefty's face changed to a pained smile when he recognized her. "Well, lookie here, the littlest Castellanos."

Clementine felt her heart clench, looking down into his eyes again, the fear she had forgotten bubbling up in her chest again. Lottie cocked her gun and held it to Lefty's forehead so hard that it indented his skin. His eyes shot back to Lottie, smile fading.

"And my least-favorite Castellanos."

"Oh, I'm so offended," Lottie said sarcastically. "Any last words?"

Clementine put her hand on Lottie's arm to stop her. "No," Clementine said.

Lottie turned to look at her. "What?"

"You promised. I have to find out what happened the night our dad died."

Lefty smiled again. "Little Castellanos, always so curious."

"Clem, it does no good. We got to get rid of him while we can."

Lefty's eyes flicked between them and he suddenly barked out a laugh. "You never told her."

Lottie and Lefty looked at each other and Clementine felt her suspicions grow. "Told me what?"

"What?" Lottie licked her lips and looked back at Clementine. She looked twitchy, eyes a little wide and panicked. "It's nothing, Clemie. Let's just get rid of him."

"You plan on this being the secret you take to your grave, Castellanos?" Lefty asked.

Clementine needed answers and Lottie clearly knew more than she was letting on. Clementine kept her gun on Lefty but uncocked the gun that Lottie had to his forehead.

"What?" Lottie cried, lowering her gun.

"Tell me what you know," Clementine said firmly. "Tell me what you're hiding or I'll never forgive you either."

Lottie shifted nervously, looking between Lefty and Clementine.

"Lottie—"

"I was tired of Dad hurting me!" Lottie blurted, tears already rimming her eyes. "I was okay taking it knowing it was protecting you, but I was tired of it. And I was a kid, I was stupid. I was tired of watching him hurt Maria and I knew it was only a matter of time until he killed you. I hated him! We were better off without him."

Clementine's blood ran cold, dread filling her stomach and making her feel sick. "Lottie. What did you do?"

"I did it for you. For *us*."

Lefty's hand crept down toward his injured knee, only to fly back up again when Lottie slapped the barrel of her gun against his temple. She glared at him warningly.

"Lottie! What did you *do*?" Clementine said, tears blurring her eyes as she forced Lottie away from Lefty with a brusque shove.

"I just wanted to scare him a bit. Maybe get him taken away. I didn't mean for anyone to get killed!"

"Are you the one who sold him out?" she asked, voice thick with tears.

"All I did was ta-take some money."

Lefty hummed. "The money that got your dear old daddy killed. Let mc think that it was him. Clever, for a little girl. Maybe too clever. And beautiful Maria, gone too."

"You. *You're* the one that got them killed?"

"Clemie, please. He was hurting our family—"

"And you ripped it apart!" she shouted, hot tears streaming down her cheeks. "You *destroyed* our family. It wasn't perfect, and yeah, Dad was mean as a snake, but it was ours—"

"You weren't safe! Dad would hit us! He said cruel things to you. It got harder and harder and it was only a matter of time before you got hurt. Really hurt. I was protecting you."

"Two people are dead, Lottie! Our sister and our dad. Because of you. We were separated for years. I was stuck living with this asshole!" She gestured toward Lefty with her gun. "You have no idea what I went through for more than all those years. I sold my body to get away from him! You forced me to sell myself!"

Lottie looked away. "I thought I was going to make it better," she almost whispered.

"Yeah, well you didn't. What were you going to do? Kill him and keep lying to me for the rest of our lives?"

"I...no! I would tell you. Eventually." Lottie's fire burned out. She let out a frustrated sigh and stepped around Clementine so she could point her gun at Lefty's forehead again. "Let's just do this bastard in and deal with this later, Clem—"

"No! Wait," Lefty said, putting a finger over the barrel of Lottie's gun. "If you let me go. I can make sure Clementine's debt is no more."

"I don't have any more debt, asshole."

Lefty's grin slid like oil across his face. "But what about the bounty on one Louis Guadalajara?"

She quickly wiped some tears away from her eyes. "I guess you haven't heard that Louis is dead."

Lefty actually looked shocked. "Dead?"

Clem looked at Lottie and nodded. "Just do it. I'm ready to be done with that chapter of my life."

"You're making a huge mistake," Lefty said, his voice a little shaky and desperate.

Clementine didn't even spare him another look, she just turned around and walked away, not even flinching when she heard the sharp sound of the gunshot behind her and the eerie heavy silence that came after it.

It was broken when she could hear Lottie running up to her and she felt tears threatening to fall again.

"Clem, wait—"

"Leave me alone."

"I'm sorry. You shouldn't have found out that way."

Clementine stopped and turned abruptly, Lottie nearly knocking into her. "You shouldn't have lied to me. You're a liar and I can't believe I let you trick me like this. You used me!"

"Clementine, come on," Lottie tried. "I was a kid."

"Leave me alone," she said, as she started walking back to their hotel. "I wish you had never come back for me!"

She didn't bother looking back to see Lottie's face as she turned the corner.

* * *

Lou had bought a bouquet of flowers down the street and washed their face in the river before coming to the saloon. They saw Butter, and Diablo, Lottie's horse, tied up outside and knew it was where Clementine was staying.

Their stomach turned with excited nerves as they stepped into the saloon, looking around for a hint of the familiar face they were missing. No one even bothered looking up at them as they walked up to the bar with a smile on their face.

"'Ello, sir," they said with a tip of their hat. "'M lookin' fer a young woman 'at's stayin' here. 'Bout yay tall, brown 'air."

Lou held the hand up at around their chest and the bartender looked at them, unamused. "Do I look like I keep track'a everybody 'at comes in and outta here?"

"Well, no, sir, but I know you'd recognize 'er. She's the most beautiful woman in town, prob'ly."

"I ain't got no one staying here but some nuns at the moment. Try the hotel next door," he said before pointedly finding himself interested in taking orders from the other customers instead. Lou turned around, confused, and started toward the front door. They were *sure* they had to be here.

Just as they were about to push through the door and leave, it swung open, nearly hitting them in the face. They blocked it with their hand just in time, looking down to see Clementine barging through it.

"Miss Clementine!" they gasped with a smile, nerves lighting anew. "Miss Clementine, I knew you were 'ere…"

Clementine just blinked, tear tracks apparent on her cheeks.

Lou frowned and instinctively reached for her. "Darlin', what's—"

"What the hell are you doing here?"

She batted their hand away and frowned so angrily that Lou took a step back and their mouth opened and closed like a fish, heart plummeting to the bottom of their stomach and making them feel ill. "I um…well, I came….lookin' fer you—"

"Why? Hoping I'd come crawling back to you? I have a little more dignity than that, Lou," she scoffed.

Lou noticed the shotgun in her hand for the first time and frowned. "No, I came to apologize—"

"Apologize for what? For being a liar? Well, it's too little too late for that."

Lou shook their head, hope slowly ebbing away. "But...I jus' wanna talk to you—"

"You don't get that privilege anymore," Clementine said, poking her finger in the middle of their chest. "I have other more important things to worry about and *you* are not one of them."

She pushed past Lou, who reached for her arm, but she violently pulled away. "I said, leave me alone!"

It caught the attention of a burly man at a nearby table who stood up and frowned at Lou. "This fella botherin' you, ma'am?"

"Yes, they are," she said simply before stomping toward the stairs.

Lou's heart shattered and they were sure they were about to be sick. They stared after Clementine, still pathetically clutching the flowers as they watched her walk away. But they didn't even get to watch her walk up the stairs because the big burly man grabbed their arm, turned them back toward the door, grabbed the back of their pants and lifted them as he threw them out. They flew through the air spectacularly, falling hard on the ground and rolling with the force of his throw.

The drunken laughter of the other patrons mocked them as they lay on the ground in pain, their barely healed arm throbbing anew from their graceless landing. But at least the physical pain distracted them from how their heart felt like it was nothing more than a gaping wound in the middle of their chest.

CHAPTER NINETEEN

Lou lay on the ground for a moment, the pain in their shoulder radiating down their fingers. One of the flowers had made its way to their mouth, and as they sat up, they spit it out, staring balefully at smashed petals all over the front of their shirt. The sight did nothing to soothe their aching heart. They brushed them away and looked back at the saloon, the laughter and loud conversation still mocking them, even if it wasn't directed at them. Throwing the pathetic bunch of flowers to the ground, Lou pushed themself up with their hands on their knees and brushed off the dirt.

"What the fuck are you doin' here?" Lottie's voice came, accompanied by the clicking of a gun's hammer.

Lou rolled their eyes and faced her, not even bothering putting their hands up. "I jus' came'a see Miss Clementine—"

"Yeah? That seemed to work out for you."

"I ain't interested in being kicked while I'm down, so if you coul' excuse me." Lou tipped their hat sarcastically before turning away, but Lottie quickly stepped in front of them.

"You stay away from Clementine—"

"What the hell do you think I'm doin'?" Lou said, the sadness making it harder to control their emotions. They wanted to lash out and cry and scream, but they tugged on the sleeves of their shirt instead, straining to regain any semblance of their dignity. "Now if you'll *excuse me*."

The hammer of the gun clicked back into place as Lou unhitched Trigger.

"Wait!"

Lou straddled Trigger and he snorted, nosing toward Lottie. "Make up your mind."

"Where the fuck are you going?"

"Back to mah camp outside'a town. See ya 'round."

They clicked their tongue and kicked Trigger into a trot, steering him out of town. Their shoulders fell a little further with each moment, their throat choked with tears. They coughed and rubbed at their eyes, willing the sadness back inside. By the time they got back to the camp, the tears were streaming down their face.

Sliding off Trigger, they managed to make a small fire. Setting out their blanket roll, they sat down and crossed their legs. The fire flickered pathetically and usually Lou would try to stoke the flames, but at this moment they felt too paralyzed with grief to even worry about it.

They weren't sure what they were expecting when they went to go see Clementine, but they didn't expect her to yell in their face about being a liar. They figured she was right, though. They were a liar. They hadn't been straight with her about the past or about Inez. They pulled their hat off and let it fall beside them, reaching into the saddlebag for a flask.

They took a long swig, washing down the choking tears as their vision blurred.

Maybe they should just go home and forget this ever happened? Clementine didn't want them after all, so what was the use of staying put? Or perhaps they could just try one more time? They couldn't give up on Clementine. Not that easily.

* * *

"Clementine. Let me in," Lottie said softly from behind the door. Clementine huffed from where she lay on the bed staring angrily up at the ceiling.

"No!"

"My whiskey is in there! I don't want to pay for this overpriced bullshit downstairs."

"Too bad! I don't want to see you."

There was silence on the other side of the door and for a moment she thought Lottie had left.

There was another soft knock and Lottie's voice came muffled through the wood. "I saw you kicked Ramirez out," she snorted. "You should've seen how far they flew when they got thrown out. It was pretty impressive."

Clementine felt a wave of guilt but shut her eyes and tried to push the thoughts away instead. "Yes, well. I'm tired of you both. I wish you both would just leave me alone. For *once*."

"Fine."

She could practically see Lottie's sad blue eyes. There was a pause and then she heard heavy boots walking away and down the hall. Her stomach ached, and she could feel the hot tears pressing behind her eyes. The reality of being alone had finally settled over her. The sounds of the bar floated up from below, and she could hear a muted grunting in the room next to her. She wrinkled her nose as her overactive imagination took over. She let her mind linger too long and it turned from a man hunched over a woman, who was overselling her pleasure, into Lou hovering over her.

Strong arms wrapped around her waist, as she threaded her fingers into silky dark strands and tugged Lou's lips to her own. Lou was naked and covered in a thin layer of sweat, making their tan skin glisten as they fucked her, thick biceps and forearms flexing. She dug her heels into the base of Lou's spine, leaving angry red marks along their back. Her hand found its way to the bruise still on her collarbone, left from Lou's mouth. She pushed down on it, hissing and shivering from the sting, her face hot.

She cleared her throat, forcing herself out of her daydream despite the incessant pounding between her legs. She turned on her side and buried her face in her pillow. The fact that she still wanted Lou just made her angrier. She didn't *want* to want Lou. She didn't want to miss their smile and laugh and the way they would tip their hat at her. She missed their arms around her and smelling their sweet scent under whatever chore they had just finished. Sometimes it was hay or sometimes it was the cows, which might not have been as pleasant, but was still comforting.

She didn't *want* to want any of that. She was still mad at them, but she felt her walls breaking remembering how they looked down in the saloon with those flowers. They were just so stubborn and proper and she hated to admit that she loved them. She could stay mad, but all she wanted to do was hold them in her arms and bury her face in their neck. And to kiss them and maybe fuck some sense into them.

She pulled a pillow over her head with a groan, trying to drown out the noises of the saloon. She knew what she had to do.

Lou eventually got their fire going a little better, the liquor taking the edge off the cold of the night and a little of their grief. They didn't want to get too drunk tonight, just wanted enough to relax and really feel sad.

Tonight they just wanted to stare at the stars and be sad about Clementine. They didn't want to give up, not yet, but it was hard not to lose hope.

They had just started relaxing and were considering finally undressing, when in the distance they heard a familiar rhythmic sound. They paused, straining to listen.

Lou squinted into the darkness, heart rate elevating as they recognized the sound of a horse approaching. Their hand hovered over their gun just in case the visitor was less than friendly. The ring of light that their fire cast finally reached the approaching horse and she relaxed to see Butter, Clementine on her back, riding toward the camp. Lou dropped their hand from their gun and couldn't help but smile, even while their eyes were still swollen from tears.

"Miss Clementine," they said as she slid off her horse. She was in her nightgown, shawl over her shoulders as she approached. "Is e'rythin' all right? What're you doin'—"

Before they could get their sentence out, she leapt at them, one hand gripping the back of their head and the other wrapping around their neck. Her lips were on Lou's in an instant, and, just as needy, their hands found Clementine's waist. They stumbled back as thcy gained their bearings, kissing her back just as hard as they were being kissed.

Her other hand went to their shirt, finishing undoing the buttons and pushing it over their shoulders.

Their brain caught up with the moment and they realized that Clementine was right here kissing them. After she told them to leave. They never wanted to stop kissing her, but confusion made them reach up and grip her wrists, pushing her away and putting some distance between them for a moment.

"Miss Clementine," they said, gasping for breath. They chuckled and gently sat them both down on the bedroll. "What about wanting me to leave?"

"I'm sorry," Clementine said. "I was mad at Lottie and I was still jealous about Inez and I took it out on you. I shouldn't have done it."

"You ain't mad at me?"

"No."

"But you sure that wasn't about me? Sure felt like it was about me."

"It's not about you. Even if it was you didn't deserve that. I love you."

Lou felt their heart speed up and relief spreading through them. "I love you too, Clem."

Clementine smiled brightly and leaned down to kiss them again. Lou's entire body warmed and they sighed against her mouth. Their kisses deepened, Clementine's tongue flitting along their bottom lip, and they pulled away.

"What?" Clementine breathed.

"Don'tcha think we should take it slow? Court a little?"

She shook her head, licking her lips that were red and parted, looking entirely too inviting for the level of self-control Lou was trying to have right now.

"We've been through so much, and I've waited long enough."

Lou nodded, and her hands immediately found their way into their shirt, smoothing along the plane of their stomach and exposing their binding . Clementine's eyes darted down quickly, cheeks tinting as she crawled into Lou's lap with her knees on either side.

She shrugged off her shawl and returned her hands to Lou's chest. "I want you, cowboy," Clementine whispered, deliberately brushing their lips together as Lou ran their hands up her sides. "I don't want to wait any longer."

Lou swallowed thickly, chin tilting up to chase Clementine's lips with their own. Clementine smirked, pulling back so her lips danced just out of reach as she ran her finger over Lou's bottom lip.

"'Re you sure?" Lou asked again, hands flexing on her hips, itching to touch the strong thigh that they could see as her nightgown inched higher.

She didn't answer. Instead she leaned back on her heels and grabbed the edges of her nightgown. Brown eyes locked with hazel as she pulled it over her head, leaving her completely naked and straddling Lou. Their eyes wandered down Clementine's exposed collarbone to her breasts, nipples tight in the night air. The fire flickered over her skin, casting shadows in the lines of her stomach muscles and her hip bones that led to the dark curls between her thighs.

Lou's hands slid up her thighs, gripping them tightly as they both surged forward, lips colliding again. Her tongue brushed along the seam of their lips and Lou met it with their own. Their hands cupped behind the back of her thighs and up to her ass, squeezing the firm flesh.

Her hips pressed against Lou's stomach and they could feel the heat radiating from between her thighs. Fine hands pushed their shirt and vest over their shoulders but they got caught on their bent elbows. Lou wanted to feel every inch of Clementine's skin—her hands and lips. To ravage her and love her and taste every inch of her.

They kissed Clementine's jaw, tasting the hint of rosewater on her skin. Lou's teeth pulled her earlobe as their hands cupped her breasts in their palms, groaning at the touch. Her nipples pebbled in their palms, and they rubbed their thumb over them.

She shivered under their hands, cupping their chin and kissing them again. Their kisses were desperate, all tongue, as she pushed their shirt the rest of the way down. They nipped at her bottom lip as she tore off their shirt, throwing it away from them.

Lou's hands went to her back, pressing between her shoulder blades so that their torsos were tight together, skin to skin. The feeling of their breasts pressing together made Lou sigh, the arousal between their thighs pounding and making their hands surer in their exploration.

Her tongue brushed along the roof of their mouth and her hips pressed tight against Lou. Even through the thick material of their pants, Lou could feel the heat pouring from between her thighs and groaned.

They wanted to take things slow, to make love to her like she deserved, but it felt like every small moment of sexual tension that had built up through the months was finally pouring out between them, crackling through the air like electricity during a storm. Lou's hands desperately slid over every inch of her skin, itching to feel her. Lou sat up on their knees, Clementine's ankles locking behind her back as they kissed, and flipped them on the bedroll so that they hovered above her.

Her legs tightened around them and Lou ground into her. She gasped, fingers tightening in their hair as their hand caught the back of Clementine's knee and lifted her leg higher. They stared deep into hazel eyes as they pressed into her, determined to make her gasp and claw at their back. They weren't disappointed.

"Lou," she whispered, one hand snaking between them and trying to push their pants down their legs, only succeeding in getting tangled in the gun belt still around their hips. She only got their pants so far, leaving them hanging low on Lou's hips.

"I need you."

"I'm right here, Miss Clementine," they said, a hand cupping her between her thighs.

She sighed at the new sensation and ground herself into Lou's hand. Their fingers slipped through slickness, pleasure hitting them right between the legs. Lou ducked their head and kissed along the column of Clementine's neck as their fingers pressed through silky heat.

The air around them felt thick, hot with arousal and anticipation as she lay prone under them. They scraped their teeth over her pulse point as their fingers circled her clit.

"God, yes," she breathed, chin tilting up to the night sky as her hips moved with Lou's fingers. They bit lightly at her neck, sucking the skin just enough to leave a red mark. Nothing crazy, but just enough that she would have no problem remembering what had happened that night.

Lou pulled back to look at her when their fingers moved from her clit to her entrance. She panted, legs flexing against their waist. They could get drunk with the power of it all, but Lou didn't want to wait any longer.

They slowly pushed two fingers into her, watched her eyebrows furrow and jaw unhinge as they explored her. Lou groaned at the tight, velvety feeling, leaning down and kissing Clementine again as they began to thrust, their hips following through each movement.

Lou pressed their forehead to Clementine's, fingers curling inside of her at a measured pace. She tangled her hands in Lou's hair, her lips seeking Lou's again as she moaned. Lou's thumb circled Clementine's clit, and she tightened around their fingers as they brought her closer.

The sharp bite of her nails clawing at their back just spurred them on, their thrusts getting harder and their kisses a mess of tongue and teeth.

"F-fuck, *Lou*," Clementine cried when she came, clamping down around Lou's fingers.

Still, Lou kept pushing into her, sweat rolling down their bodies. Their skin was slick and Clementine fluttered against Lou again, the telltale signs of a second orgasm. She let out a high-pitched whine as she came again, wetness flooding Lou's palm as they kissed her down from her high.

Lou slowed their kisses, her body relaxing and thighs releasing the tight hold they had on their hips. They couldn't keep the smug smirk off their face when Clementine grunted as their fingers slipped out of her. Hazel eyes fluttered open again, her smile slow and honey sweet.

"Wow," Clementine managed bonelessly.

Lou planted soft kisses all on her face, kissing her nose and chin and eyebrows all the way up to her hairline, darkened with sweat.

"Wow," Lou agreed, pride filling their chest as they ran their hand over her firm thigh that still bracketed their hip. "Yer so beautiful."

She blushed and it was one of the sweetest things Lou had ever seen. The girly blush turned deadly as a smile crawled over her face.

Without warning, she flipped them and just barely kept them on the bedroll. "Now, cowboy, I do believe it's my turn for a ride."

"Tired, darlin'?" Lou asked softly, planting a soft kiss on the side of her head.

She just nodded, resting her forehead in the crook of Lou's neck. They smelled like sweat and sweetness and dirt and sex. Things felt so perfect, but there was still plenty she wanted to talk to Lou about. They were lying on top of Lou's bedroll, bodies still cooling as they embraced under the stars.

"You wore me out."

"Good, that was the plan."

"Don't think you can distract me though."

"From what?"

"I have some questions for you still."

"Ask me anything."

"I just need you to be honest with me. One hundred percent honest. About everything."

They nodded as Clementine scooted back a little to better look them in the eyes.

"Tell me what you wanna know."

She played with the edge of Lou's hair. "Inez."

"I was young. We both were. I 'ad just joined the Army and we were movin' through Louisiana when I met 'er. We fell in love, fast. I tol' 'er I wasn't actually who she thought I was, and she loved me anyway. But she wanted more from me 'an I could give'r. She wanted me to go back'a France with 'er and be this buttoned-up 'usband I couldn't be. I realized I didn' love'er like I thought I did. I was too much of a coward to say anythin'. So when ev'rythin' happened with Juanita and the Army wantin' me dead, I used it as my chance to run. Left 'er with a note that said they wanted me dead an' I was leavin' to protect 'er." Lou sighed and looked between them. "I ain' proud'a what I done."

"And what exactly happened that chased you away and put the bounty on your head? Juanita told me but I want to hear it from you."

"I killed some men," Lou said, looking up at her briefly before looking between them. They recounted the story that Juanita had already told her, tears filling their eyes as they finished. Clementine kissed the tears that had leaked down their cheeks.

"You did what needed to be done."

"I promise not to lie to you again."

Clementine remembered one of the last conversations she had with Lou, and her stomach twisted like Lou had just told her to leave again. She licked her lips and pulled her hands away from Lou's. "You told me to go," she whispered, unable to keep the edging of hurt out of her voice. "Why?"

Lou ran a hand through their hair and it stuck up at an odd angle. They scooted to the edge of their bedroll so that their knees bumped against hers again. "Miss Clementine, I am a lotta things, but I ain't never claimed to be smart. When I tol' you to go, I thought you wanted to go, I thought you'd be better off without me."

"Why would you think that?"

"I ain't nothin' but trouble fer ya if you haven' noticed."

"Maybe it's me that's been trouble for you."

The corner of Lou's mouth tipped up in a smirk and they said lowly, "I think you know you ain't been nothin' but trouble fer me, darlin'. Jus' maybe not in the same way 'm meanin'."

Clementine shot them a look but couldn't help the small smile that twitched on her lips. "Don't try to distract me, cowboy."

"I would never."

"You told me to leave."

"I thought it was what you wanted. What you needed," they said, voice pleading. "You pushed me away after we kissed and I thought *maybe* you didn' wanna kiss me no more, anyways. An' then when I came lookin' fer you and you told *me* to leave…it hurt."

Some of her resolve fell when she saw their eyes, big and sad looking at her.

"I wasn't necessarily fair to you either," she said, taking their hands again. "I'm sorry for pushing you away. I was just upset about Lottie and I thought you were being fickle with me, and Inez…"

Her gaze flickered to Lou who looked even sadder. "What about Inez?"

"She's just so pretty. And tall and rich and *beautiful*. I guess I was intimidated."

Lou squeezed her hand and laced their fingers together. "Ain't no reason to be intimidated, Miss Clementine."

She looked back up at Lou just as they lifted her hand to their lips. "'M sorry fer lyin' and 'm sorry for telling you to go. If you gimme another chance I promise, I will make all 'is up to you."

She sighed and held Lou's face between her hands. "You know I'll give you another chance, silly." She smiled, thumbs brushing over the high part of their cheekbones. "You know I'm not letting you go so easy."

The smile that pulled on Lou's lips made her heart swell and any resentment in her chest simply floated away. She leaned forward and kissed Lou, a joined exhale that curled to the sky like smoke. They pulled away, foreheads close together as they just let the stillness settle over them. They were okay. Things would be *okay*.

"I love you."

"I love you too, Clemie."

She pecked Lou's lips and buried her face into their neck again. The familiar scent of Lou wafting over her and the feeling of being completely in their arms... Sleep lay heavy on Clementine's body and she drifted to sleep.

CHAPTER TWENTY

Lou woke up slowly the next morning, the rising sun warming up the outside of the tent and casting a dim light inside. They sighed and stretched, the delicious soreness just reminding them of last night's activities. Their limbs felt heavy with satisfaction, and they could feel the little love bites Clementine had left along their collarbone and chest just starting to smart.

They smirked, eyes still closed as they licked their lips just to get the hint of Clementine's taste still lingering.

Their body thrummed with residual energy from the night before, remembering Clementine's skin under their hands and lips, tasting every inch of her. The slow steady build of arousal had already started between their thighs and they became painfully aware that she wasn't beside them. They rubbed their eyes before slowly opening them. The tent was small and there was definitely nowhere to hide.

They had pulled Lou's bedroll into it last night in an attempt to gain some privacy just in case someone happened to ride by. But they were close to the river and far enough from the road that Lou didn't see that happening.

For a moment Lou felt dread starting in their belly. Had Clementine regretted everything and left, leaving Lou behind, naked in the tent, while she took off with Lottie to Lord knew where?

Lou heard some rustling outside and almost called for Clementine when the flap opened and she stepped inside with a flourish. The dread was forgotten and Lou's eyes went wide. She had Lou's white shirt on, a little wrinkled, but buttoned up midchest and the hem resting high on her thighs. She even had Lou's gun belt slung low on her hips, looking too heavy for her frame. She was looking at them from under the brim of their hat, a knowing smirk on her face as she used her finger to tip it toward Lou.

"'Owdy, darlin'," she drawled.

She hooked her thumbs in the belt and swaggered over to them. She was short enough that she barely cleared the highest part of the tent, the hat catching on the top and scooting back on her head a little bit. She let the facade fall for a moment, pulling the brim back down.

Lou raised an amused eyebrow even as their gaze tried to drink in everything in front of them, particularly where the shirt was just barely covering the tuft of curls between her thighs.

"Ya know, it ain't proper'a be out there only wearin' this."

She wiggled her eyebrows at Lou. "I'll show ya what's proper, sir."

"You makin' fun'a my accent?" Lou teased, sitting up and reaching for her.

"I would neva'," Clementine said, voice still warm and drawn out like homemade taffy. She danced just out of Lou's reach, hands resting on the butt of Lou's guns. "'M jus' sayin', little sir, yer too beautiful to be 'round these parts by yerself."

"*I'm* the lil' one?" Lou said, managing to slip a hand around the back of her thigh and bringing her close enough to kiss her groin over the shirt.

She threaded her fingers through their hair, tugging and tilting their face so that she could lean down and kiss them. Lou let out a long sigh, both hands gripping the back of her thighs.

Lou hummed against her lips and tried to pull her down into their lap, but she resisted.

Lou growled in frustration, hands squeezing her ass as they kissed her stomach. "Miss Clementine—"

"Yes, cowboy?" she said lowly, her put-on accent gone as she held Lou's chin between her thumb and pointer finger, brushing their lips together softly.

"You fucked me with your guns on last night," she said, kissing them slowly so that their tongues molded together. Lou's entire body thrummed with arousal, thick and hot in their veins. Clementine whispered against their lips, "I want to return the favor."

She undid the buttons on her shirt as she sank into Lou's lap, opening the front so that her smooth, tan skin was on display. Lou leaned forward and kissed between her breasts, nose nuzzling the side of one before nipping at the skin. She hummed and finished pulling the shirt off her shoulders, leaving her only in the gun belt.

"Miss Clementine, that's 'cause last night I was too much in a hurry to take 'em off," Lou said, pulling back to appreciate the glorious sight in front of them before reaching down and pulling the belt through its buckle to take it off. "But today we 'ave the luxury of takin' our time. An' I certainly plan on takin' my time."

Lou set the belt aside, leaving Clementine bare and straddling them.

She gently guided Lou's mouth over her nipple, which they gladly took between their lips.

"You wanna do that?" she gasped, back arching as she pressed her breast deeper.

"Darlin', there're a lotta things I'd do'ta ya. A lotta improper things."

They leaned back to the ground and guided Clementine's hips so that she was straddling their face.

Clementine never wanted to leave the tent. She could stay there naked with Lou forever, hands and mouths exploring each other. Their callused hands moving over her skin made her wet almost instantly, and she couldn't get enough. But as they lay entwined in each other, their bodies slick with sweat and the air thick with the smell of sex, it became increasingly clear that they were starving.

Lou covered her with their jacket and they went to the nearby river to cool down and wash, which just led to Clementine being pressed up against a rock as Lou pleasured her. Not that she was complaining.

She never wanted to stop touching Lou because she was worried that when she did, this would all be a dream and she'd be stuck back in Lefty's camp waiting to be rescued. It felt like everything had been a dream. She somehow ended up on this kind rancher's farm, someone she thought would be dead before letting her near them. For months her mind had been filled with thoughts of kissing them and touching them and now that she'd had it all, she didn't want to be without it ever again.

Lou carried her back from the river and she couldn't keep her lips off them. Their entire chest was ravaged, small bites and bruises dotting the skin. She just wanted to let everyone know they were hers and no one else's. Just the thought of someone touching Lou like that made Clementine grip them tighter.

"Miss Clementine, we mus' get dressed," Lou said when they got to the camp, tipping their chin down and kissing her softly.

She grumbled but let herself be put down. She would have to somehow get Lou out of the habit of calling her "Miss" anything, though admittedly the name was sweet and it did something to her when Lou was over her and saying it. She shivered at the thought before looking back at Lou, who regretfully was pulling on their pants.

She picked up Lou's binding bandage from where they had thrown it last night and came up behind them.

"Let me," she said, kissing their shoulder softly as she wrapped the bandage around their front. They worked together, Lou holding and tucking as she wrapped it around them. When it was tight and Lou was satisfied, she tucked it in and kissed along the edge.

With a wistful sigh, she slipped her nightgown back on and shrugged on Lou's coat to cover her until they got back to the saloon where her clothes were.

Riding apart from Lou felt akin to torture when they had just spent all night and the day skin to skin. She hummed softly as they rode, anything to distract her from being too far apart.

They dismounted at the saloon and Clem immediately gravitated back toward Lou, wrapping her arms around them and snuggling into their chest.

"Miss Clementine," Lou chuckled, kissing the top of her head before gently prying her off them. "We're in public."

"I don't care." She pouted, but she looked up and saw Lou's eyes darting nervously around at the people passing, and realization hit her. It wasn't just about propriety, not always anyways. Lou was good and noble and protective, but they were also diligent. They'd faced things Clementine hadn't even thought of, living their truth every day, and it had made them extra aware of the world around them.

Clementine, for the most part, had been living in a bubble—a horrible, sterile bubble where she'd had to do things she never wanted to think about again, but in a way she'd been sheltered from the outside world. Lou knew what people did and said to those who were different.

Their eyes softened when they didn't see a threat. "Ain't proper," Lou teased with a small smile, kissing the tip of her nose tenderly.

She melted at the gesture and took Lou's arm to enter the saloon. Lou pulled out a seat for her at an isolated table in the corner, but she squeezed their arm.

"I'm going to go see Lottie." She looked down at herself and laughed. "And maybe put on some clothes. I'll meet you back down here. Okay?"

"All right, darlin'. I'll get us food."

She gave their arm one last squeeze and headed up to the room. She knocked and heard a grunt of acknowledgment from the other side. She tried the door and sighed when it wasn't locked. Lottie lay half on the bed, her top half bent over the side, staring at a map as she kicked her legs in the air. There was a half-drunk bottle of whiskey on the floor beside her. Clementine's stomach dropped at the sight.

"Where are you off to now?" she asked quietly. She should have known it would only be a matter of time before Lottie took off again. There had been a part of her that hoped Lottie might stay around now that they were finally together again, but clearly that wasn't the case.

"I don't know," Lottie mumbled, barely looking up. "You and Ramirez off makin' babies all night?"

"Don't change the subject," Clementine said, even though she had to push down her smile from remembering the night before. She poked her tongue into the side of her cheek and went over to her trunk to get a dress. "Are you leaving? Again?"

"Did you make up with Ramirez?" Lottie said, pointedly looking at Clementine. She could see Lottie's eyes taking in the bruise on her neck before looking back in her eyes.

"Well...yes—"

"Then what else am I supposed to do?" Lottie said with a dismissive shrug. "You have them and you're mad at me. It's time to go again."

"I don't think it's quite fair that you're making me choose between my sister and my...my Lou. You can't blame me for *you* leaving *me* again. I had a reason to be upset."

"I want you to understand why I framed our dad—"

Clementine took the map from her hands and pulled her up by the arm so they were both sitting on the edge of the bed together. She looked her directly in the eyes. "Then tell me."

"Dad hurt us. He hurt *you*. He wasn't a good man. I wanted to get rid of him but I didn't want him to *die*. I just wanted Lefty to scare him a little. Maybe set him straight. It went wrong." Her voice broke and Clementine's stomach dropped. "It went so, so wrong. I got Dad and Maria killed and y-you were stuck with that *monster*."

Clementine looked down, breathless for a moment at the memory, sharp and fresh. "You were young, Lottie. You were young and stupid. I forgive you for that. But why didn't you tell me? You should have told me."

"I didn't want to lose you after I'd finally found you," Lottie admitted, so softly she could barely hear her. "I wanted to be your big sister that saved you, not your big sister that ruined your life. I had to grow up fast, Clem, and it didn't teach me to be soft."

Lottie stared blankly at the wall, tears silently falling down her. For a moment, Clementine saw the scared little girl who shoved her under the bed and told her not to come out under any circumstances. The little girl who always defended her and put herself in the middle of her and their dad when he was in a mood.

She sighed as something within her finally released, and Lottie looked at her. Clementine nodded and forgiveness fell over them like a warm blanket. Lottie sniffled and tipped over so her head was in Clementine's lap. Clem ran her fingers through her sister's hair, while taking the whiskey bottle and setting it on the nightstand.

"You didn't ruin my life. They say everything happens for a reason. Right?"

"What reason would this be?"

"Maybe all of this was so that I'd find Lou."

"You really think Ramirez is worth all this?"

"I think they might definitely be. I love them."

Silence settled between them for a moment before Lottie spoke up. "I guess I should start being nicer to them."

"Does that mean you're gonna stay?"

"What am I gonna do if I stay? Just watch you and Ramirez make puppy dog eyes at each other? You don't need me."

"Are you telling me that you're jealous? Jealous that I have Lou?"

"I'm not...No," Lottie said with a wrinkle of her nose. "I just don't have the tendency to stay where I'm no longer needed."

Clementine stood and fetched her dress, stepping behind the changing screen. "What makes you think you're not needed?"

"You have Lou. And as much as I would love it if you chose someone who hadn't slept with an entire saloon full of girls, I can't really tell you who to fall in love with."

"That doesn't mean I don't need you. You're my sister. I've been without you for a long time. I don't want to lose you again."

"I love you. But sharing a very small, very drafty cabin with you two in your newly married bliss isn't exactly my idea of a good time. And I doubt it is for either of you."

"You wouldn't stay in the cabin—"

"And I'm not living in a barn and I'm not going to build a house anywhere—"

"Lou is building the new house. They might be okay with you staying, especially if you help them finish building it."

Lottie looked dubious but sat up in the bed anyway. She held her hands palm up with a wry smile. "Do these hands look like they do manual labor?"

"Those hands look like they need to find some honest work to do before they find themselves in jail—or worse."

Lottie sucked on her teeth and looked away with a shrug. "I guess I could be convinced."

Clementine felt a smile bloom on her face and she jumped up and down in excitement. She balled her hands into fists and held them in front of her face to try and keep in her excitement. "Really?"

"Yes," Lottie said, more firmly this time.

Clementine threw her arms around Lottie's neck and kissed her cheek. Lottie grumbled in displeasure, even if Clementine saw her lips quirk in a brief smile.

Lottie's arms wrapped around her, and she squeezed her even tighter. "You won't lose me, Clem. I promise."

"I'm holding you to that," she said before finally releasing Lottie. "Now, Lou and I are getting breakfast downstairs. Put your stupid map away and join us."

Lottie balled up the map haphazardly and shoved it off to the side. "You two aren't gonna be feeding each other or some shit? Right? I don't think my stomach can handle the public displays."

"We can control ourselves, Lottie."

They started down to meet Lou. She watched Lou looking all around the saloon, face unreadable as they took in the surroundings. Their eyes finally caught Clementine's and a smile cracked their hard facade, brown eyes lighting up and making her feel warm all over. She smiled back, waving shyly at Lou who only smiled wider.

"Ugh, what happened to controlling yourselves in public," Lottie said, moving past Clementine to Lou's table.

Moment broken, Clementine followed Lottie the rest of the way down. As soon as Lottie sat down, she pulled the plate that was in front of Lou in front of herself.

"Thanks, Ramirez," she said, digging into the plate of beans, eggs, and sausage.

Clementine sat down and pushed Lottie's shoulder. "Lottie!"

"It's fine, darlin'," Lou said, putting her hand over Clementine's and squeezing. "I'll get another."

Before they could even get up, one of the girls appeared with a fresh plate. She winked at Lou and squeezed their shoulder before going back to her rounds. Clementine raised an eyebrow at Lou, jealousy making her a little hot under the collar.

"Who is that?" she asked nonchalantly.

"No one I know, Miss Clementine, rest assured." They winked at her and picked up their fork. Clementine's heart fluttered, all traces of jealousy gone.

"You two are insufferable," Lottie said through a mouthful of eggs.

"I'm okay with that," Clementine said with a wide grin before digging into her breakfast.

Later they made their way back to the ranch. Lou and Clementine rode side by side up front, little bits of conversation flowing naturally between them but mostly just riding in silence, save for stealing little glances and smiles at each other. Clementine would rather they were on the same horse, Lou's arms around her, but she knew Lou would protest.

Lottie rode behind them, singing songs very loudly and badly as they went, three horses in trail behind her. Lefty's gang had fractured into chaos with the murder of their boss, no one sure who was responsible and every man suddenly a suspect. In the midst of all this turmoil, Lottie had slipped a stable hand a few dollars and casually claimed his mount and two others from the town stables. Now Lottie belted out the lyrics to "Home on the Range." Clementine was surprised she was sober with the way she was carrying on.

After camping along the river for another night, they finally breathed a sigh of relief, arriving at Lou's land with bodies tired and horses worn. The barn wasn't big enough for their three horses along with the other three they had brought back, so Lou fed and watered them in the corral as Lottie got settled out in the barn.

Clementine went inside, only lighting the candle next to the bed. She was tired from the journey, and while part of her felt like she could fall asleep, she also ached to feel Lou in the comfort of their shared bed and not on a bedroll in the middle of a field somewhere.

She stripped her dress off, leaving on her corset and underskirt. When Lou came into the cabin, she was attempting to undo the laces, but Lou's eyes devoured her form, and suddenly all she could focus on was how Lou's tongue darted out to wet their lips.

"Miss Clementine," Lou greeted, taking their hat off and hanging it near the door.

"You know you don't have to call me that anymore," she said as Lou pulled their suspenders off their shoulders and walked up to her. She was helpless but to just stand there as Lou smoothed their hands over her hips and pressed into her. She smiled up at Lou as she briefly touched the collar of their shirt. "Clementine would do."

"Ain't proper to call a lady by 'er first name if you ain't familiar," Lou said, voice quiet as they let their hands roam to the front of her corset, pulling at the laces. The restriction on her torso loosened, but it was just as hard to breathe with the way Lou was looking down at her.

"I think we're pretty familiar, don't you?" She smiled, slowly unbuttoning Lou's shirt, pleased to see they weren't wearing an undershirt.

"I mean, if we ain't married."

"So you're okay lying with me out of wedlock, but not calling me by my first name?" she asked, tilting her head with the teasing smile still in place.

"Maybe I jus' like callin' you that, *Miss Clementine*," Lou said lowly, as the corset came loose enough that Clementine's torso was mostly exposed through the laces. Lou ducked their head, lips brushing teasingly over Clementine's.

"Then it's a good thing I like it when you call me that," she said, pushing their shirt off their shoulders and letting it whisper to the floor. She ran her hands over the front of Lou's chest, bumping over the binding and waiting for Lou's nod before untucking the end. She pulled the end so it fell to the floor, before reaching down to undo their pants. She let her tongue peek out and taste the seam of Lou's lips as she pushed her hand into their pants and cupped them over their underwear.

Lou groaned, pressing forward to seal their lips against Clementine's. She sighed into the kiss, feeling Lou's heat in her palm. She let Lou push her back onto the bed, lying down slowly with their lips still together.

Her heart felt like it was beating out of her chest, one hand gripping Lou's strong shoulders to keep them close. They went to pull away and she groaned in protest, but Lou's fingers hooked into the waistband of her underskirt and pulled it down, satisfying her for the moment. The sheets of the bed were cool on her skin, something to soothe her overheated body as she watched Lou stand and push their pants down, leaving them in just the underwear that landed above their knees.

"Off," Clementine whispered, pulling at the waistband.

Lou smirked and pulled her hand away as they approached the bed. She felt displayed on the bed, her thin corset open with the strings hanging loosely along her stomach. It was open just enough to cover her nipples, the lace tickling her sensitive skin. She was sure she looked as turned-on as she felt, her entire body flush and lips swollen.

"Miss Clementine," Lou said as they crawled onto the bed, straddling her calves. Their voice was thick and sweet as molasses, and she just wanted to taste the words coming from their lips. "I'll tell you to the day you won't 'ave me anymore. Yer the most beautiful woman I've ever seen."

She shivered at Lou's words, and their callused hands running from her knees to her thighs. Their hands settled over her hips, thumbs brushing through damp curls and teasing her swollen sex. They slotted themself between her knees. She could feel Lou's hips where she needed them most, their underwear the only barrier.

"Louie," she moaned, hands tangling in Lou's hair and drawing their lips together again. Lou pinned her hands over her head on the pillow. A rush of arousal hit her between her thighs and she mewled against Lou's lips, tipping her hips toward Lou as best she could, practically pinned to the bed.

Lou was so sweet and gentle most of the time that when a little more of their rougher, baser side came out, she discovered that she loved it. That was why she found herself pushing back against Lou's hands briefly, just to feel them pinned back down. She squirmed under Lou, hooking her leg around Lou's thigh and tugging them down.

"Let me take care'a you, Miss Clementine," they whispered against her lips, a hand sliding hot between them before they entered her with a hard thrust.

Her back arched as she gasped in pleasure, hands itching to grab at Lou and run her nails down their back. Lou swallowed her moan when callused fingers pressed into her front wall and her entire body thrummed. Their thumb came up to press against her clit and her leg tightened around Lou's hips, the only part of them she could grip.

"Fuck, Lou," she gasped, hands balling into fists. "I...*fuck*."

Lou kissed along her jaw, nipping at the skin as they went, their fingers doubling their pace. Her hips tried to chase Lou's hand, but their tongue and teeth on her ear distracted her. She felt the fire smoldering in her stomach, ready for the flames to burst and consume her, so Clementine turned her head and their lips met messily as she came.

All she felt was their tongue. Warmth and sheer pleasure spread through her stomach, as she shuddered against them.

She wasn't sure if she was silent or screaming, but her mouth felt dry, heavy breaths escaping her lips. Lou gently kissed her, pecking her lips softly as they both caught their breath. Their hand loosened on her wrists and she fell bonelessly back to the bed. She hummed, arms barely able to wrap around Lou's neck.

She couldn't even bring herself to be annoyed at Lou's cocky smile, hair falling into their face as they looked down at her. "You know how'a take care'a yer woman, cowboy," she muttered with an exaggerated accent, kissing them slow and deep.

"Always at yer service, Miss Clementine," Lou whispered as they kissed again.

CHAPTER TWENTY-ONE

Lou pulled the bandana from their back pocket and wiped the sweat from their forehead before it could drip into their eyes. They set their hammer down, balancing it on the roof beam as they looked down to where Lottie nailed a final bit of siding. They could already feel the burn starting on their shoulders and groaned. Clementine would definitely kill them for getting burned. There were only so many times she would rub milk on their reddened shoulders without getting rid of their favorite shirt when they weren't looking.

They looked down at the light buckskin shirt they had gotten when they traded Lefty's horses with the Shoshone tribe. Clementine had been thrilled to translate again. She was pleased to discover that she still remembered the language, having not had a chance to use it since leaving Lefty's camp. They traded the horses for some supplies and the buckskin shirt that had no sleeves and felt like heaven in the heat, but it left their shoulders exposed.

Every time Lou would come in with some redness starting on their skin, Clementine would *tut* and roll her eyes.

Lou stuffed the bandana back in their pocket and looked at their progress. The house was mostly done. Lottie just needed to finish siding the house and Lou had to do the roof, and then they could move on to the interior. Lou had managed to get their hands on a catalog of furniture and was letting Clementine pore over it so they wouldn't have to.

"Hey, Ramirez," Lottie called from below. "Come down, I have water."

Lou climbed down the ladder and waited for Lottie to be done with the ladle and bucket before taking their turn.

Things with Lottie had been better. At first she had been fairly cold toward Lou, but after a particularly successful night of drinking together, Lou had managed to earn some of her affections—at least enough that she stopped glaring at them any time they went to the saloon or even looked at Clementine.

"So, Lou, when are you going to make my sister an honest woman?"

Lou choked on the water, coughing so badly that Lottie had to pat their back.

"Jesus, don't act so shocked, or I'm going to get the wrong idea."

Lou shook their head and wiped her mouth with their arm. "No, I wanna— We're practically married, ain't we?"

"If something happens to you, Clementine will get nothing."

Surprisingly, Lou hadn't really thought about it. They figured that since they and Clementine were living under the same roof and building a house, they were married. Now that they acknowledged it anyways. They had spent enough time denying their feelings for Clem, but now they didn't see the point. Anyone could see how devoted they were, they didn't need some piece of paper from the law to prove anything. They rubbed the back of their neck and looked off toward the river.

"Listen I jus' ain't thought about it lately. I'll work it out."

"Soon. You'll work it out *soon*."

"*Soon*."

"I'm not going to let my sister live in sin," Lottie said, while she crossed herself piously.

Lou snorted and Lottie turned sharply to look at them. With a shrug, Lou smiled. "Soon."

"She's gonna be wanting a baby soon too," Lottie added with a raised eyebrow. "How are you gonna pull that one off?"

Lou frowned. A baby? They'd never talked about babies. Lou wasn't even sure if they wanted one.

Clementine called them from the cabin and Lou gave her another look.

"Soon!" they promised, distracted, before they headed in for lunch.

* * *

Clementine stood in front of the finished house, looking up at it with wide eyes. It looked at least three times as wide as the cabin, with a pitched roof and a window for the attic. The porch jutted out in front with a railing around it and Clementine could already see herself and Lou sitting on that porch come next summer.

Lou had let her pick out the furniture, but then wouldn't let her into the house until they deemed it finished.

She felt Lou's arms encircle her waist from behind and leaned back into them, turning her head to kiss Lou's jaw.

"Ready to see our new 'ome, darlin'?"

"Very."

"Great," Lou said, squeezing her lightly and kissing her cheek. They pulled away and scooped Clementine up in their arms like a bride.

She squeaked in surprise, arms going around Lou's neck as she leaned comfortably into their chest. "Always the gentleman."

"Well, I gotta carry you over'a threshold," Lou said as they walked Clementine up the porch steps and pushed open the door with Clementine still in their arms.

"I thought that was after you got married."

"We ain't known to be doin' things in the right order, darlin'," they reminded her as they dramatically took a large step over the threshold.

"I guess not," she said, too distracted taking in the house to remind Lou again that they should just get married already.

Lou slowly lowered her to the ground as she looked around. The house started with a hallway, another door directly across from the front one for the summer when they needed a good breeze. To the left was the living room, stone fireplace against the wall, and a davenport and a couple of chairs gathered near it. Clementine warmed, remembering several evenings of watching Lou's back flex as they unloaded that very stone from the wagon.

She walked down the long hall and opened the door beside the living room to reveal their bedroom. She moved in awe, looking at the other bedroom across the hall and the kitchen beside that, all far bigger than the tiny cabin she'd just left.

"This is amazing," she said to Lou, who wore a proud smile. "This is our home."

"Indeed it is, darlin'." Lou wrapped their arms around her waist, widening their stance so they could be the same height as her. "Welcome home."

She felt something slide into place in that moment, something in her chest that had been floating, waiting to feel comfortable. Maybe it was Lou talking about their home that did it. Maybe it was their smile.

"Our home," she repeated, hands tugging on Lou's collar so she could kiss them properly.

* * *

"Clem, you should see Ramirez right now. They're arm deep in that fucking cow," Lottie said as she came into the house for more rags. "If I were you, I'd be jealous."

"Very funny, Lottie," Clementine sighed as she made a stew, tasting it before adding more salt. "Calf coming along okay?"

"Seems to be, according to Lou," Lottie said. "It's pretty disgusting. You're gonna be getting that smell off them for a week. At least."

Just then, Lou came in with a large smile, hair sticking up at odd angles and something stuck in it that Clementine didn't want to think about.

"Calf's 'ere! An' she's beautiful."

Clementine nearly dropped the salt shaker in excitement. "Can I go see her?"

"'Course, I'll be out there."

Lou left just as fast as they came and Lottie looked annoyed.

"You got a weird one there," she said, gesturing toward the door.

"They're not weird," Clementine defended, a wave of affection rolling over her. "But they are mine."

Lottie gagged and rolled her eyes, picking up the basket of rags and turning toward the door.

"Get over it, Lottie!"

Lottie just flipped her off as the door closed behind her.

"'Ello, darlin'," Lou said, setting their hat on the hook and shrugging off their thick jacket, hanging it on the coat stand. They rubbed their hands together to get some more warmth in them, letting the fire roaring in the hearth do its magic.

Clementine hummed and looked up from whatever project she was knitting, only briefly.

"Hey, baby," she smiled with a wink. "I made you some dinner."

"Yer the best," they said, wandering over to where Clementine was sitting. They leaned down and kissed her softly with a smile, when their eyes caught the project Clementine was working on in her lap. The knitting needles were paused over some light-pink-looking thing.

They paused, frowning down at the project that looked like…booties. Confusion and fear battled in Lou's mind as they watched her knit. No one they knew was having a baby. And that definitely looked like baby booties.

Lou cleared their throat and went into the kitchen, scooping some stew into a bowl as their mind went through all the possibilities. There was no way Clementine was pregnant, of course. It was impossible. But maybe she was hinting at something? That she wanted a baby?

They remembered Lottie's conversation from just a few weeks ago.

Was Lou going to have to find a way to get Clementine a baby? They had just started settling into their own! They weren't even married yet! Even though Lou had a ring tucked into their drawer waiting for the perfect time.

They carried the food back into the living room where Clementine sat, still knitting. "I ain't ready for a baby," Lou blurted.

Clementine frowned. "What?"

"I'm sorry, I jus' ain't ready fer a baby."

"Honey, what are you talking about?"

"I'm ready to get married, but that's 'bout it," Lou kept going, nervous lips unable to stop. "I know I shoulda asked you a long time ago but I jus' liked what we 'ad. But I'll make an honest woman outta ya once spring comes."

Clementine's mouth opened and closed, struggling to find words. She looked confused, but also elated and that made Lou's stomach warm.

"First things first, why do you think I want a baby?"

Shoveling a big bite of the stew into their mouth, Lou shrugged and pointed toward the thing in Clementine's lap.

"Ain't those baby shoes?"

Clementine giggled, picking them up to show Lou. It was two long bootie looking things, bigger than any baby feet Lou had ever seen, connected by a string.

"It's for the calf. For her ears so she doesn't get frostbite."

"Oh."

Lou felt relief and embarrassment at the same time and leaned over their bowl to try and hide their blush.

"Is there a reason you assumed I wanted a baby because of this?"

"I don' know. Lottie mentioned you'd be wantin' one."

"Since when do you listen to Lottie?"

"She is yer sister. I thought there might be some truth to it."

"If I want a baby, I'd be telling you, not my sister. But back to the important thing, you wanna marry me up?"

Lou smiled back as they took the last bite of stew. "I do, Miss Clementine."

"Does that mean you wouldn't call me 'Miss Clementine' anymore?"

"Only when you wanted me to," Lou said, setting their bowl aside.

Her eyes purposefully looked them over and she held out her hand to Lou. "I want you to call me that right now," she said, voice low.

Lou stood and easily picked Clementine up bridal style, the two of them smiling happily at each other.

"Whatever you want, Miss Clementine," Lou said, walking her toward their bedroom. "Whatever you want."

Bella Books, Inc.

Women. Books. Even Better Together.

P.O. Box 10543
Tallahassee, FL 32302
Phone: (800) 729-4992
www.BellaBooks.com

More Titles from Bella Books

Mabel and Everything After – Hannah Safren
978-1-64247-390-2 | 274 pgs | paperback: $17.95 | eBook: $9.99
A law student and a wannabe brewery owner find that the path to a fairy tale happily-ever-after is often the long and scenic route.

To Be With You – TJ O'Shea
978-1-64247-419-0 | 348 pgs | paperback: $19.95 | eBook: $9.99
Sometimes the choice is between loving safely or loving bravely.

I Dare You to Love Me – Lori G. Matthews
978-1-64247-389-6 | 292 pgs | paperback: $18.95 | eBook: $9.99
An enemy-to-lovers romance about daring to follow your heart, even when it's the hardest thing to do.

The Lady Adventurers Club - Karen Frost
978-1-64247-414-5 | 300 pgs | paperback: $18.95 | eBook: $9.99
Four women. One undiscovered Egyptian tomb. One (maybe) angry Egyptian goddess. What could possibly go wrong?

Golden Hour - Kat Jackson
978-1-64247-397-1 | 250 pgs | paperback: $17.95 | eBook: $9.99
Life would be so much easier if Lina were afraid of something basic—like spiders—instead of something significant. Something like real, true, healthy love.

Schuss – E. J. Noyes
978-1-64247-430-5 | 276 pgs | paperback: $17.95 | eBook: $9.99
They're best friends who both want something more, but what if admitting it ruins the best friendship either of them have had?

Printed in the USA
CPSIA information can be obtained
at www.ICGtesting.com
JSHW082237260324
59949JS00001B/2